ROBERTA KRAY

DOUBLE CROSSED

SPHERE

SPHERE

First published in Great Britain in 2021 by Sphere

1 3 5 7 9 10 8 6 4 2

A CIP catalogue record for this book
is available from the British Library.

ISBN 978-0-7515-7698-6

Typeset in Garamond by M Rules
Printed and bound in Great Britain by
Clays Ltd, Elcograf S.p.A.

Papers used by Sphere are from well-managed forests
and other responsible sources.

MIX
Paper from
responsible sources
FSC® C104740

Sphere
An imprint of
Little, Brown Book Group
Carmelite House
50 Victoria Embankment
London EC4Y 0DZ

An Hachette UK Company
www.hachette.co.uk

www.littlebrown.co.uk

DOUBLE CROSSED

1956

1

Liv Anderson checked out her reflection as she walked through the hotel lobby. Without make-up and with her long dark hair lying loose around her shoulders she looked younger than she actually was, closer to sixteen or seventeen than twenty-one. An innocent abroad. A girl ripe for the picking. Her shoulders were bare, her skin smooth and unblemished. The skirt of her pale blue summer dress swung around her legs.

She could still recall the terror she'd felt on the first occasion – the thumping of her heart, the burning shame, the desire for the ground to open up and swallow her – but familiarity had blunted its edge. With every month that passed her confidence was growing. Now only a few residual nerves fluttered in her chest. The rights and wrongs no longer bothered her; life ceased to be black and white when the rent needed paying, and scruples were only for people who could afford them.

Liv went into the cocktail lounge and quickly surveyed the room. She approached the bar, ordered a small lemonade and took the drink over to an empty table. The chosen man was sitting a few feet away from her. He was middle-aged, over-weight with a jowly face, receding hairline and a gold band on his finger. She watched him out of the corner of her eye as she sipped the lemonade. She knew his type: a married businessman away from home, bored and on the lookout for something or someone to distract him.

She crossed her legs, opened her handbag, took out the small *A–Z* street atlas of London and flipped to the page that covered most of the West End. With her forefinger she traced the various roads while she peered, sighed, frowned and waited for him to rise to the bait. It didn't take long.

'Excuse me,' he said. 'But would you like some help? I know London quite well.'

She smiled. 'Oh, how kind. I'm trying to find the best way to Trafalgar Square, but it seems so complicated. I've really got no sense of direction at all.'

He stood up, came over and sat down beside her. 'Trafalgar Square, eh? Well, that's not too far off. Are you here on holiday?'

'To see my uncle, but he's been called away. He won't be back until tomorrow.'

This was how it always started. And where it led was always the same, too. Introductions were made: he told her his name was George Barnes – probably a lie – and she said hers was Nancy Cook. She told him she had never been to London before. He explained the most straightforward route to Trafalgar Square and she flattered him and said how clever he was. Then he advised her against going there at night. 'A pretty girl isn't safe alone. There are all sorts roaming around. It's fine during the day though. You should wait until the morning.'

She nodded at his wise advice and thanked him. He was sitting too close, his arm touching hers. His gaze lingered on where the thin cotton of her dress covered her thighs. They chatted for a while. She finished her drink and he offered her another. 'How about a Martini?' She said she wasn't sure but let herself be persuaded. The cocktail was a strong one and she pretended it had gone to her head, giggling too much and fanning her face with the *A–Z*. 'Is it just me or is it hot in here?'

The bar was filling up, growing ever noisier. Eventually, inevitably, he suggested going to his room. 'It'll be quieter there. I can order up some drinks and we can have a proper chat.'

It had taken less than fifteen minutes. As they stood in the lift together, Liv thought about what was coming next – the hot breath on her neck, the groping and grunting – and mentally rolled her eyes. She could smell the sweat oozing from his pores and caught a whiff of musky aftershave. The only consolation was that it would soon be over. Easy money, she told herself. Better than slaving all week in a typing pool. And she chattered on, talking mindlessly like the naïve girl she was supposed to be.

Once they were in his room and the door was shut behind them, he didn't waste any time. Now they were alone the sham façade of propriety quickly slipped. Almost immediately his hands were on her, his fingers clawing at her dress, his mouth slobbering over hers. She turned her face away and tried to push him off.

'What about that drink?' she asked.

'After,' he said. He took her arms, propelling her towards the bed. 'Come on, love. Don't be a tease.'

But things were moving too fast. She wrenched herself free and backed away from him. By now her clothes were in disarray, one shoulder bare, and she was looking thoroughly dishevelled. He moved towards her again and she skirted round the big double bed. She could imagine this same scenario taking place all over the country – the predatory male and the girl about to be seduced – and felt a surge of loathing for the creature in front of her.

'Nancy,' he wheedled. 'Don't run away. We're friends. You like me, don't you?'

Liv stared at him. His mouth was smiling, but anger flashed in his eyes. She smiled back, forcing her lips to curl, making her expression more amenable. She wasn't taking any chances. Even the most mild-mannered of men could turn nasty if they didn't get what they wanted. 'Of course I do.'

'Well then.' He sat on the bed and patted the space beside him. 'Come and sit down.'

Like a chicken walking towards a fox, Liv slowly retraced her steps. George's lustful gaze was fixed on her, waiting for her to be within striking distance. She sucked in a breath and girded herself for the next act in this sordid little drama.

The moment she was close enough, he reached out, grabbed her wrist and pulled her down on to the bed. Then, before she could wriggle free, he'd climbed on top of her and pinned her with the weight of his body, forcing her legs apart as he groped for his flies. So much for romance, she thought, as she lay passively beneath him, her eyes fixed on the ceiling. Her body was still but her mind was racing. This was the point where she always started to panic, knowing it could all so easily go wrong. He was struggling with her panties, trying to pull them down, when salvation finally came.

The hammering on the door was loud and insistent. 'Nancy! Nancy!' And seconds later, discovering that the door was unlocked, Pally stormed into the room with a face like thunder. 'What the hell is going on in here?'

Panicked, George rolled off Liv, leapt up and fumbled with his zip, trying to manipulate his private bits into a less public location.

Liv let out a cry. 'Uncle David!' Then she covered her face with her hands and pretended to weep. 'It was him. I-I didn't want to. I only came up for a chat and then ...'

'It wasn't like that,' George protested. 'I didn't ... Nothing happened.'

'Nothing?' Pally roared, rage emanating from every pore. 'Do you call this *nothing*? Do you have any idea how old this girl is? It's disgusting, disgraceful. What kind of a man are you?'

'You've got it all wrong. I didn't know she was ...'

Pally, tall and intimidating, glared down at George. 'Spare me the excuses. You've got eyes, haven't you? She's still at school, for God's sake.'

George squirmed and spluttered and stared wildly round as though looking for an escape route. But Pally was standing between him and the door, and jumping out of the window was hardly an option when they were five flights up. 'I didn't know, did I? She didn't tell me that. We had a drink and then—'

'Oh, that's your game, is it? Get her drunk and take advantage!'

'No, I didn't ...'

But Pally had turned his attention to Liv. 'Nancy, go to your room.'

Liv, still snivelling, stood up and rearranged her dress. 'What are you going to do?'

'What do you think? Call the police, of course.' Pally strode over to the phone, his jaw set. 'This is a matter for the law.'

'You can't do that,' Liv said. 'What will Daddy say? He'll be angry with me. He'll go mad when he finds out.'

The colour had drained from George's face. 'There's no need to get the police involved. It was a genuine mistake. If I'd thought, even for a second, that she wasn't—'

'It's a bit late for that now,' Pally said.

'Please don't, Uncle David,' Liv pleaded. 'Everyone's going to find out. It'll be in all the papers and ... Please don't!'

Pally hesitated, his hand on the phone. 'So he's supposed to just get away with it? The man's a degenerate. He should be behind bars.'

'But ... but ...'

'Go to your room, Nancy. Right *now*. I'll deal with this.'

Liv bowed her head and slipped out. As she was closing the door behind her, George was already launching into a desperate attempt to save himself from public disgrace. 'I've never done anything like this before. I swear I haven't. I don't know what came over me. It'll never happen again. Surely there's some way we can ...'

Liv, smiling, knew that there was always a way. After a suitable period of outrage, 'Uncle David' would give in and reluctantly agree to some reasonable financial recompense for the trauma she'd endured. And she didn't feel bad about this. Why should she? George hadn't felt bad when he'd tried to get her drunk and invited her up to his room. Men like him never had regrets until the point they got caught out.

She hurried along the corridor, took the lift down to the foyer and walked out on to the street. Then she strolled to the corner and lit a cigarette while she waited. The light was fading, sliding into dusk, but the air was still warm. Soon she'd be back in Soho with money in her pocket and the rest of Friday night to enjoy herself. Life was good.

2

Liv finished her cigarette and gazed back towards the hotel. Pally never took longer than he had to. The threat of the police, of involving the hotel manager, was usually enough to loosen the victim's wallet without too much debate over the matter. Adept at what he did, calm and unflappable, Pally always played his part to perfection – even if his timing did leave something to be desired on occasion. She thought of George sprawled over her on the bed, and gave a shudder. Another minute and she'd have been in serious trouble. Still, those were the risks she took and the rewards made it worthwhile.

It was Verity, a girl who lived across the landing in the boarding house, who had introduced Liv to Pally, and Pally who had introduced her to the badger. The badger game was an old one, but men still fell for it. It was as though their brains went out of the window as soon as sex was on the table. Thoughts of their wives, their reputations, were thrown to the wind the moment a pretty girl came into view; lust replaced reason, and all good sense was lost.

A few minutes more passed before Pally finally emerged from the hotel and began to walk towards the corner. Despite her confidence in him, she released a small sigh of relief. Things could go wrong even with the best-laid plans. Quickly she scanned the street looking for a black cab and raised her arm as soon as one came into view. Pally was grinning as he caught up with her, climbed into the back and gave his instructions to the driver. 'Dean Street, please, mate.'

Liv spoke softly so the cabbie wouldn't overhear. 'You took your time.'

'A man and his money aren't easily parted.'

'I meant earlier. Cutting it a bit fine, weren't you?'

Pally raised his eyebrows. 'I'd have called it just about perfect. Only fools rush in. Isn't that what they say?'

'Yes, well, George was the impatient sort. The creep was all over me.'

'When have I ever let you down?'

'There's always a first time.'

'Never,' he said. 'Trust me.'

Liv did trust him, although not over everything. 'How much did you get?'

'Half a ton.'

Liv studied him closely, searching for the tell, for the sign that he was holding out on her, but Pally never gave much away. Her half was nothing to complain about – twenty-five quid was three times what she'd have earned in a week in the typing pool or as an usherette – but she had a suspicion that he often took more than his fair share.

'What?' he asked.

'Nothing.'

'I thought that was a pretty decent result. I mean, he's hardly Rockefeller, is he?'

'No, it's good.'

'So what's with the face?'

Liv knew better than to start throwing accusations around. Their partnership, even if it wasn't completely equal, was still a profitable one. And she needed him more than he needed her. He could easily find another girl, but she'd be hard pressed to find another Pally. Who else could walk into a hotel bar and spot a mark straight away? He had a sixth sense, an instinct. Deciding to keep things light, she laughed and said, 'It's that wig. You never look like *you* in it.'

Pally touched his head, grinning again. 'I'll take that as a compliment.'

With his fake grey hair and staid navy suit, Pally was a vision of middle-aged, middle-class respectability. He should have been on the stage, she thought, with his talent for play acting. No one could feign outrage like him. Or know exactly how much could be screwed from a victim. He was a born conman.

Liv took her compact out of her bag, examined her face in the mirror and then put on some lipstick. She had fallen a bit in love with Pally at the start. He was good looking, smart, funny and kind. And he always took care of her. No one had done that since her mum had died. So, perhaps unsurprisingly, she'd developed some romantic notions before Verity had put her straight.

'You've no chance there, love. You're not his type.'

And Liv, still as innocent as a lamb back then, had said: 'Why? Does he prefer blondes?'

Verity had snorted into her vodka. 'I've no idea, but he certainly doesn't prefer women. He's as queer as they come, Liv. Didn't you realise?'

Liv, of course, hadn't. She was a small-town girl and where she came from such things were never talked about or at least not with any openness. At first, she'd been disappointed, but now she reckoned it was for the best. This way they could go on working together without any messy complications.

Pally took off his tie, slipped it into his pocket and unbuttoned the top of his shirt. Then he placed his hand on her knee and squeezed it. 'We make a good team, you and me.'

'The best,' she said.

'Same time tomorrow?'

'I'll meet you in the caff.'

3

There was nowhere quite like Soho. It was brilliant and dreary, uplifting and depressing, full of hope and riddled with desperation. Liv revelled in its contradictions. She was fascinated by the narrow knot of streets and everything that lay within. Even the smells – Turkish coffee, Russian tobacco – made her senses tingle. Here there were no moral boundaries, no restrictions, so long as you stayed under the radar of the police. Here there was a different rhythm, an alternative beat to the rest of the city.

It was almost a year now since Liv had chucked in her job, packed a bag, caught a train and come to London. Her mother's sudden death had left her not only bereft but homeless, too, and a fresh start had seemed the best way forward. She had no regrets about the move. The streets might not be paved with gold but there was money to be made if you were young and fearless and knew where to look.

At the moment, however, the only place she was looking was through the window of a café and along Old Compton Street. She was waiting for Pally to show up, hoping that he hadn't forgotten they were supposed to meet. He'd been drunk last night, pissed as a newt, but that was nothing new. The last time she'd seen him had been after eleven when they'd left the pub. He'd staggered off towards the Gargoyle club, arm in arm with some bloke she'd never seen before. 'Come with us,' he'd said. But she hadn't fancied playing gooseberry.

She looked up at the clock on the wall – a quarter to six – and wondered how much longer to wait. Sometimes Pally disappeared for days, even weeks, on one of his gambling sprees, returning either triumphant in a new suit of clothes with money in his pocket or down at heel without a penny to his name. He always took the latter philosophically, saying that was just the way it was, that Lady Luck hadn't been shining on him that time.

Pally was a gambler when it came to men, too. It could be a tricky business picking up a mate when the law decreed that your lusts were illegal. But sex, sex of all kinds, was everywhere in Soho. For Liv, who had been raised in a stifling bubble of respectability – always behave with decorum, never act immodestly – it had been something of a revelation. She had grown up with the word 'no' echoing in her ears: she couldn't do this and she couldn't do that, and she certainly couldn't do the other. Reputation was everything. Being female meant living like a nun until you were married. Not that she blamed her mother for being so strict; sticking to the rules was the only way to survive in a small town, especially if you had something to hide. Secrets had to be securely buried. Once the tongues started wagging there would be no end to the rumours and gossip.

Liv gazed down at the table. She didn't want to think about the past, about what her mum had told her. It only made her feel sad and angry and confused. Why *had* she told her? Perhaps it had been too much of a burden to carry alone. Or perhaps she had just been worried that Liv would find out one day anyway and that it was better to come clean than to face the repercussions of having hidden the truth.

The door to the café opened and Liv looked up expectantly. But it wasn't Pally. The man who'd come in was almost as tall but he was dark haired, broader in the shoulder and wearing a smart, expensive suit. In his thirties, probably, although it was hard to tell with some blokes. For want of anything better to do, she watched as he went to the counter and ordered a cup of tea. Everything about him screamed gangster – from his clothes, through the way he stood, to the flashy gold watch on his wrist. Soho was full of them.

As he turned around, she quickly averted her eyes and gazed out through the window again. She was aware of him walking in her direction but presumed he was heading for one of the empty tables behind her. The café was quiet and there was plenty of space. It was a surprise, therefore, when he stopped, pulled out a chair and sat down opposite her.

'Hello, Liv.'

Liv stared at him, bemused. Had they met before? In a pub, maybe, or in one of the clubs? She didn't think so. He was the sort you remembered. 'I'm sorry, but do I . . . ?'

'Lincoln,' he said. 'Tom Lincoln.'

The name didn't ring any bells. Frowning, she examined his face more closely – slate-grey eyes, full mouth, a cleft in his chin – before it occurred to her that he was just some bloke on the pickup. 'Well, Mr Lincoln,' she said drily, 'it's lovely to meet you but I'm actually waiting for someone.'

'You've got time for a chat, then.'

There was something about his tone that unnerved Liv. 'I'll pass, thanks.'

'It wasn't a request.' Lincoln leaned forward and growled softly, 'Don Moody has a bone to pick with you.'

Liv's anxiety levels shot up. Moody was a West End villain with a none-too-pleasant reputation. Not the type of man you wanted to be on the wrong side of. 'I don't understand. Why should . . . I've never even met Mr Moody. What are you talking about?'

'No, but you have met a business associate of his.'

'Have I?'

'Mr Hallam.'

Liv stared blankly back. 'You've got the wrong person. I've never heard of him.'

'Perhaps you know him better as George, George Barnes. I believe you made his acquaintance yesterday at the Chesterton Hotel.'

A jolt of alarm passed through Liv and her body stiffened. Suddenly her mouth was dry. A cold knot was twisting in her guts as she tried to hold his gaze – and her nerve. 'I've . . . I've never been to—'

'Please don't waste my time, Liv. Or should I call you Nancy? The thing is, Mr Moody isn't happy. He's not happy at all. You see, it makes him look bad when someone he's invited to London, someone he's hoping to do business with, gets stung by a pair of two-bit con artists.'

Liv could have gone on protesting her innocence, but suspected it was pointless. Somehow Moody had managed to identify her and now wasn't the moment to try and figure out how. She was in big trouble. Realising that appeasement was probably the best way forward, she gave a rueful smile and said: 'Well, we weren't to know George was a friend of Mr Moody's, were we? It was a genuine mistake. I'm sorry.'

'Oh, you're sorry. That makes it all right then.'

'What more can I say?'

'It's more what you can do.' Lincoln drank some of his tea and put the cup back down. 'We'll start with the money, shall we?'

Liv hesitated, but then opened her bag, took out her purse, removed the notes, put them on the table and regretfully pushed them towards him.

Lincoln picked up the five notes and frowned. 'What's this?'

'Twenty-five quid.'

'And the rest?'

'That's my half. It's all there.'

'Hallam gave you a ton.'

Liv quickly shook her head. 'No, *half* a ton. Fifty. I swear. That's all we got.'

'Are you calling Hallam a liar?'

'No, but . . .'

'A ton,' Lincoln said. 'That's how much Mr Moody has returned to Hallam, and that's how much he wants back.'

Liv didn't know if Hallam was the liar or Pally was. 'I can't give him what I haven't got.' To prove her point, she opened her purse again and showed him the inside. 'Look, nothing else, see? It's empty. I haven't got any more.'

Lincoln's eyes bored into her. 'You've got a problem, then.'

'I'll get it,' Liv promised rashly. 'I'll pay him back. I promise. Every penny.'

'And when will that be, exactly?'

'As soon as I can, but I need some time. A week or two. But I'll get it. I will. You can give me a bit of time, can't you?' Liv's voice was pleading. Seeing him unmoved, she quickly hiked up the drama and wiped away an imaginary tear. '*Please*. I really am sorry. We never meant to . . . I'll sort it out. I won't let you down.'

Lincoln studied her for a few seconds and then gave a hollow laugh. 'Bravo,' he said. 'A lovely performance. But if you're trying to appeal to my better nature, it's a hopeless cause.'

Liv pulled a face. 'You can't blame a girl for trying.'

'Don't get smart with me, love.' Lincoln pushed back his chair, stood up and then leaned down towards her again. 'I'll see you soon. One chance, that's all you've got. Oh, and that person you're waiting for? If it's Pally I wouldn't bother. He's . . . how shall I put it? . . . somewhat *indisposed* at the moment.'

Liv gave a start, her eyes widening. 'What have you done to him?'

'Nothing that he didn't deserve.'

'And what's that supposed to mean?'

Lincoln didn't reply. He simply smirked, straightened up and walked away.

Liv held her breath and didn't release it again until after Lincoln had left the café. Shivers were running through her. She leapt to her feet – she had to go in search of Pally – but then immediately sat back down. What if it was a trick? What if they hadn't found him at all, but were just waiting for her to lead them to him? No, she'd seen the expression on Lincoln's face. They'd caught up with him all right.

She waited for a couple of minutes, glancing up and down the street to make sure Lincoln was really gone, before standing up again. Her legs felt shaky, but that wasn't going to stop her. She steadied herself against the table before heading for the door. Pally was out there somewhere and she had to find him.

4

Ralph McCall had come to the café to work on a piece he was writing for the *West End News*. The girl had arrived shortly after him and he'd been surreptitiously watching her ever since. She was worth looking at – a slim brunette with dark eyes and a sulky mouth – and now, as she was leaving, his gaze followed her all the way to the door.

He wondered how old she was. Well, old enough to be consorting with villains, that was for sure. There had been a quiet but clearly acrimonious exchange between her and the bloke before she'd handed over some money. Her pimp? Ralph wouldn't have taken her for a whore, not from the way she was dressed, but appearances could be deceptive. Soho was swimming in ladies of the night; they came in all shapes and sizes and catered for every taste.

Ralph watched the door close behind her, thought about her for a few more seconds and then turned his attention back to his notebook. He scored through a few lines and frowned. It was hard to create any attention-grabbing copy when all you had to work with was the week's proceedings at the local magistrates' court: a tedious procession of pickpockets, petty thieves and tarts. What he wanted was something juicy to get his teeth into.

He lit a cigarette and pondered on his career. It wasn't panning out quite as he'd envisaged. He had peaked too soon, perhaps, getting his first job on the *Hackney Herald* at the age of eighteen. Within two years he had moved from the East End to the West, believing then that it was only one small step to a position on a national. For ten years he'd been trying, but every time he applied, he got knocked back. Now, with his thirtieth birthday approaching, he was starting to think it would never happen. There was nothing fundamentally wrong with the *West End News* – it was a weekly paper, published every Thursday, with an average circulation and a modest reputation – but it was hardly cutting edge. He was a man who had ambition and what he needed was a big scoop, an exclusive that would propel him from obscurity into the inner sanctum of Fleet Street.

Ralph pulled on his cigarette and released a long, narrow stream of smoke. He deserved better, he knew he did, but opportunities always seemed to pass him by. Take the latest scandal, for example. Most of London's crime reporters were currently in Eastbourne where Scotland Yard had been called in to investigate a society doctor called John Bodkin Adams. There were, incredibly, suspicions that he could have murdered over four hundred of his patients. Now *that* was a story. And who had the editor sent to cover it? Henry bloody Squires, of course.

When Ralph had complained, he'd got short shrift.

'I can't afford to send you both,' Arthur Neames had said. 'Anyway, you should be grateful. With everyone else out of the way, there won't be any competition if something big breaks here.'

Which was small consolation. Especially as the chances

of anything decent occurring were slim. He felt passed over, ignored, as though all his hard work counted for nothing. Henry's glory days were long gone, but his reputation endured. Neames wouldn't get rid of him and for as long as he stayed Ralph would remain in his shadow.

He took a few more resentful puffs on his cigarette before angrily stubbing it out in the ashtray. He gazed across the café and out of the window. Soho was always busy but never more so than on a Saturday night. The place was a cesspit, heaving with pimps, whores, ponces, thieves and gamblers. Temptation lay all around like tiny drops of glittering poison.

He flipped shut his notebook and shoved it into his pocket. It was time to get positive, to put aside his bitterness and make things happen. Soho was full of stories, full of secrets and lies. All he had to do was go out there and dig. What the readers wanted was murder and mayhem, sleaze and depravity – and he was just the man to give it to them.

5

Liv had been searching for half an hour, visiting all of Pally's usual haunts. She went in and out of cafés and pubs, asking anyone she recognised if they'd seen him, but the answer was always the same. If she'd known where he lived, she'd have gone there too, but she didn't have a clue. Pally flitted from place to place, never staying anywhere for long. He wasn't a man for putting down roots.

As she tramped the streets, she was growing increasingly anxious. What if he was lying in some alleyway, bleeding to death? Should she ring round the hospitals? What if he was already dead? Panic seeped into her. But surely they wouldn't have gone that far? She reassured herself with the thought that if Mr Moody wanted his money back, he wouldn't get it by killing Pally.

Eventually she decided to try the French again and headed back to Dean Street. The pub's real name was the York Minster but none of the regulars ever called it that. Pally had told her it was because Charles de Gaulle had once written a speech there, but she didn't know if it was true or not. She didn't even know why she was thinking about it. Just something to distract her, to take her mind off the awfulness of what was happening.

She quickened her pace until she was almost running. *Please God, let him be here.* The French was his favourite drinking hole, the place to hang out until the clubs opened later in the evening. She girded herself for disappointment as she pushed open the door, but miraculously her prayer was answered. Pally was sitting at the bar with his back to her.

Liv rushed over 'Pally! God, I've been looking everywhere for you. I . . . ' But relief quickly switched to horror as he turned. His face was a bloodied mess: two black eyes, a split lip and a busted nose. 'Jesus! The state of you!'

Pally gave her a rueful smile. 'I'm all right, sweetheart. At least I will be when I've had a few more of these.' He lifted a glass to his mouth, wincing as the Scotch touched his lips. 'I went to the caff but you weren't there. I figured you'd find me here eventually.'

Liv cursed herself for not waiting longer. 'You should go to the hospital.'

'What for? There's nothing they can do.'

'They can clean you up, check that nothing's broken.'

'I prefer my own methods.' Pally knocked back the rest of his Scotch and raised his hand to get the attention of the barman. 'Put another one in there, will you. And whatever the lady's having.'

'I'll have the same,' Liv said, feeling in need of something strong to take the edge off. She grabbed a stool and sat down beside Pally. 'Did Lincoln do that to you?'

'Who's Lincoln?'

'Tall bloke. Dark hair. One of Moody's charming helpers. He came to the caff.'

Pally's eyes flashed. 'Did he hurt you? If he laid one finger on you, I'll—'

'No, nothing like that,' Liv said quickly, wondering what Pally could have done about it anyway. He could barely sit up straight, never mind wreak retribution. Still, she appreciated the thought. 'He just told me the error of my ways and relieved me of every penny I had.'

'Bastard.'

'Did he rob you too?'

'*They*,' Pally said indignantly, as if he might have stood a chance against one. 'There were two of them. A real pair of goons. They grabbed me on the way to the caff. And yeah, they took most of it.' He grinned, leaned down with a groan and removed a rolled-up fiver from his left sock. 'Not all of it, though.'

The drinks arrived and Pally pushed the note across the counter. The barman seemed unfazed by his appearance, as if it was perfectly normal to see his customers with their faces bashed in. Perhaps it wasn't that unusual. Soho was the kind of place where people often crossed the line – and just as often paid the price for it.

Liv grabbed her Scotch and took a large swig. 'So what are we going to do?'

'Do?'

'About the money. Moody wants the rest of it.'

'Moody's going to have to wait.'

'Lincoln reckons George gave us a ton. Why does he think that?'

Pally laughed. 'Yeah, well, that's what's called a profit margin.'

'It's double what we got.' Liv hesitated and then asked, 'Isn't it?'

'You know it is. Moody just wants his pound of flesh. Fancy

old George being a wrong 'un. I'd never have pegged him. Christ, I must be losing my touch.'

Liv shook her head. 'Don't say that. I didn't notice anything, either. I mean, he was just another mark. There was nothing to . . .'

'I messed up.'

'We *both* did,' Liv insisted. While Pally stared ruefully into his Scotch she wondered when George had realised he'd been conned. Perhaps he'd suspected even as Pally was putting on the squeeze, but hadn't been sure enough to call his bluff. He wouldn't have wanted a visit from the law, not if his business was less than legitimate. Too many awkward questions. 'How do you think Moody knew it was us?'

'Some snitch,' Pally said. He looked up from his drink and stared accusingly round the French. 'Some toe-rag must have put the finger on us.'

Liv wrinkled her nose. It was true that the West End was full of grasses, full of lowlifes prepared to sell anyone down the river for thirty pieces of silver. None of them could have known for certain that she and Pally had been at the Chesterton, but their names could have been put forward as possible suspects. From that point on they'd have been in the frame, and with the descriptions George had provided, it wouldn't have taken long for Moody to figure it out. A grey wig only went so far in disguising your identity. 'How are we going to get the money if we can't work?'

'Like I said, he'll have to wait.'

And it would be a while, Liv thought, glancing at Pally. Another two weeks, maybe three, before his face healed. Pally couldn't play the part of Mr Respectable when he looked like he'd been in a street fight. 'I doubt if Moody is the patient sort.'

'Then we'll just have to keep our heads down.'

'Like we're doing now, you mean?'

Pally shrugged. 'He's made his point. There won't be any more trouble tonight.'

Liv hoped he was right. Pally never seemed to worry much about money – easy come, easy go – but being short always made her nervous. She had a few quid stashed away at her lodgings, but that wouldn't last long, not after she'd paid her board, bought food and the rest. If only she'd put a bit more aside, but it was too late to fret about that now. With her only source of income cut off for the next few weeks, she would have to find another way to earn a living.

'Cheer up,' Pally said. 'It's not the end of the world. We'll be back in business before you know it.'

6

By the time she was on her third Scotch, Liv's spirits were starting to improve. There was no need to stress. This was just a bit of bad luck. Pally was right: it wasn't the end of the world. She still had options. She could type. She had shorthand. She had a reference. She'd be able to find some temporary work to tide her over – and, hopefully, keep Moody at bay.

The more she drank, the less anxious she became, and by ten o'clock she was in a mood approaching optimism. Bad things happened and you simply had to roll with them. By now she and Pally had moved away from the bar and taken a table near the door. People they knew came and went, all of them sympathetic, and most of them buying drinks. Suddenly life didn't seem so bad.

Verity came in with a bunch of other girls from the Windmill, the whole crowd laughing and joking. When she saw the state of Pally, she instantly stopped smiling, broke away from the group and came over to talk to him. He gave her the same tale he'd been telling everyone else – a random attack in the street from a couple of robbers – and she widened her blue eyes, clicked her tongue and cursed his assailants.

'In broad daylight too! Bleedin' thugs! Those buggers need locking up. Is it agony, hon? Have you seen a doctor?'

'He won't,' Liv said.

'You could have broken something.'

'That's what I said.'

Pally waved away their concerns. 'If it was anything serious, I'd be dead by now.'

Someone else came to the table and while Pally was distracted, Verity sat down beside Liv, leaned in and asked softly, 'So what's the real story?'

'He got jumped by a pair of Don Moody's goons.'

'You're kidding? What did he do to upset Moody?'

'We picked the wrong mark yesterday. Turns out the geezer was a business mate of his. Now Moody wants the money back – well, more than the money. Extra on top. Double, in fact. Like we can just spirit *that* out of thin air.' Liv dived into her Scotch, took a large swig and put the glass down. 'I had to hand over everything I had, the whole bleedin' lot.'

'Oh God, were you there when they beat up Pally?'

'No, I was waiting for him in the caff. Some bloke called Lincoln came in, gave me what for and got me to empty my purse. I reckon he'll be back in a week or two to get the rest.'

'What are you going to do?'

'Give it to him, of course. I'm not going to mess with the likes of Moody. Trouble is, Pally's out of the game for a while so I'll have to find some other way to raise the cash. It's back to the typing pool, I suppose.'

Verity squeezed Liv's arm. 'I'm sorry, love. I could get you an audition at the Windmill if you like. They're always looking for girls and the pay's not bad.'

'I couldn't.'

'Why not?'

Liv arched her eyebrows. 'Well, I can't sing, can't dance and I'd die of embarrassment if I had to take my clothes off. Apart from that, nothing.'

'Oh, you soon get used to it. Everyone feels like that at first. And anyone can dance with a bit of practice.'

'I'll think about it,' Liv said, even though she knew she wouldn't. There wasn't much she'd refuse to try, but baring her breasts to the world was one of them. It was a step too far. Although she was used to being leered at by men, she recoiled from the thought of doing it on stage.

'We're going to the Gargoyle later. Why don't you come along? It'll cheer you up. Cynthia knows some chap who's a member so he can sign us all in.'

'All right,' Liv said. 'Why not?' With her finances taking such a serious knock, she probably wouldn't get many nights out over the next few weeks. And this one wouldn't cost her a bean. The Windmill girls were always in demand – men queued up to buy them drinks – and they were good fun too.

'I need a pee,' Verity said, rising to her feet. 'See you in a minute.'

Liv watched as she pushed her way through the crowd. Verity was a tall, pretty blonde with a bubbly personality and a big heart. They'd met at the boarding house, shortly after Liv had come to London and she couldn't have asked for a better friend. Smiling, she sat back, happy at the prospect of a few more hours of oblivion. She liked the Gargoyle, a private club where there weren't any boundaries. The lower classes mixed with the upper, poets with bankers, artists with villains, drunks with dreamers. You could be queer or straight or anything in between and nobody gave a damn.

Five minutes passed and then five minutes more. Pally was busy recounting his story again, telling it to someone new and embellishing the truth as he went along. By the time they got kicked out of the pub, he'd probably be claiming to have fought off a pack of wolves with his hands tied behind his back. Still, she didn't blame him. After what he'd been through today, he deserved his moment in the spotlight.

Liv glanced around the pub, searching for Verity. It took a while but eventually she spotted her, speaking to a bloke at the bar. The two of them were standing close, their bodies almost touching. She didn't think anything of it – Verity was always being chatted up – but then the man, who'd had his back turned, moved to the side to let someone pass, and she saw his face for the first time. Her heart leapt into her mouth. God, it was Lincoln! It was Tom bloody Lincoln!

A stream of questions rushed into her head: what was his game? Why was he here? Why was he talking to Verity? Just a coincidence or . . .? She half rose to her feet, but then quickly sat down again. What was she going to do – storm over there and cause a scene? That wouldn't achieve anything, other than letting Lincoln know he'd got under her skin.

She continued to stare, willing Verity to break away from him and come back to the table. But Verity only threw back her head and laughed. She was about to tell Pally, but then had second thoughts. He might do something stupid. What if he decided to confront Lincoln, to have a go, to try and perform some drunken heroics? He'd end up on his backside, looking even worse than he did now.

Liv crossed her legs, uncrossed them, drank some Scotch, lit a cigarette and smoked furiously with her eyes fixed on Lincoln. Perhaps she should go over to him. Should she? And say what? She had the feeling that he was, in some subtle way, attempting to intimidate her – I know where you drink, I know who your friends are – but wasn't sure if it was the booze making her paranoid.

Eventually, after what felt like an eternity, Verity came back with a glass in her hand and a smile on her face. She sat down, looked at Liv, frowned and said, 'What's wrong?'

'That's *him*,' Liv hissed softly. 'That man you've been talking to. He's Tom Lincoln, the sod who took all my money.'

'What? No way! What?'

They both looked towards the bar, but Lincoln had disappeared.

'What did he say to you?' Liv asked.

Verity shook her head. 'Nothing. Well, nothing about you or Pally. God, if I'd known who he was, I wouldn't have given him the time of day.'

'It's not your fault.'

'He was just making small talk, the usual stuff. He seemed nice enough. He bought me a gin and . . . Jesus! Was he one of the thugs who beat up Pally?'

'I don't think so. He wouldn't want to get blood on that nice, smart suit of his, would he? No, I reckon he left the dirty work to someone else.' Liv scanned the bar again, but there was still no sign of him. 'He's up to something. Do you think he followed me here?'

Verity looked doubtful. 'I mean, he could have, but why would he? He's already got what he wanted.'

'Not all of it.'

'It could just be chance. Lots of people drink here.'

'I've never seen him in the French before.' Although, Liv conceded, the place was often so crowded, he could easily have been here without her noticing. But something in her gut told her she was right to be suspicious. 'I don't like it.'

'He's gone now. There's nothing to worry about.'

Liv wished she had Verity's confidence, but it was hard *not* to worry. Lincoln's appearance had put her back on edge. She drank the last of her Scotch and gazed regretfully into the empty glass. Last orders had already been called, and the customers were starting to leave. Pally was on his feet too, wincing as he pulled on his jacket. 'Come on, lovelies,' he said. 'The night is young.'

They all made their way towards the door where Cynthia and the other Windmill girls were waiting, and then spilled out on to the street in a frothy, laughing mass like they'd been popped straight out of a champagne bottle. It was only as they were setting off for the Gargoyle that Verity stopped abruptly, took Liv's arm and said, 'Oh God, I've just remembered something. That Lincoln asked if I had any plans for the evening and I told him I was going to the Gargoyle.'

'What?'

'He probably won't show up, and if he does I'll give him what for. You'll be fine. It doesn't matter. You'll be with the rest of us.'

Liv, whose mood had already taken a downward turn, suddenly lost her desire for any further carousing. 'Actually, I think I'll give it a miss. I've had enough. I'm going to go home.'

'No, don't do that. Come on, don't let him get to you.'

But he already had. The Gargoyle was a large club with plenty of places to lurk. She couldn't bear the thought of Lincoln being there, spying on her, watching her every move. How could she relax when she knew he could be in the shadows somewhere? 'It's not that,' she lied. 'I'm just not in the mood. You go. Go and catch up with the others or you won't get in.'

Verity glanced to her right. The rest of the crowd were turning into Meard Street, the sound of their footsteps changing as they moved on to the cobbles, their voices shrill on the cool evening air.

32

'Go on,' Liv urged again. 'I'll be fine. I'll see you tomorrow.'

'Are you sure?'

'I'm sure.'

Finally, Verity left, and Liv began her short journey home. She was never bothered walking about at night on her own. Soho was always busy and, despite its reputation, she usually felt safe and secure as though nothing bad could happen to her here. But it was different tonight; she had Lincoln on her mind.

It was just as she reached the end of Dean Street and turned into Shaftesbury Avenue that the back of her neck started prickling. She kept glancing over her shoulder, sure that he was there, but every time she looked, he was nowhere to be seen. Just her imagination playing tricks? Just the whisky blurring reason? But compared to Pally, she knew that she had got off lightly. Perhaps Lincoln wasn't finished with her yet.

Now she was wishing that she hadn't separated from the others. Safety in numbers, right? She upped the pace as she crossed Shaftesbury Avenue and then turned left until she reached Whitcomb Street. Not far now. The boarding house was only a hundred yards away. It was quieter here, off from the main thoroughfare, and she felt more vulnerable. There was still an occasional car passing by, but otherwise the street was deserted. She muttered to herself as she walked, an encouraging pep talk on how she shouldn't let her imagination run riot. 'There's no one there,' she repeated several times. 'No one, no one.'

By the time she was approaching the house, her nerves were frayed. Fear had partly sobered her up, but she still stumbled a little as she hurried on. She fumbled in her handbag for her key, plucked it out and immediately dropped it. Cursing softly, she stopped, bent down and snatched it off the pavement.

It was as she straightened up that she heard the sound – a soft, mocking laugh floating on the air. She whirled around but the street was empty. Where had it come from? For a moment she stood very still, straining her eyes, straining her ears, but there was nothing to see and nothing more to hear. She held her breath. She could feel the fast thump of her heart in her chest.

Adrenalin eventually propelled her forward, along the last few yards. The house was in darkness and it took her a few frantic seconds to insert the key into the lock. Her hand was shaking as she turned it, pushed open the door and almost tumbled over the threshold. With relief, she closed the door behind her, switched on the dim light, crossed the hallway and ran up the stairs.

7

Slug waited until he heard the door close before stepping back out on to the pavement. He had tailed the girl from the French, keeping his distance, ducking in and out of shop doorways in order to keep out of sight. She must have either sensed his presence or been the nervous sort because she'd kept glancing back over her shoulder. This had made the whole enterprise more interesting, more of a challenge, but he'd been the winner in the end. She hadn't spotted him and that was all that counted.

He knew whose house it was – it belonged to Dora Marks – so he knew too that the girl must be one of her lodgers. He tugged his cap down over his eyes as he passed. With hunched shoulders, he walked quickly on before crossing the road, turning right into Coventry Street and heading back towards Soho. His mouth twisted into a freakish grin. It had scared her when he'd laughed, which was why he'd done it. There was no fun in the game without fear. He gave a snort and wiped his nose on the back of his sleeve.

Slug was used to staying out of sight. He had spent the war

on the lam, keeping his head down and dodging the attentions of the military police. And even now, eleven years after peace had been declared, he still lived in the shadows. He was happiest under the cover of darkness, slithering quietly from place to place. The West End was where he roamed, and Soho was where he felt most at home; there was no alleyway, no dark corner or filthy crevice that he wasn't familiar with.

In a peculiar way, he missed the war. The blackouts and the Blitz had provided endless opportunities for gain. Even the clumsiest dip could pick a pocket or two in the pitch black. And there'd been plenty to be salvaged from the bombed-out buildings. This was classed as looting, of course, but personally he'd never seen the harm. Finders, keepers. And it wasn't as if the stuff was much use to the poor dead sods buried under the rubble.

Some men had made their fortunes from the war, flogging goods on the black market or from forging petrol coupons. Most of them were still around, only now they'd moved into clubs and gambling and girls. It was to these men that Slug made himself useful, gathering information about their enemies: who they were meeting, who they'd fallen out with, who was planning what – all the rumour and gossip from the underworld. He frequented the same places as the villains did, keeping his ear to the ground, watching everyone and everything.

No one noticed Slug, or if they did, they classed him as irrelevant; just a scruffy old bloke with his nose stuck in a pint. Sometimes, if he needed extra cash or felt he had been slighted in some way, he would even pass on leads to the law. He didn't feel bad about grassing. Why should he? It was every man for himself in this world. He had loyalty to no one, just as no one had any loyalty to him.

He thought about the dark-haired girl and grinned again.

He had no idea why Lincoln wanted her address, wanted her followed, and didn't care either. It was no concern of his. So long as he got paid, he never asked any questions. He was glad, though, that she'd split off from the others and not gone on to a club. That would have meant standing around for half the night, kicking his heels while he waited for her to come out again.

Girls, in Slug's experience, usually meant trouble. This one had looked faintly familiar when Lincoln had pointed her out in the French. He reckoned he had seen her around – he had a good memory for faces – in another pub, perhaps, or in one of the many Soho caffs. The whole area was swarming with tarts, with toms and strippers and exotic dancers, all of them relying on the lusts of men to make a living.

Slug's own lusts were a private matter. He kept them close to his chest, wrapped up tight and away from public view. There had been that unfortunate incident during the war, but he didn't tend to dwell on that. For some reason, however, it had crept back into his head tonight. The woman had been slim with white-blonde hair and had smelled of cheap scent. Sometimes he'd be walking down a street and he would get a whiff of that perfume again. It would bring him up short, an unwelcome reminder, and send a tremor through his body. A misunderstanding, that's all it had been, and if the silly bitch hadn't kicked up such a fuss, he wouldn't have been forced to do what he had.

He tried to push away the memory and concentrate instead on the here and now. There was nothing to be gained by reliving past mistakes. And anyway, it had not been entirely his fault: her mouth had said one thing while her eyes said another. Crossed wires, mixed signals, an accident. These things happened. Time passed and it was no longer relevant.

Slug pushed on and soon he was absorbed back into the heart

of Soho, into its rowdy nightlife and squalid diversions. He kept his eyes open and his ears pricked. As he walked along Brewer Street, he bent to pick up a half-smoked cigarette lying in the gutter and dropped it into his pocket. Waste not, want not.

8

Liv woke with a hangover on Sunday morning. Too much whisky had left her with a dry mouth, a dull headache and a fog in her brain. Why did she never learn? Now she would feel like hell for at least half the day. She lay for a while, her eyes screwed up, gazing at a thin ribbon of light sliding between the curtains. At first it just seemed like any other morning after the night before, but gradually the reason for her overindulgence began to leak into her head, a steady drip of unwelcome information: Pally, George, Lincoln, the debt she owed to Moody. She groaned, rolled over and buried her face in the pillow.

What she longed for most was to go back to sleep, to forget about it all, but there was fat chance of that. Now that she'd remembered, she couldn't stop going over everything that had happened. From the moment she'd sat down near George Hallam, from the moment she'd got out her *A–Z*, she'd been on a hiding to nothing. If only she could turn back time, but unfortunately that option wasn't open to her.

Despite being cocooned in the bedclothes, Liv shivered when

she thought about Don Moody. He wasn't the kind of man to let these things go. He'd want his money no matter what, and sooner rather than later. And Lincoln, of course, would be on her back until she delivered. She wondered how Lincoln had found her, how he'd known she would be at the caff. Had she been followed? Or had Pally told the goons who'd beaten him up? There was no point in asking him – he was bound to deny it – and it didn't really matter. They'd have found her eventually, one way or another.

Once Liv realised that more sleep was an impossibility, she got up, pulled on her dressing gown, picked up her washbag and towel, and padded along the landing to the bathroom. Thankfully it was empty. She had a pee, washed her hands and face, brushed her teeth and frowned at her reflection in the mirror. Not a pretty sight. Her face was less than radiant, her eyes puffy and half closed. She rubbed her temples, trying to dispel the ache. She felt lousy. Still, it was probably nothing compared to what Pally was feeling this morning.

'I will never drink again,' she muttered.

This was a resolution often made and never stuck to. There was too much temptation in Soho, too many opportunities. Somehow, she always ended up in one pub or another, and no matter how many hangovers she endured, she still went back for more. The booze helped her deal with things, helped her forget, but the pain and confusion were still there when she sobered up again.

As she walked back, she paused outside Verity's door and listened. All quiet. She hadn't heard her come home so it must have been late. Had Lincoln shown up at the Gargoyle last night? She wanted to find out, but it would have to wait. It could be hours before Verity surfaced. With a sigh, she returned to her room.

Liv got dressed in a pair of navy slacks and a lightweight

cream sweater. She pulled back the curtains and looked out at a cloudy August sky. It was still summer but already there was a nip of autumn in the air. Lowering her gaze, she glanced along the street, remembering her panic when she thought she was being followed. From now on she would take more care; men like Moody and Lincoln wouldn't have any qualms when it came to terrorising women. They'd put the squeeze on their own grannies if it meant a few extra quid in their pockets.

She cursed the day she'd walked into the Chesterton. Bad luck didn't even begin to describe it. Although she didn't exactly live within the confines of the law, she'd always managed to steer clear of trouble and had deliberately kept her distance from men she viewed as serious criminals. But there was no avoiding them now. She'd have them on her case until the debt was settled.

Liv retreated from the window, brushed her hair and went downstairs. Her landlady, Dora, was hunched over the kitchen table checking her pools coupon against the football results in the Sunday paper. Aline Bowers, who had a room on the top floor, was sitting beside her, neatly sewing a button on to a white blouse.

'Morning,' Dora said.

'If you can call it that,' Aline said drily.

Liv ignored her. Aline couldn't open her mouth without something scornful coming out of it. 'Morning,' she said back to Dora. 'Is there a brew going?'

'On the stove, love. Help yourself.'

'Ta.' Liv poured herself a cup from the teapot, added milk and sugar and gave it a stir. She sat down and nodded towards Dora's coupon. 'Any luck?'

Dora put down her pencil and shook her head. 'Not even close. Maybe next week.'

'You're wasting your money,' Aline said. 'I don't know why you bother.'

'You won't be saying that when I'm riding around in my Rolls Royce.'

Aline bit off a piece of thread with her teeth and lifted up the blouse to view her handiwork. 'No good ever came of gambling. The devil's work, that's what it is.'

'Well, the devil's welcome to throw a few quid my way any time he feels like it.'

Aline tutted.

Liv wondered if she should start doing the pools. A good win was just what she needed, the answer to all her problems. She blew on the surface of her tea and took a sip.

'Aren't you going to have some breakfast?' Dora asked.

The thought of food made Liv's stomach turn over. 'Maybe later. I'm not that hungry at the moment.'

Aline, guessing the reason for her lack of appetite, shot her a disapproving look. Liv pretended not to notice. The mere hint of a girl having a good time was usually enough to send the older woman running for her bible. A devout Catholic, Aline went to early morning Mass every Sunday where she probably prayed for the black souls of her fellow lodgers. A hopeless cause if ever there was one.

'Was it busy last night?' Dora asked. 'You look tired.'

Liv nodded, the motion causing her head to hurt more. She tried not to wince. 'It's always packed out on a Saturday. You'd think there was nowhere else to go in London.' So far as her landlady was concerned, Liv still worked as an usherette at the Odeon in Leicester Square, the job she'd had when she'd first rented the room. She'd kept her subsequent change of employment under her hat. Although Dora was a broad-minded sort of person, her liberality didn't quite extend to having con artists living under her roof.

From tomorrow, however, Liv would be searching for a more legitimate way to make a weekly wage. Her heart sank at the prospect. She certainly wasn't going back to the cinema where she had to be constantly on her feet, and on her guard too against all the chancers trying to touch her up in the dark. No, a dull but sensible position in a typing pool would do until Pally's face had healed and normal service could be resumed.

'And down the pub after, I suppose,' Aline said, pursing her lips.

'Only for a quick one,' Liv lied. 'No harm in that, is there?'

Dora chuckled. 'No harm at all, love. You enjoy yourself while you're young.'

'It's what the enjoying leads to,' Aline said. 'That's the trouble.'

Liv raised her eyebrows, sat back and studied the two women. She had never understood what they had in common, other than having lived in the same house for over twenty years. They were like chalk and cheese, physically and temperamentally. Dora was in her early seventies, small and plump, round as a dumpling, easy-going and personable, whereas Aline, in her fifties, was tall and skinny, narrow-minded, severe and judgemental. Liv couldn't see what united them unless it was simply familiarity.

'You should think on,' Aline continued. 'That's all I'm saying. God sees *everything*.'

Normally Liv would react to Aline's insinuations, come back with some retort, give as good as she got, but this morning she was too hungover to even bother trying. Instead she just let it wash over her, certain that God, if he even existed, had better things to do than to watch her every move.

A copy of the *West End News*, a few days old, was lying on the table and Liv pulled it towards her. She never normally read the paper but began leafing through the pages in the hope it would save her from having to make any further contribution to the conversation. Perhaps, if she looked absorbed enough, she'd be left in peace to finish her tea.

A few quiet minutes passed and then suddenly her pretence at being interested in what she was reading became real. It wasn't so much the story, a piece on a possibly murderous Eastbourne doctor, as the byline that caught her attention. The article had been written by a man called Henry Squires and that name meant something to her. She drew in an audible breath.

Dora looked up from her own paper, glanced at what Liv was reading and said: 'It's shocking, isn't it? I mean, a doctor. Who'd have thought it? None of us are safe in our own beds these days.'

Aline clicked her tongue. 'I don't see how you come to that conclusion. You don't live in Eastbourne, you're not his patient and you're not rich enough to be bumped off for your fortune. As such, I can't see you as being in any imminent danger.'

But Dora, who liked a bit of drama, refused to concede the point. 'Well, you don't know how many of them are at it, do you? This could be the tip of the iceberg. There might be doctors all over the country doing exactly the same thing.'

'Hardly likely.'

'But not impossible.'

'He's not even been found guilty yet. You can't believe everything you read in the papers.'

While the two of them continued the debate, Liv gazed down at the byline. After she had come to London, one of the first things she'd done was to find a phone box and make a call to the *Daily Mail*. 'Could I speak to Mr Squires, please?'

The man on the other end of the line had sounded harassed. 'Sorry, who? What was the name?'

In the background she'd heard chatter and the noise of clacking typewriters. 'Mr Squires,' she'd repeated. 'Henry Squires.'

'Mr Squires doesn't work here any more.'

'Oh, all right. So could you tell me where—'

But he'd rung off before she could even finish the question. It had been a setback, but not too much of a disappointment. After nineteen years she could hardly have expected Squires to be at the same place. And at least the man hadn't said he was dead. That was something. She could have tried a few other papers – had intended to, in fact – but somehow had never got around to it. Or maybe her courage had just drained away. Tomorrow, she'd kept telling herself, until weeks and then months and now almost a year had gone by.

Seeing his name in bold print felt like a sign to Liv. It was time to face up to the past. As a local reporter, Squires would cover Soho and all the surrounding areas. It was possible, she thought, that she'd even passed him in the street or stood beside him in a pub. How strange was that? She closed the newspaper, checked the address on the back – Tottenham Court Road – and resolved to finally do what she'd been putting off for way too long.

Liv finished her tea, stood up, washed the cup at the sink and left it to dry on the drainer. 'I'm going out for a walk. I need some fresh air.'

'Take your brolly,' Dora said. 'It looks like rain.'

9

Before leaving the safety of the doorway, Liv glanced quickly up and down the street, checking there were no suspicious characters lurking in the vicinity. She didn't need more surprises coming her way, from either Lincoln or any of Moody's other goons. When she was sure the coast was clear, she set off at a brisk pace, partly to try and shake the cobwebs from her fogged-up head but mainly so she wouldn't get cold feet and change her mind. Determination was what was required now. She had to hold her nerve and not shy away from the truth, no matter how unpleasant it was.

While she walked, she tried to figure out what she'd say to Henry Squires. It would be a surprise her turning up after all these years. She put together some sentences, a way of introducing herself, but they all sounded wrong. Frowning, she sought better ones. Would the office even be open? She presumed it would; the news didn't stop happening just because it was the Sabbath.

In the distance she could hear church bells ringing. They

reminded her of all the times she had gone to church with her mum, week in, week out, always neat and respectable in their Sunday best. What had her mother so ardently prayed for, kneeling down with her pale face covered by her hands? Probably that the secret would never come out, that the sins of the father would not be delivered on the daughter.

When she thought of her mum, Liv got an ache in her chest. It was impossible to accept that she'd never see her again, talk to her again, wake to the sound of her moving around. All that had been safe and comforting was gone; her anchor had been snatched away. Without her mum in her life, nothing seemed that important any more. Except, perhaps, the unravelling of the past.

Liv strode on until she came to Cambridge Circus, where she turned up Charing Cross Road and then on to Tottenham Court Road. Here she slowed as she checked the numbers on the doorways and counted them off until she found the right building. It was a shabby block of offices, in need of a coat of paint, with several metal plaques attached to the outside wall, including one that said *West End News*.

She hesitated, took a few deep breaths and stepped inside. A wide reception desk was situated to one side of the foyer, but there was no one behind it. Even without the list of businesses on the wall, stating where they could be found, she would have known where to go. Voices floated down from the first floor along with the steady clack and ting of typewriters.

Liv climbed the stairs, her fingers gripping the metal banister. When she came to the top, she didn't stop – this was no time to be having second thoughts – but walked purposefully through the open door. Instantly she was assailed by the smell of sweat, cigarette smoke and ink. There were three men inside, two of them sitting behind typewriters, the other hunched over a pile of papers with a pencil in his hand.

As soon as she entered everything fell silent. The men all lifted their heads and stared at her, a slightly startled expression on their faces as though they'd never seen a woman in the office before. She glanced at each of them in turn – she had no idea what Henry looked like – but only one, the one with the pencil, seemed to be of the right age.

'I'm sorry to disturb you,' she said to him. 'I'm looking for Henry Squires.'

'Sorry, love, he's away.'

'Do you know when he'll be back?'

'A day? Two days? There's no telling with Henry. Is it anything urgent? Do you want to leave a message?'

Liv, disappointed, shook her head. 'No, it'll keep. Thanks.'

She quickly withdrew, feeling like an intruder in the very male space, but had barely started down the stairs when the youngest of the three men caught up with her. He was a skinny bloke in his late twenties with short straw-coloured hair and sly, eager eyes.

'Ralph McCall,' he said. 'How do you do?'

Liv nodded, smiled faintly, but didn't reciprocate with her own name. This, however, didn't deter him.

'I was wondering if I could be of any help? I'm Henry's right-hand man, you see. We work together all the time. If there's anything . . .'

'Thank you, but no. It's personal.'

'He might not be back for quite a while.'

'Your associate said a day or two.'

'It could be longer. But, like I said, we work together, so anything you want to tell him, you can tell me. We could get things started, save some time.'

Liv's smile had faded. Her tone, when she spoke again, was firm. 'And like *I* said, it's personal. There's no story here, Mr McCall. This was just a social call.'

'So you know Henry, then?'

'I really have to go.'

Liv began walking down the stairs, but McCall wasn't giving up. He stuck to her side like some stray dog who'd sniffed out a pork chop in her pocket.

'I've seen you before, haven't I?' he said. 'You were in Joe's yesterday. Old Compton Street, right?'

Liv was starting to regret that she'd ever come here. She neither admitted nor denied that she'd been in the café but just kept on walking.

'I was sitting across the other side and saw that bloke come over to talk to you. If you're in some kind of bother . . . '

Liv stopped, stared at him and said: 'If I was in some kind of bother, Mr McCall, I'd go to the law, not the press. But as it happens, I'm not, so if you don't mind, I really have to get on.'

'Are you sure? Because . . . '

But Liv was already heading down the stairs again, walking fast, almost running in her determination to shake him off. She reached the bottom, flew across the foyer and hurried out on to the street. Even there she didn't feel entirely safe from his attentions. She crossed the road and glanced back. The doorway was empty. Good, he was gone. But her relief was short-lived. When she lifted her gaze to the first-floor window she saw him standing there, watching her.

10

As Ralph McCall turned away from the window, he felt the irritation that comes with letting something promising slip through your fingers. He had not been firm enough, persuasive enough, friendly enough. She hadn't trusted him and now she had gone. Damn it! He should have stuck with her, tried harder. He shouldn't have let her dismiss him so easily. The girl knew something; he had seen it in her eyes. And he had seen the worry on her face in the café yesterday. She had come here prepared to spill the beans, to tell all, but only to Henry Squires.

Ralph cursed softly under his breath. Why had she chosen Henry? He'd been famous once – well, as famous as any reporter could be – but she wasn't old enough to remember those days. Personal, she'd said, but that could mean anything. From the way she'd hesitated at the office door, her gaze falling on each of them in turn, he had the feeling she had never actually met Henry before.

He wondered if he should go after her, try again. It might not be too late. He retraced his steps, returning to the window, but already she was out of sight. For a while he gazed along the almost empty road before accepting defeat and sitting back down. Frustration nagged at him and he typed with only half his mind on what he was doing, his fingers bashing absently against the keys as he put the finishing touches to the story he was writing.

The completed piece was hardly riveting, just another column filler about a brawl that had taken place in Greek Street with a few local villains trying to knock seven bells out of each other. The story was hardly new – Soho was awash with criminals, major and minor, all jostling for position in the West End – but he had embellished it with a few quotes from witnesses and for a bit of extra colour had added some made up ones of his own.

Ralph pulled the sheet of paper out of the typewriter, reread it, reckoned it was the best it was going to get and immediately turned his attention to more interesting things. The girl jumped into his thoughts again. He had a gut feeling that he was on to something with her, that what he'd witnessed yesterday was more than just a grubby exchange between a whore and her pimp. And now that he'd talked to her, he was even more convinced. She had been well spoken – not that that was any guarantee of virtue – and smart enough to not give anything away. She had been defensive, evasive and far too eager to get shot of him.

Or was he just creating drama where there wasn't any? Perhaps the bloke she'd met in the café had been nothing more than a money lender, one of those greedy, grasping sharks who never let go once they got their teeth into you. But then why come to Henry? No, it had to be something juicier than that. Blackmail, perhaps. Yes, that would explain why she was so wary. Except, as she'd said herself, she'd go to the law rather than the press if she was in any serious kind of trouble.

He went over his brief exchange with her, searching for more clues. She didn't come from round here, that was for sure: her accent was southern but not London. Close up she'd looked a little older than he'd originally thought, not a teenager but not long into adulthood, either. He had caught a whiff of alcohol and toothpaste on her breath. What else was useful? Nothing much: an attractive girl, money changing hands, a villain, something that she needed Henry's help with. On the surface it didn't exactly add up to the story of the century, but his reporter's nose wouldn't stop twitching.

He was still pondering on it all when the door at the rear of the office opened and Arthur Neames stuck his head out. 'McCall!'

Ralph jumped up and hurried over. 'What is it?'

'It's your lucky day,' Neames said. 'I've just got word that a body's been found down an alley off Dean Street. You'd better get yourself over there, see what you can find out.'

'Man or a woman?'

'I've no idea.'

'Foul play, do you think?'

'Are you still here?'

'Okay, okay, I'm on my way.'

Like a warning, Neames called after him, 'Henry's back tomorrow morning.'

With those unwelcome words ringing in his ears, Ralph hurried through the office, picked up a notebook and grabbed his jacket off the back of his chair. He took the stairs two at a time and hurtled through the foyer. Outside a thin drizzle had started to fall. He turned up the collar of his jacket, raised his eyes to the heavens and prayed that the corpse wasn't just some old tramp who had drunk himself to death. Murder was what he was hoping for, and that the victim was female. It always made for better copy. The public was more sympathetic to the killing of a woman, and more fascinated by it.

By the time Ralph got to Dean Street it had been sealed off by the police and a three-deep crowd had gathered. The onlookers bobbed up and down, straining their necks to get a better view. He sidled up to an elderly lady wearing a stripy headscarf and asked innocently, 'What's going on here, then?'

The old dear turned her pale, eager eyes on him and said, 'Found a body, ain't they?' She swiftly crossed herself. 'Poor soul.'

'A body? Lord, how awful!'

'A couple of kids found her. She was just lying there in the alley with all the rubbish.'

Ralph's ears pricked up. 'So it's a woman, then?'

'That's what they're saying. Poor thing could have been there for days.'

'Do they know what happened to her?'

The old lady, clearly reluctant to relinquish her position as the fount of all knowledge, frowned while she thought about it. 'Well, someone did for her, that's for sure. It weren't natural, if that's what you're asking.' She gestured towards the police. 'They wouldn't all be here if it were.'

The woman to her right, only slightly younger, couldn't resist putting her oar in. 'I heard someone say her throat had been slit.'

'Strangled. That's what I heard,' another voice piped up.

Knowing he had learnt all that he was going to and that they were now in the realm of rumour and Chinese whispers, Ralph looked around, spotted a uniformed constable he knew called Green and ambled over to him.

PC Green gave an exaggerated sigh. 'I was wondering when you'd show your face.'

'Nice to see you too,' Ralph said. 'Suspicious death is it?'

'Could be.'

'Aw, come on,' Ralph said. 'You got an ID yet?'

'I can't tell you that.'

Ralph wasn't deterred. Green was one of those cops with an inflated sense of his own importance, the type who liked to be in possession of information other people wanted. Eventually, after a bit of gentle persuasion, he'd give up what he knew. 'A woman, right? Is she local? Come on, mate, help me out here. I'll find out eventually so why not tell me now?'

Green put his nose in the air.

Ralph changed tactics. 'Who's in charge of the case, then?' He glanced along Dean Street towards the place where the dark mouth of the alleyway opened. Standing on the corner was a detective talking to a couple of uniforms. 'Ah, DI Bentley. Perhaps I'll have a word with him instead.'

'Bentley won't tell you nothin',' Green said firmly.

'Maybe he will, maybe he won't.' Ralph turned as if to walk off, but Green, unwilling to give up any possible advantage that might be coming his way – usually a few free pints down the pub – quickly stopped him in his tracks. 'All right, hold yer horses. I might have something for you. Don't suppose it'll do any harm.'

'Go on then.'

Green lowered his voice, paused for dramatic effect and then said softly, 'It's Moll, Moll Ainsworth.'

'Are you sure?'

'Course I'm sure. I've nicked the poor cow often enough.'

Moll was familiar to Ralph from her regular appearances in the magistrates' court for soliciting. A middle-aged, local tom, she had always accepted her fines with quiet resignation and then immediately gone out on to the streets again. He felt a stab of inappropriate disappointment that the victim hadn't been younger, prettier and more glamorous. 'A punter then, you reckon?'

'Like as not,' Green said. 'Strangled by the looks of it, but we'll know more later.'

Ralph wasn't shocked. The unfortunate truth was that toms were always in danger of being beaten up, or worse. He felt sorry for Moll in a vague sort of way, but most of his pity was reserved for himself. Although he would still have a story, it would not be as sensational as he'd hoped.

'Someone said she was found by a couple of kids.'

'You shouldn't believe all you hear. The street cleaner found her, clearing up after last night,' Green said. 'You know what state this place gets in on a Saturday.'

'Must have been a nasty surprise. You got a name?'

Green stared at him. 'You've had enough from me. You'd better push off before the guvnor spots us.'

Ralph grinned, glanced towards DI Bentley, gave a nod and wandered back towards the crowd. In his head he had already started to compile the piece – the *gruesome* discovery of the body, the *appalling* crime, the *vile* act of a stranger – trying to make the best of the situation. What you needed for this kind of reporting was a good supply of adjectives. To add to the atmosphere, he thought he might have the church bells tolling; it would add a suitable air of doom and gloom.

He was scanning the area, mentally noting other details that could be useful, when he suddenly spotted the dark-haired girl. She was pacing the pavement with anxious eyes, gazing towards the alley and then back at the crowd. Ralph could see she was distressed. Never one to miss an opportunity, he walked over to her and said, 'Hello again.'

She stared blankly back at him for a second before the penny dropped and she realised who he was. 'Oh, hello.'

Ralph could have taken offence at her failure to immediately recognise him – barely fifteen minutes had passed since they'd first met – but decided, in the circumstances, to give her the benefit of the doubt. 'Are you all right?'

'Not really,' she said. 'Look, do you know what's going on? Everyone's saying that a body's been found and . . . Some friends of mine were out drinking round here last night and I'm worried that it might be one of them. God, it probably isn't, but I just need to know. Have you any idea who it is?'

Had Ralph been a more empathetic or kinder sort of person, he would have put her out of her misery straight away, but instead he said: 'I do, as it happens. I was just talking to one of the coppers.'

She waited expectantly and when he didn't continue, prompted, 'Please, if you know anything . . .'

But Ralph wasn't prepared to give up what he knew unless he got something in return. 'Sorry, I didn't catch your name.'

'My name?'

'Yes. I mean, you know mine so . . .' Ralph gave a shrug.

A frown appeared between her eyes as she weighed up the pros and cons of revealing her identity. It didn't take long. 'Liv,' she said tightly, 'Liv Anderson.'

'Well, Liv, are any of your friends called Moll?'

She shook her head.

Ralph smiled. 'Good. You've not nothing to worry about then.'

She didn't smile back. 'Thank you,' she said through gritted teeth, before walking off.

Ralph called after her, 'Hey, Liv!'

She turned, glowering. 'What?'

'If you still want to see Henry, he'll be in the Eagle tomorrow at about half twelve. It's down the road from the office.'

'I thought he was away.'

'He is, but I've just heard he'll be back tomorrow. If I were you, I'd try and catch him while you can. He could be out of London again in a day or two.'

'Are you sure he'll be there?'

Ralph barked out a laugh. 'Absolutely sure. Henry's always in the pub at lunchtime. It's a given.'

She considered this for a while with her eyes fixed on him. 'Oh, right.' That frown reappeared on her forehead as she shuffled from one foot to the other. 'Only it's been a while since I last saw him. I'm not sure if I'd ... erm, even recognise him now.'

'Oh, you can't miss Henry. I shouldn't think he's changed a jot in the last twenty years.'

'Hasn't he?'

Although Ralph was enjoying watching her squirm, he also wanted her to show up and so decided to give a helping hand. 'Big man, thinning hair, always wears a tweed jacket? You can't miss him. He'll be sitting at the bar.'

She nodded. 'I'm not sure about tomorrow. I've got a lot on.'

'Just trying to help,' Ralph said. 'It's up to you.'

11

Liv rose early on Monday morning. There was a recruitment agency on Oxford Street and she wanted to be there, first in the queue, when they opened at nine o'clock. She went to the bathroom, had a wash, brushed her hair and twisted it into a roll at the nape of her neck. Back in her bedroom she went through the clothes in the wardrobe and chose an outfit with care. What she needed was something smart but sensible, something that said she was the kind of girl who could be trusted. In the end she settled on a plain beige suit with a white blouse, put it on and stood back to view the effect in the mirror.

Liv sighed at her reflection. The suit made her look like someone she wasn't, but that, of course, was precisely the point. For the next few weeks, she would be a different Liv Anderson, one who worked nine to five, five days a week, and was grateful for the meagre salary at the end of it. Her spirits took a dive. But there was no other choice; Moody wanted his money and she would have to pay.

The events of yesterday morning sprang into her head. It had been a shock when she'd come across the crowd in Dean Street and heard that a body had been found. Pally had been her first thought, that Moody's men had finished what they'd started. And then, when she'd heard the victim was a woman, her fears had shifted on to Verity. She'd presumed her friend was safely tucked up in bed, but what if she wasn't? What if she hadn't come home last night? Panic had swept through her. It had been that unpleasant reporter who'd eventually put her mind at rest, but only after he'd forced her to reveal her name. She hadn't liked the man when she'd first met him and liked him even less now.

Liv took one last glance in the mirror, decided she was looking as respectable as she ever could and headed downstairs for breakfast. Dora and Aline were sitting at the kitchen table, tucking into bacon and eggs.

'Well, we don't usually see *you* at this time of day,' Aline said disdainfully.

'That's because I work late,' Liv said. 'But I've got things to do today. I'm going down the agency to try and get a new job.'

Glee jumped into Aline's eyes. 'Oh, the cinema sacked you, did they?'

'No, they didn't. I haven't been sacked. I'm just sick of being on my feet all night. I fancy a change.'

'You look very smart, dear,' Dora said. 'I'm sure you won't have any trouble finding something else.' She half rose from her chair. 'Let me do you some breakfast. I'm out of bacon but I can fry you some eggs.'

Aline pursed her lips. 'She doesn't pay for a cooked breakfast.'

But Dora wasn't so mean minded. 'Just this once won't hurt. It's hungry work job hunting. You need a good meal in your belly.'

Liv was tempted to accept the offer just to spite Aline, but in truth she couldn't face fried food this early in the morning. 'No, no, it's fine. Stay where you are. I'll have a slice of bread, though, if that's all right.'

'Help yourself, love.'

Liv cut the bread and spread some butter on it. Meals had originally been included in the price of her lodgings, but with the hours she kept it had made sense to renegotiate the terms. This had suited them both. Dora had less cooking to do, and Liv could eat when and where she liked – usually in a Lyons Corner House or in one of the cheap caffs in Soho.

Dora put down her knife and fork, shook her head and said, 'I still can't get over poor Moll.' She glanced at Aline. 'I warned her, didn't I?'

'You did,' Aline said.

'I saw it clear as day.'

'What did you see?' Liv asked. She had only found out yesterday that Moll Ainsworth had been a 'client' of Dora's, one of the many women who came to the house to have the tarot read. Although Liv scoffed at the notion of any kind of fortune telling – her mother would have called it dangerous nonsense – she was secretly afraid of those cards. There was something dark about them, something sinister.

'It was written,' Dora said. 'I told her I saw danger. I told her to take care, to watch her back, but she didn't listen. Moll always went her own way.'

'You did tell her,' Aline agreed, staring fiercely at Liv as though she had voiced an opinion to the contrary. 'I was right here. I heard every word.' She patted Dora's hand. 'You went white as a sheet when those cards showed up.'

'I should have done more. If I'd only—'

'You did what you could,' Aline said. 'It was God's will. Don't go blaming yourself for what can't be changed.'

Liv thought it was strange how Aline, who disapproved of almost everything – drinking, smoking, dancing, gambling, sex – was more than tolerant of the dark art of tarot. There was no understanding some people. And had Dora really foreseen Moll's awful fate? It was probably just a coincidence. Even so, she gave a small shudder as if someone had just walked over her grave.

Dora took a handkerchief from her sleeve and dabbed at her eyes. 'I know, I know. But poor Moll. It won't be the same without her.'

Aline nodded. 'She was a character, that's for sure.'

'She was.'

Liv had always refused to have a reading. Despite her professed scepticism, she still had a sneaking worry that if Dora could see into the future then maybe she could see into the past, too. In her head she could imagine the deck laid out across the table. And then that one card flipped over to reveal ... the hangman. Just the thought of it sent a sliver of ice sliding down her spine.

Aline finished her breakfast, pushed back her chair and stood up. 'Well, some of us have got work to go to. See you later, Dora.' She shot a fleeting glance at Liv but didn't wish her luck in her job search or even say goodbye.

After the front door had closed, Liv said, 'I sometimes think Aline doesn't like me much.'

Dora blew her nose and put her handkerchief away. 'Oh, don't mind her. It takes her a while to warm to people.'

Liv raised her eyebrows. She had lived in the house for almost a year and Aline's feelings towards her still hadn't risen above freezing point. Changing the subject, she asked, 'Do you think they'll catch him, Dora? The sod who killed Moll.'

'Let's hope so, love, but I'm not holding my breath. The law don't go out of their way when it comes to the likes of her. Think they bring it on themselves, don't they? Like the women are just asking for it. Anyhow most of the rozzers round here are too busy collecting backhanders from the local villains to bother themselves with any proper investigation.'

'It's murder, though,' Liv said. 'It shouldn't matter who the victim is – or what they do.'

'It shouldn't,' Dora agreed, 'not in an ideal world, but it ain't ideal and that's the truth of it. You girls should be careful out there. Now he's got the taste for it, there's no knowing who he might pick on next.'

Liv remembered walking home on Saturday night, certain she was being followed. Well, not certain exactly, but suspecting it at least. And she had come from Dean Street, hadn't she? That was where Moll's body had been found. Liv shivered. What if she hadn't walked quickly enough, if she'd lived a bit further away, if . . . but what-ifs were guaranteed to send you round the bend. 'I'll be careful,' she said. 'I promise.'

12

As Liv strode up Wardour Street, trying not to dwell on what had happened to Moll, she turned her thoughts to Henry Squires instead. If the agency had some immediate work for her, she wouldn't be able to make the appointment today. That's if she even had an appointment. The creep McCall hadn't made it entirely clear as to whether Henry would be expecting her or not. She had got the impression it was more of a casual thing – if you want to talk to him, he'll be in the pub – but wasn't entirely sure.

Liv wanted to see Henry, but at the same time she didn't. That's why she'd been putting it off for so long. There was so much she wanted to know – and so much she feared knowing. During the past year, she'd frequently convinced herself that the past was best left buried, that she should just move on and find a way to live with it, but then the old questions would start nagging at her again. In her heart she knew that she'd get no peace until she'd properly faced up to the horror of it all.

Oxford Street was busy and she had to weave a path through

the surging crowd. So many people with somewhere to go. And soon she'd be one of them, joining the daily grind of nine to five, part of the regular swarm descending on the West End. Her heart was not lifted by the prospect. Still, it wouldn't be for ever. Soon she and Pally would be back working together.

Although what she did with him often scared her, it gave her a strange kind of thrill, too. She'd been shocked when Verity had first explained what would be required of her – respectable small-town girls didn't lure men into hotel rooms in order for them to be blackmailed – but then the more she'd thought about it, the less averse to the idea she'd become. Why not? Men who cheated on their wives, or at least intended to, deserved everything that was coming to them. And where had the constant struggle for respectability ever got her mother? Dead from cancer at forty-three, that was where, with nothing to show for her life but years of grief and pain and disappointment.

It hadn't taken Liv long to make up her mind. After all, she'd come to London to get a fresh start, to reinvent herself and break with the shackles of the past. She hadn't wanted to live by the rules any more, rules that only seemed designed to keep people in their place. No, it was time to do things differently. Teaming up with Pally hadn't just been financially advantageous, but also a way of hitting back at all those dull hypocrites who said one thing and did another.

Liv was almost at the agency now. She stopped to stare in a shop window, to check out her reflection and make sure she was looking neat and tidy. It was only as she was smoothing down her hair that she became aware that hers wasn't the only face reflected in the glass. Startled, she turned to find Tom Lincoln standing behind her.

'What are you doing here?'

'That's not much of a welcome,' he said.

'Are you following me? What do you want?'

'Let's get a coffee,' he said. 'We need to talk.'

Liv, who had no desire to talk to him, quickly shook her head. 'I can't. I have to get a job and the agency opens at nine. If I don't get work, I can't pay back—'

Lincoln waved away her objections. 'Five minutes won't make much difference. Anyway, I might be able to help you out on that front.'

'What do you mean?'

'We'll get a coffee and I'll tell you.'

'Why can't you tell me now?'

Lincoln frowned, clearly getting annoyed by all the questions. He glanced around and looked back at her. 'Because I'd rather go somewhere more private. Come on, I know a place just along here.'

He strolled off and Liv trailed behind like a recalcitrant child. Whatever Lincoln had to tell her was unlikely to be good. And she didn't believe their meeting was a coincidence; he *must* have been following her. This made her feel both angry and afraid at the same time. She glowered at his back, wishing their paths had never crossed in the first place, rueing the day she and Pally had ever set foot in the Chesterton.

Lincoln turned off into a side street and walked a few more yards before arriving at the door of a shabby-looking café. Inside the walls were stained yellow with nicotine and the air smelled of hot oil and fry-ups. The early morning rush was over and only a few customers remained. A waitress was clearing up the breakfast things, piling greasy plates and cutlery on to a tray.

'Two coffees when you've got a minute, love,' Lincoln said to her, before heading for an empty table away from the window.

Liv pulled out a chair, sat down opposite him and said with more confidence than she felt, 'So?'

Lincoln studied her for a moment as if trying to decide whether her attitude was as disrespectful as he thought it might be. Then he asked abruptly, 'Can you type, do shorthand, all that stuff?'

Liv didn't answer straight away, wondering if it was better to admit or deny it.

Lincoln scowled. 'Jesus, it's not a difficult question. Yes or no?'

Liv considered lying, but then realised he might already know the answer. Could he? Unwilling to take the risk she eventually gave a small nod.

'Good,' he said. 'I might have just the thing for you. There's a man called Hugh Garvie who's in need of a secretary. He runs a property company in Bloomsbury – development, rentals, that kind of thing. I reckon you'd be ideal for the job.'

'Why can't Mr Garvie find his own secretary?'

'He thinks he can. He's even placed some adverts in the papers. But I'm sure if you apply, the position will be yours.' Lincoln gave a sly grin. 'Yeah, he likes pretty girls. I'm sure you'll fit the bill just fine.'

Liv wrinkled her nose. The more she heard, the less happy she was becoming. 'So why exactly do you want me to work for this Garvie?'

'Let's just say Mr Moody has an interest in him – and what he's up to.'

'Oh, so you want me to be a spy. Is that what you mean?'

Lincoln's eyebrows went up. 'There's no need to take that tone about it. You're hardly Miss Morality.'

Liv bristled. 'You don't know anything about me. Nothing.'

'Enough to know you can spot a good deal when you see it.'

'And what's good about this one?'

'You get a job that pays, you get to meet your rent, you stay on the right side of Mr Moody and you prevent any more unfortunate *accidents* happening to Pally.'

Liv glared at him. 'That's blackmail.'

'Call it what you like. I call it a win–win situation.'

In Liv's experience there was no such thing – someone always lost – so she was thinking fast, trying to figure out how best to turn all this to her advantage. Aware that she had little choice in the matter of the job, she was determined to broker the best possible deal she could. 'And if I do it will Mr Moody write off the debt? All of it, I mean, mine and Pally's. We'll be quits, yeah?'

'You don't want much, do you?' Lincoln sat back and folded his arms across his chest. 'I suppose it's not out of the question, so long as you come up with the goods.'

'And what *goods* are you after, exactly?'

'Everything,' Lincoln replied. 'The whole shebang. Everything that Garvie's doing, everyone he's seeing, everyone he calls or who calls him. The big stuff, the little stuff and whatever falls in between.'

'How long for? How long do I have to keep working for him?'

'Until Mr Moody's satisfied that he knows all there is to know.'

'That could be months,' she said.

Lincoln lifted and dropped his heavy shoulders. 'That's down to you, love. The quicker you dig the dirt, the sooner you'll be out of there.'

Liv locked eyes with him, trying not to show any sign of weakness. 'There's still one little problem, though. You can't be sure that Garvie will employ me. Lots of girls could be apply-ing for the job.' She added drily, 'One of them might be even prettier than me.'

'You'll have to use your charm, then. I'm presuming you can do charm?'

Liv curled her lip. 'I can't *make* him take me on. If someone else has more experience, he might—'

'You don't have to worry about that, not with the glowing reference you've got.'

Liv frowned. The only reference she had was from Beacons, the lighting company she'd worked for back home, and although it was adequate it could hardly be described as glowing. 'What reference? I don't understand.'

Lincoln sighed and rolled his eyes as if she was being particularly slow on the uptake. He opened his mouth but closed it again as the waitress arrived with the coffees. After she'd gone, he leaned across the table and said, 'Your reference from Lord Carbrooke.'

Liv was none the wiser. 'I've never heard of Lord Carbrooke.'

'You worked for him for two years. He highly recommends you.'

'And why should he do that?'

Lincoln shovelled sugar into his coffee and gave it a stir. 'He and Mr Moody have come to an arrangement. Our peer of the realm has a fondness for gambling, but unfortunately – for him, at least – he's been on something of a losing streak recently. As it happens, he's run up quite a debt at one of the clubs.'

Out of curiosity, Liv asked, 'How much?'

But Lincoln shook his head. 'Enough for him to be . . . cooperative.'

Liv had some sympathy for the lord; she knew how it felt to be in debt to Don Moody. 'But he doesn't even know me.'

'He doesn't need to. All he has to say is that you're smart, reliable, efficient and, most importantly of all, *discreet*. That's your get-out clause if Garvie becomes too curious about your former employer. Good secretaries don't blab, right? They keep quiet about the public *and* the private lives of the people they work for.'

'Are you sure the reference will be enough to get me the job?'

'It'll be enough to get you an interview, a foot in the door –
the rest is up to you. But Garvie's a snob, a social climber; he'll
be impressed by the Carbrooke connection. Odds are that he'll
jump at the opportunity to employ a lord's former secretary.'

'Let's hope so.'

As if hope had nothing to do with it, Lincoln sneered and
said, 'Just don't screw it up.'

Liv smiled thinly back. Now that the deal was done, she
relaxed a little, drank some coffee and gazed at Lincoln over
the rim of her cup. He was handsome, she thought, but not
attractive. His face had a hard, stone-like quality and his eyes
were cold. He was the sort of man you could never really trust.

Lincoln stared right back at her. 'Garvie's going to ask why
you left your last job. Tell him you've been caring for an elderly
relative, a sick aunt. That should explain it.'

'And has this aunt passed or has she made a full recovery?'

'Best kill her off, I reckon. We don't want Garvie worrying
that you might up and leave if she falls ill again.'

'Poor auntie,' she said. 'So what next? Where do I apply?'

'You don't need to worry about that. I'll organise the application once we've got a few things sorted out. Let's start with
your name. What's Liv short for? Olive? Olivia?'

'Olivia.'

'Right, well, I suggest we keep that, just in case you bump
into someone you know when you're with him. We'll only
change your surname. Anything you fancy?'

Liv thought about it, glancing around the café in search of
inspiration. Her eyes scanned the walls, but there was only a
poster for Bovril on display. As this didn't seem quite suitable,
she kept on racking her brains.

'And not your mother's maiden name,' he said. 'That's too
easy to trace.'

She could have told him that Anderson *was* her mother's maiden name, but she hadn't shared that information with anyone in London. 'Kent, then,' she said, resorting to the name of the county she'd grown up in. 'Olivia Kent.'

Lincoln scratched his chin while he considered it. 'I suppose it'll do. We'll give you a different address, too, and a different date of birth. When were you born?'

'The third of May,' she said. 'Nineteen thirty-five.'

'I'll change it to something else. And I'll make sure you get all the details we're using before the interview. Someone will drop them off at your house.'

Liv noted that he didn't ask for her address which meant that he already knew it. Well, of course he did. How else could he have found her this morning? She wanted to ask if he'd followed her home on Saturday night, but wasn't prepared to give him the satisfaction of knowing that he'd spooked her.

'And one more thing,' Lincoln continued. 'You don't tell anyone about our arrangement, right? Not Pally, not your other friends, no one. Is that clear? If I hear you've been talking . . . '

'You won't.'

'Good.' Lincoln finished his coffee and put the cup down on the table. 'I reckon we're done here – unless there's anything else?'

Liv, never one to pass over an opportunity, decided to chance her arm. 'Actually, there is something. I'll need a decent outfit for the interview.'

'What's wrong with what you've got on?'

Liv glanced down at the suit she was wearing and looked up again. 'This is fine for the typing pool, but it's not what you'd call classy. I mean, it's hardly the sort of thing a former secretary of Lord Carbrooke's would wear, is it?'

'So buy something else.'

'I would, only I'm a bit short at the moment on account of . . . ' Liv smiled sweetly at him. 'Well, you know why.'

Lincoln's face tightened as he tried to weigh up the balance between the sense in what she was saying and his reluctance to give back any of the cash he'd originally taken from her. His brow furrowed and his cold eyes bored into her. Eventually, he took out his wallet, pulled three notes from it and threw them on the table. 'There.'

'Five would be better,' she said cheekily.

Lincoln snarled. 'Don't push your luck.'

Liv quickly picked up the notes and slipped them into her pocket before he could change his mind. 'Ta.'

'Don't let me down,' Lincoln said as he pushed back his chair and stood up. 'I don't like being disappointed.'

Suddenly a disturbing thought jumped into Liv's head. 'This Garvie,' she said. 'Is he dangerous?'

Lincoln leaned down towards her, his mouth sliding into an evil grin. He left a short dramatic pause before he said softly, 'Not as dangerous as Mr Moody.'

13

Ralph was typing up his copy for the Moll Ainsworth murder when Henry strolled in with a copy of *The Times* under his arm. It was already getting on for eleven. The old hack gave a lazy wave in Ralph's direction, headed towards the door marked EDITOR, knocked and went inside. Ralph stared at the closed door for a while, praying that Henry hadn't returned with something so sensational that it would knock his own story off the front page.

Since yesterday, Ralph had been busy gathering information on the killing in Dean Street. He'd talked to the street cleaner and got his reaction to finding the body, talked to the local residents, some of the other toms and, of course, the police. To date, DI Bentley didn't seem to be making much progress on the case, but that was hardly surprising; all sorts frequented the streets of Soho and most of them were dubious. Tracking down Moll's regular clients wouldn't be an easy task and, anyway, the man who'd murdered her could well have been a stranger.

It was ten minutes before Henry emerged from the office. Did he look pleased with himself? It was hard to tell. Neames would have gone through his copy with a fine toothcomb, careful not to let anything slip by that could result in a lawsuit. Libel was a tricky business and a small paper like the *West End News* couldn't afford to get embroiled in expensive litigation. John Bodkin Adams – whether guilty or not – might be tempted to make an example of them.

Henry sat down at the desk near the window, opened his copy of *The Times* and started reading. Ralph squirmed in his seat, desperate to know how successful his rival had been in Eastbourne.

'So, what's the news on Doctor Death? Has he been arrested yet?'

Henry looked up. The end of his bulbous nose was tinged pink, either from the coastal sun or, more likely, too much booze. 'Not yet.'

'And will he be?'

'Your guess is as good as mine.'

This was obviously untrue – Ralph hadn't been the one with his ear to the ground in Eastbourne – but he tried not to let his irritation show. Henry, as usual, was keeping his cards close to his chest. 'What do the locals reckon?'

'The worst, like they always do.' He looked back down at his paper, read the headlines, sighed and said, 'Bloody Eden's going to lead us straight into another war if he doesn't watch out.'

Ralph, who probably didn't pay as much attention as he should to national events, hadn't been taking much notice of what the prime minister was up to. 'How do you figure that out?'

'Egypt, Nasser, Suez,' Henry said. 'It's a disaster waiting to happen. The man's a bloody fool.'

'Another war, though.' Ralph had only escaped the last one by the skin of his teeth and had no desire to be part of any future hostilities. 'Is it really that bad?'

'Don't you read the news, lad?'

Ralph knew that Henry didn't like him. Back in time, when he'd first started working on the *West End News*, he'd thought this was because the older man viewed him as competition, but now he suspected it was down to something more personal. A superiority complex, that's what Henry had. He reckoned he was a cut above. 'I've been busy.'

Henry threw him a disdainful look.

The familiar resentment flared in Ralph, but he made an effort not to show it. 'You had a visitor while you were away. An old friend of yours.'

'Oh, yes?'

'Liv Anderson.' Ralph watched him closely, looking for any signs that he recognised the name, but there were none. 'She called by yesterday.'

Henry shook his head. 'Doesn't ring a bell.'

'A girl. Young. She said she knew you. I think it was important, at least I got that impression.'

'She'll come back, then,' Henry said, showing little interest in the matter.

'I told her you'd probably be in the Eagle at lunchtime.' Ralph was pretty certain he'd be there – Henry rarely missed his lunchtime pints – but he wanted to make sure. 'Around twelve-thirty. That's what I told her. I said she should be able to catch you then.'

Henry gave a nod, muttered something unintelligible and went back to reading his paper.

Ralph resolved to go to the pub, too. He'd find a place where he could watch the two of them without being seen. There was more to all this than met the eye.

14

Liv was at a loose end now that her plans for the morning had been disrupted by Tom Lincoln. She'd been window-shopping for the past few hours, roaming up and down Oxford Street, while she tried to think through this whole new situation. It would be easy enough to blow the interview, to make herself so disagreeable to Garvie that he wouldn't want to employ her, but that would only make matters worse. No, not getting the job wasn't an option. Moody would get the hump and probably double the debt . . . and take out his rage on Pally, too.

She wondered why Don Moody was so interested in Garvie. Whatever the reason it wouldn't be good. If she wasn't careful, she'd end up in the middle of it all. Collateral damage. Wasn't that what they called it? She'd have liked to find out more about her future employer but wasn't sure how to do it. Having been sworn to secrecy about the arrangement, she could hardly start asking around.

Liv's fingers closed around the pound notes in her pocket. She had no intention of spending them on any new clothes – her wardrobe was full of smart stuff – but the cash would come in useful until she got her first pay packet. She grinned, thinking how she'd got one over on Lincoln, but her smile quickly faded. It was a minor victory compared to what he'd got in return.

Now that she wasn't going to the agency, Liv had no reason not to see Henry Squires. Well, only her own cowardice. Perhaps she'd had enough drama for one day – the encounter with Lincoln had left her on edge – but, on the other hand, she didn't want to stand him up if he was actually expecting her. That wouldn't be a good start to what she hoped would be a fruitful meeting. Or was she just kidding herself? Perhaps she was the last person he'd want to see after all these years.

She checked her watch, saw that the French was about to open and decided to make her way back to Soho. If she was going to see Henry, she'd need a drink first, a drop of Dutch courage to steady her nerves. The French was the only pub she felt comfortable about going into on her own; there was nearly always someone there she knew.

Her high-heeled shoes were beginning to pinch and she was glad when she finally got there. As she pushed through the doors she glanced along the road to where the police tape was still blocking off the alley. Quickly she averted her gaze. She didn't want to think about Moll Ainsworth and how she had died.

Inside, the first person she saw was Pally, sitting at the far side of the pub with an empty glass in front of him. He looked like he'd just rolled out of bed, and probably had. His clothes were stained and crumpled as though he'd grabbed whatever was lying on the floor and put it on without a second thought. His fair hair was uncombed and sticking up in tufts. Usually he was quick to bounce back from any form of adversity, but today he appeared to have the weight of the world on his shoulders.

Liv went to the bar where Verity was standing with a couple

of Windmill girls. None of them were drinking alcohol – it wasn't allowed before they went on stage – but they were just as loud and giggly without it. She smiled and said hello to them. Verity broke away from the others and came to join her.

'How's the job hunting going? Have you found anything?'

Recalling Lincoln's warning about keeping their arrangement secret, Liv said: 'I think so. I've been to the agency and there's a secretarial job I might be suitable for. Fingers crossed. I should know in a few days.'

'I'm sure you'll get it.'

'I hope so. Do you want a drink?'

Verity shook her head. 'No, I'm all right, ta. I have to go in a minute. We only nipped in on our way to rehearsals. Cynthia wanted to see Geoff, but he's not here. They had a big bust-up last night, apparently. He accused her of seeing someone else behind his back.'

'And is she?'

Verity laughed. 'Oh, probably. Cynthia's always in demand.'

The talk of Cynthia reminded Liv of something she'd meant to ask. 'Did that Lincoln bloke turn up at the Gargoyle on Saturday?'

'No, I don't think so. I didn't see him.'

The barman came and Liv ordered a vodka and tonic for herself and a double whisky for her partner in crime. While she was waiting for the drinks she leaned towards Verity and said: 'Pally still looks in a bad way. Do you think he's all right? Maybe we should try and persuade him to see a doctor.'

Verity glanced over towards the table. 'Oh, it's not the beating. Well, not *just* that. He's upset about Rosa. It's her birthday today.'

'Rosa?'

'His sister. She died during the war.'

'In the Blitz?' Liv asked, surprised that she'd never heard about her.

Verity screwed up her face, lowered her voice and said: 'No, it was awful. Not that the Blitz *wasn't* awful but . . . she was murdered, poor girl. She was only twenty. And they never got the bastard who did it, neither. Pally was away when it happened, serving in France. He's never really got over it. Well, you wouldn't, would you? She was the only family he had left.'

'That's terrible. God. He's never mentioned her.'

'No, well, he doesn't talk about her much.' Suddenly Verity seemed to regret her indiscretion. 'You won't say anything to him, will you? I probably shouldn't have . . .'

Although Liv felt hurt by Pally's failure to even mention the fact he had a sister, never mind how she'd died so tragically, she was quick to offer reassurance. 'No. No, I won't. I promise.'

The drinks arrived and Liv paid for them. She took them over to the table where Pally was absently running his index finger through a small puddle of beer. 'Do you mind if I join you?'

Pally looked up, smiling when he saw her – or perhaps when he saw the whisky. 'Course not. Take a pew. Why should I mind?'

'You look deep in thought.'

'Do I?' He picked up the whisky as soon as she put it down, lifted the glass and said, 'Cheers! Ta, love, you're an angel.'

Liv tried not to stare at his damaged face. The bruises had spread, turning into torrid shades of ochre, brown and purple. 'How are you doing?'

'I'm all right. Yourself? How's the job hunting going?'

Liv shrugged. 'Not so bad.'

'Have you found something?'

'I might have. I'll know in a day or two.'

Pally drank some more whisky and looked at her. 'What's the job, then? Who are you going to be working for?'

'Some company or other.' Liv had Lincoln's warning ringing in her ears again. 'It doesn't matter. I won't be there for long.'

'How do you know? You might like it.'

'Yes, there's nothing like nine to five to get your blood racing.' And then, wanting to change the subject before she had to answer any more awkward questions, she said, 'Are you sure you're all right?' She flapped a hand in the general direction of his face. 'I mean, apart from the obvious.'

Pally hesitated for a moment but then grinned and said: 'It's the obvious that's bothering me. When you're this handsome, these things matter.' He gingerly touched his cheek and winced. 'How would *you* like to look at this in the mirror every morning?'

'It's not that bad. It'll heal up soon.'

'Thank you, Dr Anderson.'

'You're welcome. And that's it? That's all you're bothered about?'

'It's enough. Although, come to think of it, the prospect of Mr Moody's thugs paying me another visit doesn't do an awful lot for my peace of mind.'

'You don't have to worry about that any more.' As soon as the words were out of her mouth, she regretted them. Quickly she tried to cover up the slip. 'I mean, he knows you can't work looking like that. He'll give us some time to pay the money back. And I told Lincoln, told him on Saturday, that I'd get work, that I'd start to pay off the debt.'

'I hate to tell you this, hon, but Moody isn't a reasonable man. Or a rational one.' Pally ran his fingers through his rumpled hair. 'And it shouldn't all be down to you. I'll pay you back once we start working again.'

'I know you will,' Liv said. 'You just concentrate on getting better, yeah?'

Pally took another large swig of whisky and lapsed into silence.

Liv wondered why he hadn't told her about Rosa. Although he'd known Verity for longer, she'd still thought they were close. You had to trust each other when you did the kind of work they did. She wanted to say something kind, something comforting, but couldn't risk breaking Verity's confidence. Suddenly, it occurred to her that Pally had occasionally raised the subject of family but she had always closed him down, concerned that such a conversation could lead to difficult questions about her own background. So maybe it was her own fault that he'd kept this tragedy from her, and maybe she had to stop being so afraid of her own past.

'Now you're the one lost in thought,' Pally said.

Liv smiled. 'Nothing worth sharing.' She took a few quick gulps of vodka and pushed the glass across the table. 'Here, you can finish this if you want. I've just realised I'm supposed to be somewhere.'

As she left the pub, Liv resolved to tell Pally everything once all the Moody business was settled – and once she'd faced up to her own demons. There shouldn't be secrets between friends.

15

The Eagle was shabby, dimly lit and about as charmless as a pub could be. As soon as she stepped inside, Liv had second thoughts, although this was more down to cold feet than the uninviting nature of the decor. She stopped dead in her tracks and might have turned around and fled if someone hadn't come in behind her, forcing her to move forward.

The bar was to her right and she immediately saw a middle-aged man matching the description Ralph McCall had given her. He was standing at the counter, hunched over what remained of a pint of Guinness. His belly protruded lazily over the waistband of his trousers and he had thinning, sandy-coloured hair. She took a deep breath and advanced.

'Mr Squires?' she asked.

The man, still examining the liquid blackness of his drink, turned his face to look at her. 'The very same,' he said. 'And let me guess, you must be the mysterious Liv Anderson?'

'Not that mysterious. So Ralph McCall told you I'd be here, then?'

'He said it was important.'

'I never said that exactly. I just . . . ' She stopped, realising she was getting sidetracked and gave a nod. 'But yes, it is important. At least to me.'

Henry raised a quizzical eyebrow. 'How can I help?'

Liv paused and cleared her throat before proceeding. 'I want to talk to you about . . . about someone.' She faltered again, her nerves getting the better of her. 'This is in confidence, isn't it? You won't tell anyone else?'

'Of course not. Unless you're about to confess to something dreadful. You're not going to do that, are you? No gruesome murders or the like? My stomach's not as strong as it was.'

Liv was aware that he was only trying to put her at ease, but his words made her flinch. She was tempted to make her excuses, turn around and walk away, but knew she wouldn't have the courage to return. It was now or never. Quickly she blurted out the truth before she could change her mind. 'I'm Paul Teller's daughter.'

Henry visibly recoiled, shock registering on his face. His mouth opened but nothing came out. He stood staring at her, his eyes wide and disbelieving as if a ghost had just materialised in front of him.

'I'm sorry,' she said. 'I didn't mean to surprise you. Anderson was Mum's maiden name. She went back to it after . . . well, you know why.'

Eventually Henry found his voice. 'Heavens,' he said. 'Little Liv. My God, it must be twenty years since I last saw you. You were just a toddler then.' He gazed intently at her and slowly shook his head. 'And how is your mother?'

'She passed away, I'm afraid. Cancer. It was over a year ago now.'

Henry's face twisted a little. 'Oh, I'm so sorry to hear that.

She was a fine woman, very fine.' He leaned forward, gently patted her arm and straightened up again. 'Good Lord, where are my manners? Let me get you a drink. Brandies all round, I think. Then we'll sit down and have a proper catch-up.'

Liv didn't protest. A strong drink was just what she needed. Although the initial hurdle had been jumped – that was a relief – there was still a long way to go. She had a jumble of questions in her head, all of them vying for priority, and was wrestling with where to start.

Henry caught the attention of the barman, put the order in and then drained what remained of his pint. He put the glass down and gazed at Liv again. 'Look at you. I can't believe that you're all grown-up already. It hardly seems like yesterday since ...' He released a long, heavy sigh. 'Where does all the time go? Are you living in London or just on a visit?'

'I've been here a while. I kept meaning to come and see you but ...' She gave him a rueful smile. 'It's easy to put things off, isn't it? Then the days turn into weeks and the weeks into months and before you know it almost a year has gone by. So, anyway, here I am, *finally*. I hope you don't mind.'

'Why should I mind? Of course not. It's good to see you. I would have kept in touch with your mother, but I had no idea where she'd gone. She told me she was moving, that she'd send her address once she was settled, but I never heard from her again.'

'We went to Kent,' Liv said. 'I suppose she wanted a fresh start.'

'That's understandable.'

The drinks arrived and Henry paid. They carried them over to a nearby table and sat down. Liv took a gulp of brandy and felt a wave of warmth spread through her. 'You must wonder why I'm here, though.'

'Well, I'm presuming this isn't just a social call.'

'I need your help, you see. There's no one else I can ask. I want to know about my father. Everything. Everything you can tell me.'

Apprehension flickered across Henry's face.

'I know what he did,' she said. 'I mean, I didn't, not for a long time, but when Mum fell sick, she told me. I grew up believing that he'd been killed in the war, that he was a good man, an honourable one, that he'd sacrificed his life for his country, but it wasn't exactly like that, was it? I need to understand what happened.'

Henry shook his head. 'It's not always wise to rake up the past.'

'*Please*,' Liv pleaded, good sense being the last thing on her mind. 'Now Mum's gone, you're the only person left I can turn to. I know you might not have all the answers, but you must have some. You were his colleague, his friend. You must have an idea.'

'I wouldn't know where to start.'

'You could tell me about Irene Lister,' Liv said, trying to keep the bitterness out of her voice. 'Tell me what was so special about her that made him happy to destroy his family.'

'I don't think your father was ever happy, not about any of it. He never meant to ... no, he just got himself into one unholy mess. He did love you and your mother, only ... '

'He loved Irene more.'

'Differently, perhaps,' Henry replied, trying to be tactful. He dived into his brandy before continuing. 'What can I say about her? She was a fascinating woman – clever, beautiful, spirited. She was an actress, you know. The stage mainly, but a few films, too. Of course, all that came to an end after ... Anyway, that's not important. They met in thirty-six and your father became infatuated by her.'

'How did they meet?'

'Through Nicky, I think. Her husband, Nicky Lister. He owned a club in Mayfair, one of those slightly eccentric places where the intelligentsia liked to gather – the politicos and the literati – and where they all rubbed shoulders with the more mundane forms of human life. Eden it was called – like the prime minister. Your father was writing a piece about it. I presume Nicky introduced him to Irene and . . .' Henry rubbed his face. 'Are you sure you want to hear all this?'

'I'm sure.'

'Only—'

'I'm sure,' Liv insisted again.

Henry's eyes grew sad. 'Don't judge him too harshly, my dear. Try not to hate him. Your father was a good man at heart.'

'A good man? And how do you come to that conclusion?' Liv stared at him, frowned and gave a hollow laugh. 'Good men don't kill other women's husbands. Good men don't hang for murder.'

16

Even as the words came out of Liv's mouth, her face was starting to crumple. It was the first time she'd said it out loud and the sheer act of doing so provoked equal feelings of horror and relief. But she wasn't going to fall apart. Quickly she reached for the brandy and gulped down two large mouthfuls. It had the effect, if nothing else, of a temporary numbness.

Henry patted her on the arm again. 'And now I've upset you. I didn't mean to—'

'You haven't,' Liv said. 'It's not your fault. Really. It's just . . . I've not been able to talk to anyone since Mum died. And even when she was alive, she could hardly bear to speak about it. I'm grateful to you. I really am.' She could hear the tremor in her voice, but pushed on regardless. 'So my father fell for Irene. How long did it go on for, this affair?'

Henry hesitated and briefly looked away from her. 'According to her, there was no affair.'

'What do you mean? Of course there was. There must have been. What are you saying?'

'I'm saying that your father might have fallen in love, but his feelings weren't reciprocated. According to her, nothing ever happened between the two of them.'

Liv's body stiffened, her eyes widening with incredulity 'And you really believe that?'

'Everyone said that she and Nicky were happy, a perfect match. They'd only been married for a year.'

'That doesn't stop some women. It doesn't mean anything. She must have given my father a reason to . . . to do what he did.'

'Perhaps it was just simple jealousy,' Henry said. 'He couldn't bear the thought of the two of them together.'

'Or maybe the marriage wasn't as happy as everyone believed. You don't know what goes on behind closed doors. Everything can look fine on the surface but underneath . . . well, she might have realised she'd made a mistake. That's possible, isn't it? And she wanted a way out.' Liv could feel her thoughts getting tangled up as she tried to make sense of the senseless. 'Then my father came along and she persuaded him to help.'

Henry gave a half shrug, the sort of shrug that implied she was clutching at straws. 'The kind of help where he shoots her husband dead in the middle of a crowded club? It's not the most subtle way of solving the problem, or of eliminating the competition.'

Liv couldn't argue with that. She wasn't even sure why she was trying to shift the blame, or at least some of it, on to someone else. Her father had made his own choices, been responsible for his own actions – unless he'd been completely out of his mind. A shiver ran through her. What if madness ran in the family? It could be lurking deep inside her, too. Maybe that was why she needed to find a rational explanation for the inexplicable. 'Did he ever talk to you about her?'

'He didn't confide in me if that's what you're asking, but I was aware that something had changed, that he wasn't himself.

And I guessed that he had feelings for Irene. It wasn't difficult. I saw the way he looked at her whenever they were in the same room: he couldn't keep his eyes off her.' Henry gave another of his deep sighs. 'I suppose I thought that he'd get over it. People do. I thought it was just infatuation. If I'd had any idea . . . but hindsight's a wonderful thing, isn't it?'

'Do you think Nicky Lister knew how my father felt?'

'Oh, yes, I should imagine so, but it wouldn't have bothered him. He wasn't the insecure type. And it was nothing unusual. Half the men in London were besotted with Irene at one time or another. He probably saw it as a compliment.'

Liv wondered if Lister had been quite so blasé as Henry was suggesting. Could her father have been goaded by him on that fateful night? Except that didn't explain why he'd turned up at Eden with a gun in his pocket. Premeditation was the only thing that explained that.

'Why do *you* think he did it?' she asked. 'I mean, more than jealousy, surely? To do something so awful, so extreme. He must have known he couldn't get away with it.'

Henry, put on the spot, could only shake his head.

Liv, following her own fractured train of thought, carried on speaking. 'There were witnesses – lots of them. Do you think he'd gone quite mad? Had he lost his mind?'

'Passion can do strange things to people, take them over, turn them into someone else. Even make them go down roads they'd never normally consider. I meant it when I said your father was a good man. For all the years I knew him, he was. The person he became in the last few months – well, that wasn't him, not the real Paul Teller.'

Liv's fingers tightened around her glass. She had no idea who the real Paul Teller was, and Henry, she suspected, was only trying to make her feel better.

'All he wanted was a family,' Henry persisted. 'I remember when you were born: he couldn't have been happier.'

'Well, that didn't last for long.' Liv, who was starting to feel emotional again – tears were pricking her eyes – made an effort to hold herself together. She had come here wanting to know more about her father, but hadn't bargained on how painful it would be.

'I suppose the papers were full of it,' she said. 'Do you keep records at your office, copies of old articles? I'd like to see them if that's possible. And if it's not too much trouble.'

'There's nothing in them, nothing worth reading, at least. I hate to besmirch my fellow reporters but they don't always take much interest in the *facts* of a matter. Rumour and gossip, speculation, hearsay – that's all you're going to find. Believe me, they're not worth a second glance.'

But Liv stood firm. 'I'd still like to read them.'

'If you're looking for answers there, my dear, then you'll be disappointed. Your father took those to the grave with him.'

Liv knew that her father had never explained anything, not even in the short letter he had written to her mother from his prison cell. All he had said was that he was sorry, that he had never meant to hurt her, that he hoped one day she could forgive him. 'Not answers, no, but it would be interesting to get some background. I'd be really grateful.'

'I'll see what I can do,' Henry said reluctantly.

'Thank you. Perhaps we could meet up again next week. Would that be convenient?'

'Next Monday should be all right. I can't see a problem with that. Do you want to meet back here or would you prefer somewhere more salubrious?'

Liv, guessing that this was the place where Henry felt most comfortable, decided not to suggest anywhere else. 'This is fine. Around the same time, then?'

Henry nodded. 'I'll be here.'

As she stood up to leave, another thought jumped into Liv's head. 'Do you know what happened to Irene Lister?'

Henry took a fraction too long to answer, as though he was weighing up the pros and cons of feeding Liv's desperate desire for information. 'I think she may have remarried. I'm not sure, though. It was all such a long time ago. All I do know is that she never worked as an actress again. No one would employ her after Lister's murder.'

'But she claimed she had nothing to do with it.'

'No smoke without fire. Isn't that what they say? The law might have cleared her of any wrongdoing, but the public weren't quite so forgiving.' Henry stood up too and stared directly into her eyes. 'Look, Liv, please be careful. Don't let yourself get dragged down by all this. You've got your whole life ahead. Don't let it be ruined by the past. These things can eat away at you, take over.'

Liv nodded and smiled as if she was taking everything he said on board, but in fact the only words that were resonating with her were 'No smoke without fire'. Just because it was a cliché didn't mean it wasn't true. If Henry couldn't provide the answer to why her father had murdered Nicky Lister, then perhaps Irene could. All she had to do now was find her.

17

Ralph McCall had gone into the Eagle the minute it opened, securing a good spot near the back where he could hopefully merge into the background whilst still retaining a clear view of the bar. Henry was a creature of habit and always sat in the same place. It was not, perhaps, entirely ethical to spy on your colleagues, but he felt his subterfuge was justified. There was now no doubt in his mind that the Anderson girl was known to Henry. The old hack didn't buy a drink for just anyone, and especially not one as pricey as brandy.

The conversation between the two had been intense. They had moved from the bar to a table and Ralph had had to shift to his left and strain his neck to keep them in sight. He hadn't been able to hear any of the exchange – a huge frustration – but had seen Liv's face and the expression on it. If ever a girl was upset, it was her. And Henry had touched her on the arm more than once, a sure sign of familiarity. Ralph, who didn't like being kept in the dark, frowned with irritation. If only he'd been able to lip-read . . .

Liv Anderson had just left, and now Henry was heading for the Gents. Grabbing the opportunity, Ralph scooted out from behind his table and quickly exited the pub. He had only just cleared the door when a small, rat-like man rushed out right behind and barrelled straight into him.

'Oi!' Ralph protested, rubbing his elbow.

The man stepped to one side and glared back at him. 'Shouldn't be standing in the bleedin' way then, should you?' His breath, stale and rancid, flew up into Ralph's face.

'And you should watch where you're going.'

The rat snarled, showing a row of sharp yellow teeth, muttered something unintelligible and scurried off. Ralph watched until he disappeared into the crowd, peeved at not getting an apology but unsurprised by it. The Eagle wasn't the sort of pub where you expected good manners from the customers, or any manners at all, come to that.

He moved away from the door and paced the pavement for a while, smoking a cigarette while he waited to put the next part of his plan into action. While he was mulling over the scene he'd witnessed in the pub, it occurred to him that maybe Liv was in *that* sort of trouble, the sort where she'd shortly be putting on weight and anticipating the pitter-patter of tiny feet. But then why would she turn to Henry? Unless he was the ... but God, the very idea of it was preposterous! No self-respecting girl would look twice at the likes of that old man. Still, he found the idea amusing.

What he didn't find so amusing was that he might get caught out himself if he wasn't careful, and made a mental note to buy johnnies. Pauline had been dropping hints recently about getting engaged and the last thing he needed was to find himself obliged to marry her. What was it with women that they couldn't just enjoy the moment, but always had to be wanting more? He had told her that he didn't have the wherewithal to get hitched, that weddings cost money, but none of that seemed to put her off.

The truth was that he had no intention of ever marrying her. The thought of waking up to her face every morning sent a chill down his spine. Not that she was ugly, but she was nothing special, either. She had one of those gossipy, scatterbrain sorts of mind, and a tendency to get on his nerves. Her attractiveness, he'd noticed, only increased in direct proportion to the amount of beer he had drunk.

When he felt that sufficient time had elapsed, Ralph went back inside the Eagle and walked over to the bar. Henry had resumed his position at the counter and was gazing pensively into mid-air. 'Ah, I thought you might be here. Can I get you a drink?'

Henry's eyes flashed with suspicion. 'What are you after?'

'Don't be like that,' Ralph said, smiling amiably. 'Can't a man buy his colleague a pint without his motives being called into question?'

'*Some* men,' Henry said pointedly. 'But if you're buying, I'll have another brandy, ta.'

Ralph wasn't overly pleased at having to fork out for a brandy, but he ordered it anyway, along with half a mild for himself. He turned to Henry again. 'On the hard stuff, eh? Had some bad news?'

'Just come out with it, lad, whatever you want to know.'

Ralph glanced round the pub, at the brown walls stained with nicotine and the sawdust on the floor. The place was seedy, almost squalid, and had a pungent odour about it, a grotesque mix of dirt and sweat and unwashed clothes, all underlain by the slight but pervasive whiff of urine. 'You could start by telling me why you even drink in this joint.'

Henry smirked. 'It's the only place I can get any peace and quiet.'

The drinks arrived and Ralph paid for them, hoping the expense would prove to be a worthwhile investment. 'Cheers!' he said, lifting his glass. Then, seeing that Henry was still waiting for some kind of explanation as to his presence there, he quickly added: 'Actually, I was hoping to pick your brains about Moll Ainsworth. I've got the bones of the story, so to speak, but I need to flesh it out a bit. I don't suppose you know if she had any family, a husband, kids, anything like that?'

'Your guess is as good as mine.' Henry swirled the brandy around his glass, gazed down at it for a moment, took a swig and licked his lips. 'Although, now I come to think of it, I reckon there might have been a husband way back in the day. Couldn't say if he was still around, though. And don't ask me what his name was 'cause I don't have a clue.'

'What kind of bloke lets his missus go on the game?'

'A poor one or a sick one or a downright nasty bastard. Who's to say? It doesn't always do to judge.'

Ralph could have taken offence – Henry's response had something of the put-down about it – but he had bigger fish to fry. 'And what about kids?'

'Can't help you there. Although if she had, they'd be grown up by now. Have you tried asking round the other girls?'

'Most of them don't want to talk.'

'Yes, well, they're none too keen on the press. You have to build up trust with them, build a rapport.'

And there it was again, Ralph thought, that little dig. And stating the bloody obvious, too, as if he was still some kind of rookie who needed the ropes explained to him. But he kept the smile on his face, pretending he was grateful for the advice. 'I'm sure you're right.'

94

'It's a bad business. She was a good sort, old Moll. Bit of a mouth on her but no real malice. Let's hope it was a one-off and we haven't got a bloody nutter on the loose.'

Ralph nodded and agreed even though he privately hoped for the opposite. A psychopath stalking the streets of Soho was just what he needed to get his career back on track. He thought of the headlines and the opportunities and gave a deep inner sigh. Then, remembering his purpose for actually being there, he asked casually, 'Oh, did that girl turn up, the one who wanted to see you?'

'Yes,' Henry said shortly.

'Good, that's good. Was it anything important?'

'Something and nothing.'

'Ah, right.' Ralph, irked that he was being lied to, decided to go for a little provocation. 'Quite a looker, eh? I wouldn't mind ten minutes with her.'

Henry glared at him. 'Show some respect, lad. She's a decent girl.'

'You do know her then? Only you said you didn't recognise the name when I mentioned it this morning.'

'Listen, when you get to my age, you're lucky to remember your own name, never mind anyone else's.'

Which didn't answer Ralph's question and left him wondering why Henry was being so evasive. He didn't believe that 'something and nothing', not for an instant, but hadn't quite figured out if this was a personal matter or a professional one. If there was a good story brewing then he wanted to be in on it. 'It's a small world, though. I saw her on Saturday afternoon at Joe's, the caff on Old Compton Street. She was with some rum-looking bloke, well dressed, had the whiff of the thug about him.'

'The whiff?'

'He just gave that impression, that's all. She didn't look too happy. I think he was hassling her for money.'

Concern appeared on Henry's face, deep lines furrowing his forehead. But he was quick to try and cover up any worries he had. 'Well, it's none of my business – or yours, come to that.'

'I just thought you ought to know, in case . . .'

'In case what?'

'Just trying to be helpful. Sometimes people aren't all they seem to be.'

Henry glared, knocked back his brandy and put the glass down on the counter. 'Thanks for the tip, son,' he said curtly. 'I'll bear it in mind.' And then, without so much as a goodbye – or a thank you for the drink – walked out of the pub.

Ralph stayed at the bar, convinced he'd touched a nerve and glad of it. Yes, he'd rattled the old hack, there was no doubt about it. He drank his mild, feeling a warm wave of satisfaction roll over him. He might not have got to the bottom of who Liv Anderson really was, but from Henry's reaction he knew she was important. And, as Henry had claimed to not even know her yesterday, that could only mean that he was hiding something.

18

Slug muttered as he walked, still narked by the altercation outside the pub. Because he was small and shabby, he was used to being looked down on – in every sense. Taking offence had become second nature to him. He collected all the jibes, the insults and slights, and stored them away for future reference. One day he would get his own back. He had been born with few advantages, but his ability to hold a grudge was one of them.

Still, it wasn't all bad. He had things to be pleased about, too. Slug didn't believe in fate or coincidence or good luck, but only in being in the right place at the right time. And today, at the Eagle, had been that time. There was nothing unusual about Henry Squires propping up the bar, but when the girl had turned up – the girl Slug had followed on Saturday night – he'd known there was a few bob to be made. There was someone who would pay for the information.

When he got close to his destination, he went to the usual phone box, made a call to the Paradise and asked to speak to

Tom Lincoln. While he hung on, he could hear voices in the background, the chink of glasses and the tinkling of a piano. He waited impatiently, hoping his money wouldn't run out.

The Paradise was just one of Moody's clubs, most of which were a cover for illegal gambling. Gambling was a mug's game, but there were plenty of mugs in the world. Even now, in the middle of the day, there would be suckers chancing their arm on the turn of a card. He could see the appeal, of course – the hope of a big win – but it was always the banker who came out on top in the end.

Eventually there was a voice on the other end of the line. 'Yeah? Lincoln.'

'It's me,' Slug said. 'I've got something for you.'

'Can it wait? I'm kind of busy at the moment.'

'You'll want to hear this. It's about the girl.'

'What about her?'

'Meet me by the bins.' He rang off quickly before Lincoln could interrogate him any further. He could have told him over the phone, but then he'd have to wait for the money. This way he'd be paid here and now and have the satisfaction of a few notes in his pocket. Plus, if he played it right, there could be a chance of some ongoing work.

Slug left the phone box and crossed the road to the Paradise. He sidled round the building, leaned against the wall and rolled himself a skinny cigarette. The stink of the bins rose up into his nostrils, but it didn't bother him. In fact, he positively welcomed it. Bad smells were, if nothing else, a guarantee of privacy.

It was another ten minutes before Lincoln finally put in an appearance. Slug could tell he was in a bad mood – trouble in the club perhaps – and so he didn't beat around the bush. Sometimes it was good to take your time with a story, to eke out the details one by one, but this wasn't one of those occasions. 'I just saw your lady friend,' he said. 'In the Eagle. She had a meet with Henry Squires.'

Lincoln stared blankly back at him. 'Who?'

'Chief reporter on the *West End News*,' Slug said. 'And very cosy they looked, too. Chatting away like there was no tomorrow. I thought you'd want to know.'

'Did you catch any of it?'

'Nah, I weren't close enough. Couldn't risk moving in case they sussed me. But Henry Squires don't waste his time on just anyone.'

Lincoln's face had taken on a darker look.

Slug continued to pile it on. 'And it's never good news, right? Not when someone starts talking to the press. Those reporters, they make a bleedin' living out of other people's misery and they ain't the sort to have any sleepless nights over it, neither. And the thing is, Mr Lincoln, it weren't just one of them reporters in the Eagle, but two. Another one was there, sitting right across from me and watching them both like a hawk.' He paused to catch a breath before adding: 'A younger bloke who works for the *News*, too. McClean, McGregor? Something like that. Anyway, I reckon his job was to follow her when she left but he didn't make much of a job of it. He was still standing on the pavement when I got out there.'

'Do you know where she is now?'

Slug didn't, but unwilling to admit to it he hazarded a guess. 'Last time I saw her, she was heading towards Soho. Do you want me to try and find her?'

Lincoln shook his head. 'She won't have gone far. Leave it to me.'

19

Liv had taken a circuitous route back to Soho, trying to get her thoughts in order as she walked. She wasn't sure if it was the brandy or the meeting with Henry that had unleashed the tumultuous emotions in her. A combination of the two, probably. Anger and bitterness vied with pain and confusion, but intertwined with it all was a sense of relief that she finally had someone to talk to about her father. But could she trust Henry? It was too late now to ask that question.

Eventually she had found her way here to Joe's. In the hope of reversing the effect of the brandy, she had ordered a chicken omelette and a strong coffee. She sat by the window and ate the omelette without really tasting it. Her gaze flew continuously to the world outside, but she saw nothing. Her thoughts had turned inward. Now it was only the past that mattered, the whys and the wherefores. There were so many more things she wished she'd asked Henry, but they'd have to wait.

Liv had hero-worshipped her father as a child, creating a fantasy about him in her head. The greatest lie, of course, was that he'd died valiantly, loving his wife and daughter. Nothing could be further from the truth. Her stomach turned over as she thought about Irene Lister. It was hard to imagine the pain her mother had endured, the betrayal and shame and humiliation. No wonder she had changed her name, fled London and sought sanctuary in the little town of Maybury. Even then she must have lived with the dread that one day her true identity would be discovered.

Liv only possessed one photograph of her father, a picture of him standing outside the flat in Archway where her parents had started their married life. She could see herself in his features, in his wide eyes, the curve of his cheekbones and dark brown hair. And suddenly she was back to worrying about what else she might have inherited. Maybe, hidden deep within her, in her cells, in her bone and tissue, in her very heart, lay the seeds of something terrible. *Madness*. The fear crept under her skin and made her shudder.

How could love be so destructive? She didn't understand it. She had drunk with men, laughed with them, slept with them, but had never felt the overwhelming passion that had possessed her father. And she never would. No, she'd fight it tooth and claw. She'd fight it with her very last breath. She resolved there and then to always stay in control, to sheathe herself in armour, to never let herself be consumed. It was the only way, she decided, to stay sane.

There was a limit to how much introspection anyone could endure, and after a while Liv returned to the present. She drank what remained of her cooling coffee and wondered if she should go and look for Pally. He would probably still be in the French, although it would be closing soon. But perhaps he didn't want company at the moment. Perhaps he'd prefer to be alone.

In some respects, she and Pally were similar, both putting

on a face against the world, both refusing to bow down to convention, but she wondered how well you could ever know another human being. The Maybury people who would have claimed to know her mother – friends, neighbours, her work colleagues at the library – would have described her as a quiet, pleasant woman. None of them had seen beyond the façade to the frightened, haunted person she had really been. And Liv hadn't, either. Not until near the end, when the truth had leaked from her mouth like poison.

In the end, Liv decided to go home. It had been an eventful day, first Lincoln and then Henry, and she needed some time to come to terms with it all. She had a sudden longing to be cocooned within the four walls of her room, to lie down on her bed and close her eyes. It would be a blessed relief to escape from reality for a while.

Liv didn't notice much as she hurried through Soho and made her way to Whitcomb Street. She was in sight of the house when it happened. If she had been less distracted, she might have clocked the grey saloon parked by the lamp-post or heard the sound of the car door opening and closing shortly after she'd passed it. Instead, she was only barely aware of footsteps behind her before she was grabbed by the arm and roughly yanked around.

'What's your bloody game!' Lincoln hissed into her face.

Liv, taken by surprise and utterly bewildered, struggled to get free, but his hold only tightened. 'W-what are you doing?' she stammered. 'What do you want?'

'I knew I couldn't trust you. Girls like you don't think twice about screwing people over. It's second bloody nature, isn't it?' His eyes flashed with anger. 'The minute I turn my back you go running to the newspapers. Offering you a good deal, are they, to spill your guts and sell Mr Moody down the river? Well, if you think you're getting away with it, you're a bigger bloody fool than I took you for.'

Light was finally dawning in Liv's startled brain. 'No, you've got it all wrong. I was just—'

'The only thing I got wrong was ever believing a word you said. Jesus, I don't know why I wasted my time on you. But I'll tell you something for nothing, if anything appears in that rag about me or Mr Moody, you'll be sorry you were ever born.'

Liv's confusion was rapidly being replaced by indignation. She gave up struggling to free herself – it was pointless – and, deciding that attack was the best course of defence, confronted him instead. 'If you'd just shut up for a moment, I can explain what I was doing with Henry Squires.'

'Ha!' he said triumphantly. 'So you're not denying it. You *have* been to see him.'

'Did I ever say I hadn't? And no, I don't damn well deny it. Why would I? But it's not what you think. It didn't have anything to do with you or Don Moody.'

'And you really expect me to believe that?'

'Are you going to listen to me or not? God, if you didn't go around spying on me you wouldn't be jumping to these ridiculous conclusions.' Liv was thinking on her feet, desperately trying to win him round. She certainly wasn't going to tell Lincoln the whole truth, but she had to tell him some of it. 'Henry's an old family friend. I've known him for years. He used to work with my dad. We meet up every now and again, have a chat, have a drink – and that's all there is to it. It had nothing to do with our arrangement.'

'So it's just a coincidence that you decided to catch up with him today, straight after you talked to me?'

'It wasn't straight after, nothing like. It was hours later. If I'd been that desperate to "spill my guts", as you so nicely put it, wouldn't I have gone to see him immediately?'

'Not necessarily.'

'Look, so far as he's concerned, I'm a nice respectable girl and that's the way I want to keep it. And what story do you think I'd be selling him, exactly? That I'm a con woman who makes my money by picking up cheating husbands? That I relieved a mate of Don Moody's of a few quid and now he wants his money back? Come on, it's hardly something I'd want to broadcast to the world.' Liv was talking quickly, earnestly, trying to convince him. 'And how on earth would I work again after I'd made all these scandalous confessions? I may not be trustworthy, Mr Lincoln, but I'm not completely stupid. I'm hardly going to throw it all away for the sake of a stupid headline.'

Some of what she said must have got through to him because Lincoln finally released her arm. A flicker of doubt crossed his face but he wasn't quite ready to concede defeat. 'That depends on how much they're paying you.'

Liv rubbed the place where his fingers had gripped her, thinking of the bruises that would be there tomorrow. 'We're talking the *West End News* here, not some national with a hefty budget. I don't imagine they ever pay for anything. And do you really think any amount of money would be worth crossing Don Moody for?'

'It might if you're thinking of doing a disappearing trick, taking off, going somewhere else.'

'This is where I live. I'm not going anywhere.'

'So you say.'

'Because it's the truth.' Liv rubbed at her arm again, gazing resentfully at him. 'You could have just come and asked me about it. You didn't have to—'

104

'You have to see it how it looks,' Lincoln said, with no hint of an apology for the pain he'd inflicted.

'Well, how it looks isn't always like it is. I've got more to lose than to gain by going to the press. Surely even you can see that.'

'Yeah, well, you could be cooking up all sorts. I know what the press are like, always rooting around for dirt.' Then something else seemed to occur to Lincoln. His eyes narrowed into slits. 'And if your chat with Squires was so damn innocent, what was the other one doing there?'

Liv gazed up at him, bewildered again. 'What other one?'

'The other reporter, the younger one. McGregor or whatever his name is. Why was he there too?'

'There wasn't anyone else. It was just me and Henry.'

'Not *with* you. In the pub. Watching.'

Liv found herself on the back foot again. She presumed he meant Ralph McCall. Had he really been there? She hadn't noticed him, but that wasn't surprising. She'd been too wrapped up in talking to Henry to pay much attention to the other customers. 'I don't know any other reporters,' she lied, deciding this was safer than admitting that their paths had crossed yesterday, a fact that might raise even more suspicion in Lincoln's mind.

'From what I've heard he couldn't take his eyes off you.'

'Perhaps he was just admiring the view.' Then, seeing that her flippancy hadn't gone down too well, she quickly went on in a more serious tone. 'Reporters are interested in everything, especially what their colleagues are up to. And the Eagle's the nearest pub to the *West End News*. Lots of the staff must drink there.'

'So why did he follow you out when you left?'

'He didn't,' Liv said. 'At least, if he did, I didn't see him, and I certainly didn't speak to him. Who's been telling you all this?'

'That doesn't matter.'

'It matters to me. Isn't that why we're standing here now? Isn't it why you think I'm double-crossing you? Look, I can't stop you believing whatever you choose to believe, but none of it's true. I really have known Henry for years. And there's nothing going on, nothing at all.'

'I don't like coincidences.'

'So what do you want to do? You want to call off the whole Garvie business?'

'I haven't decided. I'll have to think about it.'

And how long is that going to take? Liv almost snapped, but had the sense to use a more placatory tone. 'Well, let me know when you make up your mind.'

'If we drop it, you'll still owe the money,' Lincoln said sourly.

'And I'll pay it back. I said I would, didn't I?'

Lincoln was glaring at her like she was something he'd found on the sole of his shoe. 'You'll do that all right. And while I'm thinking it over you can stay away from Henry Squires – and any other reporters, come to that.'

Liv gave a light shrug of her shoulders. 'Fine. If that's what you want.'

As the exchange appeared to have reached its natural conclusion, Liv started backing away, eager to make her escape. But Lincoln clearly had to have the last word.

'Don't disappoint us, love. Mr Moody won't take kindly to it.'

20

Liv was shaking by the time she got inside the house, a delayed reaction to the shock of her clash with Lincoln. She stumbled up the stairs, rushed along the landing to her room, pushed open the door, flung herself on the bed and waited for her heartbeat to slow. She had stood up to the man but had she convinced him? If she hadn't, she was going to be in even bigger trouble with Don Moody.

It had been bad luck being spotted with Henry in the Eagle. Now Lincoln thought she was conspiring against him and things were ten times worse than they had been before. She wondered who'd grassed her up. The barman, perhaps, but how would he have even known who she was? Or Ralph McCall. Was it possible that Moody had the reporter in his pocket? Except Lincoln had called him McGregor. And come out with all that stuff about him following her out of the pub. No, that didn't make any sense unless it had been a ploy to put her off the scent.

On reflection she decided it had probably been neither of

them, but some third party who Lincoln had employed to follow her. As soon as this thought entered her head, she jumped off the bed and went over to the window. She gazed down on the street. Lincoln and his car had gone, but there were plenty of other people walking past. She looked for someone suspicious, someone who was loitering, but couldn't find anyone who fitted the bill. Still, she resolved to keep her eyes open whenever she went out, to be alert to any possible tail.

It was an unpleasant notion, the idea of someone watching her every move. And an inconvenient one, too. She might have to change her next meeting with Henry, arrange to see him somewhere else, but she'd cross that bridge when she came to it. Their meeting wasn't for another week and a lot could change in seven days. If the Garvie business fell through, Lincoln would in all likelihood call off the tail.

Liv leaned against the window frame, wondering whether it would be better or worse if she didn't have to go through with the secretarial job. Better in that she wouldn't have to spy on some stranger, but worse in that she'd still owe the money to Moody – and probably interest on it, too. Neither scenario was ideal, but she would have to deal with one of them.

Hopefully Lincoln would make up his mind sooner rather than later. The money she had wouldn't last for ever and she'd need to find some kind of job if she was to keep on paying her rent. She had a sick feeling in her stomach that could have been a result of the dubious food that came out of Joe's kitchen, but was more probably down to the recent confrontation. There was only so much turmoil anyone could take in a day.

She stayed at the window, scrutinising every passer-by. This man, that man? Or perhaps it was a woman. But no one gave the house a second glance. Eventually, when her vigil yielded no results, she gave up and retired to the bed where she kicked off her shoes and sat with her knees pulled up and her back against the wobbly headboard. What now? It was just a waiting game.

Patience, however, wasn't one of Liv's greatest attributes. She had struggled with it as a child – at home, in school, in church – and little had changed. For as long as she could remember she had been straining at the leash, always wanting tomorrow to be here today. Being patient, even if it was a virtue, seemed to involve an unnatural level of self-restraint. She couldn't quite see what was so virtuous about it when all it involved was doing nothing.

Her gaze roamed the room, taking in the faded flowery wallpaper and the dark brown furniture. Everything was old and worn, including the carpet, almost threadbare with its green pile long since trodden down. It could have been a gloomy place if it hadn't been for the two big windows allowing the light to flood in, and the bright yellow vase – a purchase from the market – that sat on the bedside table. For all its shabbiness, she still loved it. It was a room of her own and she was happy here.

What she feared most was losing that happiness. What if Lincoln, out of spite or revenge, decided to report her and Pally to the law? Perhaps George Hallam could even be persuaded to give evidence against them. It was unlikely but not impossible. If she was exposed, there would be shaming and public humiliation. She shuddered at the thought.

Liv wrapped her arms around her knees. Although she wasn't ashamed of her excursions with Pally – she was doing women a favour, after all, teaching all those lecherous cheating no-good husbands that they couldn't get away with it – she knew that society would judge her. She would be held up as an example of female moral deficiency and punished accordingly. The city Liv sneered at the hypocrisy, but the small-town girl in her recoiled at the prospect. That was the problem with the past; it could never quite be shaken off.

The way women were treated constantly appalled her and although things were changing, they were not changing fast enough. Men still ruled the roost. They ran the country, got the best jobs and, on the whole, viewed women as little more than breeding machines. Cooking, cleaning and babies were all the female of the species were good for. They were second-rate citizens, too brainless or too 'emotional' to be granted any real power.

Liv had done well at school, but it had only got her as far as the typing pool at Beacons. The sheer stultifying boredom of the job had driven her to distraction. Still, she might have accepted that as her lot if it hadn't been for finding out the truth about her father. Once that genie was out of the bottle it could never be put back in. She wasn't going to live like her mother had, trapped by rigid convention and other people's rules. There had to be something more, something better.

Liv's thoughts were interrupted by a loud knocking on the front door. Because the law had been on her mind, she immediately jumped to the conclusion that it must be them. Oh God! Fear swept over her. Lincoln had done his worst and now she was about to face the consequences. With her heart thrashing she leapt up from the bed, quickly crossed the room, opened the door and went out on to the landing.

Leaning over the banister, she looked down. Dora was padding across the hall, her slippers slapping softly against the lino. She had to stop herself from calling out, 'Don't open it! Please don't open it!' Her fingers tightened round the wooden rail while the rest of her body battled with the fight-or-flight signals pulling her in different directions. Should she run upstairs to try and hide or stand her ground and protest her innocence? Paralysed by indecision, she did nothing.

The door was opened – Liv couldn't see who was standing on the other side of it – and there was a murmur of voices. The breath caught in the back of her throat. Then the door was closed and Dora began to retrace her steps towards the kitchen. Behind her walked a woman in her fifties, scrawny and sad-looking with an old black handbag hanging off her arm.

Liv released a long and grateful sigh of relief. It was only one of Dora's clients, here for a tarot reading. The women always had a certain look about them, down at heel and careworn as if they carried the burdens of the world on their shoulders. They came for a glimpse of the future, for hope, for a light at the end of the long dark tunnel. They left with expectations and a few less shillings in their purses.

Retreating back into her room, Liv smiled wryly at how she had overreacted. The trouble with being on edge, with being under pressure, was that you ended up a nervous wreck. Of course Lincoln would never go the police. It wasn't his style. How could she ever have believed it? Men like him, like Moody, had their own way of doling out retribution. Her smile quickly faded. There was little consolation to be found in that particular thought.

21

For the next few days Liv was in limbo, unsure as to which way Lincoln was going to jump and equally dreading either of the outcomes. She considered going to the agency and trying to get some temporary work while she waited, but somehow couldn't summon up the enthusiasm. For the most part she stayed in her room, reading books and magazines or watching the world go by from the window.

Occasionally she ventured out for a walk but never went far. During these excursions she spent much of the time trying to figure out if she was being followed. She would constantly glance over her shoulder or stop abruptly and turn around. But her tail was either non-existent or too good to be spotted. She kept her eyes peeled for Henry and Ralph McCall, too. It would be just her luck to bump into one of them after Lincoln had made clear that there was to be no further contact.

She had, of course, no intention of obeying Lincoln's instruction when it came to meeting Henry Squires. But she didn't want to get caught in the act, either. She would have to make alternative arrangements either through a phone call or by letter. It was too risky to go back to the Eagle.

From time to time, she popped into the French to see if Pally was around, but there was no sign of him. She tried Joe's too without success. Perhaps he was doing the sensible thing and keeping his head down until the business with Moody was sorted. She missed his company, but it was probably for the best. After a few drinks, she might be tempted to tell him about the Garvie job. Pally could keep a secret – she was pretty sure of that – but it wasn't worth taking any chances.

By Thursday, Liv's anxiety levels were growing. Why hadn't Lincoln been in touch? She needed to know what was happening, to be aware of where she stood, so she could make the appropriate arrangements. He was probably doing it deliberately, leaving her to sweat. Dora, surprised to find her in the house so much, worried that she was 'under the weather' and insisted on feeding her hot soup, even though the temperature was 75 degrees outside.

'I'm sure it's nothing,' Liv said, thinking it was best to go along with the diagnosis rather than try and come up with another explanation for why she was so down in the dumps. 'Perhaps I'm getting one of those summer colds.'

'You girls should take better care of yourselves. That's what happens when you burn the candle at both ends.'

'I've not been burning *that* many candles.'

Dora raised her eyebrows but was tactful enough not to mention the numerous occasions she must have heard her and Verity stumbling in at two or three in the morning. 'Nothing else bothering you, then?'

'Like what?'

'I don't know. Man trouble, perhaps. Only I noticed … I wasn't snooping, dear, I promise … I just glanced out of the window and saw you arguing with that young man. Monday, was it? He didn't look best pleased, whatever it was about.'

Liv, put on the spot, tried to keep her tone dismissive. 'Oh, *him*. That wasn't anything. You know what some men are like: they buy you a drink and think they own you.'

'You'd tell me, though, if you were in any kind of trouble?'

There was something about the way she said 'trouble' that alerted Liv to the underlying meaning. 'God, no. I'm not ... no, there's nothing to worry about on that score.'

'Glad to hear it. Only there are people who can help if you ever get in a jam.'

'I'm not, I swear,' Liv said quickly, before Dora could direct her towards the nearest backstreet abortionist. 'I'd tell you if I was.'

'You didn't mind me asking, did you? I don't mean to cause offence'

'None taken,' Liv said.

'Only it's always the woman who pays the price. I can't tell you how many girls have sat at this table, hoping against hope that the cards will say they're not in the family way and that the only thing they've got is indigestion.'

'Wishful thinking, I suppose.'

Dora shook her head. 'It's a man's world, that's for sure.'

Liv couldn't argue with that. It seemed that men had everything their own way, had their cake and ate it. And what choices was a woman left with if she got caught out? She could try to bully the man into marriage, raise the kid on her own, have it adopted or risk her life with an illegal termination. It was enough to put you off sex for ever. 'Do you think it will ever change, Dora?'

Dora chuckled softly. 'Not in my lifetime, love.'

Liv finished her soup, stood up and carried the empty bowls

to the sink. 'Thanks for that, Dora. It was lovely. I'll do the washing-up.' She put the kettle on the hob and while she was waiting for it to boil sat down again and took a look at the local paper. Moll Ainsworth's murder was emblazoned across the front. 'Have you read this?'

'Not got a good word to say about her,' Dora grumbled. 'You'd think it was her fault she got murdered, not the bugger's who did it. They're all the same them reporters: can't see the wood for the bleedin' trees.'

Liv read through the article and understood what she meant. The fact that Moll had worked as a prostitute was the main focus, the implication being that by doing what she did she had virtually brought it on herself. There was nothing about the person she'd been, her character or personality, and there was little sympathy expressed for her as a victim. It was a story big on sensationalism and small on detail. Somehow the paper had managed to get hold of a photograph, an unflattering mugshot that must have been taken after one of her many arrests. The piece, unsurprisingly, had been written by Ralph McCall. It didn't improve her opinion of him.

'Says here the police are still making enquiries.'

'Is that what they call it? I doubt they'll be putting themselves out.'

The kettle came to the boil and Liv rose to her feet, put some water in the sink and started washing the pots. There was a clatter at the front door, a rattling of the letterbox, and Dora went off to investigate.

'Bit late for the postman.'

Dora came back waving a large brown envelope. 'It's for you, love. Someone must have dropped it off.'

Liv dried her hands and took the envelope. Her name had been printed in bold block capitals on the front. Without thinking she tore it open and partly pulled out the contents, discovering a sheaf of papers that Lincoln must have put together. Immediately she saw that the top sheet was from Hugh Garvie, inviting her for an interview. The rest, she presumed, was the background information she'd need to complete the deceit.

Dora was waiting, curious.

'Oh, I've got an interview for a job,' Liv said. 'Tomorrow morning at ten o'clock.'

'Well done, love. I'm sure they'll take you on.'

'I hope so.'

'Anything interesting?'

'Just secretarial, but it looks all right.' Liv quickly pushed all the papers back into the envelope again, and before Dora could ask any more questions said: 'Well, I suppose I'd better go and get some typing practice in if I want to stand a chance of getting it. I'm a bit rusty.'

'You'll be fine. It'll soon come back to you.'

Liv thanked Dora again for lunch and went upstairs to her room. So, Lincoln had finally made up his mind. She wasn't sure if she was more relieved or alarmed by this. A bit of both, probably. She was under no illusion, however, that this meant he trusted her. More likely he'd decided that another opportunity like this wasn't going to come around in a hurry and with time being short – too short, perhaps, to find anyone else – had chosen to take a chance with her.

She sat down on the bed and emptied the envelope. Beneath the letter confirming her interview was a copy of her application for the job – or rather the application Lincoln had made. It was short and to the point, setting out her experience and expressing her enthusiasm for the post that was on offer. Her address was given as Duncan Terrace in Islington, her date of birth as 4 January. She committed these to memory and also made a mental note to practise the signature allegedly belonging to Olivia Kent in case she was asked to sign anything else.

The next sheet of paper contained a copy of the reference from Lord Carbrooke, a glowing testimony that would have made her blush had any of it been true. She was described as loyal, hard-working, efficient, intelligent and discreet. He stressed that she would be an asset to any employer and expressed regret at how the unfortunate business of her aunt's illness had meant she could no longer go on working for him.

'Very impressive,' she murmured. Unless Mr Garvie got an application from the queen's secretary, she should be in with a chance.

The rest of what she'd been provided with was information relating to the lord himself. He had a wife, Clara, and two grown-up children called William and Margaret. There was a country estate in Norfolk and a London house in Belgravia. In the past he had served as an MP, but was now retired. There were lists of his business interests and his favoured pastimes. Gambling, unsurprisingly, wasn't mentioned. Numerous press cuttings showed him at public functions with and without his wife. He was a portly gentleman with a wide face, a couple of chins and thick grey hair.

Liv studied all the pictures until she had his image imprinted on her mind. She read and reread the information about him. What she didn't want was to get caught out by some random question Garvie might ask her. Lincoln wouldn't be happy if she blew it at the last hurdle.

Once she was sure that she was up to speed, Liv rose to her feet, took down her Olympia from the top of the wardrobe and set it on the dressing table. The portable typewriter had been a gift from her mother just after she'd left school, a second-hand machine to give her some practice while she was searching for a job. She rolled in a sheet of paper and began to type, clumsily at first, but then with more confidence as her fingers remembered what to do and where they were supposed to be. For the next couple of hours she clattered away until she was certain of being competent enough to pass any test Garvie might throw at her.

22

Ralph McCall was feeling pleased with himself. A front-page story was not to be sneered at and he reckoned he'd done a good job, good enough hopefully for Arthur Neames to take notice and push some more interesting assignments in his direction. Moll Ainsworth had, inadvertently, done him a favour. The *West End News* had been published today and would already be gracing thousands of tables in local households, cafés and pubs. Murder always boosted circulation figures, even if that murder was of a common prostitute.

The only fly in the ointment was Henry's double-page spread on pages two and three. It was headlined A TOWN IN FEAR, and although it contained nothing new about the facts of the case, he'd managed to imbue the piece with a sinister edge, somehow capturing the atmosphere of Eastbourne and its shocked residents. The article, a rare departure from local news, was both compelling and darkly masterful. Ralph had read it with dismay; it took a little of the gloss off his own achievement.

Peace and quiet reigned in the office. This wasn't unusual

for a Thursday when most of the small band of reporters took a break after the frenetic Wednesday that always preceded publication day. Ralph had chosen to come in for two reasons, one of which was to ingratiate himself with Neames, the other to keep an eye on Henry. He'd been doing the latter since Monday, still convinced that the old man was on to something with Liv Anderson and looking for evidence to back up his hunch.

Other than the odd occasions when Henry was sent out of the city, like the recent Eastbourne jaunt, he rarely strayed far from the office and yet was always able to conjure up a story as if from nowhere. This increased Ralph's resentment towards him. The bastard used the minimum of effort to produce the maximum result. How did he do it? Neames could present Henry with an assignment that appeared on the surface to be as insubstantial as air and yet he would always manage to make something solid out of it, something that drew the readers in and made them laugh or curse or cry. He could, as Ralph's mother would have put it, make a silk purse out of a sow's ear.

Ralph slurped his mug of tea and watched his enemy surreptitiously. He had never found out why Henry had left the *Daily Mail*. No self-respecting journalist would ever normally resign from such a paper – a national with a huge circulation – to work for a rag like the *West End News*. He had made discreet enquiries but come up with nothing. If anyone did know they weren't prepared to say.

Henry had once travelled the world, met the famous and infamous, drunk with statesmen, gangsters, killers and film stars. He had, in his day, been a force to be reckoned with. Respected in Fleet Street, feared by law breakers and loved by the public, he had been at the peak of his career when he'd suddenly decided, for no apparent reason, to throw it all in. Where Henry had once spent his time hounding crooks or exposing injustice, he now seemed content to loll around the office – or the Eagle – only rousing himself when a deadline beckoned and some action became essential.

That Henry had been so careless with his success felt almost like a slap in the face. The man had possessed everything Ralph had always wanted and yet he'd chucked it all away. This act, so apparently wanton, only increased Ralph's feelings of bitterness. He would have revelled in having even half of Henry's reputation, would have given his right arm for it.

'Some people,' he muttered under his breath.

Ralph's perseverance eventually paid off. At around four o'clock the office junior, Clive, approached Henry's desk, put a brown cardboard file down on it and said: 'Here's those old cuttings you were after, Mr Squires. That's all we have here but if you need more I can go up to Colindale.'

Ralph's ears had pricked up but he was taking care not to look like he was interested. The British Newspaper Library was housed in Colindale so Henry was clearly researching something. To do with Liv Anderson? He didn't have any proof as yet, but that's what his instincts told him.

Henry opened the file, flicked through the contents and nodded. 'No, that's fine. Thanks, lad, you've done a grand job.'

Clive beamed like he'd just been handed a gold star by his favourite teacher. 'Always happy to help, Mr Squires.'

Ralph rolled his eyes. Whenever he asked Clive for some help, the little bugger always claimed he was too busy. Preferential treatment, that's what Henry got. Which only provided another reason to dislike him.

The next half-hour was an agony for Ralph. He dreaded Henry standing up, putting on his jacket, tucking the file under his arm and heading off for home – or the pub. Either way it would mean he wouldn't get to see what was in the damn file.

He sat in a misery of impatience, his fear of missing out almost too much to bear.

Then he got a stroke of luck. Clive went out to post the mail, and minutes later Henry lumbered to his feet and sauntered towards the Gents. Ralph waited until the door had closed before leaping to his feet and rushing over to the older man's desk. He had one fast glance around to make sure he was completely alone before opening the file and quickly rifling through the contents. What he found both baffled and intrigued him: a small pile of photostats relating to the murder of a man called Nicky Lister. Ralph had never heard of the bloke. He checked the date across the top of one cutting – April 1937 – and wondered why the hell Henry was so interested in a killing that had taken place all those years ago.

Afraid of getting caught in the act, Ralph didn't linger. He closed the file and returned to his own desk. Without sitting down, he scribbled Nicky Lister's name and the date of the murder in his notepad, slipped the pad into his pocket and left the office. As he hit the street he considered jumping on the Tube and going to Colindale, but when he checked his watch saw that it was already too late. By the time he got there the library would be closed. It would have to wait until tomorrow.

With no immediate desire to go home, Ralph strolled into Soho. He went to Joe's, ordered a coffee, found an empty table near the back and spent the next few minutes smugly congratulating himself on discovering the contents of the file. But what did it all mean? Why was Henry rooting around in the past? He had to be on to something big.

Then, from nowhere, a horrible thought occurred to him. What if this was just some kind of prank, a set-up by Henry, a lesson in not poking his nose into other people's business? He could be about to embark on a wild goose chase. It had been too convenient, perhaps, for both Clive and Henry to be out of the room at the same time, the file left unattended.

The idea of being taken for a fool made his blood boil, but the more he thought about it the less he believed it to be true. No, he was barking up the wrong tree. The old hack was just careless, and too stupid to realise that Ralph had been watching his every move. Henry had underestimated him and he was going to pay the price. Wherever he was going with this story, Ralph would be hot on his heels. He might have lost out on Eastbourne but he wouldn't let this slip through his fingers.

23

Liv rose early on Friday morning, had a bath, did her hair and make-up and then dressed carefully in a moss-green dress with matching jacket. The suit was elegant and expensive, an outfit that announced (in a subtle kind of way) that she possessed both taste and confidence. The shoes she chose were high-heeled, but not too high, and showed off her slim calves and ankles. Her stockings were sheer. A dab of Chanel No. 5 provided the finishing touch.

She stood back and viewed the effect in the mirror through critical eyes. Not bad. She made a few adjustments to her hair. Everything had to be perfect if she was going to look the part, if she was going to look like the sort of girl a lord might once have employed. Carbrooke would have been as meticulous in his choice of secretary as he was about the clothes he wore and the restaurants he dined in.

At half past nine, Liv set out for her appointment. She took the shortest route, skirting round Soho, walked at a smart pace and arrived in Bedford Square with time to spare. It was impossible to fault Garvie's office location. With its lines of fine Georgian houses and a private leafy garden set in its heart, the square was probably one of the most attractive in London. She located the right number and then, as she was early, took a stroll around.

While she walked, she kept her eyes peeled for Lincoln. He had to be here. She was sure of it. He'd want to check that she had turned up for the interview. But as hard as she looked, she couldn't spot him. Keeping out of the way, then. But he'd be showing his face once she got out, keen to discover if she'd got the job or not.

Just before ten, Liv approached the building again. She examined the gold-coloured plaques – Garvie & Carr were on the ground floor – and tried the door. It wasn't locked. She stepped inside with nerves fluttering in her chest. She couldn't afford to blow this. If Garvie rejected her, chose someone else instead, Lincoln would presume she had deliberately messed up.

In the hallway a staircase rose up to her right. To the left was a long corridor and off this, only a few feet away, was the open door to an office where a woman was sitting behind a desk, her fingers pounding at the keys of a typewriter. Liv took a deep breath, reminded herself of her fake credentials, painted on a smile and walked confidently into the room.

The woman stopped typing and looked up at her. The look wasn't friendly. 'Can I help?'

'Good morning. I'm Olivia Kent. I have an interview with Mr Garvie at ten o'clock.'

The woman nodded and waved a hand towards a brown leather sofa. 'Take a seat. He'll be with you shortly.'

Liv sat down and glanced around. It was an airy, spacious room, even with the banks of filing cabinets. Pictures of London were on the walls, framed prints of the Thames, Parliament and Westminster Abbey. Two healthy palms, their green fronds bending gracefully, filled the far corners. There was an empty desk at right angles to one of the windows with a pleasant view across the square – hers, perhaps, if she managed to secure the job.

She looked back at the receptionist. The woman was a bleached blonde in her late thirties, trying hard to look much younger. Her hair was crimped into tight waves and her lipstick was a garish red. When their eyes met, Liv smiled. 'Have you worked here for long?'

'Fourteen years. Give or take a month.'

'That's quite a time. You must be happy here, then.'

'Well, it suits *me*,' the woman said tightly. 'It might not be for everyone.'

'No, of course not. But Mr Garvie must be a good boss if you've worked for him for this long.'

'Actually, I work for Mr Carr in the main. We deal with the residential side of things.'

'Ah, I see. So have there been many applicants for the job?'

A gleeful, slightly sly look came into the woman's eyes. 'Oh, yes, he's been interviewing all week. It's been like Piccadilly Circus in here.'

Liv wasn't overjoyed by this news. With so much competition for the post, she could still lose out. Perhaps the reference from Lord Carbrooke wouldn't impress Garvie quite as much as Lincoln thought it would. She would have to pull out all the stops, launch a charm offensive and give it everything. There was no way she was leaving here without that job in her pocket.

The telephone rang and the woman picked it up. 'Yes, Mr Garvie. Yes, I'll do that. I'll send her along right away.' She put the phone down and said primly: 'Mr Garvie will see you now. It's the room straight ahead at the end of the corridor.'

'Thank you.' Liv rose to her feet and made her way down the hall, pushing back her shoulders as she walked. She paused for just long enough to gather her thoughts, to inhabit the mindset of Olivia Kent and then knocked lightly on the door.

'Come in!'

Liv depressed the brass handle and went inside. Hugh Garvie rose from his chair as she approached, smiled and held out his hand across the wide mahogany desk.

'Miss Kent. How nice to meet you.'

As their hands linked, she saw his eyes quickly rake her body, an appraisal so fleeting that had she blinked she would have missed it. But she hadn't. And it told her everything she needed to know. She was familiar with that predatory look, had seen it too many times before in the quiet surroundings of all those hotel bars.

'Do take a seat,' he said.

'Thank you. And thank you for inviting me here today.'

As Liv sat down, she was already busy making her own appraisal. Garvie was, she estimated, in his early fifties, a slim, hawkish-looking man with a shock of silver hair brushed back from his forehead. His height was average, his suit expertly cut and his brilliant white shirt probably from Jermyn Street. Everything about him screamed money and success.

Garvie made a show of looking down at her application form as if reminding himself of who she was. 'Ah, yes, of course. You're the young lady who used to work for Lord Carbrooke.'

'That's right. I was very fortunate. He was an excellent employer; I learnt a lot in the years I was with him.'

'What were your duties, exactly, if you don't me asking?'

Liv reeled off the answer she'd already prepared. 'Shorthand, typing, answering the phone, dealing with the correspondence and making travel arrangements. It was always very busy, but that's what I liked about it. I'm not afraid of hard work, Mr Garvie. I always give one hundred per cent.'

'But the property business, Miss Kent. Do you have any experience of that?'

'Lord Carbrooke had a lot of business interests, some of them connected to property. I can't claim to be an expert but I do have some experience. And I'm quick to pick things up.'

Garvie nodded. 'Good, good. But what are we talking about here? What property interests exactly?'

Liv saw the trap for what it was and responded accordingly. 'I couldn't possibly discuss that, Mr Garvie – just as I'd never discuss your business with anyone else. It's a matter of trust, isn't it? Trust and discretion.' Then, worried that she might be coming across as a touch holier-than-thou, she crossed her legs to reveal another tantalising inch of stocking, and smiled sweetly. 'I think loyalty is very important.'

Unable to resist temptation, Garvie's gaze flew to her legs where it lingered for a few lascivious seconds before rising to her face again. 'I couldn't agree more.'

While the interview was proceeding, Liv was also taking in the office. With its wood-panelled walls, deep pile carpet and expensive furnishings, it fell just short of ostentatious. He was clearly a man who liked to display his wealth but not to flaunt it. She was gradually getting the measure of him.

As Garvie expressed his condolences over her late aunt, he watched her closely. Liv was careful with her response, aiming for the right balance between being suitably sad yet not so distressed that she might be liable to burst into tears at inappropriate moments. The man was not, she suspected, overly tolerant of emotional women.

'It's been a while now,' she said. 'I've had time to come to terms with it. Aunt Enid always said that you have to look forward, not back. I think that's so true, don't you?' Then, without waiting for an answer, she quickly added, 'Yes, I believe I'm quite ready for a new challenge.'

A few more questions, none of them difficult, eventually brought the interview to a close. Although she thought it had gone well, she wasn't going to count her chickens. She still expected him to say that he would be in touch, that he had other applicants to consider, but instead he sat back, folded his arms across his chest and stared at her.

'You know, Miss Kent, I've still got other girls to see but I do feel that you could fit in very nicely here. If I offered you the job, would you be able to start on Monday?'

Liv, relieved, was quick to respond. 'Yes, of course. That would be perfectly acceptable. Thank you. I won't let you down.'

'I'm glad to hear it. Nine o'clock, then. Muriel will show you what's what and sort out the paperwork on Monday.'

'Thank you,' Liv repeated, rising to her feet.

Garvie made no move to stand up or shake her hand again, so she wished him goodbye and left. As she walked back down the hall, she felt the adrenalin kick in, the satisfaction of a job well done. Now that it was over, she knew that Lincoln had been right all along – the Carbrooke connection had been too much for Garvie to resist. She hadn't even been asked to take a typing test. But her part in the proceedings hadn't been entirely negligible. Hugh Garvie would never have employed her if he hadn't liked what he'd seen and wanted to have it.

Muriel was still clacking away at the typewriter as Liv walked past. She thought about popping her head round the door and announcing the good news, but suspected the joy wouldn't be shared. She would have to work on Muriel, find a way to ingratiate herself. If anyone had the dirt on Garvie, it would be her.

24

Liv bounced out of the office with a spring in her step. Yes! It only struck her as she walked across the square that Pally wasn't here to share the triumph. Usually it was the two of them, partners in crime, co-conspirators revelling in their success and sharing out the spoils. It didn't feel the same without him. And whose fault was that? She scowled, thinking of his bruises, of what Moody's thugs had done to him. And from there it was only a small leap to Lincoln and all his demands.

She had just reached Tottenham Court Road when she felt the presence at her side. As if her resentment had conjured him up, Lincoln suddenly fell into step beside her. 'Well?'

'Well what?' she snapped, knowing exactly what he meant but unwilling to give him the good news he wanted before she had to.

'Tell me you didn't screw it up.'

Liv didn't reply straight away. She carried on walking, not even looking at him. She heard the edge in his voice, the concern that something had gone wrong. She was quietly pleased.

Most of the power was on his side but now she had the chance to get a little of her own back. Not quite a taste of his own medicine but as close as she was likely to get.

'Sometimes people just don't like you. A good reference doesn't guarantee anything.'

They were walking close enough for her to feel his body stiffen. 'Jesus! All you had to do was *get* him to like you. How bloody hard is that? You don't usually have a problem. What was so different about today? Damn it! Do you have any idea how rarely an opportunity likes this comes along?' Lincoln thrust his hand into his pocket, pulled out a pack of cigarettes, took one out and lit it. He expelled the smoke like a dragon blowing fire. 'I knew I couldn't trust you! I knew I should have gone with someone else.'

Liv gave a shrug, said nothing, safe in the knowledge that he couldn't do anything too terrible to her when they were out in public. Anyway, she was enjoying herself. It was worth winding him up just to see him suffer. Now he knew what it felt like to be on the receiving end, to not always have things go his own way.

'So I've got to go and tell Mr Moody that it's all been a waste of time, that he's getting nothing back, that Carbrooke's reference is now a worthless piece of paper. You think he's going to be happy about that?'

'All right. I get it.'

'Do you? Only that's not what I'm hearing. You reckon you can just walk away from this? Well, you can't. We had a deal and you screwed up. This isn't over, not by a long chalk.'

'You made that perfectly clear the last time we met.'

Lincoln continued in much the same mode, berating and blaming until they had reached St Giles Circus. By this time Liv had heard enough. She moved to the inner edge of the pavement, out of the flow of pedestrians, stopped and turned to face him. 'Did I tell you I hadn't got the job?'

Lincoln, caught on the hop, frowned down at her. 'As good as.'

'No, not as good as at all. I made one comment and you jumped to conclusions.'

His jaw slackened and hope sprang into his eyes. 'So what are you saying?'

'Of course I got it. I start on Monday, all right. Happy now?'

Lincoln's face relaxed as relief washed over him. But the benign expression didn't last for long. Almost instantly his eyes hardened again, anger filling his voice. 'So why the hell did you pretend you hadn't?'

'I didn't pretend anything,' she lied. 'If you didn't like the sound of your own voice so much, I could have told you five minutes ago. It's been hard to get a word in edgeways.'

Naturally, Lincoln didn't say 'Well done' or offer her any words of congratulation. She hadn't expected it. He still had the hump because she'd let him sound off for so long. She had made him look foolish and his male pride was hurt. Instead, he said curtly: 'I'll see you next Friday. Six o'clock at Joe's.' It was an order not a request.

Lincoln turned to go but Liv stopped him. 'Hang on. I still don't know what you want me to do there – at Garvie's, I mean. What exactly are you after?'

'I've already explained that.'

Liv thought back to their conversation in the shabby café. 'Yes, but don't you think "everything" is just a tiny bit vague? Can't you be more specific?'

'No,' he said.

'You don't know what you want or you don't want to tell me?'

Lincoln took another deep drag on his cigarette. His tone was peevish, full of irritation. 'What don't you understand about everything? It seems pretty straightforward to me.'

Liv decided not to provoke him any further; it was too much like prodding a sleeping tiger. Anyway, she had probably got away with as much as she was going to. 'All right. Fine. Everything it is.'

Lincoln gave her a searching look as if suspecting some trickery in this sudden acquiescence. A grim smile appeared on his lips. 'Six o'clock at Joe's, then. Don't be late.'

Liv watched him walk off, wondering at her own perversity. Winding him up like that hadn't been the smartest thing to do in the current circumstances. He wouldn't forget it in a hurry, but for now – while he needed her – it would remain on the back burner, a grudge to be settled at a later date.

25

DI Jack Bentley, returning to the scene of the crime, stood in Dean Street and peered down the narrow alleyway. It was five days since Moll Ainsworth's body had been found and he was no closer to discovering who'd killed her. His gaze took in the blackened brick walls, the row of bins and the litter scattered around them. At night, away from the street lamps, there would be very little light, which was why, of course, it was a popular venue for the local toms. Not that any of them would be using it again in a hurry, not until memories faded and convenience replaced fear.

He knew there was no physical evidence here – the forensics team had already swept the area and found nothing useful – but what he was searching for was something less tangible. A feel for what had happened. A sense of the sequence of events. He lifted his face and sniffed the air as if, hidden in the atmosphere, a clue was waiting to be given up.

In his head he reviewed what they already knew: Moll had visited the Black Bull at eight and the French at ten – a couple of breaks, a few drinks to ease her through the soul-destroying hours of Saturday-night business. Although how much business was actually on offer? She had hardly been in the first flush of youth and there was plenty of competition. Punters couldn't have been that easy to come by.

This was why, perhaps, she had gone with someone who might not have smelled completely right. The girls usually had a nose for the wrong 'uns. Moll hadn't been some raw recruit in from the country, naïve and inexperienced – she'd been walking these streets for years – but desperation might have dulled her judgement.

DC Hemmings scuffed the toe of his shoe against the pavement, and sighed. 'What exactly are we looking for, guv?'

Bentley glanced at him before gazing back down the alley. Hemmings wasn't a bad cop but he was young and impatient, more interested in action than contemplation. Still, at least he was straight, which was more than could be said for some. Well, for the moment he was, but how long would he stay that way? West End Central was almost as corrupt as the villains who ran Soho. Eventually even the good cops slid into the mire, tired of swimming against the tide and unable to resist the lure of easy money.

'It always pays to have a second look, and a third come to that. Things get missed. You have to try and get inside the head of the killer, think like he was thinking.'

'Just a punter, wasn't he? After a bit of how's your father.'

'And then he strangled her. Why do you think he did that?'

Hemmings shrugged, uninterested in motivation. 'Probably one of those blokes who hates toms. He has it away with her and then . . . Or perhaps he just didn't want to pay.'

'The girls always get the cash up front. Moll wasn't a fool; she wouldn't have set foot in that alley until she'd seen the colour of his money.'

'He could have taken it back after he killed her.'

'So why didn't he take the rest of it? When she was found she still had a few quid shoved down her bra. No, it doesn't add up.' Bentley shook his head, unsure of where any of this was taking him. 'The pathologist found some fibres during the autopsy. He reckons she was strangled with a silk scarf. What do you make of that?'

Hemmings frowned, unable apparently to make anything much out of it. 'So she was wearing a scarf. What's odd about that?'

'No, she wasn't. Not a chance. Moll would never have worn a scarf when she was working. None of the girls do. It's just asking for trouble.'

'So the killer was wearing it. A toff, then. Or one of those arty types – there's plenty of them drink down the French.'

Bentley nodded. 'Or maybe stashed in his pocket. Our killer could have come prepared.'

'Premeditated, then. But who'd want to kill Moll Ainsworth?'

'Someone clearly did. Or perhaps they were after any tom and she was just unlucky. Either way, I'm going to nail the bastard.'

There was a vehemence in his voice that made Hemmings stare at him for a moment. 'So what now, guv?'

'You go and talk to the girls, anyone who's around at the moment. See what they can remember about Saturday night.'

'But we've already done that.'

'So do it again. Try and jog their memories. Our killer must have walked along Dean Street with Moll. Someone must have seen them.'

Once Hemmings had gone, Bentley took a few steps into the alley. He reached out a hand and touched the damp, grainy brick. If only walls could talk. It would make his job a damn sight easier. His gaze dropped to the ground, to the sheets of newspaper that had blown in and the fag ends that people had chucked as they went past. He thought about the street cleaner, John Harrow, the man who'd discovered the body. A suspect? He didn't think so. Although there were some murderers who liked to be at the centre of things, who couldn't resist the danger of being involved, he didn't believe Harrow fitted the bill.

Bentley raised his eyes again. He knew that it wasn't good to be too emotional about a victim, but what had happened to Moll both angered and moved him. Splashed across the front cover of the local paper, she had become more important in death than she had ever been in life. He wasn't the sentimental sort but he reckoned she deserved more than that. Moll had been walking these streets for as long as he'd been policing them, their lives running in an odd kind of parallel. Now he was getting on too, his usefulness receding, his retirement looming on the horizon.

Bentley winced a little when he thought about retirement. What the hell would he do with himself? Take up golf, perhaps, or gardening. Or maybe get one of those part-time security jobs where he sat around all day waiting for something to happen. No, that wasn't for him. He erased the very idea of it and returned his attention to the matter in hand.

Moll had lived in Bridle Lane. The second-floor rooms she'd rented had been cramped and dark and stank of damp. Barely habitable but cheap. Her few possessions – some clothes and a small amount of costume jewellery – hadn't taken long to go through. There had been no letters or paperwork of any kind. A single framed photograph had graced the bedside table: a much younger Moll with a baby in her arms. The first thing she had seen every morning when she woke up, the last thing she saw before she went to sleep. And he had known from that picture that this was a place she had never brought punters.

Bentley wondered where the child was now. Adopted, perhaps, or given to a relative to raise. Maybe it had not survived. They had been unable to trace any of Moll's relations. There had been nothing in the room to help, and the other girls hadn't heard her talk of anyone. To all intents and purposes, she'd been alone in the world.

Something about Bridle Lane rang a bell in the back of his mind, an old case, a piece of the past he couldn't quite get a grip on. The harder he tried the more elusive it became. But it would come back to him eventually. Once he stopped fretting about it, his unconscious would start sifting through all the debris in his head, rooting through old crimes, old names, distant investigations, until it finally rose to the surface.

He stood for a while longer, his thoughts fixed on Moll. Then he turned and retraced his steps to the opening of the alley. There was nothing more he could do here. Time was slipping by and with every day that passed the chances of finding the killer grew slimmer. A local or a visitor? A regular or someone she didn't know? He didn't have the answers, but he wasn't giving up. With a firm step he set off to find Hemmings.

26

It was two years since rationing had come to an end, but Liv still found it a novelty that there was so much food to buy in the shops. She remembered the queues, the tiny portions, the constant eking out. Now she flitted from baker to greengrocer to butcher without having to think twice about whether what she wanted would be available or not. She bought bread, eggs, lettuce, potatoes, tomatoes and slices of ham. Money would be tight until she got her first wage packet so eating at home would be more economical than eating out.

As she carried her shopping back towards Whitcomb Street, she reflected on the morning. Well, it hadn't gone too badly. She had managed to hold her nerve, secure a job and provide Lincoln with a short-lived but entirely pleasurable dent to his confidence. She'd had worse days.

The knowledge that she'd be trapped in a regular job for the next few weeks – maybe even longer – dampened her spirits a little. Being at the beck and call of Hugh Garvie wasn't anything to look forward to, either, but it would be worth it in the end. She'd be free of Moody and she'd never have to see Lincoln again. Both good causes for celebration. At lunchtime she'd go to the French and see if Pally was there.

As soon as she entered the house, Liv knew that no one else was in. It had that peculiar quality of all empty houses, a kind of hush as though it was holding its breath until the residents returned. Aline and Verity would be at work. Dora must have gone shopping or to visit a friend, but would probably be back soon; she never went far, not with her rheumatism.

Liv took the groceries through to the kitchen, opened the door to the pantry and stacked her purchases on the shelves. Dora had talked about buying a fridge, but nothing had come of it yet. Perhaps it was a luxury too far. She put the kettle on the stove and while she was waiting for it to boil went upstairs and changed out of her good clothes. Once she was dressed in slacks and a blouse, she felt more relaxed, as if the business part of the morning was over.

By the time she came downstairs again the kettle was whistling. She made a pot of tea, left it to brew and wandered down the hall into the living room. The room, spacious but somehow cosy, looked out on to the street. It was full of old-fashioned furniture: a big, battered sofa and a couple of easy chairs, an oak sideboard, a writing bureau and a glass cabinet containing porcelain figures, along with other assorted knick-knacks. There were two tall lamps with tasselled shades and an aspidistra in a blue pot. The only nod to modernity came in the form of the television, which had pride of place to the right of the hearth.

On the mantelpiece, flanked by a pair of china dogs, was a clock and two framed photographs, one of Dora's husband and the other of her son, Larry. Larry's picture must have been taken in his late teens; the eyes that gazed into the camera were pale, the mouth unsmiling. He had a sad, almost tragic look about him, as if he already knew what was coming. Liv winced when she recalled asking Dora about the pictures shortly after she'd moved in.

'That's my husband, Albert,' Dora had said. 'And that's my poor Larry. Sadly, they're not with us any more.'

'Oh, I'm so sorry.'

'You learn to live with it, my dear. What else can you do?'

And Liv, who at the time was suffering the awful grief at the loss of her mother, had wanted to ask how. She hadn't, of course. How could you? She was starting to understand, however, how the pain gradually faded. There was still a gaping hole in the centre of her life, still a void that could never be filled, but she was dealing with it better now. At least she didn't wake up every morning with an ache so intense she could barely get out of bed.

Thinking of her mother reminded her of Henry Squires. Her gaze fell on the writing bureau, its lid still down from where Dora must have been using it earlier. Inside was a pad of Basildon Bond, envelopes, stamps, pens, bills, letters, rubber bands and numerous other bits and bobs that had found their way into the cubbyholes.

Liv sat down in front of the bureau and pulled the pad towards her. Quickly, she wrote a note to Henry asking if they could meet on Monday at Amelia's instead. The café, halfway between his office and hers, seemed a safer bet than the Eagle. She still had no idea who'd tipped off Lincoln and wasn't going to take the chance of them doing it again.

Once the note was written she put it in an envelope, printed out the address of the *West End News* and attached a stamp. Then, as a second thought, she wrote PRIVATE in block capitals in the top left-hand corner. She didn't want that McCall reading it. Returning to the kitchen, she dropped the envelope into her handbag – she could post it later on her way to the French – and then took out her purse, found a threepence to cover the stamp

141

and the stationery and went back to the living room to leave the coin on the bureau.

Across the hall was the old front parlour, the room Dora now used as her bedroom. The door was ajar and the scent of talc and lavender water floated out. Liv, tempted to peek inside, hovered for a moment but resisted the urge. Curiosity killed the cat, as her mother had always said. Not that she'd ever understood the phrase. What cat? And what had it been doing? It was a question, she suspected, that she'd never get the answer to.

In the kitchen, Liv poured out the tea and sat down at the table. She'd barely taken a sip when she heard the front door open and close. Voices travelled down the hallway – cross voices. Dora and Aline at loggerheads again. What was Aline doing off work? The thought had barely entered her head before the exchange made her prick up her ears.

'You should go to the police, Dora. You have to tell them.'

'I don't have to do anything of the sort. Moll was wrong. She made a mistake.'

'You're the one making the mistake. For God's sake, what if you're next?'

'Don't be ridiculous!'

'So it's just a coincidence, is it?'

'Yes, that's exactly what it is.'

Liv had one of those awkward moments, wondering whether she should do something – cough, move the chair, shout out 'Hello' – to let them know she was there, but by the time she'd decided that she probably should, the two women had already reached the kitchen.

Aline stopped dead in her tracks, flustered. 'Oh, I thought you were out at some interview.'

'I was,' Liv said. 'But now I'm back.' She glanced from one to the other. 'Is everything all right?'

It was Dora who answered, bustling in with a wide smile on her face. 'Just Aline overreacting, as usual.' She paused as if trying to estimate how much Liv might have heard, perhaps quickly replaying the conversation in her head. 'She thinks I should go to the law about Moll.'

'Why? Do you know something?'

'Nothing they'll be interested in. Best not to waste their time, I reckon.'

Aline put her handbag on the table and untied her headscarf. 'All I meant was that any detail might be useful. Moll seemed worried about something when she was here. She wasn't herself. She was ... preoccupied. Yes, she was definitely preoccupied.'

'And you think the law are going to want to know that?' Dora said. 'Moll always had worries. There was nothing new there.'

Liv, recalling an earlier conversation about Moll's tarot reading, said: 'But didn't you warn her that she might be in danger? That would have worried anyone.'

'Before that,' Aline snapped. 'She had something on her mind even before Dora dealt the cards.'

'Did she say what it was?' Liv asked.

'No,' Dora said firmly. 'She didn't say a word.'

Liv noticed Dora throw Aline a warning glance and knew immediately that they were about to close ranks. Whatever the truth was, neither of them was going to reveal it to her.

'Yes, well,' Aline said. 'I suppose it is all a bit vague. I just thought ... '

'Is there tea?' Dora asked, leaning over to touch the pot. 'I'm gasping for a brew.'

'It's just made,' Liv said.

There was one of those awkward silences while Dora busied herself with cups and milk, and Aline hovered beside the table before eventually sitting down. Liv could feel the tension between them. She was curious but knew better than to pursue it. The subject, so far as Dora was concerned, was closed. Aline, she suspected, had more to say but wasn't going to say it in front of her.

'So, no work today?' Liv asked Aline, resorting to chit-chat.

'I took the day off.' Aline's voice was sullen. 'Dora and I were planning a trip to the coast, but she changed her mind at the last minute.'

'I'm not in the mood for gallivanting round Southend,' Dora said. 'It doesn't seem right, not at a time like this.'

'A walk along the front. It's hardly gallivanting. A bit of fresh air would have done you good.'

Dora put a cup of tea down in front of her. 'Anyway, I can't walk far, not with my knees. Maybe tomorrow.'

'It'll be too busy tomorrow. You know I don't like crowds.'

Dora sat down, looked at Liv and said, 'Sorry, love, we haven't even asked how your interview went.'

'Not so bad, thanks. I got the job. I start on Monday.'

'Well done! That's good news. Not that I doubted it for a minute, a smart girl like you. It was never going to be a problem. They're lucky to have you.'

Aline, who rarely enjoyed anyone else's good fortune, asked drily, 'So who is the lucky employer?'

And Liv, who wasn't going to take the risk of telling anyone about Garvie & Carr, found herself having to prevaricate again. 'No one special. Just a property company, but it'll do for now.'

'You won't get far with an attitude like that.'

'Oh, leave the girl alone,' Dora said. 'She's young. She's got plenty of time to make her way in the world.'

Aline pursed her lips. 'All I'm saying is that it doesn't hurt to put some effort into things. No good ever came from being slapdash.'

'And no good ever came from interfering, either.'

Liv, who could sense another row brewing, made a show of looking at her watch. 'Is that the time already? Gosh, I have to go. I promised to meet a friend for lunch.'

27

As she left the house and headed for Dean Street, Liv was still thinking about what she'd overheard. *For God's sake, what if you're next?* That's what Aline had asked. But why, and what had she meant by it? Moll Ainsworth had clearly said something that had got Aline in a tizz, but it wasn't anything Dora was prepared to repeat to the law. Liv could understand that. Avoiding the police was second nature to most people round here, no matter how innocent you were. Proffering information was tantamount to opening your front door and inviting in trouble.

Aline's words were still playing on her mind as she stopped to post the letter to Henry. It had been an odd thing for her to come out with. The suggestion that whoever had killed Moll might come after Dora too was a disturbing thought. Not that Dora had taken it seriously. She'd brushed it off, scoffing at the very idea. Maybe Aline *had* been overreacting. Sudden death, especially one as violent as this, could do strange things to people.

Liv took the envelope out of her bag and slid it through the slit of the pillar box. It would be delivered tomorrow and even if Henry wasn't in the office over the weekend, he should still get it by Monday. She could have tried calling the *West End News* but suspected that the odds of catching him there were slim. Journalists, by the very nature of their work, tended to be out and about for most of the day. Leaving a message wasn't a viable option either, not with that awful Ralph McCall nosing around.

As she started walking towards the French, it occurred to Liv that she had never even set foot in a pub before she'd come to London. The hostelries of Maybury hadn't welcomed the fairer sex, unless they were standing behind the bar: women belonged in the home, chained to the kitchen sink, not out enjoying themselves. It had been a revelation to discover that most of the West End pubs, and especially the Soho ones, were of a more liberal frame of mind. Between them, Pally and Verity had opened her eyes and shown her the best places to go.

It was Pally she was looking for as she pushed open the door and stepped into the French. And she didn't have to look very far. There he was, leaning casually against the bar with one elbow on the counter. She had a moment to take him in, to see him as a stranger might, a handsome man, albeit one who had suffered some adversity recently. His face, although it was starting to heal, still bore the evidence of the beating he'd taken.

He must have felt her gaze on him because he turned his head, grinning when he saw her. 'Hello, sweetheart. Let me get you a drink.'

She asked for a half of light, thinking it wise not to hit the hard stuff at this early hour. 'Ta. How are you doing?'

'On the mend. You can't keep a good man down. Or me, come to that.' He caught the barman's attention, ordered the drink, asked for it to be put on his slate and turned back to her. 'How goes it with you?'

'My last weekend of freedom before I join the masses. I start work on Monday.'

'Better make it a good one, then,' Pally said. 'What's the job?'

'Typing, filing, making tea. I can't tell you how much I'm looking forward to it. Still, it won't be for long.' Liv, who was starting to get adept at avoiding the question of who exactly she was working for, quickly changed the subject. 'Where are you staying at the moment? Have you got a place?'

'I'm at Geoff's for a week or so, or until he gets sick of me. Brewer Street. It's the flat above the off licence on the corner.'

'Cynthia's boyfriend?'

'Ex-boyfriend. He's been crying into his beer for the last few days.'

'Oh, yes, Verity mentioned something.'

'I've told him she's not worth the grief. No woman is.'

Liv raised her eyebrows.

'Present company excepted,' Pally said, grinning again. 'I mean, come on, it's not the first time she's cheated on the poor bloke. You'd think he'd have learnt by now.'

Liv's drink arrived. They carried their glasses over to a table and sat down. Although the pub had only opened fifteen minutes ago, it was rapidly filling up. For some people, it appeared, the weekend had arrived early; it might only be Friday lunchtime but celebrations were already getting under way.

'Have you ever been in love, Pally?'

Pally gave a snort. 'What do you think? Love's for idiots, for dreamers. It's just an illusion, a trick of nature, a way to keep the babies coming. Can you imagine me getting all dewy-eyed over someone? It's not my style, hon. I'm not cut out for happy ever afters.'

For all his denial, Liv didn't quite believe him. 'There must have been someone.'

But Pally wouldn't be drawn. Instead, he sighed and said, 'I suppose it's only a matter of time before you fall for some smooth-talking chancer and walk off into the sunset.'

'You don't have any worries on that score. I'm staying permanently single.'

'I'll remind you of that when you're standing at the altar promising to love, honour and obey.'

'If that ever happens, you have my permission to shoot me.'

While they were talking, Liv noticed a man working his way round the pub, going from table to table, holding out a photograph. He looked familiar but it took her a while to recognise him as the cop she'd seen in Dean Street last Sunday. Her thoughts flew back to Moll and what Aline had said. Pally was also saying something, but she wasn't really listening.

'Liv?'

'Huh?' she said, returning her attention to him.

'Am I boring you?'

'Sorry, I was just . . .' But she never got a chance to explain. The cop had finished with the last lot of customers and was now approaching their table.

He stood over them, smiled politely and said, 'My name's DI Bentley and I'm investigating the murder of Moll Ainsworth.' He held out the photograph. 'This is her. Were either of you in here last Saturday night?'

'Probably,' Pally said. 'We usually are.'

'Do you recall seeing this woman at any time during the evening?'

Liv stared at the photo, the same one that had been on the front of the paper. 'I didn't see her, but it was busy. It's always busy.'

'No,' Pally said. 'Sorry.'

DI Bentley nodded, looked as though he was about to move on, but then stopped, frowned and said, 'It's Mr Palliser, isn't it?'

'You remember me, then.'

Liv felt a palpable tension between the two men and glanced from one to the other. It was rarely good news when you were recognised by a cop. She saw Pally's face tighten and wondered if Bentley had arrested him in the past.

'Of course. It's been a while. You've been in the wars by the look of it.'

Pally touched his eye. 'Oh, this. It's nothing. I took a tumble. You know what it's like when you've had one too many beers.'

Bentley inclined his head slightly as if trying to recall the last occasion or perhaps any occasion when he'd been in such a position. He opened his mouth, hesitated and then said, 'Well, thanks for your time.'

The cop had only taken a few steps towards the next table when Pally called after him, his voice tight and angry. 'Let's hope you do better with this investigation than you did with Rosa's.'

Bentley stopped, turned around and the two men locked eyes. 'I hope so too.'

'That bastard's still out there somewhere.'

'I haven't forgotten.'

'Eleven years,' Pally said. 'There's not much chance of catching him now, is there?'

'There's always a chance.'

'I won't hold my breath.'

Bentley looked suddenly weary, as though burdened by the failures of the past. Liv might almost have felt sorry for him if her loyalties hadn't lain so completely with Pally. The cop nodded again and moved on.

Pally watched him for a moment and then lifted his glass and took a drink. He gave Liv a sideways glance. 'Rosa was my sister in case you're wondering. Although I don't suppose you are. Verity never could keep her mouth shut.'

It was the first time Liv had heard that edge of bitterness in his voice, although she suspected it was directed more at the cop than at Verity. She briefly laid her hand on his arm. 'I'm so sorry, Pally.'

'That's the trouble. As soon as people find out they get all weird and pitying and don't know what to say.'

Liv, who *didn't* know what else to say, chewed on her lower lip and stared at the bar while she tried to think of something suitable. She understood what it meant to want to keep things quiet, to not want to shout your anguish to the world, but her situation was different to his. Any thoughts of sharing the truth about her father instantly evaporated. This wasn't the time or the place.

'Oh, don't mind me,' Pally said, smiling as he nudged her elbow. 'I didn't mean anything by it. It was just a surprise seeing old Bentley again. I thought they'd have put him out to grass by now.'

'I take it he never got far with finding out who did it?'

'He didn't get anywhere. But one day ... one day I'll get justice for her.'

Liv remembered what Dora had said about learning to live with loss, but suspected that Pally never had. The brutal murder of Rosa was still as raw to him now as it had been eleven years ago.

28

Ralph had dragged Pauline into three other Soho pubs before he finally hit pay dirt at the French. It was eight o'clock, crowded and there weren't any free tables. He bought the drinks – a pint for himself, a Babycham for her – before the two of them squeezed into a smoky space at the rear of the room.

Pauline was still complaining. She hadn't been happy about shifting from the last pub and was equally miserable about having to stand up in this one. 'I've been on my feet all day, love. Can't we find somewhere with a place to sit?'

'Someone will leave soon enough. Don't you like it here? I've heard it's where the actors and artists drink. You might spot someone famous.'

Pauline brightened a little at this piece of information, her eyes darting around in anticipation. 'Like who?'

Ralph knew that the painter Francis Bacon often propped up the bar here, but also knew that Pauline would never have heard of him. She didn't do culture. All she was interested in were film stars or people on the telly. But Pauline wanted names so he pulled a few random ones out of the hat. 'Deborah Kerr, Trevor Howard, Stanley Baker? And Diana Dors, too.'

Pauline looked suitably impressed, her lips forming an ooh shape. She stood on her toes so she could see over the heads of the other customers. While she was busy searching for the rich and famous, Ralph took the opportunity to study Liv Anderson. He'd almost given up hope of finding her before they'd walked into the French. What were the odds? Well, maybe not that long seeing as he'd first noticed her in Joe's and so she probably lived round here, but he still felt as though the gods or fate or whatever ordered the universe had pointed him in the right direction.

Ralph had chosen a position that was close enough to Liv Anderson for him to watch her, without being so close that she might notice him. She was standing in a group near the bar, casually dressed in navy-blue slacks and a white blouse. Shiny hair fell loose around her face, framing wide dark eyes and a generous mouth. When she smiled, which was often, her lips parted to reveal a row of strong white teeth. He couldn't take his eyes off her. She wasn't exactly beautiful and yet she made other women seem dull and ordinary by comparison.

Pauline was wittering on and he made the occasional sound just to pretend he was paying attention. Her chatter floated over and around him – what Deirdre had said, what Mr Carter had done, why she was going to have to take back the shoes she'd bought last Saturday – a constant drone that barely penetrated his consciousness. Ralph had his mind on other things.

This morning he had spent a couple of hours at the newspaper library. He'd dug out every article he could on the Lister murder, had copies made and gone through them line by line while he was travelling back to the West End on the Tube. The killing had made the front pages in 1937, containing as it did everything the public liked best – a shocking crime, a handsome victim and a beautiful widow. Although never openly stated, there was an implication in all the articles that the dazzling Irene might not have been quite as innocent as she claimed.

He was surprised to discover that the perpetrator had been a reporter. Paul Teller had worked for the *Sunday Pictorial* and had written several stories about the golden couple before deciding to blast Nicky Lister into oblivion. Looking at the pictures of Irene, Ralph could see how a man could become obsessed. She'd been an extraordinary beauty, a little like Grace Kelly, with a seductive face and slender, shapely body.

At first, he hadn't been able to see the connection between this sensational murder and Liv Anderson. She was far too young. He had trawled through acres of newsprint before finally discovering the golden nugget: Paul Teller had been married with a wife called Jane and a two-year-old daughter, Olivia. Even then it had taken him a moment to make the leap from Olivia to Liv. And he hadn't counted his chickens: there were plenty of other girls with the same name.

His next port of call had been Somerset House, where he'd spent another long hour going through the records before coming across the written proof of Paul Teller's marriage to a Jane Anderson. It had been a eureka moment. There it was in black and white. And then it was all perfectly clear as to why Henry Squires was so interested: it might be an old story but it was one still shrouded in mystery. If Liv was about to reveal why her father had done what he'd done, it could be the exclusive of the year.

What Ralph still hadn't figured out, however, was what *he* was going to do next. Other than pushing Henry under a bus – an option he didn't entirely rule out – it was hard to see how he could prise Liv Anderson away from him. Perhaps he could approach Henry, tell him he knew what he was working on and demand to be in on the action. But he couldn't see the old hack going for that. Why would he share the honours when he didn't have to? No, there had to be another way. This could be the big break he'd been waiting for and he wasn't going to let it slip through his fingers.

Ralph was contemplating what this would mean, imagining the glory, when he got a hard dig in the ribs from Pauline's elbow.

'For God's sake. Can you stop staring at that bloody girl?'

Ralph hadn't even been aware that his gaze was still fixed on Liv Anderson. 'I'm not staring at her,' he protested, acting injured, like butter wouldn't melt in his mouth. 'It's the bloke she's with. I'm sure I've seen him before. Maybe on the telly. What do you think?'

Pauline glared at him but couldn't resist the temptation to turn her head and look just in case he was someone famous. 'No,' she said crossly.

Ralph shrugged, crunching his forehead into a frown as if still trying to place him. 'Somewhere else, then.'

'He'd be quite good looking if it wasn't for all those bruises,' she said, possibly in a pathetic attempt to make him jealous. 'But she's nothing special.'

'No,' he agreed quickly. The last thing he needed was a row. The man was tall and blond, a different feller to the one he'd seen Liv with in Joe's. Were they a couple? It was hard to tell. He was older than her, a good bit older, but some girls preferred that. He noticed the way they stood together, their arms touching, a kind of intimacy that suggested more than friendship. They seemed comfortable with each other, laughing and joking, leaning in to make themselves heard above the noise of the crowd.

'I don't like it here,' Pauline whined. 'Can we go?'

'I haven't finished my drink.'

'So finish it.'

Ralph gazed at her tight little face, at her eyes that were too close together and her lips that were too red. Once he'd made it big, once he had a few quid in his pocket and could pick and choose, the first thing he'd do was dump her. He deserved better and he was going to have it. No more listening to her inane chatter or having to account for who he chose to look at. He'd had enough. The sooner he got shot of her, the happier he'd be.

He downed what remained of his pint and placed the empty glass on a ledge. As they left the pub, he took the opportunity to sneak one last glance at Liv Anderson. She didn't know it yet, but she was the answer to his prayers.

29

Friday was payday for most workers, and it was usually an earner for Slug, too. People got careless when they'd had a few drinks – with their mouths and their money. He was spending the evening drifting from pub to pub, eavesdropping on conversations and taking advantage of the crowds to relieve unwary victims of their wallets. Soho stripped people of their inhibitions and their good sense.

Slug sucked in the cool evening air as he shambled along Brewer Street. The West End was changing as the old guard died out or retired. The likes of Billy Hill, of Jack Spot, had seen the writing on the wall. There was only so long you could hold on to power before your luck or your strength ran its course. It was smart to bow out gracefully, to leave with your reputation intact.

New faces like Don Moody were moving in now to take their place, grabbing whatever they could. This was where the money was: the girls, the gambling, the glory. Fights were breaking out over territory. Allegiances were being made and broken. There were only so many slices of pie and everyone was hungry.

Slug didn't care for Moody – the man was greedy, vicious and unpredictable – which was why he preferred doing business with Lincoln. Lincoln was no pushover but at least you knew where you stood. The bloke wasn't afraid to put his hand in his pocket. And he was always civil. Well, as civil as that shower ever were: when God was handing out the manners, he hadn't been overly generous to the villains of Soho.

There were stories Slug could tell about before the war, during the war, but he kept his counsel. *Dangerous talk costs lives*. That's what it had said on the posters, and it was still true today. It was those who liked the sound of their own voices – the loudmouths, the blatherers – who furnished him with the information he needed to scrape a living. Once the robbers and the racketeers, the thugs and the swindlers, had a few pints inside them they couldn't resist the indiscretions that would eventually put bread on his table.

This afternoon in the French, he'd seen the dark-haired girl who Lincoln had such an interest in. He'd watched her for a while but discovered nothing worth passing on. The person she'd been drinking with, a tall, blond bloke – he'd heard someone call him Pally – wasn't any kind of threat to Lincoln. If he wasn't mistaken, and he rarely was, the man was as bent as a nine-bob note. Although there had been nothing overtly queer about him, Slug had a nose for these things.

Bentley had turned up at the pub, too. He'd been doing the rounds, brandishing a photo of Moll Ainsworth. That's when Slug had scarpered. He might have something to tell Bentley about the murder, but he hadn't made up his mind yet. You had to weigh things carefully in his line of business, decide what might be more trouble than it was worth. He knew who Moll had seen – knew who he'd seen himself – but whether he was going to snitch was another matter altogether.

Slug was still thinking about this when he passed a young couple, the girl looking sulky, the bloke looking bored. He recognised the latter straight away – the reporter who'd given him a mouthful outside the Eagle. It was an opportunity too good to miss. He turned around and began to follow them.

30

Liv got up late on Saturday – it was almost midday – and grudgingly accepted her throbbing headache as an acceptable punishment for a long night of drinking and dancing. She and Pally had gone on to the Gargoyle after the French had closed, along with Geoff Dowd and a group of his friends, partying until it was almost dawn. It was the last hurrah before she started work on Monday and she'd enjoyed every minute of it.

Now, however, she was paying the price. She washed and dressed and went downstairs to the kitchen where she put the kettle on and drank some water. There was no sign of anyone else. Verity, of course, would be at the Windmill. Perhaps Dora and Aline had kissed and made up and toddled off to Southend. It was a nice day for it. Outside the sun was shining and the sky was a clear, bright blue.

Liv made a brew, opened the back door and sat down on the step. She smiled as she sipped her tea and thought about last night. The only downside had been Geoff's black mood. They had tried to cheer him up but with little success. Swinging between anger and self-pity, he had rained down curses on his faithless girlfriend, become maudlin, swore he would get his revenge and descended again into morose silence. Cynthia had a lot to answer for.

For Liv, it was all just another example of how destructive romantic love could be. She couldn't see the point of something that caused so much pain and misery. A trick of nature was what Pally had called it, but it was a malicious trick, one that turned lives upside down and transformed previously rational people into gibbering wrecks. Inevitably, her thoughts flew to her father and his obsession with Irene Lister. Had he sworn to get revenge, too?

Despite the warmth, Liv shivered. On Monday she was meeting Henry, after which everything might be clearer. Whether this would make her feel any better was a matter of debate. Still, at least she was facing it head on, looking it straight in the eye and not hiding from the truth. However awful the details were going to be – and she suspected they'd be *truly* awful – she could never find peace until it had all been confronted.

She gazed out across the small garden. Once well tended, it was now wild and neglected. Along the left side there was evidence of an old vegetable plot and to the right a row of flower beds. A few straggly roses still triumphed over the long grass, the thistles and the weeds. Dora had long ago given up on it, and no one else was interested.

Liv yawned, finished her tea and went back inside for a top-up. She had only just lifted the pot when she heard what sounded like a creak from the landing. So she wasn't alone after all. Not Dora – she couldn't remember the last time she'd been upstairs – but either Aline or Verity must be home, too. Hoping it was the latter, she put down the pot, went through to the hall and called out: 'Hello? Verity? Is that you?'

There was no response.

'Verity?'

Liv walked to the foot of the stairs and looked up. No one. She waited, listening, but everything was quiet. Perhaps all she had heard was the natural breathing of an old house, one of those strange clicks or creaks that seem to come from nowhere. She shrugged and was about to head back to the kitchen. But then she heard another sound, so slight she couldn't even give it a name: it was more a feeling than a noise, a shifting of the air, a sense of someone else's presence.

'Hello?'

Now her own voice sounded unnaturally loud, a strident call through the silence. She had suddenly become uneasy. Goosebumps spread over the backs of her arms. She held her breath, straining to listen again. Perhaps it was Verity, trying to put the wind up her. Or Aline, just being downright rude and ignoring her. She hoped for one or the other, but at the same time feared that it was neither.

Tentatively she put one foot on the bottom stair and gazed up towards the landing. A beam of sunlight slipped through the tall window, dust motes dancing in its stream. Her instincts urged her to retreat but she couldn't. And anyway, where would she go? Back to the kitchen, to cower fearfully while she waited for whoever was there to show themselves? Or out of the front door and into the street to try and find a copper on the beat? And then what would she say? That there might, only *might*, be an intruder lurking in the house? No, she had to go on. Until she was sure, until she had checked out the other two floors, she wouldn't be able to relax again.

Liv went up another couple of steps, her hand tightly gripping the rail of the banister. Her heart was beating fast, anxiety knotting her stomach as she continued the ascent. Please God, let it just be her imagination playing tricks. With everything that had happened recently – Moll Ainsworth's murder, all the bad business with Moody and Lincoln – it was hardly surprising that she was nervous.

The first thing she noticed as she rounded the landing was that the door to her room was ajar. She'd closed it, hadn't she? She was sure she had, but maybe she hadn't done it properly. She stopped dead, trying to recreate the moment in her mind, to relive her fingers on the handle, the firm click as the door actually shut. But nothing came back to her clearly.

She stood very still, aware of the hangover ache in her temples, of her racing pulse. *Just go inside and look.* But then a warning voice whispered in her head: *Don't go.* She opened her mouth to say 'Hello' again, but the word dried on her lips. What was worse, she wondered, knowing what was behind the door or not knowing?

The answer came sooner than she expected.

Her heart almost stopped as the door was abruptly flung wide open and a man flew out, barrelled into her and pushed her roughly aside. She fell with a gasp against the wall, the air knocked out of her lungs. Immediately her knees gave way and she crumpled to the floor. Before she could scream, or even think about screaming, he had hurtled downstairs and gone out through the front door, slamming it behind him.

Liv didn't get up straight away. Shock had rendered her incapable of movement. She lay sprawled on the carpet, her mind still trying to process what had just taken place. Panic coursed through her blood. She was breathing heavily, her chest heaving. The seconds ticked by. Had he gone? Yes, she had heard the door. She was safe now. He wouldn't come back.

Eventually she scrambled to her feet, rubbing her shoulder. Once she was upright again, she felt incapable of knowing what to do next, her gaze flitting blankly between her room and the stairs. How had the man got in? How long had he been there? Had he been in the house while she was sleeping? The idea of that made her go cold all over. But it was more likely that he'd entered while she was sitting on the back step, heading straight upstairs to where the valuables might be. She stuck with this theory as a less distressing one than the alternative.

Valuables. The thought finally jolted her into action. She walked quickly into her room, her heart sinking as she saw the state of it. To say that it had been ransacked was not entirely true – she'd have heard the commotion from downstairs – but it had been searched. The drawers of the dressing table had been pulled out and the wardrobe opened. Her handbag was on the bed, its contents spilled across the spread. She picked up her purse and found, unsurprisingly, that the bastard had emptied it. Not that there had been much to empty. She was glad now that she'd overspent last night, glad she'd bought too many drinks and taken Pally for something to eat.

She dropped the purse and went to check her secret stash of cash, briefly smiling when she found the five one-pound notes undiscovered in her paperback copy of *The Tiger in the Smoke*. However, she hadn't be so lucky when it came to her jewellery. He'd nicked a gold bracelet, a couple of rings, three pairs of earrings and a silver cross and chain. The cross, which had belonged to her mother, was the greatest loss. All the rest could be replaced.

Liv cursed him under her breath. What were the chances of getting the cross back? Slim, she reckoned. The lowlife would flog it as soon as he could. Her only chance would be to tour the local jewellers and pray that it turned up in one of them. Anger was gradually replacing her shock. He had no damn right to come into her home and steal from her!

She noticed that the Olympia had been laid on the bed, too. He must have meant to take it, but had fled when he'd been disturbed. She wondered if he had been as scared as her when they'd be standing either side of the door – only feet from each other, both of them probably holding their breath – and hoped that he had. It wasn't much consolation, but it was some.

Liv crossed over the landing and opened the door to Verity's room. It was hard to tell if it had been burgled or not. The place was in its usual state of disarray with clothes strewn everywhere. There was make-up scattered across the dressing table: lipsticks and eye shadows and face powder. She stared at it all for a while, trying to work out if any of the mess was down to the intruder, but couldn't come to a firm conclusion. Now that Dora's knees prevented her from climbing the stairs, it was left to them to clean their own rooms. Or not, in Verity's case.

Liv closed the door, walked along the landing and sat down on the top step of the stairs. She rubbed her shoulder again. Bad luck seemed to be following her around at the moment: first, George Hallam and now this. What was going to be next? 'Bad luck comes in threes,' her mother always used to say. It wasn't an uplifting thought.

She put her elbows on her knees, covered her face and considered all the things she could have done to the intruder if she'd been faster and braver and stronger. In her imagination she wrestled him to the ground, retrieved all her property and chased him out of the house. It was a good fantasy, but a long way from the truth.

Liv was still replaying the drama in her head when the front door suddenly opened again. She leapt to her feet but then instantly froze. Was it him? Had he come back?

31

Liv's fears were quickly assuaged by the sound of familiar voices. As Dora and Aline took off their coats, she half ran, half stumbled down the stairs to break the news to them. The words tumbled from her mouth in a rush, a garbled account that made such little sense she had to stop, take some deep breaths and try again.

'There's been a break-in. Someone's been here. I saw him. He was in my room.'

There were exclamations of shock and surprise, followed by much fussing over her from Dora. Was she all right? Had the man hurt her? After the downstairs rooms were rapidly checked – there was no sign of anything missing – she was led to the kitchen where she was made to sit down while the kettle was put on and a brew made.

Aline looked at the open back door. 'Was that how he got in?'

Liv shook her head. 'No, it was bolted. I was the one who opened it. I was sitting out there earlier. Then I came in to get another cup of tea and I heard . . . I don't know. I heard something from upstairs and thought it was Verity so I called up but . . .'

'You poor thing,' Dora said. 'It must have been a dreadful shock.'

'He took some jewellery from my room. I'm not sure if he's taken anything else.'

'You'd better check your room,' Dora said to Aline.

But Aline shook her head. 'He won't have got in there. I always keep it locked.'

This was news to Liv. She might have been insulted – it hardly showed trust in her fellow lodgers – if she hadn't had more pressing things to worry about.

'You'd better take a look, all the same,' Dora said. 'I don't understand how the blighter got in. I'm sure I locked the front door.' She frowned, trying to remember. 'Or did I leave it on the latch? Lord, I wouldn't have done that, would I?'

'You're always careful,' Aline said.

'Well, yes, usually, but I couldn't have been, could I? Not this time. Not if he just walked in like that.'

'I'll nip upstairs and then I'd better go across the road and call the police.'

Dora nodded. 'Yes, yes, the police. Of course. Thanks, Aline.'

Aline went upstairs, came back down, reported that her own room was still secured and then hurried off to ring the boys in blue.

The tea that Dora made was strong and sweet, the kind of tea that is always provided to deal with shock. She put the cup in front of Liv, sat down and patted her arm. 'I'm so sorry, love.'

'It's not your fault. You haven't got anything to be sorry about.'

'I have if I left that bleedin' door on the latch.'

'Well, so what if you did? It's not an open invitation to walk in and rob us.'

'Maybe he saw me and Aline leave and thought the place was empty.'

Liv considered this. It was possible, she supposed. He might even have knocked, perhaps while she was in the bathroom with the water running, got no response and reckoned he was on to a good thing.

'Did you get a look at him?' Dora asked. 'Could you pick him out, do you think, if you saw him again?'

Liv shook her head. 'No, it all happened too quickly. I couldn't even say what age he was, not really. He had his head down. But he wasn't very tall, not much taller than me. I think he was wearing a brown jacket but I couldn't swear to it. Oh, and gloves, yes, I think he was wearing gloves.'

'And did he say anything?'

'No, not a word. He ran straight into me, sent me flying into the wall and then sprinted down the stairs.'

Dora tutted and said, 'It's a terrible thing when you're not safe in your own home. This used to be a decent neighbourhood.'

It was about twenty minutes before the police constable arrived, at which point Liv had to go through the whole story again. The officer was middle-aged, a regular on the beat round here. He accepted the offer of a cup of tea, pulled out a chair and took out his notebook. While Liv was describing the items that had been taken, she could see Aline looking at her, like she was trying to figure out how a former cinema usherette could afford gold bracelets and fancy earrings. Worried that it might cross the constable's mind, too, she quickly said, 'The jewellery belonged to my mother. It means a lot to me. Do you think there's any chance of getting it back?'

'There's always a chance, love. Try not to worry. These things have a habit of turning up.'

After he'd noted down everything Liv could tell him, he moved on to Dora who said that although she thought she had she couldn't swear she'd locked the front door behind her. And Aline said that she hadn't been paying much attention as she was looking down the street to see if a bus was coming.

'Who else has a key to the property?'

'No one else. It's just the four of us here,' Dora said. 'Verity's at work. She won't be back until later.'

'And what about past lodgers? Could anyone have held on to a key? Or had one copied?'

Dora shook her head. 'I always take them back. And anyway, no past lodgers of mine would ever do a thing like this. I only take in good, decent girls.'

Liv sat and smiled and tried her best to look good and decent. Her smile gradually faded as an awful thought occurred to her. What if this hadn't been a random burglary? What if she'd been the intended victim all along? Whoever had followed her last Saturday night could have waited until the light had come on in her room. That way he'd have known which one it was. Lincoln could have arranged this as some kind of warning, a way of showing her that if she didn't toe the line, she wouldn't be safe even in her own home.

'Are you all right, sweetheart?' Dora asked, concern in her eyes.

'Yes, yes,' Liv said, raising a hand to her chest. 'I think it's just the shock catching up with me.'

The constable made some reassuring noises about how the man wouldn't be back, that he'd be well gone by now, but Liv was barely listening. She was too busy trying to figure out if her theory had legs. She could see how Lincoln was more than capable of arranging such a thing, but would he really go this

169

far? The answer was that she just didn't know. Maybe she was being paranoid. Or maybe she wasn't.

Liv and Aline accompanied the constable upstairs, where he had a good look round Liv's room. 'And you say he was wearing gloves?'

'I think so.'

'No chance of any fingerprints, then.'

As the constable proceeded with his examination, Aline grabbed the opportunity to give the place the once-over. Liv could see her eyes roaming across the room, taking in everything from the photograph of her mum on the window ledge, to the curtains, the multi-coloured bedspread, to the open drawers in the dressing table and then to the floor beneath them. Here Aline's eyes lingered, a frown appearing on her forehead, and Liv, following her gaze, had a sudden moment of panic. There, scattered across the carpet for anyone to see was all the paperwork Lincoln had given her about Lord Carbrooke.

Liv silently cursed. There was nothing strictly illegal about gathering information on a peer of the realm, but it wouldn't be the easiest thing to explain. She casually moved to obscure Aline's view before asking the constable, 'Is it all right if I start tidying up?'

'I don't see why not.'

Quickly she bent to gather up the papers before stuffing them into a drawer and closing it. She prayed that Aline wouldn't choose this moment to ask any awkward questions. How much had she seen? Enough, no doubt, to be curious. Liv straightened out the dressing table and placed the Olympia back on top of the wardrobe. Then, eager for everyone to be gone, she asked the constable, 'Would you like to see Verity's room?'

They all crossed the landing. When he opened the door, he said, 'Well, he's made a right old mess in here.'

Liv nodded, unwilling to enlighten either him or Aline as to its usual state. 'I don't know if anything's missing. We'll have to wait until she gets back.'

Eventually the constable was satisfied that he'd seen as much as he needed to see and the three of them traipsed back downstairs. Dora came out from the kitchen and offered the officer another cup of tea, which he refused. They were in the hall when the front door opened and Verity came in. She took one look at the constable, widened her eyes and gave an audible gasp.

'Oh God! Are you here about Cynthia?'

32

Bemused, everyone stood in the hall and stared at Verity. She'd gone white as a sheet and looked like she was going to faint. One hand had risen to her mouth and the other was gripping the banister. She swayed a little, a small, scared noise coming from the back of her throat.

'What's wrong? What's happened?' Liv asked.

Verity's gaze darted from Liv to the constable. 'Cynthia hasn't shown up at work today. She's gone missing. We can't find her. Isn't that why you're here?'

It was Aline who answered before the officer had a chance to. 'There's been a break-in. That's why he's here.'

'What?'

Liv took Verity's arm and gently led her towards the kitchen. 'Come on. Come and sit down and you can tell us about Cynthia.'

'Then you'd better check your room,' Aline said. 'See if anything's missing.'

Verity shook her head. Now she knew that the copper hadn't

172

come bearing bad news, she was starting to recover. 'I doubt that very much. I haven't got anything worth nicking.'

When they were all seated round the kitchen table, the constable took out his notebook again. Verity repeated what she'd said about Cynthia not showing up. 'It's not like her. That's why me and a couple of the other girls went over to her place at lunchtime. We thought she might be sick or something. But her flatmate said she hadn't come home last night. She wasn't worried because she thought she was with Geoff – that's her boyfriend or ... well, he *was* her boyfriend. So we went round there too but Geoff reckoned he hadn't seen her either, not since they ...' Verity paused for breath and perhaps to think about what she was saying. 'But I'm sure he's got nothing to do with it. Geoff's a nice bloke. He'd never ...'

The constable asked for Cynthia's full name and address, and Geoff's, too, carefully writing it all down. 'It's early days. I'm sure she'll turn up.'

'You don't know Cynthia. She's never missed a rehearsal. *Never.* Not in the three years I've been there.'

'And where do you work, miss?'

The constable's eyebrows shifted up when she told him. 'And when did you last see her?'

'Last night, around nine-thirty. That was her last spot. She's one of the singers, you see, not a dancer. By the time we got offstage she was gone.'

'And this Mr Dowd,' he said. 'Geoff. Did they split up recently?'

'I don't know if they split up, exactly. They had a bit of a spat, but that happens with couples, doesn't it? I'm sure it wasn't serious.'

'Do you know what it was about?'

Verity hesitated for longer than she should. Liv could see the indecision on her face and knew that she was deliberating over how honest she should be. She didn't want to land Geoff in it, but couldn't completely disregard the possibility that he had something to do with Cynthia's disappearance. 'He thought she was seeing someone else.'

'And was she?'

'She might have been,' Verity said. 'Men were always asking her out. I think there could have been someone new. That's the person you should be looking for. Whoever she went to meet last night.'

'And that couldn't have been Mr Dowd?'

'I saw Geoff last night,' Liv interjected. 'He was in the French. Then he came with us to the Gargoyle. He was with us all evening.'

The constable added this to his notebook. 'And do you know what time he arrived at the French?'

Liv frowned while she thought about it. 'I'm not sure. He was definitely there at half past ten – that's when we left – and a bit before.'

'A bit?'

'It was crowded. To be honest, he could have been there for ages. That was just the first time I noticed him.'

The constable asked a few more questions and then closed his notebook. 'I'll put a report in at the station, but I'm sure she'll turn up. They usually do. Maybe she had a drink too many and stayed over with a friend. I don't think we have to worry too much at this point.'

Aline, of course, chose this moment to darken the mood. 'There's been one murder already. Who's to say he hasn't struck again?'

'That's got nothing to do with this girl,' Dora said sharply.

'How do you know? Once they get a taste for it, there's no saying where it will end.'

Liv, seeing Verity's expression – the fear had crept into her eyes again – said, 'Let's go up and check your room.'

The two girls walked silently upstairs, not talking until they were out of earshot of the kitchen. Verity looked pale and scared. 'You don't think Aline could be right, do you?'

'No. You know what she's like. It's probably like the constable said: Cynthia had a skinful and just stayed over somewhere.'

But Verity wasn't convinced. 'She'd have phoned the Windmill if she wasn't coming in. Or sent a note or something. She wouldn't just not turn up.'

'Well, maybe she did and the message didn't get through.'

Verity brightened a little at this suggestion. They went into her room where she sighed at the mess and said, 'I don't suppose Dora was best pleased when she saw this.'

'Dora hasn't seen it. Only Aline, and she thinks the burglar did it.'

Verity managed a weak smile. She went over to her jewellery box and opened the lid. Inside was a tiny ballerina who instantly started revolving to the tinkling sound of music. After rooting through the contents of the box for a moment, Verity shook her head. 'No, he's not taken anything from here.'

'That's good. We'll let the constable know and then I'll give you a hand to tidy up.'

Verity closed the box, leaned against the dressing table, folded her arms across her chest and unfolded them again. 'I shouldn't have told him about Cynthia and Geoff rowing, should I?'

'If you hadn't, someone else would.'

'I suppose. I still feel awful about it, though. I mean, Geoff wouldn't do anything bad. He can be a touch moody but ... no, he's not the type. How did he seem last night?'

Liv kept her voice low. 'Drunk, upset, depressed.'

'Angry?'

'A bit. But who isn't going to be if they think they've been cheated on?' Liv pulled back from sharing the full extent of Geoff's black mood – and his threats. Verity was worried enough as it was. Until it was confirmed that Cynthia was actually missing it was better to stay positive. 'Anyway, he was with me and Pally at the French so he couldn't have been with her.'

'Only from half past ten.'

'That's just the time I first saw him. What did he say when you went round?'

Verity gave a tiny shrug. 'He didn't seem to care. He said it was none of his business any more. He said she was probably with her fancy man.'

'Well, he wouldn't have said that if he'd done anything bad. Wouldn't he have acted worried or concerned?'

'I don't know.'

Liv didn't know, either. The two girls stared at each other, both hoping for the best but thinking the worst.

33

DI Bentley wouldn't normally have worried. It wasn't even twenty-four hours since Cynthia Crosby had gone missing and there was nothing, really, to suggest foul play. If the police were called out every time a girl didn't turn up for work, they wouldn't have time to do anything else. But something about this case concerned him. Perhaps because of the Moll Ainsworth murder. Was it possible that Cynthia was another victim? He was disinclined to believe it, but couldn't rule it out.

He had asked the officers on the beat to be alert and to check out the alleys and the derelict buildings. DC Hemmings had been to the Windmill where it had been confirmed that she had left the building at about nine-thirty last night and that she still hadn't been in touch. Cynthia had been described as popular, reliable and a hard worker. It was agreed by everyone that it was out of character for her to go AWOL like this.

In his opinion, however, girls were rarely predictable. It wasn't completely out of the question that she'd decided, on a whim, to just take off and get away for a while. Especially after a row with the other half. The flatmate hadn't been helpful. Jennifer Bridges had only moved in a couple of weeks ago and couldn't say for sure whether any of Cynthia's clothes were missing. She also couldn't enlighten them as to Cynthia's frame of mind; they worked different hours and didn't see much of each other.

Bentley stared at the glossy photograph Hemmings had brought back, one of the publicity stills used to advertise the show. Cynthia was a good-looking redhead with a bright, shiny smile, curves in all the right places and legs up to her elbows. She was twenty-one. He could see why a boyfriend might feel insecure.

'So what do we know about this Geoff Dowd?'

'Nothing much, guv,' Hemmings said. 'He hasn't got a record. He's an artist, apparently, at least that's what he calls himself. Seems to mainly make his living from pulling pints in the French.'

'I suppose we'd better go and have a word with him.'

The two men walked to Brewer Street, weaving through the early-evening crowd. The smell of spices, tobacco and dope floated in the air. Bentley was aware of eyes sliding away from his, of guilt and evasion. Villains crossed the street when they saw him coming. Racketeers pulled their hats down over their faces, and dips dodged down alleyways. Only the toms met his gaze, unbothered by his presence, knowing that he wasn't here for them. He noticed a familiar figure huddled in a doorway, watching everyone and everything.

'There's our friend, Slug.'

'That bloke gives me the creeps,' Hemmings said. 'What's his real name, anyway?'

Bentley had to think about it. 'Suggs,' he said, when he eventually brought it to mind. 'Leslie Suggs. And he may be a creep but he's a useful one.'

'I wouldn't trust him.'

'You don't have to trust him. You just have to understand his motivation.'

Hemmings threw him a sidelong glance. 'Huh?'

'Revenge, money, mischief. Once you've worked out where he's coming from, you can figure out where to go with the information.'

'If you say so, guv.'

Bentley wondered if Slug was ever bothered by his nickname. If he was, he never showed it. Perhaps, over the years, he had grown as used to the moniker as his own lowly position in life. It was just another cross to bear, another burden among many. He remembered Slug scurrying out of the French yesterday while they were making enquiries about Moll Ainsworth. Because he knew something? Or because it had just become a habit to never be seen talking to the law? It could be worth following up, he thought, when he got the time.

It was getting on for six when they came to an off-licence and found a door to the right where Bentley checked the name tags on the bells and pressed the one that said DOWD. It was a couple of minutes before a man came down and opened up. He was tall with an angular face and longish wheat-coloured hair that was streaked with paint. The grey overalls he was wearing were splattered too, as though a rainbow of colour had exploded on his chest.

'Yeah?'

'Mr Dowd?' Bentley asked. 'Mr Geoffrey Dowd?'

'That's me. You the law?'

Bentley held up his warrant card and made the introductions. 'Do you mind if we come in?'

'Would it matter if I did?'

'It's about Cynthia Crosby,' Bentley said.

'I don't know where she is, if that's what you're here for. Those girls have already been round. I haven't seen her all week.'

'If we could just come in? We won't keep you long.'

Dowd hesitated but then stood aside to let them enter. 'Second floor.'

The three men trudged up the stairs in silence. The first thing that struck Bentley as he walked into the living room was the overwhelming smell of paint. The second thing was that it wasn't really a living room at all. There was hardly any furniture – just a battered old sofa – and most of the space was taken up with an easel and a long trestle table covered in tubes and bottles, jam jars and brushes. Canvases in various stages of completion leaned against every wall.

Dowd gestured towards the sofa. 'I suppose you'd better sit down.'

Bentley saw Hemmings give the sofa a dubious look before they took up the invitation. Dowd perched on a wooden stool and placed his palms on his thighs.

'So? What is it you want?'

Before Bentley could answer, a male voice came from a room off the back, probably the kitchen. 'Who was that, Geoff?' A moment later, Alan Palliser showed up in the doorway with a bottle of beer in his hand. 'Oh,' he said, seeing the two cops sitting there. 'Mr Bentley. How nice to see you – again.'

Bentley nodded, surprised to find him here. 'Mr Palliser. I didn't realise you too knew each other.'

'You make it sound like a crime.' He glanced at Dowd. 'You want me to clear off for a while?'

Dowd shook his head. 'No, stay, Pally. It's fine. They're here about Cynthia.'

'Oh, *her*.' Palliser swigged some beer and stared at Bentley. 'I don't see what all the fuss is about. Haven't you got anything better to do? Cynthia doesn't show up for work and suddenly you're all running around like blue-arsed flies.'

Bentley thought about Rosa and how slow they'd been to follow up on her disappearance. 'Well, perhaps we've learnt from past mistakes.'

Palliser curled his lip but said nothing.

Bentley turned his attention back to Dowd. 'Cynthia Crosby appears to have gone missing, Mr Dowd. People are worried about her.' Bentley was watching the man carefully as he spoke. 'Do you have any idea where she could be?'

'It's her new fancy man you should be asking, not me. Like I said, I haven't seen her for a week.'

'And do you have any idea of this man's name?'

Dowd barked out a laugh. 'Well, she's hardly likely to tell me, is she? Look, the two of us aren't together any more. We had a row, we broke up, and that's that. End of story. What she does now is her business.'

'You're not the slightest bit concerned?'

'Concerned about what? She'll be with this new bloke of hers. I don't know why everyone's making such a fuss.'

Bentley wasn't taking his couldn't-care-less-attitude about the break-up at face value. Beneath the surface there was something intense about Dowd, something that hinted at much stronger emotions. 'I understand you were at the French last night. Could you tell me what time you got there?'

Dowd pulled a face. 'I'm not sure. I was working here until about ten, I think. Then I went to the French. It's only a short walk from here so ... I suppose I got there about five past.'

Bentley was busy making the calculations. Even if Dowd was lying about the time he'd left the flat, it still didn't leave much of a window for him to pick up Cynthia Crosby from the Windmill at nine-thirty, take her somewhere, murder her,

181

hide the body and turn up at the pub. But it wasn't impossible. 'Can anyone verify that? What time you arrived at the French, I mean.'

'I've no idea.' Dowd looked at Palliser. 'Do you remember?'

'I think it was earlier. More like twenty to ten.'

But Bentley wasn't putting much weight on Palliser's evidence. He probably knew when Cynthia finished work and had adjusted the time of arrival accordingly. 'You work there, don't you, Mr Dowd?'

'I do some lunchtime shifts, that's all.'

'Still, it means you'll be a familiar face. I'm sure there are others who'll remember when you got there.'

Dowd shrugged. 'Maybe.'

'Do you have a car?'

Palliser put his oar in again. 'Are you accusing Geoff of something? Only if you are, I think a solicitor is in order.'

'No one's accusing him of anything.'

'It doesn't sound like that from where I'm standing.'

'It's all right, Pally,' Dowd said. 'I haven't got anything to hide. And in answer to your question, inspector, no, I don't have a car. I can barely afford to pay the rent, never mind run a motor. As you can imagine, there's not a whole lot of money in what I do.'

Bentley glanced at the canvases stacked up against the walls. They were probably what would be termed 'modern art', all squares and triangles and nothing remotely resembling what he thought of as real. His idea of art was a portrait or a pleasant landscape, not this mad jumble of shape and colour that he found both confusing and faintly alarming.

Hemmings joined in with a question of his own. 'Do you have any idea where Cynthia might have gone?'

'Not a clue,' Dowd said. 'I dare say she'll turn up before long.'

'When did you find out about the new boyfriend?' Bentley asked.

Dowd's expression darkened. 'A while ago. There were rumours doing the rounds. Whispers. You can't move in Soho without some gossip or another sharing their bad news with you. When I confronted her, she denied it, but I knew she was lying. That's why I finished it. What's the point when there isn't any trust?'

Bentley nodded. Although Dowd's tone was measured, there was still a hint of anger in it. 'And how long were you together?'

'About a year, give or take.'

'No man likes being cheated on,' Hemmings said provocatively.

It was Palliser who responded, glaring at the detective constable. 'Well, I dare say you've had plenty of experience.'

Bentley felt Hemmings stiffen and decided to bring the exchange to a close before it descended into a bunfight. 'One last thing. It's just routine, but would you mind if we had a quick look around?'

'Help yourself,' Dowd said.

Palliser moved away from the door and went to stand by the window. 'Don't forget to check under the bed.'

The search only took a couple of minutes. Bentley hadn't believed that Cynthia would be here – dead or alive – but he'd had to cover all the bases. When they returned to the living room, Dowd was on his feet, standing beside Palliser. The two of them were talking in low voices, their heads bent together, their look conspiratorial, but stopped abruptly when he and Hemmings came back in.

'Thank you for your help. Let us know if you hear from her, Mr Dowd.'

'I'll be the last person she'll get in touch with.'

'We'll show ourselves out.'

Back on the street, Hemmings, still seething from the slight he'd received, snarled and said, 'What's with that bloody Palliser?'

'He doesn't much care for the law.'

'He made that abundantly clear. And I reckon he's lying through his teeth about the time Dowd got to the French.'

'Yes,' Bentley agreed. 'What did you think of Dowd?'

'Not much. And I reckon he was a damn sight more cut up over Cynthia's cheating than he's letting on.'

'Male pride, perhaps.'

Hemmings gave a grunt. 'Calls himself an artist. Did you see those pictures? A five-year-old kid could have painted them. I'm not surprised she looked elsewhere. He's hardly got prospects, has he?'

'The mystery man,' Bentley said. 'I wonder if he even exists.'

'You reckon Dowd's making it up?'

'Well, we've only got his word for it. And it's a useful way to deflect attention from himself and on to another suspect. I could be wrong but he strikes me as the jealous sort, the sort who gets the hump if his girlfriend even looks at anyone else. He probably didn't take too kindly to her being up on stage and ogled every night.'

'I thought these artists were free and easy types.'

'When it suits them. We should have a word with Cynthia's girlfriends, check if anyone has actually seen her with this new bloke. Let's start with the girl who reported her as missing.'

'Verity Lang.'

'That's the one. Whitcomb Street, isn't it?'

As they cut down towards Shaftesbury Avenue, Bentley's brain was busily ticking over. He was thinking about Alan Palliser and trying to put his finger on what was bothering him so much. His copper's nose was twitching. A bizarre notion jumped into his head. Was it possible that he and Dowd were conspiring, playing him, trying to stitch him up in some way over this Cynthia business? Revenge, perhaps, for his failure to catch Rosa Palliser's killer. No sooner had the thought taken shape than he realised how preposterous it was. But if not that, then what? Something stank about this business, he was sure of it.

'Everything all right, guv?' Hemmings asked.

Bentley didn't express his misgivings; paranoia wasn't an attractive trait in a boss. But he couldn't let go of the suspicion he had. Like a tick on a cat, it burrowed into him as they headed towards Whitcomb Street.

34

Ralph McCall was still fuming from having his wallet nicked last night. Some bloody dip had lifted it, probably in the French, and as the banks weren't open over the weekend, he'd had to borrow a couple of quid off Pauline just to see him through. He didn't like being beholden to her, but there hadn't been any choice. Now he would have to meet up with her again on Monday to pay the money back, take her for a drink and listen to the latest episode of shop gossip whilst trying not to die of boredom. He'd gone to West End Central and reported the theft, but knew he'd never see the cash or the wallet again.

'What's eating you?' Henry asked as he took his jacket off the back of the chair and prepared to leave. 'You've had a face like thunder all day.'

Ralph wasn't about to share his sorrows. Leaving his wallet in his back pocket had been a rooky mistake, especially in Soho, and he didn't intend to give Henry the pleasure of knowing how stupid he'd been. He could imagine the old man's eyebrows shifting up while his already low opinion slipped down another few notches.

'Nothing. A heavy night last night, that's all.'

Henry gave him a long look, a disbelieving look, but didn't say anything more.

Ralph lit a cigarette and watched him leave. It would be a good few hours before he could go home himself; he was working the late shift and praying that something more interesting than the usual Saturday night bust-ups would happen. Last week Moll Ainsworth had been murdered but the odds of another killing were slight.

He thought about Liv Anderson. It was her fault, in a way, that he'd been robbed. If she hadn't been in the French, if he hadn't been so preoccupied by her, then he might have caught the thieving toe-rag trying to swipe his wallet. You could say that she owed him. He still hadn't decided what to do about what he'd found out – all that juicy stuff about her father – but he couldn't sit on it for ever. Henry would be getting the story together and if Ralph didn't move soon, he would lose the opportunity of having any part in it.

He would track her down next week, he decided. If the French was her regular drinking hole, she wouldn't be too hard to find. But what then? There was every chance she'd refuse to talk to him. And let's face it, Henry wasn't going to just roll over and let him share the credit. So . . . he'd have to play dirty. There was nothing else for it.

Ralph was still musing on what exactly this might mean when Arthur Neames came out of his office and said he'd had a tip-off. 'One of the Windmill girls, Cynthia Crosby, didn't show up for work today. The police have been at the theatre so they must be taking it seriously. Get over there and see what you can find out. Oh, and try and pick up a picture while you're at it.'

Ralph didn't need asking twice. He hot-footed it over to the Windmill with all the enthusiasm of any young man being given permission to enter the premises of a place that contained naked women.

35

There was a misunderstanding when Bentley and Hemmings first arrived at the house in Whitcomb Street. The landlady, Mrs Marks, thought they were there about a break-in, and a short confusing conversation followed where they were talking at cross-purposes. Eventually the matter was cleared up, Verity Lang was summoned from upstairs and they were led into the living room to wait for her. Tea was offered and declined.

Soon there was the sound of footsteps on the stairs and two girls came into the room, both pretty, one blonde and one dark.

'This is Verity,' Mrs Marks said. 'Verity, this is Detective Inspector Bentley and Detective Constable Hemmings. They're here about Cynthia.'

'Hello,' Verity said. She was pale and her eyes had a frightened look. 'Has something happened? Have you found her?'

Bentley shook his head. 'No, I'm afraid not. But we would like to ask you some questions, if that's all right?'

'Yes, of course. Although I'm not sure how much I can help. I told the other policeman everything I know.'

'Perhaps I should leave you to it,' the dark-haired girl said. She glanced at Bentley. 'I barely knew Cynthia. I only met her a few times.'

'No, no,' Verity said, grabbing hold of her arm. 'You've got to stay. You don't mind if she stays, do you?'

Bentley smiled. 'You're more than welcome, Miss . . . ?'

'Anderson,' she said. 'Liv Anderson.'

'Why don't we all sit down?'

'I think I'd better stay, too,' Mrs Marks said. 'I like to watch out for my girls.'

Bentley suspected it was as much about nosiness as protection, but he didn't raise any objections. Mrs Marks and the girls sat in a line on the sofa, while he and Hemmings took the easy chairs. His conspiracy theory had been reignited as he'd come face to face with Liv Anderson again, the girl who had been in the French yesterday with Palliser. He tried not to stare at her. Soho was a small place, but even so this seemed a coincidence too far. She looked ill at ease and once more he had that feeling there was something he wasn't quite grasping.

Bentley kept his eyes on Verity. 'So you saw Cynthia last night at work. How did she seem?'

'Just normal. Just the same as always.'

'Not worried about anything?'

'No, not at all. I don't think so.'

'She wasn't upset about the break-up with her boyfriend?'

Verity hesitated. 'A little, I suppose. But I don't think she thought it was for ever. They were always breaking up and getting back together. They were that kind of couple.'

'They had a stormy kind of relationship?'

Verity glanced down at the carpet, studied it for a moment

190

and then looked up again. She chewed on her lower lip as if she was afraid of saying the wrong thing. 'I don't know if I'd call it stormy, exactly. Just a bit up and down.'

'Did she say she was going out after work, meeting anyone?'

'No.'

Bentley could see how anxious the girl was. 'I'm sorry about all the questions. We're just trying to get an idea of what might have happened. Tell me about Cynthia. What's she like?'

'She's lovely, funny, kind. And she's got a fabulous voice. She could be on Broadway. That's what we're always telling her.'

'And popular, I suppose?'

'Oh yes, all the girls like her.'

'And the men?'

Verity hesitated again. 'What do you mean?'

'A girl like that – pretty, talented. She must have lots of admirers.'

There was another short silence. Verity's narrow shoulders rose and fell. 'Yes, I suppose so.'

'Anyone in particular?'

'I don't think so. I don't know. Sometimes you get men hanging around the stage door.'

'And what does Mr Dowd think about these admirers?'

The answer that came back was sharp and defensive. 'You'd have to ask *him* that.'

'Were you in the French last night, Miss Lang?'

'No, I was tired. I came straight home after the show.'

As if the landlady felt that Verity might be in need of an alibi, she piped up: 'She did, inspector. I can vouch for that. I was just on my way to bed when she came in. About ten to eleven it was.'

'Thank you, Mrs Marks.' Bentley looked at Verity again. 'I was only asking in case you'd seen Geoff Dowd in there.'

Verity shook her head. 'But you did, didn't you, Liv? You were there with Pally.'

191

Liv smiled thinly. She'd been hoping not to be drawn into all this – she had enough problems at the moment – but now she had no choice but to respond to what Verity had said. 'Yes, Geoff was there. There were a group of us. We all went on to the Gargoyle afterwards. About ten-thirty, that would have been.'

'A group?' Bentley said. 'Could you tell me who else was with you?'

'Sorry, I don't know their names. I'm sure they told me but . . . they were friends of Geoff's.'

'And do you know what time Mr Dowd arrived at the pub?'

Liv, aware that timing could be all important when it came to building a case against him, frowned while she pretended to think about it. What she was really thinking about was whether he might be guilty or not. She felt no particular loyalty towards Geoff, but he was a friend of Pally's so she did feel obliged to give him the benefit of the doubt for now. 'No, I've no idea. It was really packed. But he was there for a while before we left.'

'A while?'

'I couldn't say for sure. Half an hour? Maybe longer.'

'And how did he seem?'

'Seem?' Liv echoed, even though she knew exactly what he meant.

'What kind of mood was he in?'

'I've no idea,' Liv lied. 'I barely talked to him all evening.' If she was to tell the truth – that Geoff had been in the black mood from hell and calling Cynthia all the names under the sun – she wouldn't be doing him any favours. 'It was hard to chat with the music and everything. I was dancing for most of the evening. To be honest, I don't even know him that well.'

'But he's a good friend of Mr Palliser's.'

Liv wasn't quite sure what he was implying by the comment – that because Pally knew him well, she must too? Or that

Pally might also be involved in Cynthia's disappearance? – but she kept her cool and kept her voice neutral. 'Pally's got lots of friends.'

'Geoff wouldn't have done anything bad,' Verity suddenly blurted out. 'He loves Cynthia. He'd never . . . he wouldn't hurt her. I know what you're thinking, but he wouldn't.'

Hemmings leaned forward. 'We're not thinking anything at the moment, miss.'

'But it sounds like you are.'

'We're only trying to build up a picture. Do you know if Cynthia was seeing someone else?'

'She didn't say she was.'

'Mr Dowd thinks so. He says she denied it, but he didn't believe her.'

'Then that's who you should be looking for, isn't it?' Verity said.

'It's difficult without a name – or a description of some sort.'

Although it was Verity and the constable who were talking, Liv was aware of Bentley's eyes on her. Was he doing it deliberately, trying to make her feel uncomfortable? If so, he was doing a good job. She kept her gaze on Hemmings but could still see the inspector out of the corner of her eye. She had the feeling he knew something – about what she and Pally got up to, perhaps, or what Lincoln had persuaded her to do – and that he was playing some kind of game with her. She couldn't work out whether he had simply failed to recognise her from the French yesterday, or had deliberately not mentioned it.

Eventually, Bentley addressed her again. 'Miss Anderson. I understand it was only your property that was stolen during the break-in today.'

Liv was taken by surprise by the sudden change of subject. 'Er, yes, that's right. It was lucky, I suppose, that I was here. I

193

disturbed him before he could steal anything else. I heard a noise upstairs and . . . well, you've probably read the report.'

'It's been quite a day for you.'

And there it was again, Liv thought. Like he was hinting at something but she couldn't quite grasp what. 'I've had better.'

Bentley nodded. 'I'm sure you have.'

Liv tried to read his face. His expression seemed benign, but she sensed it was a mask. Then she started worrying about Lincoln, too, and all his suspicions; his imagination would be running riot if he heard that the police had been here twice today. But then again, she wouldn't be surprised if he'd set up the break-in in the first place. Surely, though, he wouldn't want to attract the attention of the law, not with all this Garvie business going on. Which kind of suggested that it hadn't been him. The more she thought about it, the more confused she became.

'Are you all right, Miss Anderson?' Bentley asked.

Liv quickly cleared her forehead of the frown that had settled there. 'Yes, yes, I'm fine.'

'Only you look as though—'

Dora, thankfully, interrupted at this point. 'I think the girls have had enough, inspector,' she said firmly. 'They've told you everything they know so there's no point going on at them. They're upset enough already. I suggest we call it a night now.' As if to give strength to this suggestion, she rose to her feet. 'I'll show you out.'

Although Bentley didn't look overly pleased by this summary dismissal, he didn't protest about it, either. Slowly he stood up. 'We'll leave you in peace, then. Thank you for your help.'

Liv heard a movement from outside the living-room door and knew that Aline had been earwigging. She looked at the inspector. 'You'll let us know if you hear anything about Cynthia?'

'Of course.'

As the two police officers left the room, she sat back and gave a sigh of relief.

After a brief to and fro with Hemmings, during which it was agreed that the girls had not, perhaps, been entirely honest, Bentley lapsed into silence. Although the interview hadn't shed any new light on the disappearance of Cynthia Crosby, it had provoked an interesting train of thought. He was doing a kind of chemistry in his head, randomly adding names – Dowd, Palliser, Cynthia, Liv, Verity, Rosa – in an attempt to balance out a complicated formula that was as yet beyond his comprehension.

It was only when he added Moll Ainsworth to the mix that something suddenly fell into place – not the answer to what had happened to Cynthia but to what had been niggling him at Bridle Lane. Rosa Palliser had lived there, too, renting out a room in another shabby house. He couldn't see the connection between the two murders, eleven years apart – there probably wasn't one – but he was pleased that he'd remembered. With a small grunt of satisfaction, he filed the information away in that part of his brain he reserved for miscellaneous matters of interest.

36

As Liv walked towards Bedford Square on Monday morning, she thought back over the weekend. There was still no news of Cynthia, which could be a good or a bad thing, depending on how you looked at it. She had considered going round to see Pally yesterday so she could tell him about DI Bentley's visit, but had decided to err on the side of caution. What if the flat was being watched by the police? There wouldn't be anything strange about her going there, but she didn't want the law to think that they were in any way conspiring.

Having mulled it over, Liv was now of the opinion that Geoff couldn't be guilty of anything dreadful. After all, what sort of murderer would behave the way he had on Friday night? He would be putting himself right in the frame. Surely, he would pretend he didn't care about the break-up, that he was moving on, rather than ranting like a madman? Unless it had been some sort of clever double bluff. That he couldn't possibly have killed her, because if he had he wouldn't have been shouting the odds. But the more she thought about that scenario, the more it hurt her head. It was a dangerous choice for Geoff to have made if he didn't want to end up with a noose around his neck.

Yesterday, instead of going to see Pally, she had walked to Belgravia where she had found Lord Carbrooke's house, sat down on a bench and stared at it for a while. There was no good reason for her to have committed the building to memory – Garvie was hardly likely to interrogate her on the colour of the front door – but she had felt the need. And anyway, there was no harm in preparing herself for the part she was about to play.

At precisely two minutes to nine, Liv pushed open the door to Garvie & Carr, and went inside. Muriel was already at her desk, sorting through some files. She looked up at Liv, gave a thin smile and said, 'Ah, so you're here.'

'I'm not late, am I?' Liv said, glancing at the clock on the wall.

Muriel slid a couple of sheets of paper, separated by a carbon, across the desk. She held up a pen. 'I've got your employment contract ready, if you'd just like to sign here.'

Liv took the pen, leaned down, gave herself a stern instruction to use the surname Kent and wrote her signature with a flourish.

Muriel separated the sheets, gave the copy to Liv and added the other to a pile of papers on her right. 'Mr Garvie has a meeting so he won't be in until after lunch.' Then she added, almost gleefully, 'There's plenty of filing to be done, though.'

'I don't mind filing,' Liv said, thinking that it would give her the opportunity to catch up on what Garvie was currently involved with. The quicker she found out whatever Lincoln wanted to know, the sooner she'd be out of here.

Muriel stood up. 'I'll show you where everything is.'

It was a short tour down the hallway and to the left, taking in the store cupboard, toilet and kitchen. At the latter Muriel pointed out a white porcelain teacup with a gold rim. 'That's

Mr Garvie's cup. He likes his tea at eleven, on the dot. Milk and two sugars.'

'Milk and two sugars,' Liv repeated dutifully.

'And don't forget to wash up after. Not that you need to worry about that today.'

Liv tried to make small talk, hoping to build a connection, but Muriel defeated her best efforts. Her answers were short, often monosyllabic, as if she had no interest in cultivating a friendship. Still, Liv wasn't downhearted. She would find a way, eventually, to break down the barrier.

Muriel moved briskly, not wasting any time. Before she knew it, Liv was back in the front office with a heap of papers ready to be filed. She was shown what went where and left to get on with it. The papers consisted mainly of contracts for new commercial rentals in and around the West End – pubs, clubs and shops. As she slipped them into their correct positions, she tried to remember as many names and locations as she could. Later, when she was sure Muriel wasn't looking, she would write them all down.

It was about ten o'clock when Mr Carr arrived at the office. He came over and introduced himself, shook her hand and said they were all glad to have her on board. Try telling Muriel that, she privately thought, but smiled back and said that she was pleased to be joining them. He was a smallish man and younger than Garvie by about ten years. The grey suit he wore was smart but not flashy. He was one of those people about whom there was nothing especially memorable – brown hair, brown eyes, an ordinary face – but he seemed pleasant enough and, if her first impressions were right, in possession of none of Garvie's more lecherous qualities.

Mr Carr told Muriel that he had some letters to dictate and the two of them disappeared along the hallway together. As soon as they'd gone, Liv took the opportunity to summarise everything she'd learnt this morning, jotting it all down in a notebook that she'd brought with her. Then she returned to the personnel section of one of the cabinets, where she'd filed her own contract earlier, and took down the names of Garvie's last two secretaries – Katherine Boult and Anne Harvey – along with their addresses. Now that they weren't working here any more, they might be persuaded to talk. That's if there was anything to talk about.

Lunch was taken from twelve-thirty to one-thirty, and at precisely half past twelve Liv stood up and put on her jacket. She had to meet Henry Squires at Amelia's and didn't want to be too late. As she crossed the room, she saw Muriel take a brown paper bag from a drawer and put it on her desk. A sandwich was pulled out, along with an apple.

'You're going out, then?'

'Yes, I've got some errands to run.' Then, on the spur of the moment, Liv asked, 'Look, would you like to go out for lunch tomorrow? My treat. Just as a way of saying thank you for helping me to settle in.'

Muriel hesitated, as if there might be a catch to the invitation, but the chance of a free lunch was too good to pass over. 'All right. Why not? I haven't got anything else on.'

Liv had heard more enthusiastic responses, but she smiled and nodded. 'Good. Tomorrow, then.'

Outside she walked quickly, hoping that Henry had got the note – and the information she wanted. Did she really want it? Yes, but it scared her too. She was afraid of what she might find out and how it would make her feel. The events of the weekend – the break-in, the disappearance of Cynthia – only added to her general sense of uneasiness.

Her eyes scanned the street as she headed for the café. It was not impossible that Lincoln would have a tail on her in the middle of the day, but there was nothing much she could do about it even if he had. She didn't have time to work out if she was being followed or to try and shake them off if she was. Lincoln had told her not to see Henry again and now here she was doing exactly the opposite. She could only cross her fingers and pray she was alone.

Amelia's was busy, full of local office workers, and it took her a while to find Henry. He had taken a table in an alcove near the back, away from the window and from prying eyes. She had no idea if this was deliberate – the natural caution of a newspaper reporter – or if it had been the only free table available. As she approached, he smiled and half stood up.

'Hello, Liv.'

'Sorry, I'm a bit late.'

'I've not been here for long,' he said politely, although she could see that his cup of tea was almost finished.

Henry was the old-fashioned type, she thought, the kind of man who would always arrive early if he had a meeting with a woman. She pulled out a chair and sat down. 'You got the note, then? Thanks for coming. You didn't mind us meeting here, did you? Only I'm working in Bedford Square at the moment and it seemed a good halfway point. I couldn't get away any earlier. It's my first day, you see, so . . . ' Aware that she was on the verge of rambling, she pulled herself up and said softly, 'How are you?'

'I'm very well, thank you. Let me get you a drink. What would you like?'

She asked for a coffee and Henry caught the eye of a waitress and put the order in. Then he turned to her and said: 'A new job, eh? I hope it's to your liking.'

'Yes, it's fine.' Her gaze fell on a brown envelope lying on the table. She knew what must be inside and stared at it greedily. 'You managed to find something, then?'

Henry's fingers hovered for a moment on top of the envelope. 'Are you sure about this?'

'Absolutely.'

'It worries me, you see. What you're going to read in here isn't pleasant and it isn't the whole truth, either. These are newspaper reports, remember.'

'I understand that.'

'In situations like these, exaggeration tends to be the order of the day. And what isn't known for sure tends to get made up. Don't take it all at face value.'

'The facts are still the facts, though, aren't they?'

Henry lifted his heavy shoulders in a half shrug. 'But are you prepared for them? It's going to be upsetting, Liv, no matter which way you look at it.'

'I'd rather know than not. Even some information is better than none.'

The waitress arrived with the coffee and put it down on the table along with the bill.

Henry sighed. 'It's your mother I always felt sorry for. She never really got any answers. It must have been hard on her.'

'I think she was always afraid that someone would find out who she really was. I never understood when I was growing up why she kept other people at such a distance, but I suppose she didn't want to have to lie to them. It must have been awful living with that fear all the time.' Liv took a sip of coffee and put the cup back down. She felt the familiar anger bubble up in her again. 'He must have known what it would do to her, to both of us.'

'I don't think he was in his right mind. At a guess, I'd say he was in a state of despair.'

'Despair,' Liv echoed. 'Well, Mum knew all about that.'

'Yes, she must have done.'

'And what about Irene Lister? If anyone knows the truth, it's her. Did you manage to find out anything? About what happened to her after ... Did she get married again?'

'Yes, to a man called Richard Forster.' Henry slid the envelope towards her. 'It's all in here. He was something in the City, I believe.'

'So she could still be living in London.'

'Perhaps, or they may have gone abroad. I'm sure I heard a whisper back in the day. The south of France, Monaco, somewhere like that.'

He hadn't mentioned this on the first occasion they'd met, and Liv wondered if it was true or not. 'Well, it shouldn't be too hard to find out.'

Henry looked concerned. 'You don't want to go down that road, Liv. And she isn't going to talk to you even if you do track her down. She's never talked to anyone about what happened.'

'But I'm not just anyone, am I? I'm Paul Teller's daughter.'

'Which makes you the very last person she'll want to see.'

Liv, seeing that Henry was looking increasingly perturbed, quickly backtracked and said: 'Yes, yes of course. You're right. I'm sorry. I don't know what I was thinking of. It's a stupid idea.'

Henry gazed back at her through I-wasn't-born-yesterday eyes. 'I mean it, Liv. Stay away from her. These sort of people – rich, powerful, friends in high places – aren't to be underestimated. They eat the likes of you and me for breakfast.'

'I know. I'll stay away. I promise.'

'Good,' he said, rising to his feet. 'Look, I have to go now, but you have a read through the cuttings and then get back to me when you're ready. I'm sure you'll have some questions. And even if you don't, you'll stay in touch, won't you?'

'I will. And thank you for everything. I really do appreciate it.' Liv reached for the saucer with the bill lying on it. 'Let me get this.'

But Henry was too fast for her. 'No, I'll get it. I'll pay on my way out. You take care, yes?'

'I will,' she said. 'You too.'

Once Henry had left, Liv sat for a while staring at the envelope. Then she picked up the menu and looked through it. Soup was the cheapest item on offer. When the waitress came to clear the cups, she ordered a bowl of minestrone with bread and butter. While she was waiting for her lunch, Liv went back to staring at the envelope. Strange to think of it all being in there, the tragedy of her own family played out across the pages of the newspapers. She longed to read it, feared reading it.

Behind Liv was a wall. She glanced at the tables to her left and right. No one was paying her any attention. They were all too busy eating, drinking, chatting. No one would notice what she was reading. With tentative fingers she ripped open the envelope and slid out the cuttings.

37

The reading was an agony. Although Liv had known what had happened all those years ago, actually seeing it in black and white brought a whole new level of horror. The sheer senseless brutality of it all made her stomach turn over. This was her father, her own flesh and blood, wiping out a rival's life in a split second of madness.

She could follow the chain of events – Paul Teller arriving at Eden at around nine-thirty on a Friday night, the row with Nicky Lister, the pulling out of the gun, the firing of it, the screams from the crowd – but still couldn't get inside her father's head. A crime of passion? Yes, there was little doubt about that. But what had happened to make him snap in such a dramatic and destructive fashion?

A witness standing nearby, a woman, claimed to have heard Lister laugh and say: 'Come on, old man. Don't cause a scene. It isn't worth it.' Was it that, the hint of mockery, perhaps, that had pushed him over the edge? Except, of course, he had gone there with the gun in his possession. Apparently, it had been a Colt revolver from the Great War, a gun that had belonged to his father.

He hadn't made any attempt to flee. He had fired the gun and then dropped it on the ground. Some men had grabbed him and the police had been called. Others had tried to help Lister, but it was too late: he had died instantly, the bullet passing straight through his heart. Her father had said nothing, not then and not afterwards. Well, nothing as regards an explanation. It was the first time she had seen pictures of the Listers. They had been one of those golden couples, oozing glamour and sophistication. Nicky had been good looking in a suave sort of way, but Irene had possessed a rare kind of beauty – a cool, elegant blonde with the body of a seductress and the face of an angel. Liv could see how men would fall in love with her. That figure, that hair, those eyes, that mouth. She was about as close to perfection as a woman could be.

Lunch arrived, and she held the cuttings to her chest until the waitress had left. Once the coast was clear she laid them back on the table again. She continued to read while she ate, distractedly spooning the soup into her mouth. Henry had included several reports on the actual killing, but the information in all of them was pretty much the same. MURDER IN EDEN was the most common headline, splashed across the front pages.

There had been sympathy for Irene Lister at first – the beautiful, grieving widow – but over subsequent days the tone had changed. In later press reports, when a motive was being sought, Liv's father was described as a young, handsome journalist and a close friend of the Listers. There was insinuation in that word 'close', a suggestion of something more than friendship when it came to Irene. Anonymous sources were quoted, hints dropped, oblique references made to the fact the marriage might not have been as happy as everybody thought.

And there was another marriage to consider. Liv wondered if her mother had ever suspected what was going on; if she'd sensed the change, the distance that must have grown between them. Or had her father hidden it well? She must have been used to his erratic hours and long working days, but maybe he had been absent in other ways, too. Liv thought about all the lies and excuses and deceit, the web he must have spun to keep his secret.

Liv, having read as much as she could stomach for the moment, put the cuttings back in the envelope, folded the envelope over and placed it in her bag. She finished her lunch even though she had little appetite. Starving herself to death wasn't going to achieve anything. While she nibbled on the bread and butter it occurred to her that it must have been odd for the reporters having to write about one of their own. Many of them must have known him. She had not come across anything written by Henry yet and had no idea if that was because he hadn't reported on the incident or had deliberately omitted his own articles from what he'd given her.

It was ten past one when Liv left the café and strolled slowly back towards the office. The day was warm but she felt cold and clammy. The horror of the past was settling in her bones. The world was still turning, people still milling around, but she was barely aware of any of it. Instead she was thinking of how at some point on that fateful night the law must have come knocking on her mother's door to break the news and search the flat. They would have looked for letters or diaries, anything that might help explain what her father had just done. And what had they found? Nothing. Only a woman whose heart was about to be broken, her life ripped apart.

Unwilling to return to work any sooner than she had to, Liv sat down on a bench and raised her face to the sun. Briefly she closed her eyes. The picture of Irene Lister sprang into her head. She remembered Henry's warning about staying away, but brushed it aside. Nineteen years of silence, of secrets and lies lay between her and the truth. It was time to shine a light on it all – whatever the cost.

38

Liv had to try and wipe her mind clean of murder and mayhem as she sat in Garvie's office taking dictation. He was pacing the room, frequently stopping behind her and leaning down over her shoulder on the pretext of reviewing what he'd just said, even though she was pretty sure he couldn't read shorthand. He was so close she could feel his breath on her neck, and smell it, too. He stank of alcohol. His lunch, unlike hers, had clearly been swilled down with a bottle of wine or two.

The letter was to the Westminster Council planning committee, a proposal for the development of a site called Yelland Yard. Garvie was in the process of listing all the reasons why he should be given permission to pull down the buildings that were currently there and erect a modern block of offices in their place.

Garvie stood upright, sighed and said: 'You'd think they'd be grateful, wouldn't you? The whole yard is virtually falling down – bomb damage, holes in the roofs, empty for years – and I'm offering to solve the problem. But no, they're still dragging their feet, still can't make a decision. Historical value, they keep saying.' Garvie gave a snort. 'Where's the historical value in a load of derelict buildings?'

Liv waited for a moment and then, when she realised it wasn't a rhetorical question, quickly answered, 'Absolutely. None at all. I suppose they'll come to their senses eventually.'

'Eventually can be a long time in this business, Miss Kent.'

'I'm sure you'll find a way to persuade them.'

Garvie returned to his chair, steepled his fingers and assumed a smug expression. 'Well, I am known for my powers of persuasion.'

Liv, who was glad of the distance between them, was less pleased to see his gaze sliding blatantly down her body. She sat, pen poised, waiting for the leching to stop and the dictation to continue.

'Every man has his weakness,' Garvie said. 'And his price.'

'Do you think so?' Liv asked innocently, deciding she may as well take advantage of his less than sober condition to probe a little further.

'It's usually money, but not always. Sometimes it's women or … well, perhaps I'd better not say. I wouldn't like to shock you.'

'Oh, I'm not easily shocked, Mr Garvie.'

But even with this encouragement, he didn't elucidate. He might be drunk but he wasn't *that* drunk. Instead he smiled, glanced down at his desk and up again. 'Some other time, perhaps.'

Liv, not wanting to arouse suspicion, didn't press him.

Garvie finished the letter and dismissed her. 'Get that sent out today, will you? Best to strike while the iron's hot.'

Liv returned to her office and sat down at her typewriter. Once she was sure that Muriel wasn't watching, she doubled up on the carbon paper so she'd be able to make two copies rather than one. This way she could take one home with her and pass it on to Lincoln. Through this method she hoped to accumulate enough information to eventually meet her half of the bargain.

It was mid-afternoon when a rough-looking bloke in his forties strutted into the office. He was burly, shaven-headed and had the appearance of someone Bentley would have made the acquaintance of on more than one occasion. They say never judge a book by its cover but Liv sensed that this cover could be a pretty accurate reflection of what lay inside. There wasn't just a cockiness about him, but a nastiness, too.

'Hello, darlin',' he said to Muriel. 'And how are you this fine day?'

Muriel's lip curled. 'Please don't darling me. You know perfectly well what my name is. What do you want?'

'Someone got out of bed the wrong side this morning.' The bloke sniggered. 'Is the guvnor around? I need to know about the Bridle Lane rooms. Can I clear them out or what?'

'I'll have to ask Mr Carr.'

'Well, soon as you can, darlin'. Time's money and all.'

'I'm perfectly aware of that,' Muriel said stiffly, getting up from her chair. 'Stay here and I'll find out for you.'

While she tottered off down the corridor, the bloke turned his attention to Liv. 'She's a right one, that Muriel. New here, are you? I ain't seen you before.'

'I'm Olivia,' Liv said pleasantly. 'It's my first day today.'

'Well, good luck with that.'

'Will I need it?' she asked.

He grinned and folded his arms across his massive chest. 'Mr Garvie's new secretary, are you?'

'That's right.'

'Ian Welch is the name. I collect the rents for Mr Carr.'

'Nice to meet you, Mr Welch. Have you been doing that for long?'

'Longer than I care to think about it.'

'I imagine it's not the easiest of jobs.'

Welch, having been given an opportunity to complain, grabbed it with both hands. 'Like getting blood out of a stone most of the time. I mean, they live there, don't they? They've got a roof over their heads. But when it comes to paying, you don't see 'em for dust. Or if you do, they've got every excuse under the sun – the kiddies are ill, the old man's lost his job, they ain't got bread to put on the table – but none of that's *my* problem. As I see it, you live in it, you pay for it and that's that.'

Liv was saved from having to comment on this somewhat unsympathetic approach by the return of Muriel.

'You'll have to come back tomorrow,' she said to Welch. 'Mr Carr has to ring the police before the property can be cleared.'

'So why can't he do that now?'

'He's busy. Tomorrow, all right? And you'd better make it late morning. He might not have an answer before then.'

'Suit yourself. Makes no difference to me. It's no skin off my nose if the place is lying empty.'

'Exactly,' Muriel said. 'Now, if you don't mind, I have work to get on with.'

'I can take a hint.' Welch looked over at Liv and grinned again. 'She loves me really, sweetheart. She's just got a funny way of showing it.'

Muriel sat back down behind her desk with a pained expression on her face. She waited for him to leave and for the front door to close before flapping a hand as if to waft away a bad smell. 'If I never saw that man in my life again, it would be too soon.'

'He was telling me how hard it is to collect the rents.'

'Don't believe a word he says. He loves every minute of it. Scaring the pants off people is what he does best.' Muriel glared towards the door. 'Mr Carr doesn't like his methods any more than I do, but Mr Garvie won't get rid of him. He says there's no point being soft on them ... the tenants, I mean ... or they'll just take advantage.'

Liv's opinion of Hugh Garvie wasn't improving, but she had something else she wanted to ask. 'What did you mean about having to ring the police?'

'A tenant who died. Well, she was murdered.' Muriel gave a visible shiver. 'Moll Ainsworth her name was. Bridle Lane. You may have read about it in the paper.'

'Yes, my landlady ...' Liv had been about to say that Dora had known her, that Moll had been to the house in Whitcomb Street, but stopped herself just in time. For one she was supposed to be living in Islington, and for two it might seem a little odd – to Muriel, at least – that a local tom had been a frequent visitor to Dora's kitchen. 'My landlady was talking about it the other morning. Terrible, wasn't it? Poor woman.'

Muriel lowered her voice. 'She was a prostitute, you know.'

'Oh,' Liv said.

'We weren't aware of that, of course. Not before ... I mean, this is a respectable company. We'd never have rented her the rooms if we'd known.'

Liv almost said that even prostitutes needed somewhere to live, but wisely refrained from sharing the view. It would not, she suspected, go down well with Muriel. 'So why does Mr Welch need to clear the rooms? Didn't she have any relatives who could do it?'

'Not that DI Bentley's been able to find.'

Liv flinched at the mention of the name. She vehemently hoped that his business with Garvie & Carr was over or it could

211

cause her major difficulties. What if he turned up and called her Miss Anderson in front of everyone? That wouldn't be easy to explain. Damn well impossible, more like. Then she'd be out of a job and up to her ears in it with Moody, too.

'Are you all right?' Muriel asked. 'You've gone kind of pale, if you don't mind me saying.'

'Have I?' Liv touched her face with her fingertips. 'I was just thinking about Moll Ainsworth.'

Muriel pursed her lips. 'It never ends well for women like that.'

Liv spent most of the rest of the afternoon fretting about Bentley and what she would do if he showed up at the office. Hopefully he wouldn't. Moll had just been a tenant, after all. Whatever he'd had to ask, he'd have done it by now, and probably by telephone. She had to stop stressing over it. But she couldn't. The thought of her cover being blown made her break out in a cold sweat.

39

Slug's accommodation didn't have much to recommend it, other than being free. The dark, damp cellar rooms had no electricity and no running water. He would light candles when it got dark, using them sparingly. If he needed a wash, he would use the Gents at one of the many pubs he frequented or – once in a blue moon – pay a visit to the public baths. Usually his bodily functions were adequately served by these facilities, but there was always the overgrown garden for emergencies.

The house had been condemned after the war, but no one had got around to pulling it down yet. These things cost money. He could have moved into one of the lighter, brighter rooms upstairs, but he didn't trust the ceilings. Likely to come down at any time, he reckoned, and he valued his skull too much to take the chance. The cellar had a stronger, sturdier feel to it.

Slug slept on the floor on a grubby mattress, covering himself with a coat in the summer and a ragged eiderdown in winter. An old orange box served as a table. There was a single armchair, too, battered and lumpy but still serviceable; he had found it in one of the upper rooms and dragged it downstairs. A single plate and a few pieces of cutlery, all requisitioned from one café or another, were carefully wiped clean with newspaper after use.

Although he shared the space with spiders, mice and the occasional rat, Slug was content enough with his surroundings. Preferring to roam the streets, he was rarely there during the day, and at night it was just a place to lay his head. He had no possessions, nothing he would be sorry to leave behind, and so had no fear of eviction other than the temporary inconvenience it would cause him.

It was early for Slug to be home, barely six o'clock, but he'd come back because he wanted somewhere quiet to think. He had opened the door that led out to the garden and was standing in the doorway, looking out over the long grass and weeds while he puffed on a skinny roll-up. The sky above him was blue and the air, still warm, smelled of petrol fumes and his neighbours' cooking.

The cooking smells reminded him of food and this in turn reminded him of lifting the reporter's wallet on Friday night. There had been four quid in it, not a fortune but enough to treat himself to a rare fish and chip supper and still have plenty left over. He now knew the man was called Ralph McCall: there'd been three small oblong cards in one of the slots bearing his name and the telephone number of the *West End News*. Slug had dumped them in a bin along with the wallet.

But all that was beside the point. He had a decision to make and it was a tricky one. Bentley had caught up with him an hour ago, sliding into the seat opposite his at the Marigold café on Beak Street. The inspector, for the benefit of anyone who might be paying attention, had pretended not to know him, opening his newspaper and making a show of reading the news. It was only after the waitress had delivered his tea that he'd spoken softly without looking up.

'Not avoiding me are you, Slug?'

Slug had murmured his reply. 'Avoiding you, Mr Bentley? Why would I be doing that?'

'That's what I've been asking myself. Every time our paths cross, you seem to do a disappearing trick.'

'You can't be too careful, Mr Bentley, not in my line of business. Walls have ears and all that.'

'I have the feeling there's something you're not telling me. Is it about Moll Ainsworth?'

Slug's gaze had quickly swept the café, searching for enquiring eyes. 'I don't know nothin' about that. I didn't even see her that night. I swear.'

Bentley had turned over a page of his newspaper. 'I won't be happy if I find out you've been holding out on me.'

'Not me, Mr Bentley. I'd never do that.'

'But you have heard something, right? A whisper, perhaps. A word on the grapevine.'

Slug had almost shaken his head, but stopped himself just in time. Instead he'd picked up his tea, taken a slurp and put the cup back down. He had spoken out of the corner of his mouth with his face averted. 'Quiet as the grave out there. I'll listen out, though. I'll be sure to let you know if anything comes my way.'

Bentley had given him a hard stare. 'You do that.'

That's when Slug had scarpered, not too fast like he was trying to get away again, but fast enough to prevent himself from telling what he knew. Because he'd been tempted. He'd liked Moll – they'd tramped the same streets for years – and he wanted to see her murderer caught. But he also wanted money in his pocket and food in his belly. Bentley would pay for what he knew, but someone else would pay more.

Slug took a long drag on his cigarette. He was rarely bothered by moral obligations and the tiny pangs of conscience niggling away in the back of his mind were so small as to be almost negligible. When you looked at it in black and white, it made no real difference to Moll whether her murderer was caught or not. It wasn't going to bring her back to life. She wasn't going to rise from her grave, happy and triumphant, grateful for the information he'd passed on to the law. And she'd have understood about looking out for number one. In this world you had to grab your chances when they came along.

Slug played back the scene in his head, the way he had a hundred times since he'd heard about Moll's murder. It had happened about a week before her death. He'd been in the Black Bull, minding his own business – and anyone else's he could overhear – when Moll had come in and ordered a port and lemon. The pub had been busy and she'd stayed by the counter. He hadn't thought anything of it until he'd noticed her staring, *really* staring, across the bar.

Now there wasn't anything odd about that, not in itself. Just eyeing up a prospective punter, he'd thought. Even though, strictly speaking, the girls weren't supposed to do business on the premises, it still went on. But then he'd noticed a change in Moll's face – a kind of frowning confusion – and knew that it was something more than that.

Slug had followed the direction of her gaze to a man maybe fifteen feet away, an ordinary-looking scruffy bloke with a beard, who was standing on the other side of the horseshoe-shaped bar and studying a pint of beer. As if aware of her scrutiny, he had suddenly looked up and met her eyes. Slug had witnessed that split second and seen too the moment of mutual recoiling. Moll's jaw had dropped and the blood had drained from her face.

As if she'd seen a ghost, Moll had downed her drink in one, turned on her heel and hurried out of the pub. The man had made to follow her, but then changed his mind after a few steps and returned to his pint. He'd looked worried, though, his expression dark and brooding, his hands tightly clenched.

It had taken Slug a while to place him. He was good on faces, even those he hadn't seen for years, but it must have been ten minutes at least before the penny finally dropped. The revelation when it came was satisfying. How long since he'd last seen the geezer? About ten years. He couldn't say for sure. Time wasn't a definite entity in his world, the days passing into weeks, into months, with only the change of seasons to mark the endless progression.

Slug had watched him, thinking he was taking a chance coming back here. Moll might not be the only one to recognise him. Well, she already wasn't. But the bloke must have wondered if she'd go running to the law. Slug knew better. The likes of Moll didn't grass, not even when people deserved it. However, she wouldn't have kept it to herself, either; women weren't good at keeping secrets.

Slug dropped the butt of his cigarette on the grass and ground it down with his heel. He didn't reckon it was a coincidence Moll being murdered like that, only a short while after the encounter. No, the bloke had done for her, no doubt about it; he'd panicked and shut her up, once and for all.

So, the decision was made, but Slug wasn't going to do anything about it tonight. He had money in his pocket and the pub was calling. Tomorrow was soon enough. A little chat, a few hints to the person in question and it would all be sorted. Sometimes the price of silence could be more profitable than anything else.

40

Ralph McCall had picked up Pauline after work and given her back the money he'd borrowed. Then, because he'd felt obliged, he'd brought her here, to the Lyons Corner House, where they were now eating pork chops, mash and peas, all washed down with cups of tea. She was yattering on as usual, like the spoken word was going out of fashion, an endless monologue that he'd stopped listening to about a quarter of an hour ago. When she paused for breath, he took the chance to convey some information of his own.

'You heard about that girl who's missing?'

'What girl?'

'The Windmill girl. Cynthia Crosby. I'm writing a story about her. Should be in this week's edition if she doesn't turn up before then.'

Pauline's mouth pursed at the mention of the Windmill, as though it was a den of iniquity. 'Is she pretty?'

'Yes, I suppose so. Well, it's kind of a requirement for the job, isn't it?'

Pauline never liked it when he had anything to do with attractive women, even in circumstances like these. She sawed at the pork chop with unnecessary violence. 'It's a weird kind of job if you ask me: taking your clothes off in public. I mean, it's not *respectable*, is it?'

'Of course it's not respectable. That's the point. It's why men go to the Windmill.'

Pauline glared at him. 'They should have better things to spend their money on.'

Ralph, feeling they had deviated somewhat from the original subject, said, 'Anyway, this Cynthia's been missing since Friday night. It took me hours to find anyone willing to talk about her. I reckon they've all been told to keep their mouths shut by the management; they don't want the bad publicity. I eventually managed to persuade this girl – Ruby, her name was – to give me some information. Cynthia had a boyfriend, apparently, a bloke called Geoff Dowd, but they split up recently. I reckon that puts him well in the frame.'

'What do you mean?'

'It's the first person the cops look to when something like this happens – the nearest and dearest. Ruby gave me a description of him. I even managed to get an address off her, only he won't open the door. That's not the behaviour of an innocent person, is it? If anything happened to you, I'd do everything I could to find the culprit. I'd want to cooperate with the press, get every bit of help I could.'

Pauline stopped eating for a moment, the fork halfway to her mouth. A tiny frown appeared between her eyes as though she was trying to work out if this was a compliment or not. 'He's her ex, though. It's not the same.'

'Only just an ex. And it's a bit of a coincidence that shortly after they split, she disappeared. It stinks, if you ask me.'

'But you don't know that she's actually dead.'

'No, but she might be. This girl said Cynthia wasn't the sort to just take off without telling anyone.'

Ralph was determined to get hold of Geoff Dowd, even if it meant camping outside his flat for the next couple of days. What he wanted before the *West End News* was put to bed on Wednesday night was an outright denial of any wrong-doing straight from the man's lips. Then he would be able to quote him, a quote that would draw attention to the fact that Dowd was a suspect in the matter. It might even run as the headline: EX DENIES INVOLVEMENT IN WINDMILL GIRL'S DISAPPEARANCE. A bit long, perhaps, but he'd work on it.

'So what else did this Ruby say?'

'Oh, nothing much.'

Pauline eyed him suspiciously. She wasn't big on trust. Other girls were the enemy, snipers lurking in the shadows, waiting for an opportunity to supplant her. Ralph found her possessiveness irritating. It got under his skin and made him want to be delib-erately provocative.

'She seemed a nice girl.'

'Nice girls don't flaunt themselves in public,' Pauline said tightly.

'She was very young. She couldn't have been more than six-teen. I felt sorry for her. I reckon she's scared stiff with all this stuff going on. I mean, first that prostitute being killed and now this. It's a lot to deal with at her age.' In truth, Ralph had taken advantage of Ruby's naivety to lay the cynical reporter's guilt trip on her – that to say nothing, to withhold information, could mean the difference between Cynthia being found alive or dead. He wasn't ashamed of what he'd done, and was actually quite proud of it. 'Anyway, she told me what she knew in the end.'

'For all the good it's done. You said the bloke isn't even answering the door.'

'Yeah, but I know where he lives now. He can't hide away for ever.'

'Isn't that a bit mean? Just because he doesn't want to talk to you doesn't mean he's guilty of anything.'

'If he isn't guilty, he's got nothing to be worried about.'

'I wouldn't like it if someone was knocking on my door every five minutes.'

Ralph sometimes thought that Pauline enjoyed rubbing him up the wrong way. She was always having little digs about this or that. 'It's my job, sweetheart,' he said. 'I'm an investigative journalist. We have to ask awkward questions.'

Pauline didn't look impressed. 'You work for the *West End News.*'

'Only for the moment,' he said sharply. Then, before he could lose his rag with her – no man likes a put-down – he quickly asked: 'Why don't we go for a drink? Do you fancy it?'

'No, I don't want to be late home. I've got work tomorrow.'

Ralph tried to look disappointed. 'Friday, then.'

He walked Pauline to the bus stop and waited impatiently for her bus to come. Once he'd waved her off, keeping a fixed smile on his face, he headed back towards Soho. Geoff Dowd would have to go out at some point, and he intended to be there when he did.

41

As Liv stepped into the hallway of the house in Whitcomb Street, the sound of the radio was coming from the kitchen. She could also hear Dora and Aline talking, their voices slightly raised so they could hear each other above the music.

'It's missing, I tell you,' Aline said. 'It was definitely there, on the peg in the hall.'

'But you can't even remember when you last saw it. You could have lost it months ago, left it somewhere, on the bus or . . . Have you checked upstairs? Maybe it's in your wardrobe.'

'It's *not* in my wardrobe,' Aline said insistently. 'I always leave it on the peg. That's where it stays until I need it again, along with my winter coat. I only noticed because I thought the coat might need a clean and . . . it's not there, Dora. The green scarf's gone. It's been taken.'

'Maybe one of the girls borrowed it.'

'They wouldn't do that, not without saying. Anyway, you know who's taken it. It's obvious.'

'What's obvious about it?' Dora snapped. 'I don't know why you keep saying things like that.'

Aline sighed. 'You know perfectly well. You can't keep putting your head in the sand. When are you going to come to your senses and face up to facts? He's back and you can't go on pretending he isn't. Moll told you but you wouldn't listen.'

Liv, who had found herself inadvertently eavesdropping, was now afraid to move in case she was discovered. And, of course, she was undeniably curious. Who was the 'he' Aline was talking about? And what, if anything, did he have to do with the missing scarf? The two women had been bickering on and off for the past week and now things seemed to be coming to a head.

'You should get the locks changed,' Aline said.

'It's a waste of money.'

'I saw you close and lock that door with my own eyes, Dora Marks, so don't go pretending otherwise. How else did he get in if it wasn't with a key? He didn't walk through the walls.'

'It wasn't him. It couldn't have been.'

'You won't be saying that when we're all murdered in our beds.'

Liv was reminded of Aline passing a similar comment last Friday: *You'll be next*, or something like that. A shiver ran through her.

'Don't be ridiculous!' Dora said. 'I'm not listening to any more of this.'

Liv heard the thin scrape of a chair being pushed back, and decided to make herself scarce. Quickly she went upstairs, taking care to avoid the creaking boards. Once she was safely in her room, she walked over to the window and tried to make sense of what she'd just heard. Putting two and two together, the obvious conclusion was that Aline knew – or at least thought

223

she knew – who their burglar had been. And that man was dangerous.

Liv remembered how close she'd been to him, remembered the door being flung open and her being knocked aside. Anger rose and spread in her. She could have been badly hurt or worse. Instinctively she touched her shoulder, aware of the bruise that was there from hitting the wall. Didn't she and Verity have the right to know if some madman had a key to the house? It was appalling, an outrage, to keep them in the dark. So why the hell was she skulking in her room? If she wanted answers, she wouldn't find them here. What was needed was action, and it was needed now.

Before she could think any more about it, Liv rushed out on to the landing. This wasn't the time to be holding back. She was going to confront them both, tell them what she'd overheard and demand the truth. But she had barely reached the top of the stairs when there was a knock on the front door. Damn it! She stopped in her tracks and listened.

It was Dora who answered the knock and invited the woman inside – another of her tarot clients – leading her through to the kitchen. The radio went off and there was a murmur of voices. Thwarted, Liv stood and silently cursed her luck. There would be no confrontation now until the reading was over, and that would take half an hour or so.

A few seconds later, Aline came out of the kitchen and headed for the stairs. Liv immediately drew back, returning to her room where she softly closed the door. She leaned her head against the wooden panels and waited for Aline to pass by. What now? Too impatient to sit around, she decided to go and see Pally. Even if the cops were watching the flat, she couldn't see the harm. It wasn't as if she'd rushed round straight after Bentley had paid his visit. And she wanted someone to talk to, someone she trusted.

Once the path was clear, Liv sneaked out and quietly padded down the stairs. She opened and closed the front door, careful to make only the tiniest of sounds. Then she set off for Brewer Street. While she walked, she thought about what she'd found out. Well, what she *thought* she'd found out. The two women held different opinions, and although Liv would normally be more inclined to believe Dora, she wasn't so sure in this case. Aline could certainly make a mountain out of a molehill, but on this occasion her fears might be justified.

Liv had a good look round when she got to Brewer Street. If the law were staking out the flat there was no sign of them. Although that, of course, was probably the point. Her gaze lifted to scan the windows above the shops, but all she saw were dusty panes of glass. She took one last glance up and down the street and then went and rang the bell.

Liv gave it thirty seconds, but no one came to the door. Perhaps he had gone to the French or for something to eat with Geoff. She tried again, a couple of longer rings. In this instance she got a response, although not the kind that was either expected or welcome. One of the second-floor windows was abruptly thrown open and Pally yelled down.

'For God's sake, just clear off, can't you? He doesn't want to talk. How many times do you need bloody telling?'

Liv, bemused, took a step back and stared up at him.

'Oh, shit, Liv. I didn't realise it was you. Hang on. I'll be right down.'

Relieved that it wasn't her own presence that Pally found so objectional, Liv stood and waited on the pavement.

Pally answered the door with a sheepish grin on his face. 'Sorry, love. We've had a reporter hounding us all afternoon. The bastard won't leave Geoff alone.' He looked over her shoulder, checked that the guilty party wasn't in the vicinity and quickly waved her inside. 'Come in, come in. You wouldn't believe the cheek of the sod. Goddam pariahs, the lot of them. I'd like to stuff his paper down his scrawny little throat.'

'I thought you might fancy a coffee,' she said, closing the door and following him up the stairs.

'Good idea. Geoff's been holed up here since Saturday. He could do with a change of scene. I've told him he'll go stir crazy if he doesn't get out soon, but he refuses to budge.'

Liv, who'd wanted to talk to Pally in private, now found herself hoping that Geoff would stick to his guns and stay put. She felt bad for hoping it – the poor man wasn't having the best of times – but all she wanted was half an hour alone with Pally. 'Maybe he's just not in the mood.'

'What he needs is some fresh air. It's not doing him any good, stuck inside for days on end.'

'What about that reporter, though? He doesn't want to run into him, does he?'

'To hell with the reporter,' Pally said.

'What's he called, this bloke?'

Pally glanced over his shoulder. 'I've no idea. Why?'

'There's been one sniffing round the Windmill, too. Verity said last night. It's probably the same bloke.' Liv suspected it was Ralph McCall. 'From the *West End News*, I think.'

They reached the flat and went inside. It was the first time Liv had been there and she looked around, taking in the uncarpeted, paint-spattered floor, the evening light flooding through the windows and the big splashes of colour from the canvases lined up against the walls. It was a studio rather than a living room, a purely utilitarian space. Geoff was standing by a long trestle table, cleaning brushes.

'Hi,' she said. 'Stupid question, I know, but how are you doing?'

226

Geoff shrugged. 'Keeping busy.'

'You've done enough busy for one day,' Pally said. 'Get your jacket. We're going to Joe's.'

'You go. I've got things to do.'

'Like what?' Pally said. 'Skulking in here like a guilty man? You've not done anything wrong. If you're worried about that reporter, he's well gone. And even if he does show up again, we'll soon get rid of him.'

Liv felt obliged to join in the coaxing. 'Yes, come and have a coffee. It's only down the road.'

For a moment it seemed that Geoff wasn't going to give in. He gave a small shake of his head and muttered something indecipherable. Liv's hopes rose, but were then instantly dashed.

'Oh, all right. Just a quick one.'

The three of them walked down to Old Compton Street. Pally did most of the talking, with Liv making the occasional contribution. Geoff, jumpy and anxious, kept looking around as if expecting to be confronted at any second.

'Stop stressing,' Pally said. 'There's nothing to worry about.'

'Easy for you to say. You're not the one everyone thinks murdered their girlfriend.'

'No one thinks that.'

'The law think that. Why else did they search the flat?'

'They were just covering their arses.'

The mention of murder reminded Liv of what Aline had said. She wanted Pally's advice on what she'd overheard, but didn't want to discuss it in front of Geoff. But perhaps his presence didn't matter: he was too preoccupied with his own problems to take much interest in anyone else's.

Liv took Pally's arm and leaned in towards him. 'Did Verity tell you about the break-in we had?'

227

'No, I haven't seen her since she and the others came looking for Cynthia. A break-in? Shit. That's bad. Did they take much?'

'Some jewellery,' Liv said. 'I disturbed the bloke and he ran off. But I'm not sure it was a break-in, exactly. I mean, Dora can't remember if—'

But before she could get to the point, Geoff interrupted. 'This place stinks. Soho, London, the whole damn country. I'm sick of it. It's putrid. You should get the hell out, Liv, while you still can.'

'Don't mind Geoff,' Pally said, squeezing her arm. 'He doesn't mean it.'

'I do bloody mean it. Anyone with any sense would find somewhere else to live.'

By now they had reached Joe's. They went inside, ordered three coffees and sat down near the back. Liv, having been frustrated in her attempt to explain the situation at Whitcomb Street, wasn't inclined to return to the subject. Not that she had much of an opportunity. Geoff was now on a roll, sharing his woes with everyone. Cynthia, of course, was the main target of his bitterness.

'So she just clears off without a thought, and I'm left to pick up the pieces. That's what she's like. *She* cheats on me and suddenly I'm the bad guy. How does that work, exactly?'

Liv was only listening with half an ear. Her mind was on other things. She glanced around the caff, at all the empty tables, remembering when Tom Lincoln had walked in and changed everything. The place had been quiet then, too. Recently lots of coffee bars had sprung up in Old Compton Street, all of them livelier than Joe's, most of them with music, but she and Pally always came here. It was just habit, she supposed, and a sense of the familiar.

'And now I've got the law on my back. I saw the way they

looked at me, like they couldn't wait to put the cuffs on. If she doesn't show up soon, I'll end up in the bloody slammer.'

Liv gazed across the table at Geoff. He was unshaven with dark shadows under his eyes. She studied him closely, wondering if he was capable of murder, but couldn't believe he was guilty of anything more than a seething resentment. 'Don't you have any idea where she might have gone?'

'Off with her new bloke, I should imagine. She could be anywhere.'

'Bentley was round on Saturday, asking what sort of mood you were in on Friday night.'

Geoff grunted. 'He must have been overjoyed when you told him.'

'I didn't tell him anything, other than I didn't know you very well. I said I was dancing for most of the night and barely talked to you.'

'You see,' Pally said. 'I told you Liv wouldn't land you in it.'

Geoff gave her a grudging nod. 'But what about the others? If Bentley gets to hear what I was saying, I'll be for the high jump.'

'No one's going to grass you up,' Pally said. 'Have a bit of faith.'

Eventually, after the coffees were drunk, Pally suggested going for a pint. Liv was tempted, but suspected that one drink would turn into two, and two would turn into three, and that before she knew it, it would be closing time. She dithered, but then Geoff, surprisingly, said that he was up for it, which pretty much made her mind up for her. If she couldn't be alone with Pally, she was better off going home to try and sort things out with Dora.

Liv made her excuses and left. She walked slowly home, in no hurry for a confrontation. She realised that Pally hadn't asked about her first day at work, but then he had other things to worry about. Living with Geoff couldn't be easy at the moment. And having the law poking around couldn't be much fun, either.

She had just reached Whitcomb Street, and was still in the process of figuring out what she'd say to Dora, when she became aware of someone behind her. Footsteps dogging her own. That strange prickling sensation on the back of her neck. Quickly she glanced over her shoulder and her heart sank. It was Ralph McCall on her tail, grinning like a Cheshire cat.

42

'Hello, Liv,' McCall said, falling into step beside her. 'Nice to see you again.'

'What are you doing here?'

'Oh, just out for an evening stroll. I didn't realise you knew Geoff Dowd.'

Liv kept on walking, upping her pace. The sooner she got home and away from him, the better. She wanted to tell him to shove off, to leave her alone, but feared that would only make it look like she had something to hide. 'I don't. Not really. He's a friend of a friend.'

'Well enough to go for a coffee with the bloke.' McCall shoved his hands in his pockets and did some more grinning. 'I was just passing and noticed you in Joe's.'

'What do you want?'

McCall didn't answer her directly. 'Poor Cynthia Crosby. It's shocking her disappearing like this. I presume you do know her.' A hint of mockery crept into his voice. 'Or is she just a friend of a friend too?'

Liv didn't reply.

McCall wasn't deterred. 'Three days now and still no sign. Like she's just disappeared into thin air. Worrying, don't you think? What's Geoff's take on it all?'

'Why don't you ask him?'

'Believe me, I've been trying, but he doesn't want to talk to me. Funny that. You'd think he'd be keen to have her found. I'm only trying to help. The more publicity there is, the better. Don't you think? It makes me wonder why he's being so obstructive.'

What Liv was wondering was why McCall hadn't grabbed the chance to waylay Geoff in the caff when he'd had the opportunity, and decided that he probably hadn't liked the odds. Especially with Pally looking the way he did, his face still battered and bruised. No, he'd decided to pick on her instead, to try and squeeze some information from her once she was separated from the other two. Well, he was out of luck. She had no intention of telling the creep anything.

'So what's your view on what's happened to Cynthia?'

Liv shook her head. 'Just leave me alone.'

'Don't be like that. I'm only doing my job.'

'Then go and do it somewhere else.'

McCall, who clearly couldn't take a hint, suddenly changed tack and said: 'So you and Henry managed to meet up. How did that go?'

'Fine,' she said shortly.

'The two of you must have had a lot to talk about.'

There was something about the way he said it that made her suspicious. As if he knew what their conversation had been about. But that wasn't possible. Although McCall had been at the Eagle, he couldn't have been close enough to hear. And Henry wouldn't have betrayed her. She was sure he wouldn't.

McCall carried on speaking. 'He's a good man, Henry. And he was a great journalist . . . in his day.'

'In his day?'

'Oh, no disrespect meant. Henry's probably forgotten more than I'll ever know, but he's getting on a bit now. To be honest, he spends more time in the pub than anywhere else. And the problem with drinkers, of course, is that they're not always as discreet as they should be.'

'And what's that got to do with me?'

'You know exactly what,' McCall said smugly. 'That's quite a story you've got to tell.'

Liv's heart began to thump, and she had to fight to keep her voice steady. 'I'm not telling any story. I don't know what you're talking about.'

'Have it your own way. But I think we could work well together. I could even get you a deal with one of the nationals. A link-up with one of the Sundays, perhaps. I don't know what Henry's offered but—'

'There is no offer, Mr McCall. There is no story.'

'Call me Ralph,' he said, as though they could be chums. 'It's going to be quite an exclusive, isn't it? I admire your loyalty to Henry, but perhaps it's misplaced. You have to think about what's best for you. You're only going to get one shot at this so you may as well make it profitable.'

Liv, still hoping against hope that he was only on a fishing expedition, decided to carry on playing dumb. 'I don't have a clue what you're going on about.'

'Come on, let's not dance around the houses. I know who you are, Liv, and who your father was. Paul Teller, right? The man who put a bullet through Nicky Lister.'

Liv turned cold, bile rising in her throat. 'Anderson. My name's Anderson.'

'Your mother's maiden name.'

'Who told you that?'

'Like I said, Henry's not the most discreet of people when he's got a few pints inside him.'

Liv stopped walking and glared at McCall. 'I don't believe you. You're a liar! And you can't write anything about me. If you do, I'll sue you – and your damn paper.'

'Sue us for what? For telling the truth?'

McCall's amusement – the grin was back – was almost too much for Liv to bear. She wanted to slap that smirk right off his face. 'Henry's not going to be happy when he hears about this.'

'Henry's happiness isn't my concern. Anyway, he's not in London at the moment. He's been sent away again.' McCall glanced at the watch on his wrist. 'I reckon he'll be arriving in Eastbourne just about now. He'll be gone a few days, maybe even a week. A lot can happen in that time.'

Fear and fury battled inside Liv, two strong emotions that threatened her control. 'Let's just get this perfectly clear: I'm not selling any story, not now, not ever. Can you get that into your thick skull? Henry's an old family friend and that's the only reason I met up with him. That's the beginning and end of it.'

'Except it isn't, is it? The thing is, Liv ... well, the cat's out of the bag now, so you can either work with me or against me.'

'And what the hell is that supposed to mean?'

McCall's tone turned sly, almost threatening. 'There's always another story that could be told, an interesting one about Paul Teller's daughter and her friendship with Geoff Dowd. Misfortune just seems to follow you around, doesn't it? First there was that terrible business with your dad, now the disappearance of Cynthia, and you were even there in the crowd after Moll Ainsworth's body was found. Oh, and let's not forget the curious little matter of you handing over money to a gangster.

Put it all together and people could start to think that you're more than unlucky.'

Liv's eyes flashed with rage. 'Get away from me,' she hissed. 'Get away right now or I'll scream so loud every copper in London will come running.'

McCall raised his hands, taking a few quick steps back. 'All right, all right. There's no need for that.'

'You've got five seconds.'

McCall started walking off. But he didn't go far. He had one last thing to say before he left. Looking over his shoulder, he called out: 'Sleep on it. Think it over. I'll see you soon.'

Liv turned her back on him and headed for the house. Panic was coursing through her. Could he really write a story like that? No, he was just calling her bluff, trying to force her into a corner, to make her talk about her father. A mirthless laugh slipped from her throat. As if she had anything to tell! Everything she knew, she'd got from the newspapers. But *he* didn't know that. The man was unscrupulous, twisted, a bloody snake.

Liv tried to get her thoughts straight, to work out what to do. She had to see Henry, but she couldn't, not unless she got on a train and went to Eastbourne. Even then, there was no saying she'd be able to find him. And she couldn't take time off work, not when she'd only just started. Lincoln would do his nut.

She stopped again as she approached the house, checking that McCall wasn't watching her. Perhaps he already knew where she lived, but perhaps he didn't. There was no point handing the information to him on a plate. Once she was sure that he was out of sight, she rummaged for her key, ran the last few yards, unlocked the front door and hurried inside.

43

Liv was in a state, her head spinning, as she closed the door behind her. All she wanted was to get upstairs and be alone. McCall's words echoed in her ears. His pale, hateful face loomed up in her imagination, sly and menacing. She wasn't going to let him away with it. She couldn't. But what could she do? The sound of the television, a quiz show, clapping, laughter, cut across her thoughts. She strode across the hall and had one hand on the banister when Aline emerged from the living room.

'Ah, Liv, I thought it must be you. Could I have a word?'

Liv, despite her agitation, could hardly say no. 'What is it?'

'I was wondering if you'd seen my green scarf. It was on the peg.' Aline glanced towards the coat stand. 'And now it's gone.'

'No, sorry, I haven't seen it.'

'Are you sure?'

'I'm sure,' Liv said, starting to walk up the stairs.

'What about Verity? Do you think she might have borrowed it?'

'No, not without asking.' Liv had almost forgotten about the exchange she'd overheard earlier, the very reason she'd gone out to see Pally in the first place. Now, as it came back to her, she stopped walking and blurted out the question she'd been desperate to ask. 'What's going on, Aline? I heard you talking to Dora about someone being back, about getting the locks changed. You said we could all be murdered in our beds.'

Aline's face grew tight. 'You shouldn't listen at doors.'

'I wasn't. I was on my way out and you were talking loudly. The radio was on. Anyway, what did you mean? I've a right to know. I live here too.'

'It was nothing, nothing for you to worry about.'

'It didn't sound like nothing.'

'It was only a joke. Forget it. There's no need to make a fuss.'

But Liv wasn't prepared to accept the brush-off. McCall had already stirred things up in her with his foul manipulations; anger and resentment still bubbled near the surface. She'd had enough of people trying to get one over on her. 'I don't believe you. Why won't you tell me?'

'Now you're being ridiculous.'

'It's not ridiculous to be concerned about being murdered in my bed.'

'That was just … oh, for heaven's sake! It was just a misunderstanding between me and Dora. It's all been put straight now so you don't need to be bothered about it.'

'But I *am* bothered,' Liv insisted. 'I want to know who's back. Why won't you tell me?'

'Because it's none of your business.'

'Now *you're* the one who's being ridiculous. I'm not going to stop asking until you tell me the truth.'

'Then you're going to have a long wait.'

It was at this moment that Dora appeared in the living-room

doorway. 'Stop it, you two. I can't be doing with all this rowing.' She looked at Aline and sighed. 'We have to tell her.'

'We don't have to do anything of the sort.'

Dora, ignoring her, transferred her attention to Liv and said: 'You're right, love. You deserve to know. You'd better come and sit down.'

In Liv's experience, being asked to sit down only ever meant bad news, and although she had demanded the truth, a part of her suddenly recoiled from hearing it. She braced herself as she walked into the living room and perched on the edge of the sofa. Dora sat beside her, head bowed, hands twisting awkwardly in her lap. Aline hovered near the fireplace.

Eventually, after a short silence, Dora raised her face and met Liv's eyes. 'The person Aline was referring to, dear, was my son, Larry.'

'Larry?' Liv's startled gaze flew to the photograph on the mantelpiece. 'But I thought he was ... You said ... What? I don't understand.'

'I'm sorry. I shouldn't have said what I did. It was just easier than explaining everything. And to be honest, he's been gone for so long now that it sometimes feels like he *is* dead. He had to go away, you see, and it's been over ten years since I last saw him.'

'Away?' Prison was the first thing that sprang into Liv's mind, but she kept the thought to herself. 'What happened?'

Dora hesitated. 'It wasn't his fault. He didn't do anything. But he'd been in some trouble before so he knew ... well, he reckoned the law would pin it on him. That's why he scarpered. He took off and he never came back.'

'Until now,' Aline said.

Dora gave her a sharp look. 'We don't know that for sure.'

'Moll said she saw him in the Black Bull.'

'Yes, well, Moll saw all sorts of things when she'd had one too many gins.'

As the two women glared at each other, Liv quickly jumped in. 'So what wasn't Larry's fault?'

Dora gave a long sigh, the breath coming from deep inside her. 'He was stepping out with this girl, you see. It wasn't anything serious, but then ... but then ...' Her face twisted and the words seemed to lodge in her throat.

'She ended up dead,' Aline said bluntly. 'Murdered.'

Dora shot Aline another angry look.

'What?' Aline said. 'You wanted her to know the truth, didn't you? Well, that's it in a nutshell. There's no point beating around the bush.'

A chill had descended on Liv. 'She was murdered?'

'It wasn't my Larry,' Dora said. 'I'd put my life on it. He'd never do nothing like that. He only ran because he knew what they'd think. The law would never have given him a fair hearing. He didn't have an alibi, see; he couldn't prove where he was.'

As all this was sinking in, an alarming thought leapt into Liv's head. 'Was it him? The man who was here? Was it Larry?'

Dora shook her head.

But Aline was less dismissive. 'Did he have a beard? Moll said he had a beard now.'

Liv tried to visualise the man in her mind, but it was all a blur. The intruder had rushed out of her room with his head down like a charging bull. She hadn't even been able to tell how tall he was. 'I don't know. I didn't see his face. It all happened too fast.'

'I don't think it was him,' Dora said.

'So who was it, then?' Aline said. 'There wasn't a break-in so whoever it was had a key.'

Liv's skin was prickling now, hair rising on the back of her neck. 'Did he know Moll had recognised him?'

Dora, understanding the implication, spoke through tight lips. 'Larry would never have laid a finger on Moll. He wouldn't.'

'No, sorry, I didn't mean ...' Except, of course, that was exactly what Liv had meant. If Larry was caught, if he was convicted, he'd be facing the same fate as her father. That, surely, could have been enough to make him panic, to force him into a desperate act.

'Whoever Moll thought she saw, it wasn't Larry,' Dora said firmly.

Aline, fidgeting, uncrossed her arms and then crossed them again. 'Well, someone took my scarf.'

Liv didn't see what Aline had to complain about. It was just a damn scarf. She, on the other hand, had been relieved of all her jewellery. It took a moment for her to realise what Aline was really getting at: a scarf had gone missing, Moll had been strangled, and the two events, perhaps, were not disconnected.

Dora was quicker on the uptake. 'You could have lost that scarf anywhere. And even if it was stolen, Moll was already dead by the time that man broke in.'

That was when it occurred to Liv that maybe Saturday wasn't the first time Larry had been here. With a key he'd have been free to come and go whenever the house was empty – or whenever he *believed* it was empty. Not a pleasant thought. She looked at Aline, but Aline refused to meet her gaze. They might both be thinking the same thing – they probably were – but Aline wasn't prepared to take sides against Dora.

'Anyway,' Dora said, 'I'll have the lock changed first thing tomorrow if it makes you both feel better.'

Aline nodded. 'Good. And I think we should all agree to keep quiet about ... well, about all of this for now. We don't know anything for sure, and no good's going to come from spreading it around. If Larry was here, *if* he was, he'll be well gone by now.'

Liv knew that what Aline meant by 'all' was *her*. But she wasn't going to go shooting her mouth off. Despite her suspicions over what Larry might have done, there was no firm evidence against him. She reached out a hand and touched Dora lightly on the arm. 'I won't say anything. I promise.'

Aline looked pointedly at Liv. 'It's for the best. I mean, we all have our secrets, don't we?'

Liv's eyes widened. And suddenly she thought, Aline *knows*, she knows about what my dad did. Her chest tightened as she pulled in a breath and said, 'Do we?'

'I saw those papers you had in your room, all that information about Lord Carbrooke. Now some people might find that odd, dubious even, but I'm not the sort to poke my nose into other people's business.'

Liv almost laughed with relief, and the lies tripped easily off her tongue. 'As it happens there's nothing dubious about it. Lord Carbrooke needed a secretary and the employment agency thought I might be suitable. *They* gave me those papers. They said I should know something about him before I went for an interview.'

'You?' Aline said mockingly. 'Working for a lord? That doesn't sound very likely.'

'Why not? I'm as good as anyone else.'

Aline arched her eyebrows.

'Ask the agency if you don't believe me. Anyway, this other job came up and so ...' Liv gave a shrug. She resented the attempt to coerce her into silence, but also understood that in her clumsy way Aline was just trying to protect Dora. 'I've said I'll keep quiet about all this and I will. There's no need to try and force me.'

Dora's eyes, slightly liquid, were fixed on the photograph of her son. 'Poor boy. Nothing ever did go right for him.'

Liv felt a sudden need to get out of the room, to get away from the pain and sorrow. It was like a great weight bearing down on her. Her capacity for keeping secrets was pushing at its limit, but one more wasn't going to make much difference. Quickly she rose to her feet and looked at her landlady. 'You can trust me, Dora. Thank you for explaining about Larry. I know it can't have been easy.'

Dora nodded, smiling weakly. 'You're a good girl, Liv.'

Liv went upstairs, kicked off her shoes, lay down on the bed and stared up at the ceiling. She put her hands behind her head and thought about Larry. It was a lot to take in. For all Dora's denials, it was odds on that he'd been the man she'd disturbed. Innocent or guilty of murder? She had no way of knowing. But if he had killed the girl then he could have killed Moll, too. She shivered at the awfulness of it all.

It was then that another thought occurred to her. Ten years. Wasn't that what Dora had said? About ten years since Larry had fled. If that was the case then it was possible that Rosa Palliser had been the victim. And suddenly Liv was faced with a whole new dilemma. If his sister's killer was back in Soho, how could she keep that information from Pally? But she had promised Dora to keep quiet. What to do? Nothing, she decided, until she'd found out the name of the girl. She would ask Aline when she got the opportunity.

It was a mystery why Larry had come back, a terrible risk when he was still wanted. All those years he had spent on the run, always afraid, always looking over his shoulder and then he had returned to the one place where he was in most danger. Why? Because he was sick of running, perhaps, sick of living as a fugitive. But even that, surely, was better than having a noose put round your neck.

Liv half closed her eyes, not wanting to dwell on the prospect of anyone being hanged. *Think about something else.* She knew that Aline hadn't believed her about the Carbrooke papers, but she didn't care. It would not be wise, however, for her to hold on to them. If the law got wind of Larry being in Soho they might come and search the house. There would be no reason for them to poke around in drawers, but that wouldn't necessarily stop them. And explaining why she had a dossier on a lord could prove a touch tricky.

'Get rid of it,' she murmured. 'Do the sensible thing for once.'

She could dump the papers in a bin on her way to work but a safer option, she decided, was to wait until Dora and Aline had gone to bed and then burn them in the living room hearth. Once they were ashes, it would be one less thing to worry about.

Liv stared some more at the ceiling. The room above was empty – Dora had stopped letting it out years ago – but she had a sudden horrifying notion that she might hear the creak of floorboards and the soft tread of footsteps. Who was to say that Larry wasn't hiding somewhere in the house? She had the feeling that she wouldn't sleep too well tonight.

44

It was one of those warm muggy mornings where the sun was shrouded in haze and all the odours of the city – the dust, the fumes, the human sweats and stinks – were intensified, hanging heavily in the air. Despite his perspiration, Ralph was in good spirits as he climbed the stairs to the *West End News*. He'd spent most of last night figuring out his pitch to Arthur Neames and now all he had to do was present it.

The office was quiet and he didn't hesitate. Fortune favours the brave. He walked straight across the room to the door marked EDITOR, raised his hand and knocked.

'Come!'

'Could I have a word?' Ralph said, putting his head round the door. 'Do you have a minute?'

Neames gestured him inside. His face had its usual harried look, grey and strained. On the desk, spread out in front of him, were the preliminary proofs for Thursday's edition of the paper. These would change over the following days – stuff taken out, stuff put in – in a constant cycle of revisions. 'What can I do for you, McCall?'

'There's been an interesting development in the Cynthia Crosby case. I thought you ought to know about it.'

'Has she been found?'

'No, not yet. But I've come across another girl connected to the boyfriend.'

'Ah, *cherchez la femme*,' Neames said. 'Has Mr Dowd been playing the field?'

'No, yes, I don't know yet. Maybe. Except that isn't the interesting thing about her, at least not the only interesting thing. Her name's Liv Anderson.' Ralph waited for some sign of recognition to appear on the editor's face, but nothing happened. This was odd, as Henry would usually keep Neames up to speed with any major story he was working on. 'That name doesn't mean anything to you?'

Neames shook his head. 'Should it?'

Ralph, who had been prepared with a well-rehearsed spiel on how he should be allowed to work alongside Henry on the article, now found himself in an unexpected position.

'Well?' Neames prompted.

'The Paul Teller case. Do you remember? About twenty years ago. He shot Nicky Lister after—'

'Yes, yes, I remember.'

'Well, Liv Anderson is Paul Teller's daughter.'

'Is she indeed.'

'And I'm thinking that she's got quite a tale to tell.'

Neames steepled his fingers against his chin while he considered this. 'But is she prepared to tell it?'

'I can persuade her. But I'll have to move quickly before someone else gets wind of it.'

'So what are you standing there for?'

245

Ralph grinned. 'I'll keep you informed.'

'You do that.'

As he was walking back down the stairs Ralph was convinced that he'd made an impression. Now, perhaps, his editor would finally sit up and take notice. Neames wasn't the effusive sort, not the sort to shower praise on his reporters, but there had definitely been a glint of regard in his eye.

However, there was still one fly in the ointment. What the hell was going on with Henry? Maybe he was still in the early stages with Liv Anderson and was keeping quiet until he had it in the bag. Or maybe there was another reason he hadn't told Neames. There were some reporters who supplemented their salaries by selling stories to other papers under pseudonyms. Maybe Henry was short of a few bob and had made a side deal with one of the nationals.

Ralph would have to act quickly. With Henry temporarily out of the picture, he had the opportunity to snatch the story from under his nose. But first he would have to put the screws on Liv Anderson. She was a girl with secrets and he could use them to his advantage. He had taken a punt last night when he said he'd seen her handing over money to a gangster – but she hadn't denied it. And then there was the Geoff Dowd business. Yes, put all together, there was every reason for her to finally grasp that it was better to work with than against him.

Ralph whistled softly as he walked. Already the bones of the article were forming in his head: the evil deeds of a father, the anguish of a betrayed wife and mother, a haunted childhood. Liv Anderson's life had been cursed almost from the start. And the fact that she now resided in Soho probably spoke for itself. Yes, the story would have everything that was needed for a front-page exclusive: sex, scandal and sensationalism.

45

The dense, dusty air, laden with heat, wrapped around Liv while she walked with Muriel to the café. She felt heavy and drowsy, barely capable of conversation. It was fortunate that Muriel liked the sound of her own voice and was happy to conduct a monologue that consisted mainly of gripes and grumbles about her living arrangements, the weather and travelling on the Tube.

Liv hadn't slept well. She had woken over and over again with her head full of Larry, of Rosa, of Moody, Lincoln and the reporter McCall. It had been about three o'clock in the morning when she'd suddenly had an epiphany. What did it matter if McCall published her name in the paper, if he revealed her as Paul Teller's daughter? No one she cared about would judge her. Publish and be damned! That's what the Duke of Wellington had said when he became the victim of a blackmail attempt. Well, if it was good enough for him, it was good enough for her.

Except in the broad light of day, she didn't feel quite the same level of confidence. All the attention, the finger pointing, the endless gossip. And what if they managed to get hold of a photograph? If Garvie saw it, saw her real name, he'd know she was a fraud and instantly fire her.

'Is everything all right?' Muriel asked. 'You're very quiet.'

'Yes, it's just the heat. It's draining, isn't it?'

They went into Amelia's and took a table by the window. Muriel examined the lunch menu at length, eventually choosing the chicken casserole. Liv ordered the poached fish, a meal that didn't require any effortful chewing. Muriel, made more amenable by the prospect of a free lunch, leaned forward and smiled. 'So, your second day at Garvie and Carr. How are you finding it?'

'Good, thanks. I think I'm getting the hang of things.'

'And how are you finding Mr Garvie?'

Liv tried to mentally shake off her lethargy. The whole purpose of this lunch was to pick Muriel's brains and now she'd been presented with the opportunity she should seize it with both hands. She didn't, however, want to get caught out in an indiscretion that might eventually find its way back to her boss. 'What do *you* think of him?'

Muriel had a quick look round the surrounding tables and checked that no one was earwigging. 'I wouldn't say this to just anyone, but you should watch yourself. There's a reason why his secretaries never stay for long.'

'Wandering hands?' Liv suggested.

'And the rest.'

'Tell me more.'

'You know what some men are like,' Muriel said. 'Always ready to take advantage. He's married, too, although you wouldn't think it. Prudence her name is. She doesn't come into town much, though. They've got a house in the country.'

'So, he's a bit of a womaniser?'

'More than a bit. I'm only telling you this because you seem like a nice girl and I wouldn't like him to take advantage.'

248

Liv knew there wasn't any chance of that, but she nodded and smiled and said, 'Thanks, I appreciate the warning.'

'Now Mr Carr, on the other hand, is a real gent. You don't ever get any funny business with him.'

Liv thought this was said with something almost like regret. She had seen the way Muriel gazed at Stephen Carr, her ardent eyes following him around the office. 'He seems nice.'

'Yes, I couldn't ask for anyone better to work for. He's always been good to me.' Muriel paused and then added, 'He's married too, but I don't think he's happy.'

'What makes you say that?'

'It's just a feeling.'

Liv, who wanted to get back to the subject she was really interested in, said, 'So what happened to Mr Garvie's last secretary?'

'Oh, the usual. Katherine her name was. She was stupid but pretty. They're *all* pretty. She only lasted six months. And, of course, when they leave, he always expects me to pick up the slack and do his typing as well as Mr Carr's. As if I haven't got enough on my plate.'

Liv felt faintly guilty as she said: 'Well, you don't have to worry on that score. I'm not planning on leaving in a hurry.'

'I'm glad to hear it.'

Lunch arrived and while they were eating Muriel returned to grumbling about home and her widowed mother. Liv made some suitably sympathetic noises. It was clear that Muriel was one of those disappointed women who had hoped for much from life and received, to date, very little. As she got older, even the prospect of marriage was slipping through her fingers.

Liv encouraged her to let off steam for a while before turning the conversation back to Garvie & Carr. 'This Yelland Yard development sounds big.'

'If it ever happens.'

'You don't think it will?'

Muriel gave a sniff and wrinkled her nose. 'Mr Garvie has grand ambitions, but he's still got to get it past the planning committee and get all the tenants out of the properties on Bridle Lane. Some of those houses – the ones that back on to the yard – will have to be knocked down.'

'Bridle Lane. Wasn't that where Moll Ainsworth lived?'

'I hate to speak ill of the dead,' Muriel said, with no visible signs of regret, 'but that one was always a troublemaker. She was given notice, but didn't want to move. And she was whipping all the other tenants up, too, going on about their rights and the rest of it. I mean, it's hardly Buckingham Palace, is it? You'd think they'd be glad to get out of the place.'

It instantly crossed Liv's mind that there could be a connection between Moll Ainsworth's murder and Garvie's redevelopment. With Moll out of the way, the path would be clear to evict the other tenants. But would he really go as far as to kill her? Well, when it came to big money, to big schemes, there was no saying what he would or wouldn't be capable of. Although it was, she had to admit, a bit of a leap from being an unpleasant letch to a full-blown murderer.

'Is it hard to evict tenants, then?' Liv asked casually.

'Not for the likes of Welch. He's a highly unpleasant man, as I'm sure you've already gathered.'

'Yes, he doesn't strike me as the amiable sort.'

'He's the sort who likes to throw his weight around.'

'I can imagine.'

'Shall we have a cup of tea?' Muriel said.

Liv was busy until four o'clock, when Garvie left for a late meeting and Muriel went to the post office. As soon as the coast was clear she grabbed the phone book and started hunting through the Fs. She found five Forsters but only one Richard. It was a Mayfair address – Berkeley Street – which sounded feasible. After scribbling down the details she put the slip of paper in her bag. Despite Henry's warning to stay away from Irene, Liv just couldn't. She had to see her. She had to try and get the answers she so desperately needed.

46

Liv was in the middle of mentally composing a letter, turning words and sentences over in her head and trying to arrange them into a cogent and persuasive argument as to why Irene Forster should agree to see her, when her efforts were abruptly interrupted. Ralph McCall stepped out from a shop doorway and started walking by her side.

'Hello, Liv. How are you today?'

'What are you doing here?'

'You know what. I said I'd see you soon. Now you've had time to think it over, what do you reckon to my proposition?'

Liv would have liked to tell him to shove his proposition where the sun didn't shine, but there was too much at stake. She couldn't afford to antagonise him. Publish and be damned was all very well under certain circumstances, but hers were complicated by the debt she owed to Moody. No, she had to keep him on side until she could get in touch with Henry and see if there was a way to scupper his plans.

'Time to think it over?' she said. 'It was only yesterday. I've barely had time to *start* thinking about it.'

'So how long do you need?'

Liv did her best to sound amenable. 'A few days. You can grant me that, can't you? This isn't a decision I can make overnight.'

McCall eyed her suspiciously. 'Don't try and play me. I wasn't born yesterday.'

'I'm not. I swear. You think I want to be splashed all over the papers in connection to Geoff Dowd? I mean, I barely know the bloke. You keep me out of all that and maybe we can make some kind of deal.'

'I can keep you out of it for this week,' he said. 'But after that ... well, it's up to you.'

Liv was relieved – at least it would take them past this week's edition of the *West End News* – and she forced a smile. 'Just a few days,' she said again. 'I need to get my head around it all.'

'And what about Henry Squires?'

'What about him?'

'Haven't you two got some kind of deal?'

Liv shrugged, trying to look cynical. 'Nothing on paper. Nothing signed. Let's meet up on Friday.'

'Where? How about Joe's?'

'No, not Joe's,' she said, remembering that she was supposed to meet Lincoln there. 'Amelia's. Do you know it?'

McCall nodded. 'Six o'clock?'

'Six is fine,' she said, edging away. 'I'll see you there.'

'And come on your own. Just you and me, yeah?'

'Just us,' she agreed.

Liv carried on walking to Whitcomb Street, checked that McCall wasn't on her tail, hurried straight past the house and went to the phone box on the corner. She put through a call to the *West End News* and asked the man who answered when Henry would be back.

'Thursday, I believe,' he said. 'Thursday morning. Would you like to leave a message?'

'No, that's all right. Thanks for your help.' She said goodbye and rang off, praying that Henry would follow his usual routine and she'd be able to find him propping up the bar in the Eagle on Thursday. If he didn't show then her only other options were to hang around outside the newspaper office – risky in case McCall saw her – or write another note. She was taking a chance even going to the Eagle. What if McCall was there, or one of Lincoln's spies?

As Liv made her way back to the house, she wondered how her life had suddenly got so complicated. Now she was juggling too many problems and keeping too many secrets. She longed for those days when everything had been simple. Well, relatively simple. No Moody to worry about, no Garvie, no Ralph McCall or Larry. It was odd, scary, how much could change in the blink of an eye.

Liv arrived home and tried to open the door, but the key wouldn't turn. Then she remembered about Dora changing the locks. She knocked on the door and after a short wait Aline opened it.

'Oh, it's you,' Aline said, as if she'd been hoping for someone more interesting. 'The new key is on the kitchen table. Try not to lose it. Verity's already got hers. The man came this morning before she left for work.'

Liv went through to the back, picked up the key and put it in her purse. 'No Dora?' she asked.

'She's just nipped out to post her pools coupon. I told her I'd do it in the morning but she said she wanted some fresh air.'

With Dora being out of the way, Liv grabbed the opportunity

to get some answers to the questions weighing on her mind. 'Erm ... Aline, did you know Larry? Were you living here when ... well, you know, when it all happened?'

'What do you want to know that for?' Aline answered sharply.

'I was just wondering.'

'I thought we'd agreed to keep quiet about that business.'

'We did. I will. To other people. But there's nothing to stop us talking to each other, is there?'

'Dora wouldn't want us gossiping.'

'It's not gossiping. I'm being asked to keep a secret – which I'm happy to do – but a few facts wouldn't go amiss. I was the one Larry virtually assaulted, remember? I was the one who got all my jewellery nicked.'

'*If* it was him. Dora doesn't think so.'

'But you do.'

Aline didn't deny it. 'Well, whatever. He won't be coming back, will he? Not now the locks have been changed.'

'What I don't understand is why Larry would creep around like that. If he needed help, money, why wouldn't he just ask Dora? She's his mother, after all. She's not going to turn him away, or turn him in, no matter what he's been accused of.'

'Because he's trouble, that's why. Never ask for something if you can just take it. That was always Larry's mantra. And I dare say he was worried that she might let something slip. Safer to just come in and help himself.'

'Poor Dora,' Liv said. 'She must be desperate to see him again.'

'She's better off without him.'

Liv doubted if this was Dora's opinion, but she didn't challenge it. She had one last question to ask and she tried to make it sound casual. 'So what was that girl called, you know, the one he was accused of ... the one who was killed?'

'What difference does it make what she was called?'

'I'm just curious.'

'I don't recall.'

Liv didn't believe her but seeing that she wasn't going to volunteer the name, decided on a different tack. 'It wasn't Rosa, was it?'

But Aline never got the chance to answer. There was the sound of the front door opening and closing and then the clip of Dora's footsteps on the lino.

47

Liv, disappointed, said hello to Dora and went on up to her room. Frustration gnawed at her. She should have asked about Rosa straight out instead of going around the houses. Now she would have to wait until she could get Aline alone again, although even then there was no saying that the woman could be persuaded to resume the conversation. It had been an opportunity missed. Still, it saved her from the dilemma of whether she should tell Pally or not. What she didn't know she couldn't feel guilty about.

Liv glanced around. Ever since Larry had been here, she hadn't been able to properly relax. She kept imagining him going through her things, rummaging in drawers and through her clothes. It was as though he had left an indelible stain on the place. She had given the room a good clean, but no amount of elbow grease could scrub away that sense of violation.

She gave herself a mental shake – there was no point dwelling on what couldn't be changed – and walked over to the dressing table. She opened the drawer, took out the cuttings on the killing of Nicky Lister, sat down on the bed and started to look through them again. Unwilling to reread the lurid details of the actual murder, she skipped to the latter part of the pile, where Henry had included some general information on the Listers.

Of the two, Nicky came across as the more interesting: a clever man, Cambridge educated, who had liked to work and play in equal measure. He'd been involved in politics, had clearly possessed a social conscience and had even, ironically, campaigned against the death penalty. Liv gave a wry smile at this nugget of information. At his club he had encouraged a diverse crowd, everyone from MPs, lords and ladies, to writers, artists and showgirls. The word charming cropped up more than once.

Irene, however, was defined mainly by her beauty, although this was probably more a reflection of the attitudes of the reporters than any deficiency on her part. She had, apparently, been a talented actress but less emphasis was placed on this than the loveliness of her features. Liv thought there must be more to her, that an intelligent man like her father couldn't be so besotted as to lose all sense of reason in the presence of a pretty face. But then again, she could be wrong. If her own experiences had taught her anything it was that physical desire could be a potent force.

At the bottom of the pile Liv came across a small piece on the marriage of Irene Lister to Richard Forster in 1940, three years after the murder. By then, of course, Irene's career had been on the rocks with no one wanting to employ an actress who had been so closely associated with a major scandal. Forster, a City banker, was twelve years older than her. Had she married for money? But Nicky must have left her well provided for. Perhaps she was just one of those women who couldn't bear to be alone.

Liv knew that she was making random judgements. She disliked Irene without even knowing her. But that was because the woman's version of events just didn't ring true. There must have been something going on with her father, something to have triggered such a cataclysmic reaction. If her father was mad, she thought, then Irene had helped to make him that way.

Until she got answers, Liv wasn't going to let it rest. And there was only one person who had those answers. She had to meet Irene face to face, look her in the eye and ask all those difficult questions. But getting her to agree to see her wasn't likely to be easy. Why would Irene want to meet the daughter of the man who'd murdered her husband? Especially if she had something to hide. But none of this was going to deter Liv. If you didn't ask, you didn't get.

For the next half-hour, she worked on a letter, writing and rewriting, trying to figure out not just the right words but the right tone, too. She chewed the end of her pencil, sighed and scribbled. She constructed draft after draft, dismissing each one as inadequate. Eventually she settled on a version that, if not entirely perfect, seemed at least marginally better than the rest. After carefully printing her address, she wrote:

Dear Mrs Forster,

I apologise for writing to you out of the blue. My name is Liv Anderson and I am Paul Teller's daughter. It was only recently that I discovered the truth about my father and, as you can imagine, it came as a great shock. Would you be kind enough to agree to a meeting? It would help me so much if I was able to talk to you.

Yours sincerely,

Liv Anderson

Liv stood up, carried her notebook over to the dressing table, sat down and neatly copied out the letter on to the fancy writing paper she had snaffled from work. The heavy pale blue paper would hopefully make a good impression. She pondered on whether she should use the name Olivia, but decided that her father – if he had ever talked about her – was more likely to have called her Liv.

She stared at the letter for a long time, decided that it would have to do, folded it over and placed it in an envelope. On the front she wrote out the address she had got from the telephone directory. If it was wrong, it was wrong, but she didn't think it was. The Mayfair connection was too much of a coincidence.

Liv couldn't imagine Irene welcoming the correspondence, but prayed she would have the decency to reply. Until then she would have to be patient. She would post the letter tomorrow morning and it should get there by Thursday. She stood up and put the envelope in her bag. Then – patience not being her strong point – she had a better idea. If she walked to the main post office, she could catch the last pick-up tonight. Why not? She slung her bag over her shoulder and headed out again.

48

Slug woke up on Wednesday morning with a good feeling in his guts. It was cool in the cellar and he'd slept well, his night undisturbed by scurrying mice or restless dreams. He yawned, got up, went out into the garden for a piss, went back inside and thought about the day ahead. Because he knew that on some occasions a certain level of respectability was required, he sought out the piece of broken mirror and placed it on the ledge near the open door. He examined his reflection in a disinterested kind of way, studying the lined, ageing face with its greyish skin, drooping jowls and thin lips. None of this bothered him. He saw it as no more than a mask, an artful subterfuge that enabled him to go about his business undetected.

With a blackened fingernail he picked out the gunk from the corners of his eyes, spat into his palm and smoothed down his hair. Once he was satisfied that no further improvement could be made to what God had given him, he changed into the cleaner of the two pairs of trousers he owned and chose a shirt that, if not entirely spotless, at least had fewer stains than the others.

Slug walked to the cheapest café in the neighbourhood and treated himself to bacon and eggs. He still had money in his pocket and, with luck, would have even more before the day was over. There was no one of any interest to him in the room – villains, on the whole, tended to keep late hours – and he ate his breakfast without any distractions.

It was still early when he left and so he tramped the streets until he felt that the time was right. As he sauntered along Whitcomb Street he looked up at the sky, longing for rain, for a cooling of the air, but there was no sign of any imminent change in the weather. He was not fond of the heat – it made his skin prickle and itch – and he could feel a wet trickle of sweat slipping down the back of his neck and under his collar.

Slug approached the house and gave a couple of raps on the door. He was counting on the lodgers being at work by now. This had been a boarding house for years and, as he'd hoped, it was the landlady who eventually answered his knock. She was a small, plump thing with worry in her eyes. Dora her name was, but he was careful not to be overly familiar.

'Mrs Marks?' he said politely. 'I wonder if you could spare me a few minutes?'

She looked him up and down suspiciously. 'Whatever you're selling, I don't want it.'

'I think you might be interested,' he said quickly, before she could slam the door in his face. 'It's about your Larry.'

The woman's mouth fell open and shock registered on her face. 'Larry? What? What about him?'

Slug made a show of glancing towards the neighbours' windows and lowered his voice. 'Perhaps we should continue this inside.'

'Larry doesn't live here any more.'

Slyness crept into Slug's tone. 'Not here exactly, but maybe not so far away.'

'You're talking nonsense. Clear off! I haven't got time for this.'

But Slug wasn't fooled by her bluster. She was afraid – he could see it, smell it – and he closed in for the kill. 'I saw him with my own eyes, Mrs Marks, just like poor old Moll did. In the Black Bull it was. Now you and me could talk this over in a civilised fashion or I could just pop on down to West End Central and let them know the good news. Your choice. What's it to be?'

Dora's face had gone pale. 'What are you after?'

'It's hot out here, Mrs Marks. I reckon we'd be more comfortable inside.'

Dora hesitated, clearly weighing up in her mind the option of calling his bluff and the possible consequences of such an action. Eventually, reluctantly, she stood aside.

Slug smugly entered the coolness of the house. He followed her through to the kitchen where he sat down at the table and looked pointedly at the kettle. 'A brew wouldn't go amiss.' He wiped his brow with the heel of hand. 'It's thirsty work walking those streets.'

'Whatever you want to say, say it. Just spit it out. I haven't got all day.'

But Slug wasn't going to be rushed. His gaze flitted over the kitchen – the stove, the cupboards, the shelves with their rows of pots and pans – before finally coming back to rest on Dora. 'Ain't you going to sit down?'

Dora remained standing. She folded her arms across her chest and glared at him. 'You may have thought you saw my Larry, but you're mistaken. He'd never come back here. Why would he?'

'It's a risk, that's for certain,' Slug said. 'But I can only tell you what I saw with my own two eyes. I'm good with faces. I remember people. And your Larry's pretty memorable, what

263

with his mug being splashed all over the papers back then. Ten years, is it? Something like that. Moll got a real good look at him, too. But I'm sure she told you that before . . . well, we don't want to dwell on that. Just a coincidence, I'm sure.'

'Larry had nothing to do with that. And even if he was here – and I'm not saying that he was – he'll be well gone by now. So you're wasting your time. Whatever you're after, I'm not giving it to you.'

'Best not to be hasty,' Slug said. 'The way I see it, the minute the law hears about Larry being spotted, they'll be crawling all over Soho. Bad news for him if he hasn't scarpered yet. They'll be turning this place over too, no doubt. And watching the house day and night just in case he shows his face.' Slug smirked. 'Do you really want to spend all those hours down the nick, love? They'll give you a grilling. It's a lot of trouble just for the sake of a few quid.'

'I won't be blackmailed by the likes of you,' Dora said.

Slug raised his hands in mock horror. 'Who's talking about blackmail? No one. All I'm suggesting is a little recompense for my trouble. That's fair enough, ain't it? I could just as easily have gone down the nick and told 'em what I saw. Civic duty, that's what they call it . . . although there might be some small reward for information leading to the capture of a felon. Now I'm sure your Larry never did nothin' to poor Moll, but it ain't going to look good for him, especially when he's still wanted over that girl.'

'You go and tell them, then. See if I care.'

Dora Marks spoke with bravado, but he could tell her heart wasn't in it. Slug continued to twist the knife. 'Still, I don't suppose you'd ever forgive yourself if the coppers did catch up with him. It's how it looks to that lot, not how it really is. Innocent or guilty, what do they care? So long as someone gets

264

done for it, that's good enough. And your Larry taking off like that all them years ago ain't going to impress them none.' Slug paused for breath, checked that Dora was hanging on his every word – she was – and knew that he was on the verge of victory. 'But it's up to you. No pressure. I'm not *demanding* nothin'. All I'm saying is that a friendly arrangement couldn't do neither of us any harm, or Larry, come to that.'

'I know your sort,' Dora said. 'I give you a few quid and next week you'll be back for more.'

'Ah, you've got me all wrong. What's fair is fair. I ain't the greedy sort. Shall we call it a tenner?'

'You think I've got ten quid lying around? We'll call it five and not a penny more, and that's only for the sake of my lodgers. They've had enough upset recently without a load of coppers tramping through their rooms. But if you come near here again, if you even so much as knock on the door, I'll be straight down the station myself. There's a law against blackmail. Do we understand each other?'

Slug reckoned she was bluffing, but wouldn't have bet his life on it. Although he'd hoped for more than a fiver, it was five pounds more than he'd arrived with. He reached out a grubby, greedy hand. 'Pleasure doing business with you, Mrs Marks.'

49

Dora closed the door, went through to the living room and from behind net curtains watched the man shamble off along the street. Only when she was sure he was far enough away, did she go back into the hall and call softly up towards the first-floor landing: 'He's gone now, love. You can come down.'

Larry descended cautiously, one hand gripping the banister. He was thinner than he had been, his skin grey, his body ravaged by too many years of sleeping rough. His clothes were ragged and he smelled of everything bad. 'You shouldn't have given the old bastard money.'

'He'd have gone to the law just to spite me. It's better this way.'

'He might go to the law anyway. I should get out of here.'

But Dora wasn't prepared to relinquish her son so soon. 'He won't. I can feel it. He's got what he wanted.' When Larry reached the bottom of the stairs, she stretched out a hand and touched his arm. 'This is where you belong. Come on, I'll make you something to eat. You look half starved.'

'What if someone else comes, one of the lodgers?'

'They're all out at work. It'll be hours yet before they're home.'

'You shouldn't have answered the door.'

'If I hadn't, he'd have come back later. At least it's over and done with.'

Dora shot fast nervous glances towards her boy as she lit the stove, put some lard in a pan and began frying sausages. She was afraid he'd stand up and walk out, disappear again. There was so much she needed to ask, so many questions, but she didn't want to scare him off. It was only fifteen minutes since he'd turned up at the rear of the house – he must have come over the wall – and knocked lightly on the back door.

'I can't stay here for ever.'

'No one's saying for ever. A few days, a week, just until you're back on your feet. You're not well. Anyone can see that. I bet you haven't had a square meal in months.'

Larry shifted in the chair, his posture tight and tense as if preparing for flight. 'I don't trust the man. How did he know I was here? He must have been following me.'

'He doesn't know. Relax. If he did, he wouldn't have settled for a fiver. No, he was just counting on the fact I wouldn't want the law here, wouldn't want the neighbours' tongues wagging. And that I wouldn't want a load of coppers searching Soho on the off chance you might still be hanging around.'

'I shouldn't have come back.'

'You're here now. Although why you didn't come sooner is beyond me.'

'I was going to. I meant to.' Larry raked his fingers through his unkempt hair. 'But then I got to thinking that I'd only be bringing you trouble. If they find me here – the law – you'll be done as an accessory.'

'You think I care about that? What mother wouldn't offer her son food and shelter? And you never did anything wrong.

It wasn't fair, none of it.' She thought of all the sleepless nights she'd lain in bed praying that somewhere, somehow, Larry had managed to make a new life for himself, and understood now that all the praying had been in vain. 'You want a couple of eggs to go with this?'

'Might as well. I suppose Moll told you she'd seen me in the Black Bull.'

'She did,' Dora said. 'God rest her soul. Not that I needed her to. I knew you were close by. I read it in the cards.'

'In the cards, huh?'

Dora heard the scepticism in his voice, but didn't react. Instead she asked tentatively, 'Were you worried that she'd seen you?'

Larry's eyes grew wary. 'I didn't do her in if that's what you're getting at.'

'Of course you didn't. For God's sake, why would you? Moll wouldn't have told anyone else. You know that.'

'So why are you asking.'

'All I was thinking was that it must have been a shock for you, seeing her there and knowing that she'd recognised you.' Dora sighed. 'I've been out looking for you every chance I got. I searched all over the place. Where have you been sleeping?'

'Here and there.'

'I'll run you a bath after you've eaten, then we can get you into some clean clothes. I kept everything you left behind. There are shirts and trousers and a pair of shoes. We can bring the mattress down from the empty room upstairs and put it on the floor in my room. You'll be comfy enough. And safe. No one goes in there but me. You'll have to take care, mind, when the others are home. Aline's got sharp ears; she can hear a pin drop.'

'That cow never liked me,' he said sourly.

'Aline doesn't like anyone much. It's just her way.'

Dora finished frying, put the plate in front of him and poured out two mugs of tea. She sat opposite and watched while he ate, feeling the warmth a mother feels when they're able to put food in their child's belly. For a while she was almost content. There was something she had to say, though. She knew she had to speak up, clear the air, but waited until his plate was clean and he'd lit a cigarette.

Dora got to her feet, opened the back door to let the smoke out and sat back down again. She took a quick breath and tried to keep her voice mild. 'You shouldn't have taken that jewellery from Liv's room. I'd have given you money if you'd come to me.'

'What?'

'On Saturday. You think I don't know when my own son's been in the house? She's a nice girl, decent. I reckon you had your reasons, but you shouldn't have taken her stuff.'

Larry shook his head, his eyes staring defiantly into hers. 'I don't have a clue what you're going on about, Mum. I haven't nicked nothing. I swear. This is the first time I've been here since I went.'

Dora knew when he was lying. As a kid he'd swear blind he hadn't done anything wrong, obstinately refusing to confess even when he was caught red-handed. But she wasn't going to call him on it. Later, when he was in the bath, she'd search through his pockets and see if she could find a pawn ticket. For now, she wanted to let all the bad things go, to be happy, to revel in his presence and pretend that everything was normal.

50

Liv spent most of Wednesday morning typing out contracts for new West End rentals. The law had been busy at the weekend, raiding a number of illegal gambling joints and closing them down. Now the club owners were looking for other properties in which to set up business again. She was aware of how it worked. Everyone in Soho knew, including the police: a local villain would rent out a property in the name of a so-called 'manager', pay the fine when the club was raided, and then immediately rent out another property under a different manager's name. And on it went in a never-ending cycle.

There were a lot of bent coppers in the West End, taking regular backhanders and turning a blind eye, but they still had to be seen to be upholding the law. Tip-offs were provided for when a raid was to take place so the villain in question could make himself scarce. It was a minor inconvenience for them – they would soon be up and running again – and a profitable state of affairs for Garvie, who was able to charge a hefty agent's fee every time a new contract was signed.

Thinking of the law reminded Liv of DI Bentley and her worries that he might turn up at the office out of the blue. She frequently glanced out of the window in case she spotted him strolling across the square. And what then? She could go and hide in the toilet until he'd left, but this was only feasible if his visit was a fleeting one. She could rush outside and intercept him before he even entered the building, but what was she to say? Admitting that she'd taken the job under a false name was hardly going to make for an easy conversation, especially when she couldn't think of a legitimate reason as to why she would have done such a thing.

Liv's anxiety remained with her all morning and her mood wasn't improved by Garvie's unexpected revelation in the early afternoon. She was about to leave his office, halfway to her feet, when he gestured for her to sit down again.

He steepled his fingers and looked serious, peering sternly across the desk. 'I have something rather important to discuss with you.'

Liv, fearing her deception had been discovered, felt her stomach shift. 'Important?'

Garvie continued staring for a moment and then finally said: 'A conference. I have a business conference this weekend in Essex.'

'Oh,' Liv said, relieved.

'I'm sorry this is such short notice, but I *will* need you there. If all goes well there will be agreements to be typed up. In matters of business I like to strike while the iron's hot.'

'Oh,' Liv said again, her relief short-lived.

'It *is* purely business,' Garvie insisted. 'I don't want you to be concerned on that score. I'm not the sort of boss who tries to take advantage.'

Liv thought he was precisely the sort of boss to try and take advantage, but she quickly shook her head. 'No, no, of course not. Only ... only the trouble is, I've already made plans for the weekend.'

Garvie was undeterred. 'And do you think you could possibly see your way to changing them? It's a liberty, I know, but I really can't do without a secretary.'

'What about Muriel?'

Garvie's face twisted a little. 'The truth is, Olivia, it's you I need with me. Lord Carbrooke is going to be attending and seeing as you used to work for him you could be – how shall I put it? – a useful go-between, perhaps. As you're aware he's a very influential man and I'm hoping to garner his support on the Yelland Yard development. Your presence might help smooth the path. A man like that has friends in high places. A word in the right ear and ... well, you're a clever girl, I'm sure you get what I mean.'

Liv felt like laughing in a rather hysterical way. Lord Carbrooke didn't know her from Adam. He might have written her a reference – under duress – but he had no idea what she looked like. The appalling prospect of coming face to face with him and there being not a flicker of recognition was not only mortifying but verging on the ridiculous. No, it wouldn't do. She would have to find a way to wriggle out of it. Not right now, though. She had to at least pretend to be making an effort to alter her arrangements.

'I understand. I'll see what I can do.'

'That's the spirit. Good girl. I knew I could rely on you.' And then, as if she'd already agreed to it all, he said: 'I'll pick you up on Saturday morning. About nine o'clock suit you? The traffic shouldn't be too bad.'

'Erm, I can't be absolutely sure that—'

'You'll sort it out. I've got every faith in you. Do you swim?'

Liv, thinking she must have misheard, gazed back at him, bemused. 'Pardon?'

'There's an outdoor pool at Hollinghurst. You should bring a costume. If the weather keeps up, you'll be able to have a dip. We won't be working all weekend.'

'No,' she lied. 'I can't swim.'

'A spot of sunbathing, then. There's not much opportunity for that in London. I always find the country air refreshing. It blows the cobwebs away, don't you think?'

'I dare say it does.'

'Yes, there's nothing like a couple of days in the country.' Garvie nodded, shuffled the papers on his desk, smiled brightly and dismissed her. 'Right, if you could get those letters in the post this afternoon . . .'

'Of course.'

Liv walked back along the corridor, her mind racing. Most of her thoughts were occupied by the dilemma of how to avoid the weekend away without jeopardising her job, a smaller proportion by Garvie's pathetic and somewhat creepy desire to get her into a swimsuit. She was frowning as she went into the front office and sat down at her desk.

'Muriel, do you know anything about this conference at Hollinghurst?'

'They have a few of them every summer.' Muriel pursed her scarlet lips in a disapproving way. 'Has he asked you to go with him?'

'He has, but it's rather short notice. I've already made plans, so . . .'

'He won't like it if you say no.'

'Yes, I got that impression. Have you ever been there?'

'Lord, no,' Muriel said. 'It isn't Mr Carr's thing at all.' She inclined her head slightly, making sure there was no sound that might indicate either of the bosses emerging from their offices, before adding softly, 'From all accounts there's more boozing than business, but that's only what I've heard.'

What she'd heard, Liv presumed, from Garvie's previous secretaries. 'Really?'

Muriel gave a grim smile, opened her mouth as if to elaborate, but was instantly stopped in her tracks by the ringing of the phone. 'Yes, Mr Carr . . . yes, I understand. I'll be right there.' And with that she swept up some papers from her desk and hurried off down the corridor.

Liv began typing up Garvie's correspondence, working as quickly as she could. Once the letters were done, she got them signed, put them in envelopes and dashed out of the building. If Garvie questioned her absence – she was hoping he wouldn't even notice it – she would claim she had thought the mail was urgent and had taken it to the post office straight away.

She dropped the letters in the first pillar box she came to and strode smartly on to the phone box on the corner. After pulling her notebook from her bag, she quickly flipped to the page where she had written down the number, dialled, listened to the ringing, waited for the pips to go and slid a coin into the slot.

'Paradise.'

Had Liv been in a better frame of mind, she might have been amused by the thought of reaching paradise so easily, but she was too agitated at the moment to appreciate the humour. 'Is Mr Lincoln there, please?'

'Sorry, love. He's not around at the moment.'

Liv heaved out a sigh of exasperation. 'Could you give him a message, please? Could you tell him Liv called? I need to see him urgently. I'll be in Joe's at half past five.'

'Yeah,' the man said. 'Liv, right?'

'At Joe's,' she repeated loudly. 'Half past five.'

'I heard you,' he said.

'Do you think he'll be back by then?'

'Couldn't tell you, love. He don't run all his comings and goings past me.'

'Well, if you could pass on the message when you do see him, I'd appreciate it.'

'I'll do that.'

'Thank you,' Liv said through gritted teeth, not entirely convinced that Lincoln would ever receive the information. 'Goodbye, then.'

The man hung up without saying goodbye back.

Liv placed the receiver on the hook, quietly cursed and stepped out of the phone box. Would Lincoln show up? She could only wait and see. It was going to be a long afternoon.

51

Liv was at Joe's by twenty past five, drinking a cup of coffee while she stared out of the window, impatiently waiting for Lincoln. She was relieved that Pally wasn't there and hoped it would stay that way. The last thing she needed was a confrontation between the two of them: Pally had enough cuts and bruises without adding any more to the collection. She sighed, longing for the good old days when she could do what she liked and wasn't at anyone's beck and call.

Five-thirty came and went and there was no sign. How long should she give him? Another half-hour, she decided. If he wasn't here by six, he probably wouldn't be coming. The bloke at the Paradise could easily have forgotten her message as soon as he'd put the phone down. Or maybe Lincoln hadn't gone back to the club yet. Either way it was pointless sitting in Joe's if he wasn't going to turn up.

At five to six, just as Liv was on the verge of leaving, Lincoln casually strolled in and sat down opposite her. By now she was feeling decidedly hot and bothered, while he looked irritatingly cool in his pale grey suit.

'So, what's the big emergency?'

'We've got a problem,' she said. 'There's a business conference this weekend at a place called Hollinghurst. Garvie wants me to go with him.'

Lincoln grinned. 'Good.'

'Good?'

He winked at her. 'I hear people get up to all sorts at these *business* conferences.'

Liv, annoyed, gave a snort. 'Well he won't be getting up to anything with me, I can tell you that for nothing.'

'Is that why you got me here? Christ, I thought it was something important.'

'I'm not some bloody tart,' she hissed. 'This was never part of the deal.'

'For God's sake, no one's asking to get your knickers off. What's the matter with you? I thought you could handle the likes of Garvie. I mean, you're hardly Miss Innocent, are you?'

Liv glared at him. 'You're really something else, you know that? And yes, I can deal with the likes of Garvie but that's not the problem. Lord Carbrooke is going to be there and seeing as we've never met that might just make for a slightly awkward situation.'

'Why didn't you say that in the first place?' Lincoln stood up and looked down at her. 'Come on.'

'Come on where?'

'Charing Cross Road. You want to get this sorted or not? I know a photographer there. He can take a few snaps, I can pass them on to Carbrooke and—'

Liv shrank back. 'No, no photos. I'm not having any photos taken.' Ralph McCall had suddenly sprung into her head – what *he* wouldn't do for a snap of her – and she couldn't take the chance of the pictures falling into the wrong hands. 'If I go, you'll just have to describe me to him.'

'What do you mean *if* you go?'

'I don't think it's a good idea.'

Lincoln sat back down, put his elbows on the table and glowered at her. 'Is that what you want me to tell Mr Moody?'

'I'm trying to do the smart thing here. Would he really want Garvie to find out I'm not who I say I am? I'll be out the door in five minutes flat. It's not worth the risk.'

'There wouldn't be any risk if we got some photos.'

'No,' she said firmly.

'Why not? Give me one good reason?'

'Because I don't *want* to have my picture taken, all right?'

'That's not even a reason.' Lincoln shook his head. 'Jesus, you don't like to make things easy.'

A simmering silence fell over the table. Liv was determined to stand her ground but she could tell it wasn't going down well. 'Anyway, what if Lord Carbrooke doesn't want to play along? It's one thing writing a dodgy reference, but he's going to have to lie in front of everybody.'

'You leave Carbrooke to me. He won't be a problem. You think he's never lied before? We'll just have to find a way round this. Tell me what you're going to wear on Saturday.'

'I haven't thought about it.'

'So think about it now.'

Liv, who was rapidly resigning herself to the fact she wouldn't be able to wriggle out of the weekend, made a mental review of her wardrobe. 'I could wear my dark red dress, I suppose.'

'And jewellery?'

'Now that's going to be tricky. Some burglar nicked all my decent stuff on Saturday.' Liv could see that Lincoln didn't believe her, that he thought she was trying to squeeze money out of him again. 'It's true. I swear. I caught the bugger red-handed. He flew out of my room, knocked me over and scarpered. We had the law round and everything. You can check if you don't believe me.'

'Bad luck just seems to follow you around,' Lincoln said drily.

Liv made a point of staring directly into his eyes. 'You're right. It does.'

At that precise moment the door opened and a noisy group of teenagers came in. They laughed and jostled, spreading themselves around the café and talking loudly to each other. Lincoln threw them a dirty look, but they didn't even notice.

'Let's get out of here. We can finish this somewhere else. I need a drink.'

Liv stood up. 'Not the French. Pally might be there.'

When they were outside, Lincoln said: 'Are you hungry? I'm hungry. Let's go to Wheeler's.'

'It's too expensive,' she said.

'Am I asking you to pay?'

'Well, you didn't exactly make it clear.'

'Dinner,' he said. 'On me. Is that clear enough?'

Liv, who wanted to keep on the right side of him, didn't feel she could refuse. 'In that case, thank you. I'm sure I could manage something.'

'So long as it's fish. They don't do anything else.'

'I know that. I have eaten there before.' In fact, Liv had only ever been there once, months ago, when she and Pally had got extra lucky and been in the money. They'd celebrated by splashing out at Wheeler's. The food was delicious but expensive and she was glad she wouldn't be picking up the bill.

As they walked together down Old Compton Street, Liv thought of another objection to the weekend plans and said:

'Garvie thinks I live in Islington. He'll be expecting to pick me up from the address I gave.'

'Then that's where he'll pick you up from. What time are we talking about?'

'Nine o'clock, he said.'

'Fine. I'll collect you about quarter past eight and we'll drive over there.'

'Don't come to the house,' Liv said. 'I'll meet you on the corner of Coventry Street. My landlady has already spotted you with me once. If she sees you again, she might start asking awkward questions.'

Lincoln's eyebrows shifted up. 'If I didn't know better, I might think you were ashamed of me.'

Liv gave him a brittle smile. 'Ha ha.'

'Coventry Street it is, then. Try not to be late.'

Liv was about to retort that she wasn't the one who'd turned up half an hour late this evening, but bit her tongue. It had been short notice, after all, and he might not have got the message until the meeting time had already passed. And then there was that other small detail of never biting the hand that feeds you. In her present financial circumstances, a free meal – especially one as good as this – wasn't to be sneered at.

52

Wheeler's was quiet inside. It was still early and there were plenty of free tables. The waiter clearly knew Lincoln and fussed around him, smiling widely and asking how he was. Liv sat down and was given a menu. She had a quick look round the room. Everything was much as she remembered it: checked tablecloths, long drapes at the windows and pictures with a maritime theme adorning the walls.

Liv chose the Dover sole. It was what she had eaten last time and she was more than happy to repeat the experience. Lincoln ordered the turbot and a bottle of Sauvignon Blanc. He sat back and said, 'So how it's going with Garvie?'

'Fabulous,' she said. 'It's the job from heaven, especially if you love having a boss who can't take his eyes off your chest.'

'Tiresome, I should imagine.'

'That's one word for it. Anyway, I've taken copies of all his correspondence to date, rentals and contracts and the like, and also dug out the names and addresses of the two secretaries who worked there before me. They might be useful if they're willing to talk. The last one only stayed six months so there's probably a story behind that. I'll give you all the paperwork on Saturday.'

The wine arrived and was poured into glasses. Liv waited until the waiter had gone before resuming her monologue. 'His big project at the moment is the redevelopment of Yelland Yard. You know the place, behind Bridle Lane?' He nodded and she carried on. 'He wants to pull the buildings down and put up an office block, but he's having trouble getting it past the planning committee. Oh, that's something you should warn Lord Carbrooke about. My charming company isn't the only reason Garvie wants to take me to Hollinghurst this weekend. He's hoping to get Carbrooke interested in the project and thinks my history with him could be useful.'

'I'll warn him,' Lincoln said.

'Other than that, there isn't much to report. Garvie's partner, Stephen Carr – he runs the residential side – seems all right. Not the lecherous sort, at least, so that's always a plus. There's another bloke, Ian Welch, who collects the rents. I'm not so sure about him. I'd say he's got a nasty streak.'

'What makes you say that?'

'Just the impression I get. And Muriel – she's Stephen Carr's secretary – doesn't exactly speak highly of him.' Liv took a sip of white wine, a wine that was so good she might have smacked her lips and sighed if she'd been alone. 'Muriel's worked there for years so she's got all the dirt. She was telling me about Moll Ainsworth – you know, the woman who was murdered recently? Apparently, Moll was living in Bridle Lane and causing the business some trouble. Garvie's been trying to evict all the tenants before the Yelland Yard development gets under way, but she wasn't having any of it.'

'You reckon he bumped her off, then?'

Liv sipped some more wine and peered at him over the rim of her glass. 'You can scoff all you like, but stranger things have happened. Especially when there are large sums of money at stake. And no, I'm sure Garvie wouldn't have done it himself, but it's not beyond the bounds of possibility that he got someone else to do it for him.'

'You've been reading too many detective stories.'

'I'm just giving you the facts.'

'The facts?'

'With a few extras thrown in for free.'

The food arrived and the subject of Garvie was dropped while they ate. Lincoln asked how she'd ended up in London and she gave him the same stock response she used for everyone: that her mother had died and she'd wanted a fresh start. He asked about her father and she tried not to flinch. 'He's dead, too.'

'That's tough. You got no other family, then?'

Liv, who was never far from paranoia these days, wondered if the real question he was asking was whether anyone would miss her if she suddenly disappeared. 'Why?'

'I'm just making polite conversation.'

'I've got friends. They look out for me.'

'Glad to hear it. It's always good to have friends.' Lincoln seemed amused, as if he'd guessed what she'd been thinking. 'Talking of which, how's Pally doing these days?'

'How do you imagine?'

'He's been around the block. He'll survive.'

'No thanks to you.'

'Hey, I did you both a favour. If it hadn't been for me, things would have been a lot worse. Moody wasn't happy when he found out what you two had done. I was the one who persuaded him to go easy, who convinced him that there might be a more useful way to deal with the situation.'

'Good of you,' Liv said caustically.

'I wasn't trying to be good – just practical.'

'Why do you work for that man?'

'Why do you work for Pally?'

'I don't. I work *with* him. We're a partnership.'

'For now,' Lincoln said.

'And what's that supposed to mean?'

Lincoln didn't rush to answer. He ate some turbot, drank some wine and put his glass down on the table. 'What I mean,' he said eventually, 'is that you can't play the badger indefinitely. You're going to be too old for it soon.'

'Nice of you to mention it.'

'I'm just being realistic. It's all right for Pally – it doesn't matter how old he looks – but you can't be sweet sixteen for ever. There's going to come a time when . . . well, when he might start looking around for someone younger.'

Liv frowned, resenting him for saying it. She knew that he was trying to stir things up between her and Pally, to get under her skin, to plant doubts in her mind and drive a wedge between them. But he wasn't going to succeed. Pally wouldn't dump her. They were close, partners in crime, in it for the long haul. She cleared the frown and smiled. 'I'm sure we'll figure something out. The badger's not the only game in the book. Anyway, you never answered my question about why you work for Moody.'

'Because it pays well, and it suits me. I'm good at figures and he's not. If you're going to run gambling joints you need to understand percentages. I keep everything running smoothly – and profitably – and in return I get a damn good wage.'

'You could get a damn good wage in the City if you're that brilliant, and without the worry of being arrested.'

'Oh, I never worry about that.'

284

Liv believed him, although she couldn't tell if his answer was based on a high regard for his own abilities or a complete disregard for his personal liberty. 'Have you ever been inside?'

'Only for a short stretch. And it taught me a valuable lesson.'

'Don't get caught?'

'Exactly.'

They talked on for a while until the meal was almost finished. Liv, aware of the relaxing effect of the wine, tried to keep her wits about her. There was no such thing as a free lunch – or, in this case, a free dinner. So yes, all right, he'd wanted to get up to date with the Garvie situation, but they could have had that conversation over a drink in the pub. She sensed there was something more, but couldn't quite put her finger on it. Perhaps he was just making sure that she could be trusted.

'Can I give you a piece of advice?' Lincoln said.

'If you must.'

Lincoln, not appreciating the response, gave her a pained look. 'Once this Garvie business is over, you should think about getting out of Soho. It's not a good place. It eats people up and spits them out.'

'Are you speaking from experience?'

'Yeah, I know what you think: who am I to advise you what to do, right? You don't want to hear it and especially not from me. You're young, smart, and you reckon you can beat the odds. You're sure you won't get dragged down, but everyone does in the end.'

'Why are you telling me this?'

Lincoln sat back with a strange smile on his face. 'Because I've just had a bloody good meal and I'm in a generous frame of mind. You have a look round next time you're in the French or the Gargoyle or any of those other joints you like to frequent.

Underneath all the smiling faces there's nothing but blankness: empty shells, the whole lot of them. I don't know what you're running away from but—'

'I'm not running away from anything,' Liv interrupted, defensively. 'You've got it all wrong. And isn't it a bit hypocritical you sitting there saying I should get out of Soho when you seem perfectly happy to stay here yourself?'

'It's too late for me, but you can still save yourself.'

'You're all heart.'

'I thought you'd never notice.'

Liv wondered if there was anyone more irritating than Tom Lincoln. 'Actually, if you did have a heart you wouldn't make me work for Garvie.'

'No one's making you work for him. It's up to you how you pay your debts.'

'Be good to know how long it's going to take to pay it off, though.'

'You've only done three days.'

'Three *long* days. I'm not cut out for office work. If I knew exactly what Mr Moody wanted, we could wrap this all up much quicker.'

'Haven't we had this conversation before?'

'So?'

'So I'm easily bored.' Lincoln gestured to the waiter for the bill before looking at her again. 'I can't see the point in going over old ground.'

Liv took exception to his dismissive attitude but kept her expression neutral. 'Well, thank you for dinner.'

'Pleasure.'

The bill arrived and Lincoln got out his wallet. He dropped a couple of notes on to the saucer, leaving the change as a substantial tip. They left Wheeler's and stood together on the pavement outside. He glanced at his watch. 'You all right going home on your own?'

'Would I be safer with you?'

Lincoln smiled in a lukewarm sort of way. 'I'll see you on Saturday morning, then.'

Liv replayed parts of the evening as she walked back towards Whitcomb Street. God, Lincoln was a condescending bastard. How dare he accuse her of running away? He didn't have a clue. She had come to London to find out the truth about her father. If anything, she was running *towards* things, facing them head on, confronting the past and all its dreadful consequences. She didn't need some conniving, wise-guy villain making judgements about her. And she didn't need his guidance, either. Men always thought they knew best, doling out advice like it was going out of fashion. Well, she could take care of herself. She didn't need any man to tell her what to do.

With this thought in her head, Liv straightened her shoulders and strode purposefully on.

53

DI Jack Bentley was in the Black Bull, perched on a stool beside his retired colleague Jim Arnold. They were sitting on the quiet side of the horseshoe-shaped counter, the side furthest from the door, and were able to chat in private so long as they kept their voices down.

'Any progress with the Moll Ainsworth murder?'

Bentley shook his head. There had been a time, and it was not that long ago, when he would never have discussed a case with anyone who wasn't on the force. It had been a rule he'd stuck to assiduously. But this evening, in the company of his old friend, he felt less inclined to follow official procedure. 'She was in here on the night she died. Later, she had a drink in the French. Then . . .'

'Then?' Jim prompted.

'Then nothing. She went back to work and that's the last anyone saw of her. Well, alive at least.'

'She was a character, Moll. Some disgruntled punter, I suppose.'

'No one's talking, not even a whisper. And now there's a missing girl: Cynthia Crosby. She's a singer at the Windmill. She didn't show up for work on Saturday and hasn't been seen since.'

'You reckon there's a connection?'

'I can't see it, other than the two incidents happening fairly close together. And Moll's killer didn't even try to hide the body. If Cynthia is dead, we should have found her by now.'

'Your man could have been disturbed the first time. Soho's a busy place. Perhaps he was more careful second time around.' Jim lifted his pint and took a drink. 'There are some punters, of course, who wouldn't make much of a distinction between a woman who works the streets and one who performs at the Windmill. Any girl who takes her clothes off in public might fall into the tom category for him.'

This had already crossed Bentley's mind, but he didn't want to believe – and had no real reason to believe – that he could have some kind of maniacal prostitute hater on his patch. 'Cynthia's boyfriend's, *ex*-boyfriend, isn't in the clear. She was cheating on him by all accounts.'

'No firm alibi?'

'About as firm as quicksand.'

'What's he like?'

'Arty type. Dowd's the name, Geoff Dowd. He paints that weird modern stuff: all splodges and squares and triangles. Nothing that actually looks like anything.'

'You could lock him up just for that,' Jim said.

Bentley smiled. 'Can't say I care for the bloke much, but I'm giving him the benefit of the doubt at the moment. He doesn't have any form, no record of violence or anything else, come to that. Clean as a whistle.'

'That's the problem with crimes of passion,' Jim said. 'Your normal everyday person can just snap. Something pushes them over the edge and then . . . bam!' He slapped his hand down on the counter to emphasise the point. 'Suddenly it's gone, all that natural human restraint that normally stops us from harming our nearest and dearest.'

'It's not easy to dispose of a body, though, especially if you haven't much time. To be honest, I'm not convinced she's dead.' Bentley sighed into the stuffy air of the pub. 'Maybe she decided she'd had enough of Dowd, had enough of everything and just took off. She wouldn't be the first girl to break up with her boyfriend and disappear for a week or two.'

'True enough.'

Bentley's gaze roamed the pub, lightly scrutinising the other customers. He was looking in a vague sort of way for Slug. This was one of his informant's many haunts and the old man usually showed up at some point in the evening. He still had the feeling, a hunch in his guts, that Slug knew more about Moll than he was letting on. His reflections on Moll's death quickly led him on to another victim. He turned his face to look at Jim. 'I've had Rosa Palliser on my mind recently.'

Jim screwed up his eyes while he tried to place the name. 'Rosa Palliser,' he repeated softly. 'Let me think . . . '

'It was a while back, eleven years or so. The Bridle Lane girl who was found in the river? She had a nasty head injury. It could have been caused while she was in the water, but the pathologist thought not.'

'Yes, I remember now. You always were convinced it was murder.'

'For all the good it did. We never got the bastard.'

'Loose ends, unsolved crimes: these are the things that keep you awake at night.'

Bentley nodded his agreement. Rosa's body had been hooked out of the Thames at a place called Dead Man's Hole on the north side of Tower Bridge. This hadn't provided any clues, however, as to where she might have gone in. The Hole was where the drowned turned up with such frequency that, in Victorian times, a mortuary had even been built there. Those rooms of horror were long gone now, although the structure still remained. Whenever he walked that way, he was aware of the L-shaped set of stone steps, curving under the bridge and leading to the very edge of the river.

'Her brother still lives in Soho. I saw him in the French not so long ago, and then he turned up again at Geoff Dowd's flat.'

Jim cocked his head. 'And that bothers you because . . . ?'

'I don't know. Connections?' Bentley shrugged. 'Something doesn't feel right.'

'Soho's a small place. People know people.'

'He's got a grudge and who can blame him? I just . . . I still wonder what I missed back then.'

'Who says you missed anything?'

Bentley frowned and absently turned his pint glass around. 'It was my first case after Maria died. Perhaps my mind wasn't exactly on the job.' He didn't often talk about his wife – even after all these years it was still painful – but he couldn't help wondering if his failure to solve Rosa Palliser's murder could have been as much to do with the distraction of grief as the lack of any leads.

'Don't go talking like that. You weren't the only person on the case.'

'I was the one in charge.'

'There was nothing to miss,' Jim said firmly. 'Stop beating yourself up about it. We all have cases that bug us, that keep niggling away in the back of our minds. It's just the nature of the job.' He briefly laid a hand on his friend's shoulder. 'I'm retired but I'm still waiting to catch the shit who murdered Amy Duggan.'

The name was only vaguely familiar to Bentley. He'd been on compassionate leave at the time of that case, watching Maria die a slow and painful death from cancer. The memory made him wince. He blinked twice, trying to chase away the unwelcome images crowding into his head. 'Wasn't that shortly before Rosa Palliser was killed?'

'A few weeks. No link, though. Amy's boyfriend had it on his toes before the poor kid was even cold. It gets my goat thinking of him walking around out there. He strangles the girl and then does a runner. Larry bloody Marks. I'll still have his name on my lips when I'm on my deathbed.'

It took a moment for Bentley to make the connection. 'Marks,' he repeated softly. 'He didn't have family in Whitcomb Street, did he?'

'That's the one. He lived there with his mother. It was a boarding house, probably still is. Dora Marks. A widow. She was a rum one, too.' Jim lifted his eyebrows in a cynical fashion. 'Claimed to be able to read the cards. You know, all that weird tarot shit. Like she was psychic or something. Why? What's happened?'

'I was there on Saturday about the Crosby girl. One of the lodgers, Verity Lang, reported her as missing. They work together at the Windmill. There was a burglary at the house on the same day and another girl had some jewellery taken. She's a friend of Palliser's – well, I think they both are. They both know Geoff Dowd, too.'

'Like I said, Soho's a small place.'

'Getting smaller by the minute.'

Jim drained his pint, caught the attention of the barman and ordered two more. Once the drinks had been delivered and paid for, he turned back to Bentley and said, 'Dora Marks knew Moll, you know.'

'Did she?'

'Yeah, we were watching the house for months after Larry did a runner. Moll used to show up regular as clockwork every Tuesday evening, stay for an hour or so and then get back on the streets. She was one of Dora's regular clients although God knows what she was hoping to hear. "You will meet a tall dark handsome stranger" hardly cuts it when you're in her line of work.'

'Any bit of hope is better than none, I suppose. Something to look forward to.'

'You don't believe in any of that nonsense, do you?'

Bentley gave a dismissive wave of his hand. 'It's not my cup of tea, but whatever gets you through the day. Where do you think Larry is now?'

'A hundred miles away if he's got any sense.'

'And if he hasn't?'

'What, you think he misses his old mum so much that he'd come back and risk getting nicked?'

'It's not beyond the realms of possibility. She's getting on, and people can get tired of running. They long for the familiar, for where they feel they belong.'

Jim chuckled. 'Well, if you come across him, be sure to pass on my best.'

Bentley nodded, lifted the new pint to his lips and took a drink. He was back to thinking about those connections, those linking threads that still didn't make any sense to him. When he went into the station tomorrow, he would lift the files on the Palliser and Duggan cases and take a good look at them both.

54

By the time Liv left for work on Thursday morning the first post had already come. She had rushed into the hall and snatched up the envelope as soon as she'd heard it rattle through the letterbox, but all it had been was a bill for Dora. She was disappointed, even though she knew it was too soon to expect a reply from Irene. The woman would need time to think about it all. Next week was probably the soonest she could expect to hear from her, hopefully on Monday or Tuesday. Until then she would just have to be patient.

On her way to Garvie & Carr, Liv bought a copy of the *West End News*, sat down on a bench and quickly flicked through the pages. McCall's piece about Cynthia was on page five and there was a Windmill publicity still to go with the story, a full-length picture of her looking glamorous in a long white dress with a feather boa round her neck. The report mentioned that her boyfriend, Geoff Dowd – described as a barman rather than an artist – had been interviewed by the police. It also said that he'd recently been seen in the company of an attractive brunette, the clear implication being that he could have disposed of the old to usher in the new.

But at least her name wasn't mentioned. McCall had been true to his word, although she knew it was only a temporary reprieve. If she couldn't get Henry to intervene, she might be splashed all over next week's edition. She felt sorry for Geoff, who'd remain under suspicion until Cynthia turned up. The more she thought about it, the more convinced she was that he was innocent.

Liv closed the paper, folded it over, stood up and continued on towards work. While she walked, a rather unpleasant thought entered her head. What if Moll Ainsworth and Aline had both been right about Larry being back? And what if Larry *had* been guilty of murder? It was natural for Dora to protest his innocence, to believe in him, but that didn't mean it was true. He had come back on the scene before Cynthia had gone missing and that, perhaps, was not a coincidence.

Aline's words – *when we're all murdered in our beds* – jumped into her head. She shuddered. If Larry had been the intruder, she had got dangerously close to him. She was glad now that she'd been taken by surprise and pushed aside. If she'd had the chance to confront him, to see his face, she might have recognised him from the photo in the living room. And then what? It didn't bear thinking about.

The first thing Liv was aware of as she entered the building in Bedford Square was raised voices coming from the end of the corridor. Garvie and Carr were having what could only be described as a heated discussion, not shouting exactly, but close enough. The door to Garvie's office was open and the whole exchange was clearly audible.

'It needs to be done now!'

'It's too early,' Carr replied. 'It's ridiculous. We could be looking at months before the builders go in. You haven't even got permission yet.'

'They won't be going in at all if the houses are still occupied. You know what your problem is, Stephen? You haven't got any bloody ambition.'

'And your problem is that you have too bloody much.'

Liv walked into the front office, looked at Muriel and raised her eyebrows. 'What's going on?'

Muriel kept her own voice low. 'Yelland Yard. They've been at it for the past ten minutes. Mr Garvie wants all the tenants from Bridle Lane cleared out straight away, but Mr Carr thinks they should wait until planning permission comes through for the redevelopment.'

'And who's right?' Liv asked.

'Mr Carr, of course. I mean, it makes sense, doesn't it? It's stupid having those properties empty for months on end when there could be rent coming in.'

Liv, who could see both points of view, suspected Muriel would take Carr's side no matter what. If he said the world was flat or that the moon was made of cheese, she would happily nod in agreement. Her loyalty was absolute. 'Do they often row like this?'

'Sometimes. Mr Garvie can be very unreasonable.'

Liv took off her jacket, hung it up on the peg by the door and sat down. She glanced out of the window at the square, looking at the people walking by, nervous again that Bentley might pay a surprise visit. Unwilling to spend all her working hours in a state of anxiety, she cleared her throat and asked, 'So, erm . . . I suppose all that business with Moll Ainsworth hasn't helped much.'

'What do you mean?'

'With the police and everything. When something like that

296

happens there's always so much trouble. Wasn't there a problem about emptying her flat?'

'No, no problem. Mr Carr sorted all that out.'

'Oh, right. Good. It must have been a shock when they turned up to tell you what had happened to her.'

'Nothing shocks me any more,' Muriel said. 'Especially when it comes to that Bridle Lane lot.'

'Were the police here for ages? I've had to talk to them twice about the burglary. You'd think once would be enough, but apparently not. It's just endless questions which you've already answered.'

'No, not long. I mean, it's nothing to do with us, is it? We only rented out the flat.'

Liv, relieved, began to sort through the work on her desk. It didn't sound like the law had much interest in Garvie & Carr. 'That's true. I suppose they'll leave you in peace now.'

'Once they've returned the keys,' Muriel said.

Liv's heart skipped a beat. 'What, they've still got them?'

'There's no rush. They were only spares.'

But it mattered to Liv. Would Bentley be the one to return them? Surely not. He'd have better things to do. Her eyes flew to the window again. She had hoped from reassurance from Muriel, but all she'd got was yet more worry.

55

Liv left the office at lunchtime and walked quickly towards the Eagle. She was glad to escape from what had been an uneasy atmosphere. The row had come to an end a few minutes after she'd got there, but its effects had lingered on all morning. Garvie's simmering rage had been palpable, a hot resentful anger that had been only marginally cooled by her announcement that she'd managed to change her plans for the weekend and could now accompany him to Hollinghurst.

'Good,' he'd said. 'I knew you wouldn't let me down.'

Liv didn't even want to think about the weekend, about the two long days she would have to spend trying to keep him at arm's length without damaging his male pride or giving him any reason to fire her. Perhaps she should invent a boyfriend or, even better, a fiancé, some bloke he might think twice about crossing. A boxer or a weightlifter or, God forbid, even a copper. She grinned at the very idea of it. And, looking on the bright side, maybe the whole Carbrooke thing would be a blessing in disguise. If Garvie was busy chasing the lord, at least he wouldn't be chasing her.

Once she reached the pub, Liv stood across the road for a while, trying to establish whether she was alone or not. There were so many people around that it was impossible to tell. Everyone seemed suspicious, even the woman with the kids and the shopping. She was worried about Lincoln finding out that she was seeing Henry, but even more worried that Henry wouldn't be there.

Liv had another concern as she crossed over and tentatively pushed open the doors to the Eagle. What if McCall was inside? She quickly looked around. The pub was almost deserted – no sign of her enemy – but Henry was sitting at the bar. She gave a sigh of relief, thankful that he was a man of such regular habits.

As Liv hurried over, Henry turned his head, smiled and quickly got to his feet. 'Ah, Liv. How lovely to see you again. How have you been?'

'Good, thanks. And you? How was Eastbourne?'

'A hotbed of gossip, fortunately. Let me buy you a drink. What would you like?'

Liv asked for an orange juice and when it arrived, they moved away from the bar and sat down at the same table as last time.

'You've read the cuttings, I suppose,' Henry said.

'Yes, but that's not the reason I'm here. Well, not the main reason. Something's happened and I need your help.' Liv took a breath before continuing. 'It's Ralph McCall. He's found out who I am, all about my father and everything.'

Henry frowned. 'How on earth did he do that?'

'You didn't say anything to him?'

'No, of course not. I wouldn't. Not a word.'

'He suggested that he'd got it from you, but I didn't believe him. He said you weren't exactly discreet when you'd had a few drinks.'

'Little bugger,' Henry muttered.

'He's been working on the missing girl story. You know, Cynthia Crosby? He saw me with her ex, Geoff, in a café. And now he seems to want to make something of it even though I barely know the bloke. But what he *really* wants is the inside story of why Dad shot Nicky Lister. He seems to think I'm selling you some kind of exclusive and he wants in on the action.'

'What a louse.'

'He's that all right. He was in here when we first met up, but he couldn't have heard anything.'

'Was he? I thought he came in later, after you'd gone.'

Liv shook her head. She couldn't explain about Lincoln spying on her and so she had to use some dramatic licence. 'He was sitting over there.' She flapped a hand vaguely towards the far end of the room. 'I recognised him from when I first came to your office, but I didn't think anything of it. I thought lots of you probably drank in here.'

'It's not to most people's taste,' Henry said.

'Anyway, he more or less threatened to reveal who I was in this week's paper unless I agreed to an interview. I told him I'd think about it – it was the only way to get rid of him – and we arranged to meet at Amelia's on Friday. Basically, he was asking me to dump whatever deal I had going with you and go with him instead.'

By now Henry's face was turning a deep shade of red, anger flashing in his eyes. 'You won't have to meet him.'

'Won't I?'

'I'll sort this out,' Henry said firmly. 'Don't worry. I'll have a word with the editor. The two of us go way back. Once I explain everything, he'll get McCall off your case.'

'And what if McCall goes to another paper?'

'He won't, not if he wants to keep his job.'

'He won't be happy.'

'He doesn't deserve to be. He's a nasty piece of work, that one. All reporters can fly close to the wind sometimes, but there's a limit. I won't let him do this to you.'

Liv, feeling partly reassured, sipped her orange juice. 'Thanks. I suppose I should just be open about it all, stop being so afraid. It's not my fault what my dad did, is it? Mum was just always so secretive, so terrified of anyone finding out.'

'You've a right to tell people if and when you want to. Don't ever allow yourself to be bullied into it.'

Liv knew this was good advice, although she wondered if the time would ever come when she could be completely honest and open about the past. 'I read through all the newspaper cuttings. I'm not sure I'm any the wiser, though. You were right: there aren't any answers there. And I still don't get it. What was it about Irene that made Dad so obsessed? I know she was beautiful, but . . . ' Liv gave a small shake of her head. 'Unless he was a complete fantasist, there must have been something going on between them.'

Henry studied the wall for a few seconds as if trying to gather his thoughts. Eventually his gaze slid back to Liv. 'She was a charming woman, from what I knew of her. And men can be weak creatures, easily beguiled by beauty. Look at what happened with Helen of Troy: war and carnage, ships launched, armies despatched, all for the sake of a beautiful face.'

'Except that's just a made-up story.'

'Even made-up stories have elements of the truth in them. Men are renowned for their destructive desires: reason disappears and lust takes over. From that point on, there's no saying what might happen. Whether there's encouragement or not, possession is all that matters.'

'Do you think there *was* encouragement, though? How could Irene have been completely innocent in all this?'

'We don't have the answer to that, and I don't suppose either of us ever will.'

But that, Liv thought, was where Henry was wrong. She wouldn't rest until she could make some sense of the whole damn tragedy. One way or another she would get the truth out of Irene.

56

Liv was in the front office on her own – Muriel had left early for a dental appointment – when Stephen Carr came in at about quarter past four. He laid some papers on Muriel's desk, went to leave and then appeared to have second thoughts. Turning to her, he folded his arms across his chest and said: 'Erm, I should apologise for this morning. A difference of opinion, I'm afraid, between myself and Mr Garvie. I know you've only just started here and I wouldn't like you to get the impression that we're always at each other throats.'

'That's all right. Believe me, I've heard worse.'

'You shouldn't have had to witness it. I wouldn't want you to feel awkward.'

'I don't,' Liv said. 'Please don't worry. These things happen, don't they? We can't all agree all of the time.'

'It's nice of you to be so understanding.'

Liv smiled. 'Don't give it another thought.'

Stephen Carr relaxed a little, his arms dropping back to his sides. 'Stressful times, but we'll be back to normal soon. So long as it hasn't upset you.'

'Not in the slightest.'

'Good, good,' he said. 'I'm glad to hear it.'

Liv, watching him leave, thought it had been nice of him to apologise. Garvie hadn't bothered, of course, but then he probably believed it was his right to shout what he liked when he liked and within hearing distance of whomever he liked. Consideration for the staff wouldn't even enter his head.

She resumed her typing, wondering how long it would be before Moody got what he wanted and made his move. For the first time she felt a sliver of guilt. What if whatever he was planning for Garvie impacted on Stephen Carr, too? If the business was undermined, it could damage both of them. She didn't want to be responsible for that.

'Oh, don't start going down that road,' she muttered under her breath. Now wasn't the time to be developing a conscience. She had enough problems already without inventing new ones.

At five o'clock Liv put on her jacket, told Garvie she was going, said goodbye and walked out of the building into the balmy summer air. At lunchtime, after seeing Henry, she had called in at a few second-hand jewellery shops searching for her silver cross, but hadn't had any joy. Before heading for home, she would check out the local pawnbrokers and try her luck with them. The chances were slim – the burglar could have shifted the items in a pub or further afield – but anything was worth a go.

Her first port of call was Tottenham Court Road, where she stood outside the shop for a moment and gazed at the window display. There were trays of rings, necklaces, bracelets, watches, but what she wanted to see wasn't there. She pushed open the door and went inside. The interior was like an Aladdin's cave, filled with community treasure: jewellery, musical instruments, cameras, clothes, shoes and even blankets. For those struggling to make ends meet, this was the place to raise a few bob until the weekly wage came in or times grew a little easier.

'I'm looking for a silver cross,' she told the man behind the counter. 'A small one. Less than an inch.'

'Over there,' he said, gesturing towards a row of glass-topped, waist-high cabinets.

Liv scrutinised the contents, her eyes darting from one item to the next. There were several gold crosses and a couple of silver ones, but she couldn't find hers. She didn't want to divulge that it had been nicked in case the man got shirty and thought she was accusing him of receiving stolen goods. It was possible, however, that if he *was* bent, he might keep a secret stash under the counter.

'Are these all you've got? No others?'

The man nodded towards the cabinets. 'They're all in there. Everything that's available at the moment.'

And that's when it dawned on Liv that she had probably started her search too soon. She'd presumed the burglar would have flogged the items but, if he didn't want to raise suspicion, he'd have been more likely to have pawned them and chucked away the ticket. 'How long do you keep things for before they're sold? I mean, if someone doesn't come back for them.'

'A few weeks if the interest isn't paid.'

'Do you have any silver crosses waiting to be redeemed?'

But now the man seemed to be growing wary. He gave her a long hard stare as if trying to figure out what her game was.

Liv said quickly, 'It's just that if you have, and I see one I like, I could call in again.'

'There's new stuff coming in all the time.'

Which didn't exactly answer Liv's question, but she reckoned it was the best she was going to get. 'All right, then. Thanks.'

Liv was disappointed, but not disheartened. There was still

a chance that her cross might turn up. After leaving the shop she started walking towards Whitcomb Street. She considered cutting through Soho – she could call in on Pally – but decided against it. That pig McCall might be hanging around and she didn't want to bump into him. Until Henry had got him off her back, she was better off keeping a low profile.

Dora, Aline and Verity were all in the kitchen when Liv got home. They were gathered round the table, gazing intently at the cards Dora was turning over. Liv said hello to everyone and smiled at Verity. 'You're back early.'

'It was just a rehearsal day today: they let us off at five. Come and sit down. Dora's doing a reading. I'm trying to find out what's happened to Cynthia.'

Liv looked at the cards and inwardly recoiled. She hated those swords and cups and pentacles, those kings and queens and all the other mystical pictures. 'And have you?'

'Not yet. We've only just started.'

Liv reluctantly pulled out a chair and sat down. She would have preferred to go straight up to her room, to avoid the disquieting feelings that always crept over her in the presence of the cards, but didn't want to seem unsupportive.

Aline sniffed the air, wrinkled her nose, stared at Liv and said, 'I can smell smoking. Why does the house smell of cigarettes?'

'Don't look at me,' Liv said. 'I've only just come in and I've not had a smoke all day.'

'Well, *someone* has.'

Dora interrupted the exchange. 'It must be from earlier. I had that Mrs Thorndike round. She got through half a dozen while she was here. Nerves, I reckon. She's got things on her mind, that poor woman. I opened the back door but the smell does tend to linger.'

'What can you see?' Verity asked, eager to get back to the reading.

Dora turned over another card. 'I can only see confusion. Confusion and disappointment.'

'Well, that's good,' Verity said. 'Isn't it? I mean, not good exactly, but not terrible.'

'No, I don't see anything terrible.'

'Nothing like you saw with Moll.'

Dora shook her head. 'This one,' she said, laying her fingers on the Seven of Cups, 'indicates choices, dreams, illusions. And being careful what you wish for. It's easy to be tempted by the bright lights, by the flashy things. You have to look beneath the surface. All that glitters is not gold, as they say.'

'Glisters,' Aline corrected. 'All that glisters is not gold. It's from *The Merchant of Venice*.'

Dora frowned at her. 'Does it really matter? I'm sure Verity gets my drift.'

'Of course it matters. What's the point of saying it if you don't say it properly?'

'What else can you see?' Verity asked impatiently.

But at that very moment there was a knock on the front door. Liv leapt to her feet, grateful for an excuse to escape. 'I'll get it.' She walked quickly along the hallway, hoping it was someone who'd distract them from the fate of Cynthia. Neither her hope nor her gratitude lasted for long. DI Bentley was standing on the doorstep.

57

Bentley took off his hat as he entered the house. The Anderson girl tried to usher him into the living room but he nimbly skirted around her and headed straight for the kitchen. From the hallway he had spotted the others gathered round the table and didn't want to give them time to prepare or collect themselves. The element of surprise was always useful when you wanted to catch people off guard.

'Good evening, ladies,' he said. 'I hope I'm not disturbing you.'

Verity Lang sprang up, her face pale. 'Oh, God, have you found Cynthia? Is it bad news?'

Bentley raised his palms to reassure her. 'No, no, please don't be alarmed. It's nothing like that. I just have a few more questions I'd like to ask. It may seem like I'm going over old ground, but there are a few things I need to clarify.'

Verity, relieved, sank back down into her seat.

Bentley glanced over his shoulder at Liv Anderson, who was hovering in the doorway, looking about as keen to be in his company as she'd been on the first occasion he'd visited. 'If it's not too much of an inconvenience,' he said to her.

'No, of course not, but I've already told you everything I know.'

'I appreciate that. But if you wouldn't mind running through things with me again?'

'I'll leave you to it, then,' Dora Marks said, rapidly gathering up the cards. 'Come along, Aline. Let's make ourselves scarce. I'm sure the inspector doesn't need us cluttering up the kitchen while he talks to the girls.'

'I'd rather you both stayed,' Bentley said. 'If you don't mind. You may be able to help me with another matter.'

'Another matter?'

It struck Bentley as interesting that Dora Marks, so eager to sit in on his first visit, now couldn't wait to get away. Aline, however, was the opposite; she seemed positively pleased at the prospect of remaining at the table. Rather than answering Dora's question, he addressed Aline instead. 'I don't believe we've met before. I'm DI Bentley.'

'Aline Bowers,' she said. 'Long-term resident of the house. Pleased to meet you.'

'Likewise,' he said.

'Do sit down, inspector. Make yourself comfortable.'

Dora, feeling obliged, offered him tea and he accepted. He didn't especially want a brew, but what he did want was to convey a message that he wasn't planning on leaving in a hurry. The more he put them on edge, the more he might learn. While Dora busied herself with the kettle, cups and milk, he talked to Verity about Cynthia Crosby, going over pretty much the same ground as last time, only phrasing his questions slightly differently. As he'd expected, he learned nothing new.

By the time he moved on to Liv Anderson, the tea was brewed and poured. He pressed the girl about what time Geoff Dowd had arrived at the French, what mood he'd been in, what he'd said, but she stuck to her story about barely talking to him all evening. It was only when he asked his next question that her composure showed some cracks.

'You don't perform at the Windmill, do you, Miss Anderson?'

'No, I'm a secretary.'

'Ah, right. And where is it that you work?'

'A property company,' she said.

Bentley knew evasion when he heard it. He could see she was uncomfortable and that it was an effort for her to hold his gaze. 'And which one would that be?'

As if she was toying with the idea of lying, she hesitated for just a fraction too long. Indecision flickered in her eyes. Then, eventually, she said, 'Garvie and Carr.'

'I know it. Bedford Square, yes?'

Liv Anderson nodded.

'And how long have you been there for?'

'Not long,' she said. 'I only started on Monday. Look, what does this have to do with Cynthia or Geoff Dowd?'

'It's just for the records,' he replied casually.

By now he'd been there for almost twenty minutes. Aline Bowers, he noticed, was listening intently, her lips slightly parted as she drank in every word. Dora, on the other hand, was clearly on tenterhooks, constantly shifting in her seat while she waited for him to ask about that other matter.

And so, finally, Bentley turned to her. 'I understand you knew Moll Ainsworth, Mrs Marks?'

The sudden change of subject caught Dora off guard. 'Moll? What? Yes, I knew her a little. God rest her soul.' Her right hand closed over the pack of tarot cards. 'She used to come for a reading occasionally.'

'And when was the last time she came?'

310

Dora frowned. 'Let me see. It must have been two or three weeks before she . . . I can't remember the exact date.'

'Dora warned her,' Aline piped up. 'She told her to be careful. She saw danger approaching, inspector. It was in the cards.'

Bentley privately thought that Moll Ainsworth, like all other toms, was in danger every time she went out on the streets, but wisely kept his observation to himself. 'And what exactly did you see, Mrs Marks?'

'It was just as Aline said. Something bad, something sudden and shocking. It shook me up if the truth be told. I told her to watch out, to be on her guard. I'm not a doom-monger, but the cards don't lie.'

'Did Moll seem worried about anything in particular?'

'She didn't have a happy life, but she made the best of things.'

'And you can't think of anyone who might have wished to cause her harm?'

'There's always those who want to harm others, but no, she didn't mention anyone.'

'And there was nothing else she told you, nothing out of the ordinary?'

Dora made a show of thinking about it, her forehead scrunching in concentration. 'No, I can't recall anything.' She glanced at Aline. 'Did she?'

'No,' Aline agreed, perhaps a little too quickly.

'Well,' Bentley said, getting to his feet. 'Thank you all for your time. I'll keep you informed of any developments.'

Everyone apart from Aline looked relieved that he was going. Dora accompanied him to the door, clearly eager to escort him off the premises and walking at an unusually brisk pace for a woman of her age. It was then, just as he was about to leave, that he remembered his conversation with Jim Arnold.

'I don't suppose you've heard from your Larry recently?'

Dora's mouth fell open, her eyes widening in surprise. A few seconds passed before she recovered herself, gave a hollow laugh and said, 'What? Larry? Why would I? It's over ten years since I last saw him. He's not going to set foot in London while you lot have him in the frame, is he?'

'I've no idea, Mrs Marks. That's why I'm asking.'

'Well, take it from me, he isn't. If you'd done your job properly in the first place, if you'd found out who really murdered that girl, he wouldn't still be on the run.'

'It wasn't my case.'

'You know what I mean. You lot – the law. So what's going on? What's with the sudden interest in my boy?'

'No sudden interest,' Bentley said mildly. Then, watching her carefully, he slipped in the fib. 'We received some information that he'd been seen in the area, that's all.'

'Seen in the area,' Dora repeated scathingly. 'He's not a bloody fool! You want to search the house, make sure he's not hiding under the bed?'

'That won't be necessary.'

Dora held open the door. 'You'd better get on with chasing some real criminals, then.'

Bentley put on his hat, politely thanked her for her time, said good evening and left the house. He walked along the street to where Hemmings was waiting in the car, got in and gave a snort. 'Ever get the feeling people are holding out on you?'

'Every day, guv. It's par for the course in this job. No joy, then, I take it?'

'Oh, I wouldn't say that. Maybe not joy exactly, but something not far off. Let's head back to the station and I'll fill you in on the way.'

58

Dora's heart was beating fast as she went into the living room and turned on the television. It would take it a while to warm up. She put her hand to her chest and tried to steady her breathing. Where she wanted to be was in the bedroom, trying to calm down Larry – he must have caught every word of the conversation at the door – but it would have to wait until they could talk without being overheard. Bentley's question had rattled her so God alone knew what it had done to him.

'What was all that about?' Aline asked as Dora returned to the kitchen.

'All what?'

'Just now. At the door with the inspector.'

'Nothing,' Dora said. 'Nothing important.' She set about clearing the cups from the table. 'He was asking if I knew anyone who might have been close to Moll, that's all. I couldn't help and that's what I told him.'

Aline gave her a quizzical look, but didn't pursue it.

'Can we carry on with the reading?' Verity asked.

'Not tonight, love. Once it's interrupted, the flow has gone. Best leave it for now, I think. Maybe tomorrow, or Saturday.'

'He didn't even mention the burglary,' Aline said. 'You'd have thought he'd have mentioned it, wouldn't you?'

Dora poured some hot water into the sink from the kettle. 'I suppose murder is slightly higher on his agenda than a few bits of stolen jewellery.' She glanced over her shoulder at Liv. 'No offence, love.'

'None taken,' Liv said. 'I dare say you're right. Oh, I meant to mention that I'll be away this weekend. I'm going to Kent to see an old friend.'

'That's nice. I'm sure you could do with a break.'

'Couldn't we all,' Aline said. 'I can't remember the last time *I* had a holiday.'

'It's only a couple of days,' Liv said. 'And it's hardly the Bahamas.'

Dora quickly washed and rinsed the cups, agitation making her fingers clumsy. 'I've put the telly on. I think that quiz you like is about to start, Aline.'

It was a relief when everyone finally stood up and left the kitchen, the two girls going upstairs while Aline headed for the living room. Once the coast was clear, Dora walked quietly along the hall and slipped into her bedroom. Larry was standing to the side of the window, peering out at the street from the edge of the net curtains.

'For God's sake, get away from there,' she hissed softly. 'Anyone could see you.'

'I need to get out of here. You heard what that cop said.'

'Bentley's just whistling in the wind. If he really thought you were here, he'd have come with his pals and searched the place from top to bottom.'

Larry strode over to her, his face twisted, fear and anger

colouring his cheeks. He grabbed hold of her elbow and bared his teeth. 'You gave him a goddam invitation, you stupid old cow!'

Dora flinched, but stood her ground. 'What else was I supposed to do? I mean, I wouldn't be telling him to go ahead if you were actually here, would I? And he wouldn't have asked about you if he was planning on coming back to search the place. No, he doesn't have a clue.'

But Larry wasn't listening. He started pacing the floor. 'That bloody Slug must have tipped him off!'

'Keep your voice down. Aline's just across the hall.' Dora, scared that he was about to take off and that she might never see her son again, tried harder to reassure him. 'He's just doing what cops always do, having a dig when he's got the opportunity. You know what they're like. And even if Slug did say something, Bentley wouldn't ever imagine that you'd come here.'

'I'll kill the bastard,' Larry said.

Dora wasn't sure if he was referring to Bentley or Slug. 'And where's that going to get you? Look, you're more likely to be caught out there than you are here. Wait a few days at least. You're safe here. I'm sure you are.'

'Safe,' Larry scoffed. 'I'm not bloody safe anywhere.'

'He doesn't know anything,' Dora insisted. 'Will you listen to me? You need to keep your head down, not do anything rash. Promise me. Promise me, Larry.'

Larry finally stopped pacing and sat down on the bed. 'I should get out of here right now, go over the wall at the back. I should get as far away from here as I can.'

'You should sit tight. That's the best thing to do.'

'What would you know? I should never have come back to this godforsaken hole. It was one big mistake.'

Dora could have asked why he had, but was too afraid to. She wanted to believe that Larry had missed her, missed home, that he loved her, but suspected that the answer was more mundane: he had just grown tired of running. 'Sleep on it. See how you feel in the morning.'

'Dora? Dora?' Aline's voice echoed from the hallway. 'Where are you?'

'I'm coming.'

Dora gave Larry a pleading look, but he just stood up and went back to lurk by the window. She opened the bedroom door and carefully closed it behind her.

'The programme's on. What have you been doing?'

'Looking for a handkerchief,' Dora said. 'I've got the sniffles. Maybe I'm coming down with a cold.'

While they sat on the sofa, Dora kept her eyes on the television, but her ears were pricked for any sound coming from behind her.

59

By eight o'clock on Friday morning, Ralph had positioned himself on the corner of Whitcomb Street and Shaftesbury Avenue.
It was a gamble – he couldn't be sure that Liv Anderson would
pass this way en route to wherever she worked – but he reckoned
the odds were decent enough for him to give it a try.

His mouth felt dry and stale, and a hangover was making
his head thump. Despite the headache, he lit another cigarette
to pass the time while he waited. He'd spent most of last night
in the French, drowning his sorrows while he tried to figure
out what to do next. How many pints? He'd stopped counting
at six. It was probably a good thing that Liv Anderson hadn't
showed her face or he'd have given her a mouthful. That tart
had screwed him over good and proper.

Ralph's body tensed when he thought back to the conversation that had taken place yesterday afternoon in Arthur
Neames's office. No, it hadn't even been a conversation – he'd
barely had a chance to put his side of things – but more of a
lecture. Liv Anderson was to be left alone, there was to be no

story, there were to be no revelations. From now on he wasn't to go near her. And if anything appeared in another paper, he could start looking for another job.

'Bitch,' he muttered under his breath.

There was no doubt in his mind that she must have gone running to Henry the minute the old hack got back from Eastbourne. Ralph didn't believe Neames about ... well, just about bloody any of it and least of all that Liv Anderson was an innocent victim in the whole business. The truth was that he was being sidelined, left out in the cold. The editor and Henry Squires were in cahoots, keeping the story under wraps until they were ready to go to press.

Ralph pulled angrily on the cigarette as he looked around. Shaftesbury Avenue was busy, filled with cars and buses and swarms of people on their way to work. He had no idea what Liv did for a living, but he intended to find out. It was his first step in his plan for revenge. No one stabbed him in the back and got away with it. Pretty girls like her always thought they could walk all over men like him, but she was about to get a wake-up call.

It was half past eight before she eventually appeared, strolling along Whitcomb Street in a pale pink summer dress. She walked like a dancer with her hips gently swaying. Her long dark hair was swept up and tucked into the nape of her neck. His eyes raked her body, from her head to her toes, absorbing every inch. He simultaneously loathed and desired her.

As she grew closer, he darted off to his right and slid into the doorway of a shop. Once she'd gone past, he followed at a safe distance. Already he was enjoying the feeling of having the upper hand; it gave him a sublime, almost sexual thrill. It put him back in control.

Ralph tailed her up Charing Cross Road to St Giles Circus

and then on to Bedford Avenue where she turned left into Adeline Place. At this point he hung back, waiting until she'd almost reached Bedford Square before hurrying forward again. He watched her cross the square and go into an office.

He didn't follow directly in her footsteps but quickly skirted round the square instead. As he approached the door she'd gone through, he kept in close against the buildings in case she happened to look out of a window. There were three brass plaques attached to the wall and he memorised the names – a property company called Garvie & Carr on the ground floor, a firm of accountants, Brights, on the first floor and a publishing company called Mackenzie's occupying the upper floors – before moving smartly away.

When he was clear of the square he sat down on a bench, took out his notebook and scribbled down the company names. As yet he had no idea which one she worked for, but it wouldn't be too hard to find out. All he had to do was phone each company in turn, ask for her and hang up when he got a result. And then what? He hadn't quite decided. But she had screwed with his career so he felt entitled to return the favour.

60

It was quiet in the house when Liv got up on Saturday morning. She went downstairs, made some toast and a brew, opened the back door and sat down on the step to have her breakfast. Already the air was warm, the sun rising in a clear blue sky. Ideal pool weather, she thought, pulling a face. Well, Garvie wasn't going to get the chance to see *her* in a swimsuit, that was for sure. It was bad enough having to put up with his leching when she was fully clothed, never mind giving him even more flesh to gawp at.

Thinking of Garvie reminded her of Bentley asking where she worked. Why had he wanted to know that? And he must have realised that Garvie & Carr was the company Moll had rented her rooms off, but he hadn't said anything. That was odd. In fact, everything had been odd about Bentley's visit. She'd had the feeling he was only going through the motions with his questions about Cynthia and Geoff and that he'd actually had an ulterior motive for being there.

She wasn't the only one who'd been disturbed by the

inspector's visit. Dora had clearly been rattled by it, too. Still, that wasn't so surprising bearing in mind all the Larry business. Perhaps Moll wasn't alone in having spotted him. Later in the evening, when Liv and Verity had joined Dora and Aline in the living room, Dora had been up and down like a jack-in-the-box, frequently disappearing to check the back door or the stove or to make sure she'd closed her bedroom window.

'What's wrong with you?' Aline had said. 'Can't you sit still for a minute?'

'It's my rheumatism. I can't settle. It's better when I'm up and about.'

It seemed to Liv that almost everyone in the house, apart from Aline, was distracted at the moment: Dora over Larry, Verity over Cynthia, and herself over . . . ah, it was quite a list – Moody, McCall, Bentley, Irene Forster. Each of them jostled for dominance in her mind, giving her sleepless nights and anxious days.

'Just keep a cool head,' she murmured. 'You'll get there in the end.' She was not entirely sure where 'there' was, but vaguely visualised it as being in the back of a black cab with Pally, making plans for the evening, with everything returned to normal.

Liv finished her breakfast, washed up her plate and cup and climbed the stairs back to her room. She did her hair and make-up, put on the red dress and slipped on her shoes. The weekend loomed ahead, a dark cloud on the horizon, but she resolved to make the best of it. The sooner she satisfied Moody's demands, the sooner she could have her life back.

Taking her green dress from the wardrobe, she carefully folded it and placed it inside the smart overnight bag she had borrowed from Verity. She also packed a change of underwear, her wash things, a hairbrush and cosmetics. As an afterthought she added a small towel, unsure as to whether these would be provided at Hollinghurst. Then, after one last glance in the mirror, she grabbed the bag, her jacket and handbag and went downstairs.

Liv was just about to leave when the post clattered through the letterbox and landed on the hall floor. Two letters. She bent to quickly pick them up. One was an airmail letter for Aline, which she placed on the hall table, but the other – her heart skipped a beat – was a heavy cream envelope with *Miss Liv Anderson* inscribed on the front in a neat, sloping hand. There was no doubt in her mind as to who it was from. Her impulse was to rip it open and read it, but what if it contained bad news? What if Irene refused to see her? She would only dwell on it all weekend.

She dithered, turning the letter over in her hands. Should she? Shouldn't she? In the end, as a compromise, she dropped it unopened into her handbag. Maybe she would read it at Hollinghurst or maybe she'd wait until she got home. She'd see how she felt. At least she had got a reply and that was something.

Liv checked her watch, saw that it was ten past eight and hurried out of the house. By the time she reached the corner of Coventry Street, Tom Lincoln was already there. He got out of the grey saloon and nodded. 'Morning.'

'Morning,' she said.

'I was starting to think you weren't coming.'

'Why would you think that?'

'Because you're late.'

Liv glanced at her watch again. 'By about three minutes.'

Lincoln took her bag and put it in the boot. Then he opened the passenger door, waited for her to climb into the car and closed it again. He walked around to the driver's side and got in. 'Late's late, no matter which way you look at it.'

'Long night?' she asked, staring at his unshaven face.

'They're all long nights.'

'Perhaps you're getting too old for it. Have you ever considered something more suited to your age?'

Lincoln gave her a half smile, half snarl, turned the key in the ignition and started the engine. Then, before moving off, he reached into his pocket, took out a small leather jewellery box and chucked it into her lap. 'Here.'

'What's this?'

'Well, if you open it, you'll see.'

Liv flipped open the box. Inside was a silver heart-shaped locket on a chain. She frowned. 'What's this for?'

'Because I love you so much,' Lincoln said drily. 'And because I told Carbrooke that that's what you'd be wearing: a red dress and a silver locket. It shouldn't be too hard for him to recognise you.'

'Oh, okay.' Liv put the locket round her neck and fastened it. 'Is there a mirror?'

'You don't need a mirror,' he said. 'It looks fine.'

'Since when was "fine" a suitable compliment for any woman?'

Lincoln rolled his eyes. 'It looks exquisite,' he said. 'Lovely, delightful. Can we go now?'

Liv sat back and smiled.

The roads were Saturday quiet, almost empty, and it didn't take them long to get to Islington. Neither of them spoke much on the way: Liv was preoccupied by the unopened letter in her handbag and Lincoln with . . . well, she had no idea what went on in *his* head. Tom Lincoln's innermost thoughts were, thankfully, a mystery to her.

Eventually he pulled up in Duncan Terrace – a pleasant-looking row of houses with small wrought-iron balconies on the upper windows – and they got out of the car. He retrieved her bag from the boot and they went into the ground-floor flat of one of the houses. Liv looked around, but there wasn't much to see. The flat, although clean, was only sparsely furnished.

'Who does this belong to?'

'What does that matter? You're not going to be living here.' He passed her a couple of keys on a key ring. 'Here, you'll need these for when you get back tomorrow. Do you know what time that's going to be?'

'Garvie said late afternoon. Four or five, I suppose. But you don't have to give me a lift. I can make my own way home.'

'You might have things to tell me.'

'Like what?'

'Like something useful you learned over the weekend.'

Liv hoped she would learn something useful, something so beneficial to Moody that he would instantly release her from her obligation, but the chances of that were slim. She opened her handbag, took out a folded A4 envelope and handed it to Lincoln. 'This is everything to date, all the new contracts and the rest.'

'I'll pass them on. Right, I'd better be going before Garvie gets here. Enjoy your weekend.'

Liv gave him a sceptical look. 'Enjoy? At least you haven't lost your sense of humour.'

'Two days in the country. What's not to love?'

'The company, for starters.'

'You can handle Garvie.'

'Yes, well, it's the *handling* I'm not looking forward to.'

Lincoln smirked and headed for the door. 'See you tomorrow.'

'Can't wait,' she murmured, but he'd already gone.

61

Hollinghurst was a great pile of a place, an imposing red brick construction with towers, turrets, spires and more windows than she could count. It was impressive and yet faintly monstrous at the same time, a testament to some long-dead man's compulsive need to flaunt his wealth. As they travelled the length of the drive – already lined with expensive motors – she could see that the house was set in extensive grounds that wrapped around it like a country park, the lawns wide and rolling, the multitude of plants covered in blossoms.

'Quite a showstopper, isn't it?' Garvie said.

'Lovely,' Liv said. She had spent most of the journey deflecting his endless questions about Lord Carbrooke until, sensing his frustration, she'd felt obliged to offer up some fabricated pearls of wisdom. 'All right, well, I suppose there's one piece of advice I can give you: he doesn't like being pressurised. Once you put forward your proposal you have to leave him to think about it. And not just for an hour or two. If you press him, he'll turn you down point blank. He always used to say, "If they want an answer in a hurry, there's something they don't want you to know."'

Garvie had nodded. 'Right. Good. I understand.'

Liv hoped Garvie did understand and that he'd taken her advice on board. She wanted him to spend as little time as possible with Lord Carbrooke in case the whole charade about her once being his secretary was exposed. The longer they were together the more chance there was of things going wrong.

Garvie parked the car behind a white Rolls Royce, gazed at it adoringly for a few seconds and then turned to her and asked, 'Anything else I should know before we go in?'

Liv pretended to think about it. 'Just remember what I told you. Don't try and pin him down, not straight away, or he'll run a mile.'

Two tall marble columns flanked a grand front door which led into a huge echoey hallway. Voices drifted from a distant room, the rise and fall of conversation, the sound of laughter. They were greeted by a middle-aged woman in a housekeeper's uniform who took their names and referred to a list she was carrying.

'You're in the Violet room, Miss Kent. Sarah will show you the way.'

As Sarah stepped forward, Garvie turned to Liv and said, 'I'll meet you in the drawing room. It's just down there to the right. Shall we say fifteen minutes?'

'Yes, that's fine,' Liv said, attempting to look relaxed even though she didn't feel it. The moment of reckoning was rapidly approaching. She and Lord Carbrooke would have to meet and enact a fond reunion convincing enough to fool Garvie. But what if it all went wrong? What if the lord didn't play ball, or Garvie realised it was all some terrible farce? The consequences would be dire.

These thoughts filled Liv's head as she followed Sarah up the grand stairway. The girl, who didn't look more than fifteen or sixteen, had insisted on carrying her case; she walked at a brisk pace and in silence. The Violet room was tucked away in a distant corridor and by the time they reached it, Liv wondered if she'd ever find her way back.

The room was pleasant enough, light and airy, but her eyes were instantly drawn to the two single beds, one of which already had an open suitcase lying on it. For one awful second Liv thought it might be Garvie's, even though it couldn't possibly have got here before her, but then she realised that it was full of women's clothes.

'Oh, am I sharing?' she asked.

'Yes, miss. Is that all right?'

Liv wasn't overjoyed at the prospect, but there wasn't much she could do about it. Anyway, it was only for a night. 'Yes, of course. Thank you.'

'The bathroom is at the end of the corridor.' Sarah laid her case on the other bed and departed.

After she'd gone Liv wondered if she should have tipped her. She had no idea of the protocol of country houses. It wasn't a hotel, but possibly carried some of the same obligations. She wasn't used to grand places or the people who frequented them and hoped she wasn't going to make a fool of herself.

Liv unpacked and hung up her green dress in the wardrobe. She was just wondering what to do next – there were still ten minutes left before she was due downstairs – when the door opened and a petite, pretty blonde bounced into the room.

'Oh, thank God,' she said. 'I thought I might be stuck with that awful Miriam again. Hi, hello, I'm Victoria by the way. Call me Vicky.'

'I'm Liv.'

327

'Nice to meet you, Liv.'

'You too.'

Vicky, who was wearing a white dress with the halter neck of a swimsuit showing, delved into her case and pulled out a pair of sunglasses. 'Ah, there they are.' She looked up and smiled. 'Who are you here with?'

'Hugh Garvie. I'm his secretary.'

'Ah, right, yes, I know Garvie. I don't think I've seen you here before. Is this your first time?'

'I've only just started working for him.'

'Lucky you,' Vicky said.

'Lucky me?'

'Wandering hands, yeah? I've heard he's got a bit of a temper on him, too. Likes to have his own way and doesn't take kindly to not getting what he wants.' Vicky put on the sunglasses and then pushed them back on to her head. 'Sorry, am I speaking out of turn?'

'God no, not in the slightest. So who's your boss? Who are you here with?'

'No boss,' Vicky said, grinning. 'We're only here for the pool and the free drinks. There's a few of us came down with Charlie. Charlie Mayhew? His old man's in wine.'

'What else do you know about Hugh Garvie?'

'Only what the other girls say. I don't know if it's true or not. There's a rumour about one of his secretaries, that she was—'

But before Vicky could finish, a male voice called from the corridor. 'Vicky? Where are you, sweetheart? What are you doing?'

'Just a second,' Vicky called back. Then she said to Liv, 'Are you coming downstairs?'

Liv waved vaguely towards her case. 'I just want to finish up here.'

Once Vicky had gone, Liv sat down on the bed, regretting that she hadn't got more out of her. Still, there was plenty of time. She was bound to get another opportunity, especially as they were sharing a room – and a few drinks would probably loosen the girl's tongue even more. It was no big surprise that the weekend gathering appeared to be as much about pleasure as business – Muriel had hinted at it – but hoped that all Garvie would demand from her was the Carbrooke introduction. Anything more and things could get unpleasant.

Liv waited five minutes before attempting to find her way back to the staircase. A false start led her into a dingier part of the building, presumably the servants' quarters, but eventually she got her bearings and was soon walking down the thickly carpeted stairs and into the hall. From here she only had to follow the sound of voices to discover the drawing room.

There were about thirty people gathered there, most of them male, and Liv quickly spotted Garvie. As she went over to join him, her gaze subtly roamed over the other faces. It didn't take her long to identify Lord Carbrooke. The room was dominated by a large marble fireplace upon which a portly man with thick grey hair was leaning his elbow while he engaged in conversation with an elderly gentleman.

'What an amazing house,' she said to Garvie. 'Is it very old?'

But Garvie's mind was focused only on the job in hand. In a voice that barely contained his excitement, he said softly, 'He's here.'

Liv, pretending she was unaware of this, made a show of looking around. 'Oh, yes,' she said. 'There he is.'

'Shall we go over?'

'No,' Liv said. 'Don't interrupt him. Wait until he's finished talking.' She stared across the room until Carbrooke, feeling her eyes on him, finally returned her gaze. At this point she nodded and briefly touched the locket at her throat, praying that he wasn't one of those vain men who suffered from myopia but refused to wear glasses. For a few seconds she had her heart in her mouth, but then, smiling widely, Carbrooke was suddenly striding towards them. Liv braced herself.

'Olivia! How wonderful, my dear!' Carbrooke took her hand, raised it to his lips and kissed it. 'What a marvellous surprise. I can't think of anyone I'd rather see on this lovely morning.'

Liv wondered if he wasn't laying it on a bit thick, but a quick sideways glance at Garvie informed her that he was lapping it up. 'How are you? I had no idea you were going to be here.'

'Oh, yes, one has to put in an appearance every now and again. And I'm more than well, thank you. Flourishing, in fact. I've no need to ask how you are, of course. You're looking wonderful as always.'

'And this is Mr Garvie,' Liv said as if she'd just remembered her manners. 'He's my new employer. Mr Garvie, this is Lord Carbrooke.'

Carbrooke energetically shook his hand. 'Ah, so you're the devil who stole my precious Olivia.'

'It's a pleasure to meet you, sir.'

'Mr Garvie's in the property business,' Liv said.

'Property, eh? Well, you can't go far wrong with that. I've occasionally dabbled in the old bricks and mortar myself.'

Garvie, sensing his opportunity, wasn't slow to grab it. 'It's interesting you should say that, sir. I was wondering, if it's not too much of an imposition, whether we could have a word at some point. It's in regard to a new development in the West End.'

'A new development, eh?' Lord Carbrooke winked ostentatiously at Liv. 'Is this man to be trusted, my dear?'

'Absolutely,' Liv said.

'Well, I shall take your word for it. Now I have to get back to old Peterson. I've a spot of business to attend to. He had a heart attack, poor chap, a few months ago, so I'd better get things wrapped up before it's all too late.' He laughed at his own joke and slapped Garvie on the shoulder. 'See you later, my good man. Come and find me after lunch. I'm always in a better mood when I've got some food in my belly.' Then, turning to Liv, he said pointedly, 'We must have a proper catch-up this afternoon, Olivia, just the two of us. We've got so much to talk about.'

Liv thought there was an undercurrent to what he said, something that if not exactly menacing was certainly unfriendly. It was almost as if he held her personally responsible for the whole pretence and meant to have it out with her. But she kept the smile on her face and answered with warmth, 'That would be lovely.'

62

By the afternoon, the atmosphere at Hollinghurst had changed. Business had been conducted, lunch had been consumed and it was now the time for relaxation. Liv sat alone beside the Pacific-blue swimming pool, a cup of coffee in her hand, while she watched the antics of the other guests. Inhibitions were rapidly being lowered. Voices rose, laughter proliferated and the flirtatious cries of the girls – most of them splashing about in the water – echoed in the hot summer air.

Liv heard another cork pop out of a bottle of champagne. She would have liked a glass of bubbly, but wanted to keep her wits about her. Garvie, she presumed, was talking to Lord Carbrooke at this very moment, pressing him for his support of the Yelland Yard development and probably angling for an investment, too. Once that was done with, she'd be able to relax. Or would she? Carbrooke, she suspected, had a bone to pick with her.

She lit a cigarette and returned her attention to what was going on around. Most of the men were much older than the girls, their eyes greedy for smooth young flesh, their hands eager to touch. The drunker they got, the more blatant they became. And what was in it for the girls? Opportunities, of course. The chance of a rich lover to be bagged, some expensive gifts, or at the very least a nice wodge of cash left discreetly on a bedside table. What they were doing, she supposed, wasn't that different to what she did herself: taking advantage where advantage could be taken.

Liv was still contemplating this when a dark shadow fell over her and she looked up to see a tall blond man standing over her.

'Charlie Mayhew,' he said, extending a hand. 'I don't believe I've had the pleasure.'

Liv might have given him short shrift if it hadn't been for the familiarity of his name. It was possible, she thought, that he might be able to elaborate on Vicky's interesting but somewhat limited insights into the character of Hugh Garvie. She took his hand and shook it. 'Pleased to meet you. Liv Kent.'

'Do you mind?' he asked, indicating the chair beside her.

'Help yourself.'

Charlie settled himself down. 'So, Liv, what's a pretty girl like you doing sitting all alone?'

'Just passing the time. Observing.'

'And have you drawn any interesting conclusions from your observations?'

'Only that men of a certain age can be prone to foolishness.'

Charlie glanced towards the pool and laughed. 'I can't argue with you there, but you shouldn't judge them too harshly. Everyone needs a little fun in their lives.'

'I wasn't judging. I never judge anyone.'

'Good for you. You're Garvie's girl, aren't you?'

Charlie was younger than the other men – in his mid-thirties she estimated. A flop of fair hair fell over blue eyes that seemed simultaneously amused and calculating.

'Not his girl, his secretary.'

'Well, that's what I meant,' he said.

'Of course,' she replied, slightly raising her eyebrows. 'Are you a friend of his?'

'Lord, no. I barely know the chap. He often turns up here, though. What is it he's in – insurance, finance, something like that?'

'Property.'

'Ah,' he said.

'And what about you, Charlie? What's your line?'

'Fine wines. Nectar of the gods.' Charlie extended his long legs and crossed them at the ankles. 'I have to say, if I was Garvie I wouldn't leave you unattended. Someone might come along and lure you away.'

'I'm not sure I've ever been lured,' she said. 'Is it painful?'

Charlie grinned. 'Why don't you let me introduce you to a few people?'

'Maybe later. There is something you might be able to help me with, though.' Then she gave a small shake of her head. 'No, it doesn't matter. Forget it.'

'Tell me.'

'No, I shouldn't really ask.'

'Now I'm intrigued. Come on, ask away. You can trust old Charlie. I won't breathe a word, I swear.'

Liv frowned for a moment as if undecided, but then said in a lowered voice: 'It's to do with Hugh Garvie. I haven't been working for him long, you see, and I was told . . . I know you can't believe everything you hear, but I just wondered if it was true.'

Charlie inclined his head, waiting for her to elaborate.

Liv could only take a punt based on what Vicky had told her and so deliberately kept it vague. 'Erm, something about one of his former secretaries?'

'Oh, that,' he said. 'You mean the incident during the war?'

'Yes,' Liv said, nodding as though that was exactly what she'd meant.

'If it's facts you're after, I'm on shaky ground, but if rumour and gossip will do . . . '

Liv, needing something to take back to Lincoln, smiled at him sweetly and said, 'That will do just fine.'

Charlie sat forward, had a good look round to make sure no one was close enough to overhear, and then leaned back again. 'They say he was interviewed by the police more than once, but nothing came of it. I suppose when your secretary ends up dead there are always questions to be answered.'

Liv gave a start. 'Dead?'

'Didn't you know that?' As though delighting in her reaction, his eyes brightened and the corners of his mouth twitched. 'Oh dear, I didn't mean to shock you. Apologies. I'm always putting my foot in it. I suppose, with your current situation, it must make you a little nervous.'

'Only if he was guilty of killing her.'

'Well, rumour has it that their relationship wasn't confined to the office. He denied it, of course – the affair, as well as the murder – but mud does have a habit of sticking.'

Liv's mouth had gone dry. She swallowed hard. 'What happened to her?'

'She was strangled, I think, or was it stabbed? No, I can't remember. Still, the end result was the same, no matter what the method.'

'Do you know her name?'

Charlie shook his head. 'I can't help you there. Are you all right? You've gone rather pale.'

'Have I?' Liv forced a shaky smile. 'I suppose it's not every day you hear that your employer has been a suspect in a murder case.'

'To be fair, nothing was ever proved against him.'

'But was anything proved against anyone else?'

'I don't believe so,' Charlie said.

Liv was thinking about Rosa. Could it have been her? She inwardly cursed, wishing that she'd told Pally about going to work for Garvie. If she had then she'd have known about all this already. And she probably wouldn't even have been here. Pally would have put a stop to it. Which could be why, she suddenly realised, that Lincoln had insisted on her keeping quiet about the job.

'Are you sure you're all right?'

'Just taking it all in,' Liv said, trying to sound calmer than she felt. 'If there's so much rumour and gossip, how come he still gets invited to places like this?'

Charlie gave a casual shrug of his shoulders. 'Business is business. Money talks and Garvie's a rich man.'

'Even if that rich man's a murderer?'

'Innocent until proven guilty. Isn't that how it goes?'

'But what do *you* think?'

'What I think is that you're wasted on a man like that.' Charlie rose to his feet, took a business card out of his shirt pocket and handed it down to her. 'Give me a ring sometime. There's more to life than typing and filing.'

Liv, still reeling from what she'd learnt, took the card and slipped it into her bag. 'I may well do that,' she said, although she knew she never would.

Charlie grinned and strolled off to join his band of girls. Liv couldn't quite figure him out. Not exactly a pimp, she thought, but not far off. A man who could be relied upon to bring pretty girls to any party, but in return for what? A chance to hobnob with the rich and privileged, perhaps, to make connections and use them to his advantage.

Liv was still musing on this, and everything else, when Lord Carbrooke sat down heavily in the chair recently vacated by Charlie, gave her a disdainful look and said, with a hard edge to his voice: 'You can tell your friend Moody that this is it. I've kept my side of the bargain and it stops here. No more! If you lot think you can—'

'You lot?' Liv interrupted.

'I've done as much as I can,' he said. 'There's a limit. Do you understand?'

Liv, already thrown out of kilter by Charlie's revelations, felt her hackles rise. She didn't much care for the peer's tone or his attitude. He might be a lord but that didn't give him the right to lord it over her. 'I have never, and never will be, a part of Moody's *lot*. And if you think I'm here by choice, then think again. Moody has us both dangling on a string. If you have any messages for him, you can pass them on yourself.'

Carbrooke, clearly surprised by the outburst, looked at her closely, frowned and said: 'If that is the case, then I apologise. It appears that we are both in a position we do not wish to be in.'

'Apology accepted. So far as I'm concerned the sooner this is over, the better.'

'Perhaps a drink is in order. What do you say? Will you be so kind as to join me in a glass of champagne?'

Liv, having made her point, decided she would be so kind. 'Thank you.'

Carbrooke raised an arm, caught the attention of a man circling the pool with a tray and quickly procured the champagne. He passed a glass to her, sighed, took a sip of his drink and said, 'So you too are in Moody's debt?'

'Let's just say I inadvertently stepped on his toes. Now I'm paying the price for it.'

'We are both paying the price, my dear. Half an hour of

337

Garvie droning on about his damned development is enough to try the patience of a saint.'

'You should try working with him eight hours a day.'

'And how long will that continue for?'

'Until Moody says otherwise.'

Carbrooke threw her a sympathetic glance. 'I'm sorry to hear it. That can't be an appealing prospect.'

'It isn't.'

'What's Moody after, do you think? What does he want?'

'Information on Garvie. Pretty much anything and everything.'

'But to what end?'

'I have no idea,' Liv said, 'and to be honest I'd rather not know.'

'That's probably wise.' Carbrooke drank his champagne and his face assumed a thoughtful look. 'Perhaps there's more to this Yelland Yard business than meets the eye.' He drained his glass, put it down on the small table that lay between them, stood up and said, 'I've enjoyed our chat, but I really must get back to London.'

'You're leaving?'

'I think it would be wise, considering the circumstances, to put some distance between myself and Hugh Garvie. Good luck, Miss Kent. Hopefully, should we ever meet again, it will be in more agreeable circumstances.'

'Yes, let's hope so.'

Carbrooke made to go, took a step, stopped and turned around. 'Just a thought, my dear, but once this is over you should probably stay away from Mr Moody.'

'I could give you the same advice.'

'You could, my dear, but I'd be unlikely to follow it. Some of us are a lost cause.' He smoothed down his grey hair and gazed at her for a moment. 'You're an attractive girl. You should find yourself a nice young man to take care of you.'

Liv gave him a wave as he walked away. She briefly considered his suggestion before deciding, on balance, that she'd prefer to be a lost cause.

It was another half-hour before Garvie joined Liv by the pool. By then she had been approached by several different men, all thinking, as she was on her own, that she was fair game. Suggestive remarks had slipped from inebriated lips and wandering hands had settled on her thighs. Unused to advances from this particular brand of the male species – those whose innate sense of entitlement led them to believe they could have anything they wanted – she had repelled their advances with cool politeness.

Garvie took off his jacket, placed it over the back of the chair and sat down looking pleased with himself. 'Quite an afternoon,' he said.

'Did the meeting go well?'

'Couldn't have gone better. Yes, indeed. Quite a success! Lord Carbrooke was most interested in my ideas. We hit it off straight away. I think I can safely say, without blowing my own trumpet, that a good impression was made.' Then, unable to resist, he asked: 'Did he mention anything to you? I saw you talking. Did he ask about me?'

Liv might almost have felt sorry for him if Charlie Mayhew's rumours hadn't been so fresh in her mind – and if Garvie hadn't chosen that moment to let his gaze slide down from her face and linger brazenly on her breasts. 'No, he didn't say anything. Just chit-chat, I'm afraid. He's always careful when it comes to business. Still, I'm sure he'll give the proposal the attention it deserves.'

'Yes, he strikes me as the sort of man who knows a good deal when he hears it. Once he's had the chance to mull it over, I'm certain he'll see the benefits. He might even have an answer by tonight.'

'Oh, you won't get another chance to talk to him today. He had to rush off. An urgent phone call from London,' she improvised, not wanting him to suspect that Carbrooke had left because of him. 'A family problem, he said.'

Garvie was taken aback. 'What, he's gone? He's left Hollinghurst? But we were supposed to have a drink this evening. I was hoping to ...' He heaved out a sigh of disappointment. 'No chance of him coming back later, I suppose? Or tomorrow?'

'I didn't get that impression. Still, at least you got the chance to talk. That's good, isn't it?'

Garvie didn't answer immediately, his attention diverted by a tall, leggy blonde emerging from the pool like Venus. She climbed the shallow steps and raised her face to the sky. Her skin, brown and wet, glistened in the sun. Water ran down the back of her thighs in rivulets and gathered at her feet.

'Small mercies,' he murmured.

Liv, who wasn't looking forward to an evening of fighting off the advances of Garvie or any other marauding male, come to that, felt her heart sink. But then an idea, albeit a slightly risky one, came to her. 'To be honest, I think the phone call was just an excuse.'

Garvie's gaze shifted from the Venus back to Liv. 'An excuse?'

'To get away from here. He doesn't really approve of ...' Liv's eyes raked the pool and its carousing occupants. 'Well, he's rather straitlaced when it comes to certain matters, almost puritanical. And very much a family man.' Warming to her theme, she continued: 'He's very religious, you know, very principled. He always used to say that you can judge a man by his actions.

340

He'd never do business with anyone whose morals might be called into question.'

Garvie stared at her and Liv wondered if she'd gone too far. She needn't have worried, though. For a while he didn't respond, a frown appearing between his eyes as he weighed up his lust against his ambition, but it was the latter that eventually won out. 'Perhaps we should leave, too,' he said regretfully.

Liv tried to keep the relief from her voice. 'Whatever you think is best.' And then, in case he had a sudden change of heart, quickly added, 'Shall I go and get my things?'

63

Garvie drove with his right elbow balanced on the ledge of the open car window. He was a man who liked the sound of his own voice and so the only contribution required of her was to provide some obligatory nods, smiles and murmurs of agreement. As they wound through country lanes it occurred to her that if Charlie Mayhew's rumours were true, she could be travelling alone with a murderer. This gave her momentary cause for alarm until she decided that no one – unless they were a psychopath – would consider killing *two* of their secretaries. Even the dullest of policemen would get suspicious.

While she gazed through the windscreen at the hedges and fields, he discoursed at length on Yelland Yard, his hopes for its development and what it would mean for the future of Garvie & Carr. 'Not that Stephen appreciates it. That man doesn't know the meaning of the word ambition. He's weak, unfortunately; he has no nerve, no backbone, no gumption.'

Liv, who suspected that what he meant by backbone was having no qualms about kicking out inconvenient tenants, couldn't resist the obvious question. 'I hope you don't mind me asking, but what made you go into partnership in the first place?'

'Not from choice, I can assure you. I only did it for my sister's sake. Celia had the misfortune to fall for a man with limited intelligence and even more limited prospects, and by the time she realised, it was all too late. Stephen never takes the initiative; he doesn't have any drive, you see, any get up and go. He's the type who prefers to stroll through life, to always take the easy option. And where does that get you?' He didn't wait for an answer. 'Always at the back of the queue is where, that's if you're even in the queue at all.'

Liv, not for the first time, felt some sympathy for Stephen Carr. Having your brother-in-law constantly on your back couldn't be much fun. For Garvie, everything was black and white, simple and straightforward; there were no shades of grey.

'He should be grateful, but I've seen little evidence of it. Still, we all have our crosses to bear.' Garvie gently drummed his fingers on the steering wheel. 'One has to take care of family. That's the most important thing.'

'Yes, of course.'

'Even if one gets no thanks for it.'

Liv suspected he enjoyed having Stephen Carr beholden to him, forever in his debt. It gave him a feeling of superiority. He could sleep soundly at night, secure in the knowledge that he was the better man.

The journey continued with Garvie dominating the conversation. Liv didn't mind. It gave her the opportunity to think about other things, like the information she had gathered for Lincoln, seeing Pally again – he was bound to be in the French tonight – and the letter in her bag from Irene Lister. She would open the letter, she decided, as soon as she got back to London.

They were not far from Islington when Garvie gave a sudden grunt, laughed and said: 'I had a very strange phone call yesterday. Some man who wouldn't give his name.'

'Oh?'

'He asked if I had a Liv Anderson working for me. When I said no, he got quite shirty, insisting I was wrong and that I might know her as Olivia.'

Alarm ran through Liv, squeezing her throat. Who the hell had that been? Not Bentley, he wouldn't have withheld his identity, but maybe that snake McCall. 'My name,' she said lightly, forcing a smile. 'Apart from the Anderson bit.'

'An unpleasant man,' Garvie said.

'Well, it can't have been me he was after.'

'Out to cause trouble, no doubt about it.' Garvie frowned at the road ahead. 'He said I should watch out, that she was trouble, that she was connected to gangsters.'

'How bizarre,' Liv said, sure now that it *was* McCall. The creep had mentioned seeing her pass money to a gangster. 'Do you think he was quite right in the head?'

'Well, I'm presuming *you* don't make a habit of consorting with gangsters.'

Liv widened her eyes as she looked at him. 'Heavens, I don't think I've ever met one in my life.'

'No, of course not. How would you? The man was clearly a crank. Maybe I shouldn't have mentioned it. I wasn't going to, but then I thought that he could have mistaken you for someone else – whoever this Anderson woman is – and that this might not be the end of it.'

'Now you're starting to worry me.'

'I'm sure there's nothing to worry about. If he calls again, I'll ring the police. They'll soon get a trace on him.'

The last thing Liv wanted was to get the law involved, but she could hardly protest about it. 'Yes, that's true. We can always go to the police. It's all very strange though, isn't it?'

'Strange indeed.'

Liv threw Garvie a few sidelong glances, trying to read his expression, wondering if the mystery caller had raised any suspicions in his mind. It was fortunate, she thought, that Lord Carbrooke had been there today to provide her with the credibility she needed. She tried not to fidget, to look unduly concerned, but this latest development wasn't a good one.

Garvie drew up outside the flat in Duncan Terrace, got out, opened the passenger door and then went to the boot to get her overnight case. 'How about a coffee before I go?'

Liv wasn't surprised by the suggestion, but all she wanted was to get rid of him. 'Would you mind awfully if we left it? I have a bit of a headache. Too much sun, probably.' She reached out and took the case from him. 'Thank you. I hope you enjoy the rest of your weekend.'

'I'll see you on Monday, then.'

'Yes, on Monday.'

Garvie, somewhat reluctantly, got back in the car. She walked quickly to the front door, got out the keys, turned, waved and went inside. She heard the car engine start up and the car pull away. 'Bloody McCall,' she said under her breath as she walked across the hall and unlocked the second door that led into the flat.

Immediately she went to the window to check that Garvie was gone. What next? Lincoln wouldn't be expecting her back so early. She was tempted to catch a bus home and call him from Soho, but that hadn't been the arrangement. No, she'd better find a phone box – there was no phone in the flat – and let him know she was back.

Liv waited five minutes to make sure Garvie was clear of

the area before strolling on to Upper Street. It was almost four o'clock and the street, caught in that time between shoppers going home and the pubs opening, was relatively quiet. She found a phone box near the Tube, slipped inside and dialled the number for the Paradise.

On this occasion the phone was answered by a woman. She asked Liv to hold on while she went to look for Lincoln. After a while the pips went and Liv had to put in more money. Just as she was starting to wonder if she had enough change to hold the line, Lincoln finally picked up the phone.

'Yeah?'

'It's me, Liv,' she said, speaking quickly. 'I'm in Islington. Garvie decided to come back early.'

'Did Carbrooke show up?'

'Yes, that was all fine. What do you want me to do now?'

'I can't get away right this minute.'

'Shall I go home and give you a ring later?'

There was a short pause. 'No, come to the Paradise. I'll send a cab for you. Don't worry, it'll be on Moody's tab.'

Liv might have protested – she had no desire to come face to face with Don Moody – but the pips were going again. By the time they'd ended, Lincoln had hung up.

She walked slowly back to the flat, let herself in and had a wander round the rooms while she waited for the cab. The place had a musty, abandoned air as though it hadn't been lived in for a while; there was dust on every surface and cobwebs in the corners of the ceilings. In the bedroom the wardrobe and the drawers were empty. There was no food in the pantry, no towels or soap in the bathroom. After five minutes she'd exhausted her examination and went to sit at the table by the living-room window.

Liv couldn't make up her mind whether or not to tell Lincoln about Garvie's mystery phone call. If she did, he might decide that her cover had been blown, and she didn't know where that would leave her as regards the debt she owed Moody. Perhaps she could have a word with Henry, instead. Although she had no actual proof that McCall had been the caller, it seemed pretty likely.

The minutes ticked by. Liv's thoughts moved on to the letter in her handbag. She got it out and turned it around in her fingers. The envelope was heavy vellum and cream coloured. She ran her tongue over her lips and stared at the writing on the front. *Open it*, a voice in her head demanded, but still she hesitated, afraid of what might be inside.

She raised her eyes to look out at the street, hoping that the cab might arrive and save her from making the decision. The space outside the house remained empty. It didn't matter how long she delayed, the contents of the envelope would remain the same, but she had to be prepared for disappointment. She knew, even as she put this argument to herself, that it was ridiculous. How could you ever be 'prepared'? It was either good news or bad and no amount of procrastination was going to change the outcome.

Before she lost her nerve, Liv took a deep breath, tore open the envelope and unfolded the single sheet of paper. Quickly she read the short reply from Irene.

Dear Miss Anderson,
    Thank you for your letter. Regretfully, a meeting between us will not be possible. There is nothing further I can tell you about the terrible incident that took place so many years ago. I do, however, wish you all the very best for the future.
    Yours sincerely,
    Irene Forster

Liv read the letter through twice and then flung it down on the table. Anger surged through her, a red flush burning her cheeks. Regretfully? That was a joke. She didn't believe the damn woman possessed a single ounce of regret. Tears of rage and frustration pricked her eyes. Irene had been her last hope, her best chance of getting to the truth, and now it had all been swept away in the space of a few lines.

64

The Paradise, situated at the Regent Street end of Great Marlborough Street, was as shabby on the inside as it was on the out. Whether this was a result of sheer miserliness or a deliberate ploy to disguise the amount of money being made – useful, she supposed, if the law came sniffing round – Liv had no idea. A red, somewhat threadbare carpet covered the floor of the foyer. To her left a bored-looking girl was sitting in a cubicle, examining her nails.

'I'm here to see Mr Lincoln,' Liv said.

The girl waved her red talons towards a pair of double doors. 'Through there.'

The red theme was continued in the almost empty room that lay beyond: red walls, more red carpet. Liv walked over to the bar at the far end and repeated the same words to the barman. 'I'm here to see Mr Lincoln.'

The barman looked her up and down, clocked the bag she was carrying and, probably, the less than happy expression on her face and instantly narrowed his eyes as though she might be the kind of girl his boss might not welcome seeing. 'He expecting you?'

'Yes. Tell him Liv's here.'

'I'm not sure if he's around.'

'Well, you won't find out until you ask.'

A familiar voice came from behind her. 'It's all right, Jamie. Get me my usual, and whatever the lady wants.'

Liv turned to find Lincoln standing behind her. She gave him a nod, turned back to the barman and said, 'I'll have a vodka and tonic, please.'

Once the drinks had been poured, Lincoln led her to a table at the side of the room and away from the half-dozen customers, none of whom seemed interested in anything other than the glasses they were staring into. Liv sat down and tried to organise her thoughts. All she wanted was to get this over and done with so she could get out of here, head over to the French and see Pally. What she needed was a friendly face and someone she could trust.

Quickly Liv began telling him about the rumours she had heard from Charlie Mayhew, about the secretary who'd been murdered and how Garvie had been interviewed by the police. 'I know it's only gossip, it doesn't prove anything, but it makes you wonder, doesn't it?'

'Do you know what the girl's name was?'

Liv shook her head. 'But I can find out.'

'And how are you going to do that?'

'I can ask Muriel, Stephen Carr's secretary. She's been there for years. She'll know.'

Lincoln stared at her like she was mad. 'Are you kidding me? What if she tells Garvie? You start asking questions like that and you'll set alarm bells ringing all over the place.'

'I can do subtle, you know. I'm not stupid. I'm not just going to ask her out of the blue.'

'Don't ask her at all. I can find out. It shouldn't be that difficult.'

'Fine,' Liv said. 'I'll leave it with you.'

'What else have you got?'

Liv went on to tell him about what Vicky had said. 'Garvie seems to have something of a reputation.'

'That's no big surprise.'

'I was going to try and find out more, but then he decided to leave so ...' Liv shrugged and drank some vodka. 'I didn't get the chance.'

'Why do you think he did that?'

Liv knew it wouldn't be wise to tell him the truth. 'I suppose he'd already got what he wanted: his opportunity to talk to Lord Carbrooke.' She didn't mention how the lord had taken off in a hurry, thinking it might get him in bother with Moody. Victims had to stick together. 'Garvie was full of it all on the way home, about how well it had gone and how he was sure he'd get the backing he needed for the planning committee. He's obsessed with the Yelland Yard development. He won't be happy when he gets knocked back.'

'I don't suppose he will,' Lincoln said, standing up.

'Are we done?' Liv asked hopefully.

'No, I just have to check something downstairs.'

Lincoln disappeared down a flight of wide, shallow stairs to where, she presumed, the casino was in operation. Liv glanced at her watch. It was almost five o'clock and a few new customers were starting to drift in. She drank her vodka and lit a cigarette. With nothing better to do, she looked around the bar, struck again by the profusion of red – red walls, red carpet, red chairs – that even the dimness of the lighting couldn't subdue. Either Don Moody was extraordinarily fond of the colour or he'd inherited it when he took over the place.

Thinking of Moody made her uneasy. She wondered if he was in the basement and her apprehension shifted into something more acute. What if Lincoln had gone down to tell him she was here? What if the two of them walked back up the stairs together? She could feel her heart start to beat a little faster. Maybe she should get out of here right now, grab the chance to run. But even as the idea entered her head, she knew she wouldn't do it. Running away wouldn't achieve anything.

It was ten long minutes before Lincoln finally returned – thankfully, alone. He didn't sit down but stood over her and said, 'Come on, let's finish this somewhere else.'

'Don't they need you here? Don't you have to work?'

'They can manage without me.'

Liv didn't even know why she was asking the questions. Just being in the Paradise made her feel anxious. But she'd been hoping that she and Lincoln could quickly conclude their business and then she'd be free of him. He, apparently, had other ideas.

Lincoln picked up her bag and they left the Paradise together. Outside on the street, he said: 'Let's go and get some food. I haven't eaten since breakfast. Greek all right with you?'

'Sure,' she said, resigning herself to at least another hour of his company. The man seemed to be in a permanent state of starvation. 'There isn't much more to tell you, though.'

'How did it go with you and Carbrooke?' he asked, as if to refute her statement.

'It was fine, good. He was very convincing. I don't think Garvie had any suspicions.'

'You don't *think* he had?'

'He didn't,' Liv said firmly.

Lincoln led her to a little backstreet restaurant in the heart of Soho. In comparison to Wheeler's, the place was pretty basic:

wooden tables and benches, bare brick walls, and a waiter who didn't seem to care whether they ate or not. When Lincoln eventually got the man's attention, he ordered *kleftiko* and a bottle of wine. 'Unless you want something else?' he asked Liv.

Liv, who was not au fait with Greek cuisine, shook her head and said, 'If that's what you recommend.'

The waiter, with no particular sense of urgency, stopped to chat to a fellow worker before delivering their order to the kitchen.

'Yeah,' Lincoln said, 'it's not exactly silver service, but it's worth it for the food.' Then, barely missing a beat, he got straight back to business. 'So, I still don't get why Garvie came back so early. If he's such a one for the girls, why didn't he take advantage of what was on offer?'

'Perhaps he's turned over a new leaf.' Liv could see that Lincoln wasn't buying it – men like Hugh Garvie didn't change their spots overnight – and so furnished him with an alternative, rather more truthful theory. 'Or perhaps he didn't want to make a bad impression with Lord Carbrooke. You know, come across as the sort of man who has no moral backbone, who spends more time chasing women than concentrating on the job.'

'Carbrooke's hardly Mr Virtuous. He wouldn't give a damn.'

'Yes, but Garvie might not be aware of that.'

Lincoln played with the cutlery on the table, shoved his knife and fork around for a while and then looked up. 'He didn't even make a move on you?'

'Nothing serious. When he dropped me off, he tried to ask himself in for a cup of coffee, but that was about it.'

'You must be losing your charms,' he said.

'I find that hard to believe.'

Lincoln gave her a dubious smile, the sort that didn't reach his eyes.

Liv ploughed on, regardless. 'There is one other thing. Garvie doesn't like Stephen Carr. Did you know that Carr's his brother-in-law? He claims he only made him a partner to help out his sister. They were rowing over Yelland Yard on Thursday, going at it hammer and tongs. There's no love lost there, that's for sure.'

Before Lincoln could respond, the food arrived, along with the bottle of wine. A silence fell over the table as they both dug in. Liv, who had not been especially hungry, now found herself enticed by the wonderful smells and the delicious tenderness of the lamb.

'It's good, huh?' Lincoln said.

'It's very good. How did you find this place?'

'A tip-off from a punter. There have to be some advantages to working at the Paradise.'

Liv drank some wine. She should probably be careful – she'd already had the vodka, and mixing drinks wasn't the best of ideas – but being less than sober felt like a necessity after everything she'd been through today. It had all been nerve-racking: the charade with Lord Carbrooke, her time with Garvie, and then the opening of the letter from Irene Forster. She thought of those dismissive words and anger rose in her again.

'What is it?' Lincoln asked.

Liv shook her head. 'Nothing.'

'Something's bugging you. You've had a face on you all evening. I thought you'd be glad to see the back of Garvie.'

'I am glad.'

'Well then?'

'It's nothing to do with Garvie.'

'So what is it to do with?'

Liv put down her glass. 'It's personal.'

'Another type of man trouble, then,' Lincoln said, grinning. 'You having a spot of romantic bother?'

'Jesus, women do have other worries, you know. They don't spend their whole lives thinking about men.'

'Okay, no need to get in a flap.'

'I'm not in a flap,' she snapped.

'You could have fooled me.'

Liv scowled at him and drank some more wine. Her problems were her business, and she certainly wasn't going to share them with him. It annoyed her, though, that he'd been able to read her so easily. She usually did a pretty good job of hiding her feelings.

Lincoln, as if pleased to have got under her skin, smirked and said: 'Come on, eat up. I know a nice little pub round the corner.'

65

Liv, initially frustrated by her failure to shake off Lincoln, was past caring by the time she'd sunk her third vodka and tonic. It wasn't exactly how she'd planned to spend her Saturday night, but it could have been worse. The pub was pleasant, busy without being overcrowded, and they'd found a table in a corner where they could continue to talk in private.

Lincoln had been asking her more questions about Garvie when he suddenly changed tack and said: 'So, this personal thing you've got going. What's all that about?'

Liv frowned at him. 'The clue's in the word personal. It's private.'

'I'll just keep asking until you tell me.'

'That's going to make for a tedious evening.'

'It is,' Lincoln said. 'Come on, it can't be that bad. Maybe I can give you some good advice. I've been around the block; there's nothing you can say that will shock me.'

'You think?'

Lincoln's eyebrows shifted up. '*That* bad, huh?'

Under normal circumstances, sober circumstances, Liv wouldn't have breathed a word, but under the influence of alcohol she decided she could safely tell him some of the story without giving him the whole. At least it might shut him up, stop him going on about it. 'All right, then. I wrote a letter to someone, a woman, a woman who'd been seeing my father before he died. They'd been having an affair. Well, I think they had, I'm pretty sure. She was married, too. I just wanted to understand what happened between them. I asked if we could meet and talk about it.' Liv stopped, took a drink and carried on. 'Anyway, to cut a long story short, she wrote back and said no.'

'And you're surprised by that?'

'Did I say I was surprised? I just thought she might have the common decency to spare me five minutes. I don't think it's too much to ask. That woman ruined my mother's life.'

'I imagine that's why she doesn't want to see you.'

Liv gave him a look. 'Yes, well, we all have to do things we don't want to.'

Lincoln took the jibe on the chin, smiled faintly and said: 'When did this happen? The affair, I mean.'

'A long time ago. When I was two. But I didn't find out about it until much later. My mum told me before she died. I've only just got the woman's address so I thought . . . '

'Thought what? What is it you want from her?' Lincoln sat back, folding his arms. 'I mean, affairs aren't that unusual. Men behave badly, women behave badly: we all do things we shouldn't.'

There was something about his blasé attitude that got under her skin. 'You don't understand.'

'So spell it out for me.'

But how could she without revealing precisely what she was trying to avoid? Instead, she said: 'Irene just carried on, got married again after her husband died, but my mum was never able to do that. She was broken by it all.' Liv reached for her drink again. 'You can't just go around destroying people's lives and then refuse to give even the smallest of explanations. Irene owes me that, doesn't she?'

'Perhaps she doesn't want her latest husband to know what she did.'

'He already knows.'

'What makes you so certain?'

Liv gave a shrug. 'Someone told me.'

'So maybe she doesn't want to be reminded of past mistakes.'

'I don't see how that's her decision to make. My father's dead, my mum's dead; she's the only one left who can shed any light on what really happened.'

'What *really* happened?' Lincoln was back to sounding nonchalant again. 'I'm not sure how much there is to explain about two people doing the dirty on their partners. They meet, they fall in love or lust or whatever you want to call it, and others get hurt. Surely you don't want all the sordid little details? I can't see how that's going to help.'

'It's more complicated than that.'

Lincoln fixed his eyes on her. 'Why do I get the feeling I'm only getting half the story?'

'It doesn't matter. Forget about it. I knew I shouldn't have told you.'

'Don't be like that.'

'I'm not being like anything.'

'Yes, you are. You're being all prickly and defensive.'

'Can we just drop this?'

'You see, you're doing it right now.'

'For God's sake,' Liv said. 'Will you stop? I don't want to talk about this any more.'

'You don't want my advice, then?'

Liv groaned. 'I already know what your wonderful advice is: it happened and I can't change it, so grow up, accept it and leave it be, yeah?'

Lincoln put two cigarettes in his mouth, lit them and passed one to her. 'Actually, what I was going to say is that if you need to talk to this Irene so much, just go to her house and see her. If you've got her address, what's stopping you? You don't have to wait for an invitation.'

'You think I haven't thought of that? I can't *make* her talk to me.'

'Sure you can. And if she won't invite you in, sit on the doorstep until she does. I dare say she'll come around to the idea eventually.'

'Or call the law,' Liv said.

'Since when were you afraid of the law?' Lincoln pulled on his cigarette and gave a low laugh. 'Anyway, I shouldn't think she'll do that. She's not going to want the local plod knowing all the seedy details of some old love affair.'

Liv turned the suggestion over in her head. She hadn't looked at it from this particular angle before and it seemed to make perfect sense. Why not? It wasn't down to Irene to call all the shots. 'Perhaps I will do that.'

But, of course, Lincoln couldn't leave it there. Having provided some hope, he promptly tried to snatch it away again. 'Although you should probably prepare yourself for the worst, for hearing things you might not want to hear. The truth isn't always all it's cracked up to be. You could end up being even more miserable than you are now.'

'Oh, thanks for that. I'll bear it in mind. And I'm not miserable, I'm just . . .'

Lincoln grinned. 'Bitter and resentful?'

Liv, who had marginally warmed to him, now found her feelings rapidly cooling. 'I'm just looking for some answers.'

'And what if you don't like the ones you get? No one really knows what goes on in someone else's marriage. You've only had your mother's version, but there's always two sides to every story. You can blame Irene for what went wrong, blame your dad, but when people are unhappy, they don't always make good decisions.'

'Are you actually trying to make excuses for them?'

'I'm being realistic.'

Liv felt a spurt of anger. 'None of it was Mum's fault. You should know when to stop talking, especially when you don't know what you're talking about.'

'All right, no need to go off on one.'

'I wouldn't have to if you weren't being so annoying!'

'I'm only trying to save you from yourself,' he said provocatively. 'Don't you think you might be overreacting to all this?'

If Liv hadn't drunk so much, she would have realised he was deliberately goading her, trying to push her into revealing more than she wanted to. Seeing red, the words shot out of her mouth before she could think twice. 'Overreacting? I'll tell you what overreacting is: it's shooting dead your mistress's husband, killing him in front of a hundred other people, it's taking someone else's life because you can't get your own way.'

Lincoln stared across the table at her.

As soon as it was said, she regretted it, but it was too late. The cat was out of the bag and couldn't be put back in. 'There! Happy now?'

If he felt shock or even surprise, Lincoln didn't show it. 'Ah,' he said, almost smugly. 'That puts a different slant on things.'

66

Liv woke to the thin, grey light of dawn slipping through the sides of the curtains. Her mouth was parched, her head throbbing. There was a short delay, a reckoning in her hungover brain, before everything started coming back to her: the Paradise, the Greek restaurant, the pub and then ... and then back to Lincoln's flat for coffee. Except they hadn't quite got around to the coffee.

God, no. A shudder ran through her. What had she done? What had *they* done? She didn't want to believe it, but the evidence was lying only inches from her. She could hear him breathing, feel the heat emanating from his body. Her instinct was to leap out of bed, to get away from him as quickly as possible, but she couldn't run the risk of waking him up.

Liv waited a minute and then very carefully, very slowly, lowered one foot on to the floor and then the other. She stopped, glanced over at him, checked he was still fast asleep and then stood up. Immediately she knelt down to gather up her clothes from the floor, took them through to the living room and hurriedly got dressed. She pushed her feet into her shoes, grabbed her handbag, picked up her case and fled the flat, closing the door softly behind her.

Outside it took her a moment to get her bearings, to work out exactly where in Soho she was. Not too far from Whitcomb Street, thankfully. She set off at a brisk pace, partly to warm herself up in the chill morning air, but mainly to put as much distance as she could between herself and Lincoln. Regret was too small a word for what had happened. She was disgusted, ashamed, mortified. She had slept with the enemy, for God's sake, with the man who'd arranged to have Pally beaten up, the man who had her working for Garvie. What was wrong with her? She bowed her head, cursed her stupidity and wished she could turn back time.

If she could have erased her memory, she would, but even through her fogged brain Liv could still recall most of the evening. The only detail that was missing was the exact moment when Lincoln had passed from being an adversary to being an object of desire. Perhaps it had been when she'd told him about her father and, just for a while, he'd stopped being such a wise arse.

The streets were almost deserted with only a few early risers – or maybe late refugees from the night before – sharing the space with her. She wondered if any of them felt as bad as she did. It had started to rain and she hunched her shoulders as she hurried on. From the distance came a gentle rumble of thunder. She was going to get soaked but there was nothing she could do about it.

Liv's thoughts slid back to Lincoln. It would be easier if she could claim that he'd taken advantage, but it wasn't true: she was the one who'd pressed him into taking her back to his flat, she was the one who'd made the first move. The sex had been fast and urgent, a thrashing of limbs, skin against skin, searching mouths and heaving breath. She briefly closed her eyes as if to blank out the recollection. Her only excuse was that fundamental need for human contact, human comfort, but even that didn't cut it in the circumstances.

By the time she reached Whitcomb Street the rain was driving down, skimming over the pavement and pooling in the gutters. Her clothes were drenched and her shoes squelched as she walked. A flash of lightning lit up the sky and made her jump. She yearned for a long hot bath and the chance to scrub away the smell of Lincoln.

Running the last few yards, she scrabbled for her key on the doorstep and let herself in. Quietly she entered the hall, laid her case on the bottom step of the stairs and headed towards the kitchen to get a glass of water. The door was ajar and she heard a sound, a gentle rustling, coming from inside.

'Dora?' she said softly. 'Is that you?'

There was no reply. She pushed open the door and went in. The kitchen appeared to be empty and the first thing she noticed through the gloom was a small rucksack lying on the table. It was a light brown colour with its flap open. A folded jumper and a shirt were lying beside it, as well as bread and cheese and cigarettes. There was barely time to take any of this in before she felt the movement behind her. She half turned but already it was too late: an arm had snaked around her neck and a hand clamped across her mouth.

Liv tried to struggle, to free herself, but his hold was too tight. Panic rose in her. A voice hissed in her ear. 'Stay still, you bitch, or I'll break your bloody neck.'

Terrified, Liv did as he said. She could feel the rage – or was it fear? – rising off him like steam. She could feel the tension in his body. Once he was sure she was compliant, he began dragging her roughly across the kitchen. The crook of his arm dug into her throat, squeezing ever harder, making it difficult for her to breathe.

She knew it was Larry – it had to be – but knowing didn't help her any. She tried to suck in some air, to think, to figure out a way to escape, but everything was happening too fast. Her heart was thrashing, her chest heaving with fright. His fingers tightened against her mouth. She felt the desire in him to hurt her, to hurt her badly. Moll Ainsworth flashed across her mind – strangled, murdered – and her head was filled with horror.

Unwilling to submit, Liv did the only thing she could and kicked out with a foot. The heel of her shoe made contact with his ankle and he flinched and cursed and staggered to one side. They collided with the table causing it to judder and to send a cup flying off the side. It smashed on to the floor, the crash echoing through the house.

'Bitch!'

With new courage, Liv kicked out again. All she had to do was hold him off for a few more seconds. Salvation was on its way. She could hear footsteps padding quickly across the lino in the hall and the next second Dora was standing at the door.

'Let go of her! What are you doing? Let go, Larry!'

Larry, obedient to his mother, loosened his grip and pushed her away. 'I caught the little tart sneaking around.'

Liv fled around the table to Dora. 'I wasn't sneaking,' she said hoarsely, touching her throat. 'I live here, for God's sake.'

'Are you all right, love?' Dora asked.

'No thanks to him.'

'I barely touched her,' Larry said, bending to rub at his ankle. 'She shouldn't creep up on people like that. What was I sup-posed to think?'

It was the first time Liv had seen him properly. He was about five foot eight, thin, bearded, with shifty, hooded eyes. An angry muscle twitched at the corner of his mouth. She didn't want to think about what might have happened if that cup hadn't fallen off the table.

Dora's gaze jumped from Larry to Liv and back to Larry before coming to rest on the rucksack. 'What's this? Where are you going?'

'Anywhere, as long as it's away from here.'

'You can't go,' Dora said. 'What about the police? It's not safe out there.'

Larry gave a snort and began stuffing the shirt and jumper into the rucksack. 'Safer than staying here. It's only a matter of time before that cop comes back. And now she's seen me,' he said, glaring at Liv. 'Best if I don't hang around, I reckon.'

'She won't say nothing. Liv's a good girl.'

'You're too trusting, Mum, that's your trouble.'

Dora stared at him. 'You were going to leave without saying goodbye.'

'Of course not,' Larry said unconvincingly. 'I'd have woken you before I left. I just wanted to get packed up first.'

Liv wondered how long Larry had been hidden for, how long Dora had been sheltering him. It made her feel sick to think of him lurking in the house. Then, realising this might be her last opportunity, she blurted out, 'What did you do with my jewellery?'

Larry scowled at her. 'I don't have a clue what you're talking about. What bloody jewellery?'

Liv persisted. 'I know you took it. Please, just tell me who you flogged it to. That's all. It's not too much to ask, is it?'

But Larry wasn't playing. 'Are you calling me a thief?' He looked at Dora. 'Do you hear that, Mum? She's calling me a bloody thief.'

Dora said nothing.

Like a man unfairly accused, Larry shook his head and muttered while he put the rest of the items into the rucksack. Then, when he was done, he fastened up the flap and said: 'Right, that's it. I'm off.'

'At least stay and have some breakfast,' Dora said. 'It's still early and it's pouring down out there. Sit down and I'll cook you something.'

'A bit of rain never hurt anyone.'

'Ten minutes,' Dora pleaded. 'What difference will that make?'

'Sorry, Mum. It's time to go.' He hoisted the rucksack on to his back, moved around the table, bent and kissed her on the cheek. 'Don't worry about me. I'll be fine.' Dora tried to hold on to his sleeve, but he pulled away. 'You take care of yourself, huh?' Then he pushed past Liv, gave her a dirty look, unbolted the back door and stepped out into the garden.

The rain was still coming down in sheets. Lightning split the sky and a loud clap of thunder made everyone jump. Larry ran to the wall, pulled himself up and dropped down the other side without looking back.

Dora stood by the door gazing unhappily into the empty space her son had recently occupied. She looked small and sad and fragile. Liv stood beside her and the two of them were quiet for a while. Liv wasn't sorry to see the back of him, but she felt for Dora.

'It won't be for ever,' Liv said.

Dora shut the door, slumped down at the table and rubbed her face with her hands. She sighed deeply and said, 'He's gone now. He won't be back.'

'He will,' Liv insisted. 'One day.'

Dora's eyes filled with tears. She took a handkerchief from

366

her dressing-gown pocket and dabbed at her eyes. 'No, he's not coming back, not ever. This is it. I saw it in the cards, love.'

Liv didn't know what to say to that so she just gently patted Dora's shoulder. Then she knelt down, collected the shattered pieces of the cup off the floor and placed them in the bin.

'Did he hurt you?' Dora asked.

'Not really,' Liv lied. 'I didn't want to wake anyone up so I was being quiet. I suppose I took him by surprise.'

Fortunately, Dora was too preoccupied by Larry leaving to wonder how Liv had got back from Kent before the first trains had even started running. 'I couldn't turn him away. He had nowhere else to go.'

'You're his mum. What else could you do?'

'He's had a raw deal,' Dora said. 'Life hasn't been kind to him.'

Larry, Liv thought, hadn't exactly been brimming over with kindness himself. She was starting to shiver, perhaps as much from delayed shock as from the wet clothes she was wearing. 'I think I'll go up and have a bath. Will you be all right? Shall I make you a brew?'

Dora heaved herself to her feet. 'No, you get on. I'll be just fine. You won't tell anyone, will you, Liv, about Larry being here?'

'No, of course not.'

Liv walked along the hall, picked up her case, traipsed quietly up the stairs and went into her room. Her hand rose to her throat, to where Larry had grabbed her in a stranglehold, and she felt the thin silver chain of the locket Lincoln had loaned her. Quickly she took it off and laid it on the dressing table. She should have left it at his flat, but it was too late now; it would have to be returned when they next met up. The thought of that moment, of seeing him again, made her stomach shift.

67

Slug thought at first that he'd been woken by the crashes of thunder or the rain lashing down. Sleepily he stirred, turned over and prepared to go back to sleep. But then the noise came again – a thin scraping sound – and he was instantly alert. The back door didn't lock and so in order to provide an early warning system against unwanted visitors he always placed a heavy stone against it. It was that stone that was moving now, being pushed slowly across the floor.

Slug leapt up and launched himself against the door. 'Who is it? Who's there?'

No one answered, but the pressure against the door continued.

'Clear off or I'll set the dog on you!'

Not strong enough to resist, Slug found himself pushed ever further back until the gap was wide enough for the intruder to squeeze through. And then, much to his dismay, he found himself face to face with Larry Marks.

'What's wrong, mate? You don't look too pleased to see me.'

'You ain't got no business here,' Slug said. 'You're on private property.'

'Now that's no way to greet a fellow man of the streets. It's pissin' down out there. You can spare a bit of shelter, can't you?'

'What do you want?'

Larry Marks wasn't big, but he was bigger than Slug and had an air of menace about him. He looked around, taking in the old brick walls and sparse furnishings. 'God, this place is a dump. Where's this dog of yours, then? The invisible hound, is it?' He laughed softly and dropped his rucksack on the floor. 'As it happens, we do have a bit of business. You remember that money my poor mum gave you? Well, she wants it back so I've come to collect.'

'We made a deal, fair and square.'

'There weren't nothin' fair about that deal and you know it.' Larry put out his hand. 'Come on, the sooner you pass it over, the sooner I'll be out of here.'

Slug retreated a few feet. 'We made a deal,' he said again. 'There's no going back on it now.'

Larry shook his head. 'But you didn't keep to your side of the bargain, did you? You went running to the law like the pissy little grass you are.'

'I ain't been near the law. Swear to God, I ain't.'

'So, just a coincidence then that Bentley came sniffing round the minute you'd got your greedy little paws on the cash?'

'I don't know nothin' about that.'

Larry snarled, showing brown, chipped teeth. 'You're a fuckin' liar.'

'Anyone could have seen you,' Slug said. 'Anyone could have tipped him off. But it weren't me. When I make a deal, I stick to it.'

'Maybe it was Moll, then, huh? You think she grassed me up?'

Larry started wandering around the room, picking things up and putting them down. 'What do you reckon? She was always a mean cow, that one.'

As Larry moved, Slug moved too, always trying to keep a distance between them. 'I don't know.'

'You don't know much, do you, old man? Except when it suits you. Yeah, she was a tight old bitch, couldn't even spare me a few quid. I mean, what's that all about?' Larry stared at Slug through cold, angry eyes. 'You're all the same, only out for yourselves. If I had my way, I'd finish off every bloody grass in the country.'

'I've told you, I'm no grass.'

'Yeah, yeah, I get it. You're clean as a whistle, a diamond, a bleedin' saint; you just like threatening old ladies. I mean, that's not nice, Slug, is it? Robbing a poor old dear like my mum. As if she hasn't got it hard enough already, paying the bills and putting food on the table.'

'I didn't rob no one.'

'Near as damn it. She didn't give it to you out of the goodness of her heart, did she? No, you took advantage and you know it.'

Slug might have retorted that Larry was hardly above taking advantage himself, but knew better than to provoke him. 'I could have gone to the law, told them I'd seen you, but I didn't. That was worth a few quid, wasn't it?'

Outside the storm was still raging. The wind rocked the derelict house and made the ceiling creak and groan. Larry looked up, frowning.

'It ain't safe,' Slug said. 'One day the whole lot's going to come down. I wouldn't hang about if I were you.'

Larry grinned. 'You trying to get shot of me, Slug? That's not very polite.'

Slug quickly dug in his pocket and pulled out a couple of

crumpled pound notes. He took a few steps forward and thrust the notes towards Larry. 'Here, take them.'

Larry snatched the cash. 'What about the rest?'

'That's it. That's the lot. It's all I've got left.'

'Been living the high life, have you, Slug? Enjoying yourself at my mum's expense?' Larry's gaze roamed around the room again, eventually coming to rest on a bottle of Navy rum sitting on the floor by the armchair. He leaned down, picked it up, unscrewed the cap and gave the contents a sniff. Once he was convinced that it was actually alcohol and not anything of a less desirable nature, he took a swig and smacked his lips. 'That's more like it. You didn't tell me you had a bottle. Slipped your mind, did it?'

'You didn't ask,' Slug said.

Larry sat down in the armchair, making himself comfortable. He drank some more rum and placed the bottle on his thigh. 'I don't like grasses,' he hissed. 'They're the lowest of the low. If you hadn't gone running to Bentley, he'd never have guessed I was back. You fucked things up for me, Slug, you fucked them up, good and proper. I could be at home right now, all tucked up safe and sound with nothing to worry about, but instead I'm sitting here staring at your ugly mug.'

'I ain't no grass,' Slug whined, even though he was aware that no matter how many times he repeated it, he wasn't going to be believed. Larry had got it into his head that he was guilty and nothing he said was going to change that. But still he tried to reason with him. 'If I'd told Bentley, you'd have been nicked by now. They'd have turned the house over.'

Larry gulped down more of the rum, his Adam's apple bobbing in his throat. 'He's just playing with me, like a cat with a mouse.'

Slug knew this didn't make any sense, but he also knew that

371

Larry was beyond logic or rationality: the bloke had a screw loose and the booze wasn't helping any. He wished now that he *had* gone to Bentley. If he'd made that choice instead, he'd still be sleeping soundly and Larry would be behind bars.

'That Moll deserved what she got,' Larry said.

Slug recoiled, his anxiety level shifting up a notch. The last thing he wanted to hear was a confession. He had his suspicions, but he didn't need the truth laid out in black and white. Once Larry did that there was no going back. He ran his tongue along dry lips, wondering if it was worth trying to do a runner. His gaze slid towards the open door.

'Do you believe in bad blood, Slug?'

'Never thought about it.'

'No, I don't suppose you have. What are you standing over there for? Why don't you sit down? You're making the place look untidy.'

Reluctantly, Slug perched on the edge of an upended crate.

'Yeah, bad blood,' Larry continued. 'That's what my dad used to say I had. You know what else he said, Slug?'

'No.'

'No, of course you don't. How could you? He said what else could you expect when you buy a baby off a whore!' Larry gave an odd laugh and raised the bottle to his lips again. 'That's where I come from, you see – I'm the son of a bloody whore! Now that's not anything a lad wants to overhear when he's fifteen, is it? That you've been sold by some tart, like some crappy object that isn't wanted any more. No, it's not what you want to hear at all.'

Slug wondered again about trying to scarper. He was closer to the door than Larry. All he had to do was climb up those steps, run around the side of the house and get out on to the street. But he didn't fancy his chances, not in this weather, and when Larry caught up with him . . .

372

'Are you even listening to me? Here I am, baring my soul to you, man to man, sharing all the family secrets and you're not even paying attention. I could take offence if I was the sensitive sort.'

'I'm listening,' Slug said. 'Yeah, it's bad. It's really bad.'

'You don't know the half of it.'

But Slug already knew more than enough. Larry was knocking back the rum now, taking one large swig after another. The younger man's voice was acquiring a slight slur to it, his expression taking on an even meaner look. Unless he did something soon there was only one way this was going to end. 'You should get out of Soho if the Old Bill are looking for you. It ain't smart to hang around.'

'There you go again, Slug, trying to get rid of me. It's getting on my nerves if you don't mind me saying. No one's going to be looking here, are they? I'm safe as houses here. Anyway, those coppers won't be out in this weather; they'll be keeping nice and dry down at the station.' Larry fumbled in his pocket, took out a pack of cigarettes, pulled out a fag and lit it. He gazed into the middle distance for a moment and then said: 'Amy got it. She understood me. You remember Amy, Slug? Amy Duggan?'

Slug quickly shook his head. 'I never knew her.'

'We had our ups and downs, but I never laid a finger on that girl. She was everything to me.' Larry's face twisted and he stared hard at Slug. 'Who do you reckon killed her, then? Who do you reckon did for Amy?'

There was something about the way he was staring that made Slug's blood run cold. Like he *knew*. Like that was why he was really here. But it wasn't possible. He was just letting his imagination run away with him. He had to keep his cool and not give anything away. 'How would I know a thing like that?

But whoever it was ... whoever it was should be bloody well strung up.'

'It's me the bastards want to string up,' Larry said.

'Yeah, well, those coppers ain't got the brains they were born with.'

Larry stretched out his legs, took a drag on his cigarette and flicked the ash on to the floor. 'Shit, I never finished telling you my story. You want to hear the end, don't you, Slug? You want to know what happened when I asked Moll for a few quid just to tide me over?'

'You don't need to tell me.'

Larry smirked. 'Well, there's no point in hearing the beginning and not the end. That's just half a story.'

'It's your business, not mine.'

Larry ignored him. 'You'd have thought she'd have wanted to help. I mean, after all these years of doing nothing. She got off light, didn't she? No food to buy, no clothes, no worries. A few quid, that's all I was asking for. Do you want to know what the old tart said, Slug? "You think I've got money to waste on the likes of you?" It's true. I swear to God. *The likes of you.* Jesus, what kind of a way is that to talk? But that wasn't all. She hadn't finished yet. "You think I'm going to give you money after what you did to that poor girl?"' Larry barked out another of his hollow laughs. 'That ain't right. That's as wrong as anything can be. It's a kick in the teeth for an innocent man. I mean, it's all very well the law putting you in the frame, but when your own flesh and blood don't believe in you neither ...'

Slug was listening, but not just to Larry's disturbing self-justification. He had lived in the house for a long time and he knew every sound that it made, every creak and groan, every sigh and rattle. But this was something different. This noise was deep, a low ominous rumble that had nothing to do with the thunder outside. He gazed up at the ceiling and noticed the bulge. That hadn't been there before. No sooner had this thought entered his head than instinct propelled him off the crate and towards the door.

Larry, his reactions dulled by alcohol, hadn't even risen from the chair before the ceiling buckled and came crashing down. Whatever he was saying was lost to the roar of tumbling concrete and brick, to the almost explosive sound of the house folding in on itself. A thick pall of dust filled the cellar like a heavy fog on a winter's day. And then there was silence.

68

Breaking bad news was part of the job, but it never got any easier. DI Bentley had prepared himself – as much as he could – for the usual outpouring of grief, for the shock and the pain, but Dora Marks was curiously calm. She sat at the kitchen table and nodded while he told her about the death of her son. She had known it, she told him: she had seen it in the cards.

'Just tell me it was quick, Mr Bentley. He didn't suffer, did he?'

'No, he wouldn't have known anything about it.' Bentley had no idea if this was true or not, but it seemed a kindness to go along with the notion. It had taken several hours for the rubble to be shifted and the body of Larry Marks retrieved. By then, even if he hadn't been killed on impact, he was beyond any earthly help. 'Mr Suggs said it happened very suddenly.'

'I don't understand what Larry was doing there in the first place.'

'We don't either, Mrs Marks. We were hoping you might have an idea.'

'Why would I? I haven't seen Larry in years.'

Bentley reckoned this was a lie, but he let it pass. 'I'm sorry to have to do this at such a terrible time, but Mr Suggs claims that Larry made a confession before he died.'

'A confession? What sort of a confession?'

'About Moll Ainsworth.'

Dora's face, already drained of most of its colour, grew white. 'I wouldn't believe anything that man told you. He was born with a lie on his lips.'

'Mr Suggs claims that—'

Aline Bowers, who had been sitting silently, suddenly interjected. 'Is it really necessary to do this now, inspector? Dora's just lost her son. Surely you can leave her in peace while she comes to terms with it.'

But Dora gently waved her objection aside. 'It's all right, love. It's got to be done eventually. It may as well be now as later.'

Bentley girded himself. 'Is it true, Mrs Marks, that Moll Ainsworth was . . . ' He paused for a moment while he searched for the right words. 'That she was Larry's natural mother?'

'Why would you say a thing like that?'

'Is it true, Mrs Marks?'

For a moment Dora looked like she was going to deny it, her eyes becoming bright and indignant, but then she sighed and said: 'They were different times back then. I dare say it would be frowned upon these days, but we were only doing what we thought was best. Me and my Albert couldn't have kids, you see, and Moll couldn't take care of the one she was expecting, so . . . so we came to an arrangement. Albert wasn't keen, but he went along with it for my sake. I told everyone I was in the family way and then a few months before the due date, I took Moll over to my sister's in Basildon and . . . well, you don't want to know all the details.' She gave a shaky smile. 'Happiest days of my life, they were, pushing that pram proudly down the street.'

'And Larry didn't know any of this while he was growing up?'

Dora shook her head. 'We thought it better that he didn't. Perhaps that was a mistake. There were always problems between him and his dad. Albert couldn't bond with him, you see, not like I did. Larry wasn't his flesh and blood and he couldn't get beyond it. It wasn't his fault; some men find it hard, I suppose, to raise a child that isn't theirs.'

'When did Larry find out?'

'He started getting in trouble when he was about fifteen, hanging around with some local lads. It was nothing serious, but Albert got upset about it.' Dora let out another long and painful sigh. 'He said something one night, something awful about what happens when you buy a baby off a whore – he didn't know Larry was in the house – and that's when it all came out. I tried to explain to Larry that it hadn't been like that, but he wouldn't listen. He wasn't bought, inspector. The only money that changed hands was for expenses and the like, you know, something to tide Moll over while she couldn't work. I just wanted to give him a good home, to love him and take care of him.'

Bentley listened, letting her tell her story without too many interruptions. There would be questions he needed to ask, difficult questions, but he wasn't in a hurry. Sometimes the truth had to be prised out slowly.

'He went off the rails after that,' Dora continued. 'It was too much for him to deal with. He wasn't a bad boy, Mr Bentley, not really. He'd have come good in the end if it hadn't been for that awful business with Amy. He didn't kill her, I know he didn't, but he was always going to get the blame.'

Bentley, thinking it best to leave that can of worms alone for the moment, stayed with the subject of Moll Ainsworth. 'After Larry found out, did he ever have any contact with Moll?'

'No,' Dora said. 'Never. And Moll always kept away from him, too. That's what she promised and she didn't break her word. I hardly saw her through the years. We only started meeting up after Larry took off. She used to come and have a reading once in a while. Albert had passed by then, God rest his soul.'

There was a short silence, after which Aline Bowers leaned forward and asked abruptly, 'What is it you're not telling us?' She stared at Bentley through accusing eyes. 'A confession, you said earlier. Did you mean about Moll being Larry's mother or did you mean something else?'

Bentley glanced at Dora. It had to be revealed but the saying wasn't easy. He sucked in a breath. His voice, when he spoke, was soft but firm. 'I'm very sorry, Mrs Marks, only Mr Suggs claims that Larry confessed to killing Moll Ainsworth.'

'No!' Dora said, half rising from her chair before slumping down again. 'He's lying! That's not true. Why would Larry confess to something he hadn't done? That Slug doesn't know what he's talking about.'

'Why would you listen to a man like that?' Aline said, quickly backing up her friend. 'It's outrageous. You've got no right to be repeating lies.'

But Bentley was already taking the clear plastic bag from his pocket. He laid it on the table in front of them. Inside was a green silk scarf. 'We found this in the rucksack Larry had with him. It will need to go to the lab for tests, but we suspect it was the scarf used to strangle Moll Ainsworth. There was a similar scarf stolen from this house, wasn't there?' His gaze fixed on Aline. 'I believe it belonged to you, Miss Bowers.'

Aline wouldn't meet his gaze. She stared hard at the scarf, gave Dora a fast, sideways glance and said: 'It's not mine. It's not the same.'

'Are you sure? Perhaps you'd like to take a closer look.'

'I know my own scarf, don't I?'

Bentley could tell by the flush in her face and her evasive eyes that she was lying. He understood why she was doing it – to try and protect Dora – but he wasn't fooled. Not that it mattered whether she admitted it or not. He was already sure that Larry had been here recently and that both the women knew it. He also knew that they'd both deny it until the cows came home.

Dora's hands balled into two tight fists. 'He could have found that scarf anywhere, could have picked it up off the street. Just because he had it doesn't mean . . . ' Her mouth quivered a little at its corners. 'I don't get how that Slug got out of the house and my Larry didn't.'

'From what I understand,' Bentley said, 'he was closer to the door. We think the building collapsed because of the storm, because of the amount of rain that had gathered on the upper floors. At some point the cellar ceiling couldn't take the strain any longer.'

'So now he can say what he likes and my son's not here to defend himself. I can't see how that's right. And why would he tell a man he hardly knew that he'd killed Moll? Why would he do that?'

Bentley could similarly have asked why Larry had told Slug about who his biological mother was – a fact Dora hadn't denied – but he wasn't there to rub salt into an already deep and dreadful wound. 'Mr Suggs claims he was drinking, that he had a bottle of rum.'

Whatever remained of Dora's composure suddenly crumbled and she buried her face in her hands. 'He didn't do it. I don't care what that Slug says. Larry would never have killed Moll.'

Aline stiffened and glared at Bentley. 'I think Dora's had enough, inspector. If that's all then you should go now.'

Bentley slipped the plastic bag back into his pocket and rose to his feet. 'My condolences,' he said to Dora, but she wouldn't look at him. 'I'm very sorry.'

Aline showed him out, bristling with antagonism. 'Larry was everything to her,' she said, as though what he'd done was Bentley's fault. 'She doesn't need all this.'

Bentley left and made his way back to the car. He didn't immediately start the engine, but sat there for a while, staring out through the windscreen while he went over the day's events. Slug had got off lightly, all things considered: a broken leg, cuts and bruises and intermittent concussion, the latter depending on whether he wanted to answer a question or not.

The whole truth was still not entirely clear. Bentley reviewed his talk with Slug, frowning as much at what he hadn't learned as what he had. The informant always had his own agenda and there were things that remained obscure, like why Larry had turned up at the cellar in the first place.

Slug had gazed at him from his hospital bed. 'Just chance, I reckon, Mr Bentley. Just my bad luck.'

'You think?'

'What other reason could there be? I barely knew the bloke.'

'*Barely* knew him?'

'I wouldn't have known him at all if he hadn't told me his name. Then I remembered all that bad business years ago with the girl. Amy something was it? Well, he starts telling me about Moll Ainsworth, about who she was and what he did to her, and that shakes me up, I don't mind saying. I'm thinking, why is he doing this?'

'And why do you think he was?'

'I'm still not sure, Mr Bentley. He wasn't in his right mind. He was drunk and I suppose he wanted to get it off his chest.'

Bentley didn't buy the story about Larry showing up out of the blue. He'd chosen to go there for a reason, but Slug was never going to tell him what it was. And if Dora Marks knew – and he thought she did – she wasn't going to tell him, either. Despite these discrepancies, he still believed that Larry had murdered Moll Ainsworth. There was no doubt about it in his mind.

This was the first matricide Bentley had ever investigated and he felt the normal revulsion at the idea of a man murdering his own mother. It went against nature, against all that was good and decent. Something had made Larry snap – the lies and deceit, his years on the run, the final rejection – and pushed him over the edge to a place he could never return from.

Bentley wound down the window and lit a cigarette. The storm had passed now, but a thin drizzle was still falling from the sky. There was another matter to address. Slug claimed that Larry had also confessed to killing Amy Duggan, but this part of his story hadn't felt genuine. Bentley was convinced that it was pure fabrication. Slug had become shifty when he talked about it, his body language changing. Why had he lied? Just gilding the lily, perhaps, stating what he believed to be obvious and trying to boost his own importance.

Bentley put it out of his mind. It was time to move on. All that was left now was the paperwork. For him it was the end of the case, the murder of Moll Ainsworth solved. For Dora Marks, of course, it would never be over. She would have to live with what her boy had done for the rest of her life.

69

Liv left the house in Whitcomb Street early on Monday morning, eager to escape the pall of grief and sadness that hung over every room. She had been scared of Larry, frightened by him, but she hadn't wished him dead. After he'd left on Sunday morning, she had hoped that she'd never see him again – and now she'd got her wish. It made her feel odd and queasy inside, as if she was partly responsible for his fate. That was nonsense, of course, but she wasn't thinking straight at the moment.

Poor Dora. What could anyone say to comfort her? Aline, out of earshot of her friend, had whispered that Larry would have hanged when he was caught, that all in all it was better this way. He had murdered Moll Ainsworth, strangled her, but the motive for the killing remained unexplained. If Aline knew, she was keeping it to herself. What she had divulged, however, was the name of Larry's first alleged victim – a girl called Amy Duggan.

With half an hour to spare before she was due at work, Liv stopped off at Joe's and ordered toast and coffee. It was too early for Pally to be up and about, but she was still relieved not to find him there. How would she ever look him in the face again after sleeping with Lincoln, after sleeping with the enemy? She cursed herself for the thousandth time. A stupid, drunken act that she could never undo. It might not have been so bad if she'd felt Lincoln was regretting it too, but she knew he wouldn't be. He'd have cut another notch on his bed post. He'd be crowing like a rooster.

Still, there had been one good thing to have come from the evening: Lincoln had made her realise that if she wanted to find out the truth about her father, she couldn't let Irene Forster call the shots. She had to take control and the sooner the better. Today, she decided, was as good a day as any. She would go at lunchtime when, hopefully, Irene's husband would be at work. Some conversations were best held in private.

Liv spread butter and marmalade on her toast, wondering if it was wrong to be thinking about these things, about herself, after what had happened to Larry. But, then again, if Larry's death proved anything it was that you never knew when the Grim Reaper might come calling. Life was short and you had to grab your opportunities when you could.

Despite all the dreadfulness, there had been some uplifting news this morning. Dora had stopped her as she was leaving the house and thrust a slip of paper into her hand.

'I found this in Larry's jacket pocket while he was here.'

Liv had tried not to smile too widely when she'd looked down to see the pawnbroker's note, a list of items including her mother's silver cross and chain. The shop was in New Oxford Street.

'I'm sorry, love' Dora had said. 'Take whatever it costs out of your lodgings. You shouldn't have to pay.'

'You shouldn't, either. You didn't steal any of it.'

Dora had hesitated, her sad eyes not quite meeting Liv's, and then said, 'I didn't tell the police he'd been here.'

'I won't say anything. I promise.'

Liv now had the note safely tucked away in her handbag. There was enough money in her purse to redeem the cross and that was all that mattered. She couldn't wait to have it in her hands. It would be like having part of her mum back again.

Once she'd finished her breakfast, Liv paid, left the café and walked through the early-morning crowds to Bedford Square. Muriel was already in the office. She lifted eager, expectant eyes to Liv and asked, 'How did it go?'

Liv, whose head was full of Larry and Lincoln and Irene, frowned and said, 'How did what go?'

'Hollinghurst, of course!'

'Oh, that.' Liv had almost forgotten about her trip to the country with Garvie. 'Yes, it was fine.'

Muriel's face fell as though she'd been hoping for some scandal or at the very least some juicy gossip. 'Fine?'

'We weren't there for long, only a few hours. We came back on Saturday afternoon.'

Muriel's eyes brightened again. 'Why so soon? Did you have a row?'

'No, of course not.'

'Did he have a row with someone else?'

'No, not that I know of.'

'So why did you come back?'

But Liv wasn't in the mood for Muriel's relentless curiosity. 'I've no idea. Mr Garvie had a few meetings and then decided to call it a day.'

'Something must have happened,' Muriel said, pursing her lips and staring accusingly at Liv as though she was deliberately holding out on her.

Liv took off her jacket and sat down. 'Is he in yet?'

'He's been in and gone out again. He's over at Bridle Lane meeting the surveyor.'

Liv's heart sank. It sounded as though Garvie was counting on Lord Carbrooke's backing and ploughing on with the plans for redevelopment. He was going to be none too happy when the bad news was relayed.

Muriel gestured towards a pile of papers on her desk. 'If you're at a loose end, you could start filing this lot.'

Liv stood up again and crossed the room to retrieve the papers. There was nothing she liked more on a dismal Monday morning than a heap of tedious filing. As she opened and closed the cabinets, she wondered how much longer she'd be stuck here. For a long while yet, she thought, unless she could produce the goods for Moody.

There was restoration work going on with the building next door and a noisy clamour cut through the usual peace of the square. Scaffolding was being erected, a procedure that seemed to involve much clattering of poles and relentless banging. Liv glanced out of the window, hoping the noise wouldn't go on all morning.

The internal phone rang, a summons from Stephen Carr, and Muriel trotted off with her notebook. While she was gone, Liv took the opportunity to rifle through the personnel files. She was thinking about what Charlie had told her at Hollinghurst, about the girl who'd been murdered, the girl who had been Garvie's secretary. Had that been Amy or Rosa or someone else entirely?

She quickly skipped back through the years – Garvie had run through plenty of secretaries – until she reached the 1940s. Then, as her fingers flicked from one brown folder to the next, she suddenly found what she'd been looking for: PALLISER,

ROSA. Her heart gave a leap. She snatched up the folder, took it over to her desk, opened it and leaned down to read the contents.

Inside, there was an employment contract, very much like her own, with Rosa's personal details on the top of it. An address had been scored out with thick black pen, and one in Bridle Lane typed above it. Was that important? The property could well have been one of Garvie's, but so what if it was? If Rosa had been working here, and looking for somewhere to live, there was nothing odd or unusual about her renting a flat from her employer. Unless it hadn't been like that. If Garvie and Rosa had been in a relationship, he might have set her up in the property, a convenient little love nest well away from his wife and the prying eyes of society.

But none of what she had in front of her proved that particular theory. DI Bentley, she presumed, would have followed up on the possibility of an office liaison in the original inquiry, although if Pally was right, the inspector's investigative abilities left a lot to be desired. And men like Garvie were proficient at lying, at covering their tracks.

Rosa's original letter of application was also in the folder. Written in a neat, sloping hand, it held an air of poignancy. It was tragic to think that within a year she'd be dead, drowned in the cold, filthy water of the Thames. Liv shuddered at the horror of it. With everything to look forward to, all Rosa's hopes and dreams for the future had been stolen from her.

If Liv hadn't been so absorbed, and the noise from the building next door hadn't been so loud, she would have heard the soft footsteps on the carpet. By the time she became aware of them and whirled around, Garvie was already at her shoulder.

'What do you think you're doing?'

Liv quickly snapped the folder shut. 'Nothing. I was just—'

'Why are you reading Rosa Palliser's file?'

387

Liv, caught in the act, racked her brains trying to come up with something credible. 'I wasn't. I mean, I was, but I found it in the cabinet for office rentals. I think it must have been misfiled. I was just trying to work out where to put it.'

Garvie glared at her, his face dark, his eyes flashing with barely suppressed anger. 'Misfiled?'

'Yes,' Liv said, deciding the only way forward was to brazen it out. 'It was in the West End section. It looks like it should be in personnel.'

Ignoring her answer, he asked tightly, 'What exactly is your interest in Rosa Palliser?'

Liv assumed a puzzled expression. 'Interest? I don't have any interest. I've never heard of her before. Is something wrong?'

At that moment Muriel came back into the room and Liv was spared any further interrogation. Muriel, sensing the atmosphere, looked from one to the other and said, 'Is everything all right, Mr Garvie?'

Garvie reached down, snatched up the folder and held it out to her. 'Could you kindly return this to its rightful place.'

Muriel took the folder, read the name on it and frowned. 'I don't understand. How did—'

'Just file it, please.'

'Yes, Mr Garvie.'

While Muriel was doing as she was told, Liv was thanking God that she'd closed the personnel cabinet before taking the folder over to her desk. She knew that Garvie didn't believe her, but there was no actual evidence to prove that she was lying. It had been a bad mistake, though. Having planted seeds of suspicion in his mind, he was going to be watching her carefully from now on.

'Now, perhaps we can all get on with some work,' Garvie said, throwing Liv one last angry look before stalking off to his office.

Muriel stared at her through curious eyes. She waited until Garvie was out of earshot before saying: 'What are you up to? What's going on?'

'Nothing. I found the file in the wrong place and I opened it to see where it should go. That's all. I don't know what he's so annoyed about.'

'He's annoyed because it's Rosa Palliser's file.'

'What's so special about Rosa Palliser?'

But Muriel wasn't falling for it. An edge of excitement crept into her voice. 'Come on, you can't kid me. Are you working for the police?'

Liv, startled by the question, shook her head. 'What? The police? No, of course not. Why would I be doing that?'

'Why would you be reading Rosa's file? It's years since ... You're up to something. Why else would you be snooping around?'

'I've not been snooping.'

'Yes, you have.'

Liv could see that this was an argument she wasn't going to win. She couldn't tell Muriel the truth, but she had to offer up something that was more believable than an outright denial. 'Well, perhaps a little bit. All right, I'll be honest,' she said, rapidly putting together her next lie. 'I was just curious about her. Rosa's brother is a friend of a friend and I heard about her murder and ... I don't know, I couldn't resist taking a look in the file. It was stupid of me. I didn't mean anything by it. You won't tell Mr Garvie, will you?'

'If he thinks you're trying to cause him trouble, he'll fire you.' Muriel glanced towards the door, checking that he wasn't in the vicinity. 'And he'll fire me too if he ever finds out I knew about it.'

'I'm not trying to cause trouble. You won't tell him, will you?'

Muriel hesitated. 'If you promise it won't happen again.'

'It won't, I swear. Thanks.' Liv relaxed a little. 'Why on earth did you ask if I was working for the police?'

Muriel shrugged. 'I couldn't think of any other reason why you'd be interested in her. I mean, they never got to the bottom of it, did they? They never found out who did it. It's an unsolved case and they don't like those.'

'No, I suppose not, but it's been over ten years now. They've probably got enough on their plates. Anyway, do I look like a police spy?'

'Well, if you looked like one, there wouldn't be any point, would there?'

Liv smiled. 'No, I suppose not.'

'I remember her brother. He came here a few times. I felt sorry for him. It was about six months after Rosa was murdered and ... well, Mr Garvie gave him short shrift. I never understood that. I mean, you'd think he'd want to help, but he couldn't get rid of the bloke quick enough. Like he had something to hide, you know?'

Liv felt a flutter of excitement. She knew Muriel didn't like Garvie, that she was probably biased, but that didn't mean he wasn't guilty. 'Do you reckon there was something going on between the two of them, between Rosa and Mr Garvie?'

Muriel hesitated, but her desire to gossip was greater than any impulse towards discretion. 'Let's just say it wouldn't be the first time. He's hardly restrained when it comes to his secretaries. I couldn't swear to it, but I've got my suspicions.'

'Did Rosa ever say anything to you?'

There was the sound of a door opening down the corridor and Muriel scurried back towards her desk. 'I don't think we should talk about this any more.'

70

At twelve-thirty Liv left the office, walked down to Tottenham Court Road and hailed a cab. It was an added expense, but would save her time. She only had an hour for lunch and wanted to make the most of it. Nerves were fluttering in her stomach as the cab wound its way slowly through the West End. The closer they got to Mayfair, the more she was tempted to lean forward and ask the driver to stop. Was this really such a good idea? Turning up uninvited at Irene Forster's house wasn't going to go down well. She'd be about as welcome as a fox in a chicken coop.

To distract herself, she thought about Rosa Palliser, cringing as she recalled how she'd been caught in the act of snooping. She should have been more careful. But maybe it hadn't been such a bad thing. Muriel, she was sure, knew more than she was saying. With some subtle probing the woman might, eventually, be persuaded to give up the rest.

As her destination approached, Liv grew ever more anxious. It was all very well for Lincoln to suggest facing it all head on, but he wasn't the one who had to do it. Confronting Irene was going to be one of the hardest things she'd done in her life. That's if she even got to speak to her. Showing up was one thing, being invited in quite another. Or maybe Irene wouldn't be there. What if she'd gone shopping or was out to lunch? What if she'd gone off on holiday and was now lying on a beach in the south of France? What if her husband was home? All these possibilities flashed through her head, providing more reasons for her to give up before she'd even started.

But she couldn't do that. If she wanted the truth, she'd have to fight for it. There was no point acting like a baby. Liv took a compact out of her bag, flipped it open and examined her face in the mirror. A pair of worried eyes gazed back at her. She redid her lipstick and patted her hair. Then, when she was sure that nothing further could be improved upon, she sighed and dropped the compact back in her bag.

The cab pulled up in Berkeley Street. Liv got out, paid and stood on the pavement. The house was directly in front of her, grand and imposing. She knew that if she hesitated, she'd be lost and so she took a deep breath, pushed back her shoulders, strode over to the door and rang the bell.

It was answered promptly by a middle-aged woman she presumed to be the housekeeper, wearing a smart black uniform with a white apron. She looked Liv up and down, quickly assessing – and probably dismissing – her right to be standing on the doorstep. 'Yes?'

'My name's Liv Anderson. I'm here to see Mrs Forster.'

'Is she expecting you?'

Liv thought this was a good sign – at least she hadn't said that Irene was out – but the question was a tricky one. Preferring not to reply with a no, she said instead: 'She might be. She sent me a letter.'

'What sort of letter?'

'A private sort of letter,' Liv said.

The woman stared at her for a moment. 'Wait here.'

The door was closed while Liv's claims were further investigated. She gazed at the panels and the paintwork while she waited, channelling her inner determination. A couple of minutes went by. Eventually the door was opened again.

'I'm afraid Mrs Forster isn't available,' the housekeeper said smugly.

Liv smiled sweetly at her. 'That's fine. Please tell her that I'm quite happy to wait – all afternoon, in fact. All night, even. I'll stay right here until she *is* available.'

'You can't do that.'

'I think you'll find I can.' Liv glanced at the houses on either side. 'Although I suppose the neighbours will get a bit curious after a while.'

The woman shut the door in her face again. Liv wondered what to do if Irene called her bluff and left her standing here. She could be stuck on the doorstep for hours, until Richard Forster came home or the police were called. And what was she going to do about work? She couldn't just not go back, not without an explanation. She'd have to find a phone box, ring Muriel and tell her she'd been taken ill. Liv was looking up and down the road when the door abruptly opened again.

The housekeeper's face was tight and disapproving. 'Mrs Forster can spare you five minutes.'

'Thank you,' Liv said, trying not to sound too triumphant. Anyway, making it over the threshold was only the first step. The hard part was still to come. She had to hold her nerve, stand her ground and refuse to leave until Irene Forster shed some light on why her father had done what he'd done.

Her pulse started racing, her heart thrashing out a beat, as she was led through a plush hall and then on towards the back of the house. The grandeur of the place alarmed her: the large gilt mirrors, the polished wood floors and the paintings on the walls. She didn't belong here – it was a house for rich people – and she felt as ill-at-ease as a country bumpkin in a palace.

Irene Forster rose to her feet as Liv entered the room. She was tall and slender and elegant, dressed in a cream-coloured suit. Her face was arresting, her blonde hair swept up behind her head. She was in her mid-forties but undeniably beautiful. No longer Helen of Troy, perhaps, but still capable of launching a ship or two.

'Miss Anderson,' the housekeeper announced coldly before withdrawing and closing the door behind her.

The two women stared silently at each other for a moment.

'Well, you certainly have your father's tenacity,' Irene said.

Liv didn't think this was a compliment and didn't take it as such. 'I'm sorry to impose on you like this.'

'No, you're not. You're not sorry at all. If you were, you wouldn't have done it.'

'If you'd agreed to see me in the first place, I wouldn't have had to.'

Irene inclined her head slightly, raised her eyebrows and gestured towards a chair. 'Please.' She waited until Liv was seated before saying: 'You think I can help you, that I have answers, but I don't. What your father did is still as impenetrable to me now as it was back then.'

Liv was unsurprised by the declaration. She'd been expecting something of the like and refused to be deterred by it. 'I don't see how that's possible. He was in love with you, wasn't he?'

'If he was, I was unaware of it.'

Liv felt a spurt of anger. 'How could you have been "unaware"? It's hardly something you don't notice.'

'I knew your father, of course I did, but we were never close.'

'Well, you would say that, wouldn't you?'

'Especially if it's true,' Irene replied calmly. 'Look, I've no idea what you've heard or read or who you've been talking to, but I never had a relationship – not of any sort – with him. Now I can say that until I'm blue in the face and you still won't believe me, but you have my word that I'm not lying.'

Irene's voice was soft and slightly husky. Liv could imagine the times her dad had listened to her, drinking it all in, hanging on her every word. It filled her with a coldness that almost made her shiver. 'So why did he do it? Why did he kill your husband?'

'I wish I could tell you, but I can't. I can't tell you what I don't know.'

Liv felt like they were going round in circles. She took a moment to compose herself and then tried a different approach. 'What did you mean when you said I had my father's tenacity?'

'Only that he struck me as a single-minded sort of person. Very determined. I suppose you have to be when you're a journalist.'

'You did take *some* notice of him, then.'

'He spent a lot of time at Eden.'

'I wonder why that was.'

'I understand how hard this must be for you, Miss Anderson, but I really can't help. We can't change the past; all we can do is learn to live with it. You're young. You've got your whole future ahead of you. You should go home, try and put it behind you and get on with your life.'

Anger flared in Liv again. 'And how am I supposed to do that? Do you have any idea what it was like for my mother, how terrible it was for her?'

Irene briefly pressed her lips together. 'You seem to be for-getting that your mother wasn't the only victim in all this. Nicky was my husband, remember? He was murdered in cold blood, gunned down right in front of me. Or do you think that's what I wanted? Do you think I encouraged your father to kill him?' She gave a small, bitter laugh. 'Well, you wouldn't be the first person to make that assumption and I doubt you'll be the last.'

'I didn't say that.'

'You didn't need to. Please go home, Miss Anderson. There's nothing for you here.'

Liv stared at her. It was odd, she thought, how beauty could be so intimidating, as though it held a peculiar power of its own. But she refused to be cowed. 'I'm not going anywhere. You *must* know something. I'm not leaving until I find out what it is.'

'Then I'm afraid you'll have a long wait.'

Frustration streamed through Liv's body. She wanted to yell and shout and scream, but that wasn't going to get her anywhere other than back out on the street or, even worse, down the local nick. Calling on all that remained of her self-control, she said: 'So what my father did was motiveless, a random act of destruction? He just walked into Eden, took out a gun and . . . Is that what you're telling me? That he was mad, insane?'

'I don't know the state of your father's mind. I don't know why he did what he did. How many times do I have to repeat that?'

'I don't believe you.'

'Then we're at something of an impasse, aren't we?'

Liv found herself suddenly tearful like some pathetic heroine who had battled her way through a dark, demon-filled tunnel only to find a brick wall at the end of it. She had hoped for light but there was none. Desperation washed over her. 'Please,' she said. 'I'll beg if I have to, anything, but I can't go on like this. It's in my head all the time. I can't get beyond it. I'm not here to cause trouble, I swear, but I think I'll go mad myself if I don't get some answers.' She gulped in a breath of air, thinking that she should probably stop, but now that she'd started, she found that she couldn't. 'Maybe I'm already crazy. I mean, I must be to come here like this and demand to be let in and ... Do you think I could be? I don't understand any of it. I can't carry on like this. I can't bear it.'

For the first time a chink appeared in Irene's composure. She leaned forward, her eyes full of concern and said: 'You mustn't talk like that. You shouldn't.'

'Why not? It's the truth. I can't take the not knowing.'

'And what if you can't take the knowing, either?'

Liv's eyes widened at the sudden and unexpected ray of hope. 'Whatever it is has to be better than this.'

Irene stood up and went over to the window where she stayed with her arms folded and her back turned. For a while she didn't speak, as though she was weighing up the consequences of what she was about to reveal. Then she slowly walked back to the chair and sat down again. She looked closely at Liv and said, 'How old are you?'

'Twenty-one,' Liv said. 'But nothing you say will shock me. I might be young but I'm not naïve.'

Irene's gaze slid away, roamed the room and eventually came to rest again on Liv's face. 'All right,' she said.

Liv's spine tensed and her hands gripped the arms of the chair. She waited, barely breathing, aware that what she was about to hear could change everything.

'Your father wasn't in love with me,' Irene said softly. 'He was in love with Nicky.'

Bewilderment was what struck Liv first. 'What? No, he couldn't have been. What are you saying? It's impossible. You're wrong. He was married to my mother. He had a child. They had *me*. How could he be ... ' Her voice trailed off as she saw Irene's expression and realised that she was telling the truth. She

397

swallowed hard and her lips went dry. 'Are you claiming that my father was homosexual?'

'You're upset. Naturally you are. You thought nothing could shock you but ...' Irene gave a tiny shake of her head. 'I'm sure he tried his best to be otherwise, to be what society refers to as normal. And I'm sure he loved you both. Nothing will ever change that. Men like your father can spend their entire existence denying their true natures, refusing to accept who and what they really are – but it's not an easy secret to live with. And the laws of this country, of course, make it something of a challenge if you're that way inclined.'

Liv was still trying to process the revelation, to get a grip on what it all meant. 'So he lied to my mother? How could he do that?'

'Don't be too hard on him. Think of what it means to dis-cover you're different, that you don't have the same feelings, the same attractions as others. I suspect he pushed it all down and buried it. I dare say it would have remained buried if he hadn't had the misfortune to meet Nicky.'

'So was Nicky ... was he homosexual too?'

'Oh, not exclusively,' Irene said. 'He liked men and women. He was never one for walking a straight line. He was charming and clever and thoroughly unconventional. So far as he was concerned rules were there to be broken; he wasn't bothered by what the law or society declared to be 'decent'. That was prob-ably what attracted your father. He realised for the first time that he didn't have to live a lie. Nicky didn't have any hang-ups, any sense of guilt about who he was or what he wanted.'

'Did you know all this before you married him?'

'Of course. He was always honest with me.'

Liv frowned at her. 'And you didn't mind? It didn't bother you that he ... that he wasn't faithful?'

'Faithfulness comes in different shapes and sizes, my dear. I understood him – and he understood me. I knew that wherever he went, he'd always come back eventually. He needed me. We needed each other.' Irene's face grew tight, perhaps at the memory of what she'd lost. Then it slackened again and she said, 'What your father did to him was unforgiveable, but Nicky wasn't entirely blameless. He picked people up like they were new toys to play with for a while. But then he'd get bored, you see, and cast them aside. Paul ... your father ... thought he'd found the real thing – true love, a soulmate, whatever else he was longing for. He was prepared to give up everything for that, but Nicky wasn't interested. He'd already moved on by then.' Irene sighed into the room. 'He was a wonderful man in many ways, but a careless one, too.'

Liv's hands were still clasping the arms of the chair, her fingers aching, her knuckles white. 'But why kill him? For God's sake, why do that?'

Irene shook her head. 'Despair, hopelessness, rage? The rejection was too much for him to bear. If you keep all those forbidden feelings buried for years, they can't just be put back where they were before. Perhaps he didn't come to Eden meaning to kill Nicky. Perhaps he only intended to wave the gun around and threaten to kill himself. Who knows? He was drunk, I think, and not in his right mind.'

'Why didn't you tell the truth? Back then, I mean? You let everyone believe it was you my father was in love with.'

'What good would it have done? Would it have helped your mother, made her feel better? No, it would have been even more painful, even more scandalous. Your father chose to keep quiet about his motives in order to protect the two of you.' She gave a light, bitter laugh. 'And before you start thinking that I tried to protect you too, I can assure you that I didn't. My reasons

399

were purely selfish. I kept silent only in order to protect myself, to preserve what little remained of my reputation.'

Liv released her grip on the arms of the chair and rubbed her face while she tried to come to terms with this new version of events. The horrors of the past closed in on her, a dead weight that pressed against her chest. She struggled to think straight. Eventually she dropped her hands and looked at Irene again. 'I don't know what to do with all this.'

'That's up to you. You'll have to find your own way of dealing with it. Just don't let it haunt you, don't let it eat you up inside.' Irene rose to her feet again. 'Now, I think it's time we brought this conversation to a close.'

71

Preoccupied by what she'd learnt, Liv couldn't recall the details of leaving the house. She thought she had thanked Irene for being honest with her, but couldn't be sure. It was perfectly possible that whatever she had mumbled had been as incoherent and confused as the mad array of emotions that were tumbling around in her head. Anger, sadness and shame battled with pity and grief as she walked unsteadily along Berkeley Street, her legs constantly threatening to buckle beneath her.

Coming to terms with it all wasn't going to be easy. Suddenly she was seeing her father in a different light, having to judge him from a different angle. It had been unfair of him to marry her mother, to lie about his real feelings, to rob her of the opportunity of a marriage built on honest foundations, but perhaps he had tried his best, for as long as he could, to be the husband she deserved. Maybe he had even come to believe that he was who he pretended to be. He had been dealt a cruel hand, forced to turn his back on his true nature by a society that would not allow him to be what he was.

The words Nicky Lister had said to him on that fateful night at Eden revolved in her mind: *Don't cause a scene. It isn't worth it.* Had that been the final straw, the breaking point? Had her father known in that moment, by that casual dismissal, that he had lost everything and there was no going back? She could not excuse what he had done, but she could understand his pain and desperation. A flame of resentment burned inside her, a bitterness at the careless way Nicky Lister had rejected him.

Liv, lost in thought, veered off the pavement and almost got knocked over. A driver honked his horn and she jumped back in surprise. Grabbing hold of a lamp-post, she tried to steady herself. This was no good. Her head was all over the place. She had to get a grip, and fast, if she wasn't going to end up splattered under the wheels of a passing car.

She glanced at her watch and saw that it was twenty past one. The last thing she wanted was to return to work – what she really needed was a stiff drink, a few stiff drinks – but she didn't have a choice. If she failed to turn up, Garvie would become even more suspicious about the whole Rosa business. Reluctantly, she waved down another cab.

Liv was still in something of a daze by the time she arrived back at Bedford Square. She hurried into the building, attempting to look less flustered than she felt.

'You're late,' Muriel said.

'I know. I got held up. Is Mr Garvie in his office?'

'No, luckily for you he had to go out again. You're already in his bad books. Where have you been?'

Liv sat down at her desk. 'I had to see someone. It took longer than I thought.'

'Are you all right?'

'Why wouldn't I be?'

'Because you look like you just saw a ghost.' Muriel stared at her. 'Has something happened? Is this about Rosa?'

'What? No, of course not.'

'What's wrong, then?'

But Liv wasn't in the mood for Muriel's relentless questioning. 'Nothing's wrong. I've just . . . I've got a bit of a headache, that's all.'

Muriel was clearly peeved by Liv's reluctance to take her into her confidence. She said stiffly: 'Mr Garvie left some work on your desk. It's those new contracts for Percy Street. He wants them done by the end of the day.'

Liv nodded and pulled the papers towards her. As she started typing, she made mistake after mistake, her fingers apparently as distracted as her mind. She cursed softly at each error, willing her hands to behave and her thoughts to stop spinning. It was impossible to concentrate after what Irene had told her. She would have liked to open the window and throw the damn typewriter out of it.

The noise from the building next door had quietened down, but Liv had enough clamour in her head to make up for it. The hours passed slowly and the afternoon felt like an eternity. At ten to three Stephen Carr put his head round the door, told Muriel he was off to meet Mr Garvie, that they wouldn't be back today and that she should lock up before she left. At three o'clock Muriel made tea, and at half past Liv took the empty cups to the kitchen and washed them up. She stood at the sink, gazing at the white tiles, wondering if Henry had known the truth about her father.

When she returned, Muriel was on the phone. 'Yes, of course, Mr Garvie. I'll tell her. No, I'm sure it won't be a problem.' She looked up, saw Liv and said into the receiver: 'Actually, she's just come back in. Would you like a word with her? No? All right, I'll pass the message on.'

Muriel put the phone down and said unnecessarily, 'That was Mr Garvie.'

'What did he want?'

'He left some documents behind and needs you to take them over to Bridle Lane. They're in a brown envelope on his desk. He said they'll meet you there at five. Do you know where Bridle Lane is?'

Liv nodded, unsure at this point as to whether to be pleased by the summons – it would mean an early escape from the office – or uneasy about having to see her boss again after their run-in this morning. 'Yes, I know where it is.'

'It shouldn't take that long to walk there. They'll be at Moll Ainsworth's old flat. I'll write down the address for you.'

Liv went along the corridor to Garvie's office, opened the door and stepped inside. It was the first time she'd ever been in there alone. Under different circumstances she would have taken the opportunity to rifle through the papers on his desk, but she wasn't in the mood for espionage or for taking any unnecessary risks. She quickly picked up the envelope and went back to the front room.

For the next three quarters of an hour, Liv worked diligently on the contracts until they were all completed. Then she put on her jacket, picked up her bag and the envelope, said good night to Muriel and set off for Soho.

72

Liv strolled at a leisurely pace, not wanting to get there too early. She slowly weaved through the crowds on Oxford Street, lost in thought and barely aware of her surroundings. After delivering the documents she intended to find Pally and to tell him all about her father. He was the one person who would understand. She supposed at some point in his life he must have faced the same dilemma: did you accept your sexuality or deny it? But Pally was a different type of man and of a different generation; perhaps the choice for him had not been so complicated.

She cut down Wardour Street and zigzagged through Soho until she came to where she was supposed to be. Bridle Lane was long and narrow, running between Brewer Street and Beak Street. It was a claustrophobic sort of place, dark and dismal, with the shabby houses rising tall on either side. She could almost feel the poverty leaking from the walls.

Liv found the number Muriel had written down for her, tried the front door and discovered it was open. Moll's old flat was on the second floor. She trudged up the bare stone stairs, aware of the silence of the building. Some of the tenants, maybe most, had already been evicted in preparation for the grand redevelopment. There was an air of abandonment, an eeriness about the quiet. The click of her heels sounded unnaturally loud and when she cleared her throat the noise echoed around her.

It occurred to Liv, somewhat ridiculously, that Garvie could have lured her here to ... to do what? To confront her again over Rosa, to try and force the truth out of her? Or maybe something worse. But she was just being fanciful. Her head was too full of violence and murder. She wasn't going to be alone with Garvie; Stephen Carr would be here, too. There was nothing to worry about.

She reached the second-floor landing and began looking for number eight. The house had been divided and subdivided into numerous flats and rooms, each one undoubtably as cramped and unpleasant as the next. Landlords like Garvie didn't care about their tenants; the only thing they cared about was the rent. Liv recalled the splendour of Irene's home and wondered at the inequality of it all.

Eventually, she tracked down Moll's old flat and knocked on the door. There was no response. She tried again, Still nothing. Liv glanced at her watch – five to five – and listened out for footsteps on the stairs. It was thirty seconds before she tried the handle and found the door wasn't locked. She tentatively pushed it open and stood on the threshold. 'Mr Garvie?'

The smell of damp floated into her nostrils. The room was small, poky rather than cosy, with peeling wallpaper and a threadbare carpet. It was sparsely furnished: an old sofa, some cupboards and a low table lying on its side with one of its legs missing. She called out again. 'Mr Garvie? Mr Carr?'

Liv decided she might as well wait inside as out. If they were running late it could be another ten or fifteen minutes before they got there.

It was as she stepped into the room that she felt it, the sense that she wasn't alone. There was someone else. Behind her. Shielded by the open door. Hiding. Another person's tense, coiled body. Another person's nervous breath. This knowledge came to her a split second before she began to turn, but already it was too late. The force of the blow, a crack to the side of her head, sent her reeling, and she staggered forward a few feet before her knees buckled and she collapsed on to the floor.

Liv, stunned by the assault, lay helplessly while her brain tried to process what was happening. There was pain in her skull, something liquid travelling down her face. The taste of iron was on her tongue. There was movement beside her. She could hear a noise, a low groan, and gradually realised that it was coming from her own mouth. Her eyes – she could not remember closing them – flickered open and she saw a pair of feet, a pair of shoes. Slowly her gaze travelled up. Above the brown, narrow shoes were slim ankles, shins, the hem of a beige skirt.

Liv had to shift her head – a painful process – to look into the eyes of her assailant. But she already knew who it was. Except it couldn't be. It was impossible. Muriel was at the office in Bedford Square. Muriel couldn't be in two places at once. In her dazed, stupefied state, this was both mystifying and bewildering, like an impenetrable magic trick.

'Don't move,' Muriel said, her voice tight and hard. 'Stay where you are. Don't try anything.'

Liv didn't need the instruction; she didn't have the strength to try anything. Her limbs, dull and heavy, had gone into a similar state of shock as her mind. She couldn't make any sense of what was going on. 'What? . . . how?' She didn't seem able to string a sentence together, either. Trying again, she murmured, 'What are you—'

'I've got a gun,' Muriel said, pointing a tiny black revolver at her. 'You do anything stupid and I'll finish you off right now. This little thing might not look like much but it'll still put a hole through your heart.'

'A gun,' Liv repeated.

'Yes. My mother used to keep it in the bedside table drawer, just in case Hitler invaded during the night. Better to be safe than sorry, right?'

The cogs in Liv's brain continued in their sluggish revolutions. A gun. Her father had had a gun, too. He had taken it with him on the night he'd gone to see Nicky Lister. What did that have to do with this? Nothing. She had to try and concentrate, to focus on the here and now. 'What are you doing?' An inane question, but it was the best she could manage.

'Getting to the truth,' Muriel said. 'Let's start with what your real name is. Kent or Anderson?'

Fresh dread crept over Liv. The game was probably up, but she couldn't be sure. Through dry lips she muttered, 'You know what my name is. Olivia Kent. My name's Olivia Kent.'

'Really? I presume Garvie told you about the phone call on Friday, about the man who rang the office?'

'Yes.'

'So?'

'I'm not the girl he was talking about. I don't understand.'

Muriel gave a snort. 'Oh, don't come the innocent with me. It won't wash. I wasn't born yesterday.' Keeping the gun pointed, she knelt down and grabbed Liv's handbag from where it had fallen on the floor. She flicked open the clasp and turned it upside down, scattering the contents on the carpet. In amongst Liv's purse, her lipsticks, perfume and all the usual paraphernalia she carried around with her, was the letter from Irene Lister. Muriel held up the envelope triumphantly. 'What's this, then? Miss Liv Anderson it says on the front.'

Liv couldn't deny it. Her eyes automatically slid towards the door. It was shut now and a key was in the lock.

Muriel followed her gaze and smirked. 'If you're hoping for Mr Garvie to arrive, you'll have a long wait. He isn't coming, sweetheart. He's in Essex with Mr Carr. They've gone to view some properties, some nice little flats near Epping Forest. It's just you and me, I'm afraid. Still, that gives us plenty of time to sort things out.'

Liv thought about the call that had come through from Garvie this afternoon, but of course there had never been a call, just Muriel talking into empty space. The side of her head was throbbing. She lifted a hand to touch the spot – wet, soft flesh – and winced.

Muriel waved the gun at her. 'Don't move, I said. It's only a cut. It's not going to kill you. Tell me who you're working with? Is it the police or the brother? Or is it that other one?'

Liv didn't know who the other one was. Moody, perhaps, although she couldn't see how Muriel would know about him. She tried to figure out what the best answer was, but couldn't come to a decision. 'How did you get here before me?' she said instead.

'How do you think?' Muriel replied impatiently. 'I got a cab, of course. Now answer the bloody question. Who are you working with?'

Liv gazed at the carpet, at the threadbare patches, the stains, the cigarette burns and the contents of her handbag. The little table still lay on its side. And next to it was the missing leg, a curved piece of wood that was splattered with red. Blood. *Her* blood. So that was what Muriel had hit her with. Not that it mattered what the weapon had been. She felt woozy and disoriented. She had to keep her mind focused, to keep her thoughts going in a straight line. 'Working with?' she repeated dully, as though the question was incomprehensible to her.

'I'm guessing the brother,' Muriel said. 'It's him, isn't it? Alan Palliser. The two of you are in this together.'

'I don't know what you mean.'

'Oh, didn't I mention it? Our mystery caller rang again while you were out this lunchtime. We had a long chat. It was very interesting.' Muriel smirked again. 'He really doesn't like you, does he? He didn't have a good word to say. A double-crosser, that's what he called you – among other things. Said you were planning on going to the papers with your story. And what story would that be? I asked him. He got all cagey, then, said I'd read about it soon enough, but that murder always made good copy.'

'Murder?' Liv groaned. *Damn Ralph McCall,* she thought.

'I mean, it all adds up now, doesn't it?'

Liv didn't reply.

Muriel poked the toe of her shoe into Liv's upper arm. 'What's the matter? Cat got your tongue? Oh, I know your game. Snooping around, spying on us, going away for the weekend with Garvie. You're a dirty little slut, just like she was. What did he tell you, then?'

'Why would he tell me anything?'

'Because Garvie's like all men; he wears his brains in his trousers. A bit of pillow talk, was it? You opened your cheap, slutty legs for him and in return he told you about Rosa? Is that how it was?'

'No. For God's sake, we didn't even stay the night.'

'That's your story,' Muriel said. 'Why should I believe anything that comes out of your mouth? You even lie about your own name. God, girls like you make me sick. All you have to do is snap your fingers and the men come running. She was just the same. She couldn't wait to get her claws into him.'

'Look, whatever you think I know, I don't, all right? Garvie hasn't said a word about Rosa. I swear. He hasn't told me anything.'

Muriel wasn't listening. She'd already made up her mind and nothing Liv said was going to convince her otherwise. 'It wasn't right what she was doing. Someone had to put a stop to it. The little bitch wasn't bothered if she ruined his life. She didn't give a damn.'

Liv felt a sliver of ice run down her spine. 'But why should you care? You don't even like Garvie.'

Muriel gave a curious high-pitched laugh. 'Garvie? This isn't about Garvie. It was Stephen she couldn't keep her filthy hands off.'

And now Liv finally understood.

'Got herself pregnant, didn't she,' Muriel continued, almost spitting out the words. 'And don't tell me that wasn't deliberate. Then she wants him to leave his wife, to set up home together and play happy families. As if Stephen could do that! Garvie was hardly going to keep him on as a partner if he deserted Celia; it would have meant the end of his marriage, his career, everything. The little whore was deluded. He didn't even love her; she was just a distraction from that vile, nagging witch of a wife of his.'

Liv partly raised a hand from the floor, trying to get Muriel to stop talking. The more she was told, the less likely she was to get out of here alive. 'I don't understand any of this and I don't want to. It's none of my business.'

A sly smile crept on to Muriel's face. 'But you made it your business, Olivia, the minute you started poking your nose in. It's way too late to start backtracking now.'

'I was curious, that's all. I wasn't ... I didn't ... Please, just let me go and I won't say a word about any of this. I promise, I swear. I'll say I fell, that I had an accident. You'll never have to see me again. I won't come back to work.'

'No, well, you certainly won't be doing that.' Then, barely

411

missing a beat, Muriel continued: 'The problem with Stephen is that he's weak. He let himself be pushed around: by Garvie, by Celia and then by that little tramp. It's not his fault. He's a nice person, you see, someone who cares. That's why people take advantage. He lets them walk all over him. That's what *she* was doing. She thought she was on to a good thing, but she had no idea. I had to put her right, didn't I? I told her there was nothing in it for her, that they didn't have a future together and if she'd have listened, if she'd just paid attention, it wouldn't have ended so badly.'

Liv stared up, horrified. There was a gob of spittle in the corner of Muriel's mouth and her eyes were strange, bright and wild, as though she had tipped over into some kind of madness. She suspected that Muriel was going through a process of self-justification and that once she had reached the end her finger would close around the trigger. Desperately she said: 'You were only trying to help him. No one can blame you.'

'Oh, you can put a stop to that. I know what you're doing. Don't think you can get round me, because you can't.'

Liv's gaze was darting between Muriel and the gun. It would be pointless trying to reason with her. All she could do was play for time, keep her talking, until she could come up with a plan. 'I wasn't ... I mean, accidents happen, don't they? If you were arguing and she fell and ... you can't be blamed for that.'

'I don't intend to be blamed for it. It's not my fault she couldn't swim.' Muriel's lips stretched into a devilish grin. 'It was all very fast. She went straight under without a sound.'

Liv nodded, the motion making a pain run through her head. 'So there was nothing you could do. I get that. But this isn't going to solve anything.'

'If Garvie hadn't opened his big mouth, we wouldn't be here now.'

412

Liv could have protested, insisted again that Garvie hadn't told her anything, but she wasn't going to waste her breath. Muriel's fear of discovery – allied, perhaps, by an understandable paranoia – had led her to all sorts of false conclusions, including the fact she was about to be exposed. And now the truth was actually out, the only way forward was to finish what she'd started.

'He knew what was going on between the two of them, but he kept quiet when the police showed up,' Muriel said. 'Not for Stephen's sake – he doesn't give a damn about Stephen – but just to save his own reputation. It doesn't look good having a partner involved in a scandal like that. He thinks he did it, that he killed Rosa and he's held it over him for the past twelve years.'

'But he's wrong.'

'That doesn't matter. Once the police find out about the affair, they'll blame Stephen for her murder. They'll hang him for it. I can't allow that to happen.'

Liv, realising that the end was approaching, knew she had no choice but to act. She tried to gather what was left of her strength, to prepare herself. If she grabbed for Muriel's legs, she might be able to topple her. There was every chance Muriel would shoot, but she was going to shoot anyway. She may as well die trying as wait for the inevitable to happen. One last question while she prepared herself.

'How are you going to explain it when they find me here?'

Muriel laughed again. 'That won't be for a long time, sweetheart. Why would they look here? And this flat's going to be empty for months, years even, until Garvie gets permission to pull the whole lot down. By the time they find you, if they find you, there won't be much left.'

Liv had a gruesome image of her body lying on the carpet, slowly rotting away. And even the smell wouldn't alert anyone

413

because there was no one left to alert. Panic rose in her. *Do it!* she ordered herself. *Do it now before it's too late!* And with that, before she could think any more about it, she half lifted herself off the floor, lunged at Muriel and wrapped her arms around her legs.

Taken by surprise, Muriel whirled her arms around as she attempted to keep her balance. Liv held on, pushing as hard as she could, using every ounce of her remaining strength. As Muriel collapsed to the ground, the two of them became entwined in a twisted force of hissing breath, of grunts and cries and flailing limbs. Liv hit out again and again, fighting for her life, trying to shake the gun from Muriel's hand.

And then it happened. Liv heard the shot and a searing pain ran through her right arm. She fell to one side, knowing this was it, knowing she was defeated. There was nothing more she could do. In a moment it would all be over. Muriel was scrambling to her feet. Liv lay helpless. She waited for the coup de grâce, for the final despatch, with tears streaming down her cheeks.

Then, suddenly, there was a loud hammering on the door, shouts and the sound of splintering wood. '*Police!*' a voice called out. But help had come too late. A second shot rang out and Liv closed her eyes, descending into a well of darkness. Noise was replaced with silence, her pain and fear dissolved and everything went black.

When Liv regained consciousness, DI Bentley was kneeling beside her. She thought she must be dying, sliding through some final hallucinogenic moments, because she was sure she saw Lincoln, too, leaning over her with concern on his face. His lips were moving but she couldn't understand the words. It was probably for the best. She couldn't think of anything she wanted to hear him say in her final moments.

73

Several hours had passed since one living person and one dead had been carefully removed from the room in Bridle Lane. Muriel, knowing it was over, had chosen to turn the gun on herself. Liv was only gradually coming to terms with what had happened and that she had somehow, miraculously, survived it. Her head had been stitched up and the wound from the bullet repaired, but the shock of it all was still with her.

Bentley, seated beside her hospital bed, had been quietly talking for the last ten minutes, going through everything with patience and care. 'So, Muriel confessed to the murder of Rosa Palliser?'

Liv nodded. 'She said she had to be stopped, that she was going to ruin Stephen Carr's life. She reckoned Garvie had said something to me, something about Rosa and Carr having had an affair. He hadn't, of course, but she wouldn't believe it.'

'Muriel provided an alibi for Stephen Carr on the night of the murder. After work, instead of going straight home, he'd gone for a walk. There weren't any witnesses, which might have put him in a tricky position, especially if the affair became public knowledge. Apparently, she suggested they should claim they were both working late and he went along with it – with gratitude, I'm sure.'

'Providing herself with an alibi at the same time.'

'Yes, a mutually beneficial arrangement as it turned out.'

'Did he love her?' Liv asked. 'Rosa, I mean. I'm presuming you've talked to him.'

'I got that impression. I think he was prepared to leave his wife at the time.'

'That would have been a misery to Muriel. He would have been kicked out of the business and she'd never have seen him again.' Liv half closed her eyes. 'Unrequited love,' she murmured, thinking of her father. 'It makes people do terrible things.'

Bentley gave her a curious look. 'Anyway, it's a good thing we were keeping an eye on you.'

'I don't understand why you were doing that.'

'I'm a man who doesn't like coincidences,' he said. 'First I see you with Alan Palliser in the French and then I find out that you're working for the same company Rosa was when she was murdered. I reckoned the two of you had to be up to something.'

Liv shook her head. 'Pally didn't know anything about it.'

Bentley raised a pair of sceptical eyebrows. 'So why the fake name, all the subterfuge?'

Liv had to think quickly. She certainly wasn't going to mention Moody or she'd be inviting even more trouble into her precarious life. 'I just saw the job advertised and thought I might be able to find out something. It was stupid, but I knew how upset Pally was about Rosa. I reckoned I could do a bit of digging and . . . I didn't tell him, though. He didn't even know I was working there.'

'And then there was the Lincoln connection.'

Liv frowned, pretending the name didn't mean anything to her. 'Who?'

'Tom Lincoln,' Bentley said. 'And before you continue down the road of never having heard of him, I'd like to remind you that we have had you under surveillance.'

The memory of Saturday night flooded back into Liv's mind. Damn it! If they'd been following her, they would have seen her meet up with Lincoln and, even worse, go back to his flat. From which, unfortunately, she had not emerged until the early hours. A pink flush suffused her cheeks, not so much from embarrassment – it was none of Bentley's business who she slept with – but because she would never cease to regret the drunken encounter. 'Oh, him,' she said as casually as she could.

'Interestingly, Mr Lincoln has been following you too. Why do you think that is?'

This was news to Liv, but she wasn't that surprised. 'I've no idea. You'll have to ask him.'

'I already have.'

'And what did he say?'

'Very little,' Bentley replied.

Liv shrugged. 'We've been on a few dates. Perhaps he's the possessive type.' And then, recalling what Bentley had said earlier, she asked, 'How is he a "connection", as you put it?'

Bentley leaned forward, put his elbows on his thighs, brought his hands together and steepled his fingers. 'For the obvious reasons: Alan Palliser is Rosa's brother, Lincoln was her fiancé and you're linked to them both.'

Shock ran through Liv, draining the colour from her face. Her voice, when she spoke, was barely a whisper. 'Lincoln was ... what? No, he couldn't have been.'

Bentley was watching her closely, perhaps trying to figure

out how much of her reaction was an act. 'You're saying you didn't know?'

'No, he never told me that.' Liv's thoughts were racing as she tried to get her head around this new bombshell. Rosa's fiancé? How could that be? Why hadn't Pally said? Why would he keep something like that a secret? Aware of Bentley's scrutinising gaze, she muttered: 'But I don't know him that well. Obviously even less than I thought.'

'You see, that puzzles me. Lincoln and Palliser have been mates for years; they even ended up in court together for harassing Hugh Garvie. They always had him in the frame for Rosa's murder. Turns out they were wrong about that. Right place, wrong person.'

Liv's lips had gone dry, her throat tightening to the point where she could hardly speak. Mates? But they couldn't be. Lincoln had arranged for Pally to be beaten up. Why would he do that if . . . but slowly she was beginning to see the light, and it wasn't the sort that brought warmth and happiness. Goosebumps crawled across her flesh. The two of them had been working together all along. The assault on Pally had been set up for *her* benefit so she'd agree to go and work for Garvie. She'd been the goat tethered to the rope, the lure, the bait.

Bentley continued to keep his eyes on her. 'I'm guessing – and correct me if I've wrong – that they decided to have another go at exposing Garvie. A risky business, as you've since discovered. If he had been the murderous sort, he could have killed you too.'

'Lucky I just had to face Muriel, then.'

'You should leave the investigating to the police.' Bentley paused for a moment. 'Is there anything else you'd like to tell me?'

Liv shook her head.

Bentley rose to his feet. 'Mr Lincoln's waiting to see you. He's been waiting quite a while.'

'Tell him to go home.'

'Are you sure?'

'Yes, I'm tired. I don't want to see him.'

After Bentley had gone, Liv slid down under the covers and gazed up at the white ceiling. A cold knot had formed in the pit of her stomach. Lincoln's deception didn't surprise her – she wouldn't have expected anything else – but Pally, the one person she'd always trusted, had also lied to her, manipulated her and, worst of all, betrayed her. She felt like the centre had dropped out of her life.

74

Liv discharged herself from hospital at a quarter to twelve the following morning. She had things to do and they couldn't wait. During the night she had drifted in and out of sleep, her mind too preoccupied by what had happened to cease its constant whirring and commit to the rest it needed. Eventually, as dawn was breaking, she had come to a decision. It was time for change. It was time to take back control of her life.

She left by a side exit just in case Lincoln was still hanging around. He'd be worried, of course, that she'd blabbed to the law and landed him in it. Well, let him worry. It was the least he deserved. She understood now who Muriel had meant by 'the other one'. Rosa's fiancé. God, she hadn't seen that coming. What a fool she'd been, oblivious to everything. There was little worse, she thought, than the knowledge that you'd been set up.

It was fortunate that the day was fine, the sky pale blue, the air warmed by hazy sunshine. She dumped her blood-stained jacket in the first bin she came to. Fortunately, her arm had only been grazed by the bullet and shouldn't take too long to heal.

It still hurt, though, and her head ached too. Still, she had got off lightly, all things considered. She could have been lying on a mortuary slab like Muriel.

As she walked, she wondered why Lincoln had been so determined to seek retribution for Rosa's death. The girl had obviously been cheating on him; she'd even been expecting Carr's baby. But then maybe it was more about getting revenge on the man who'd stolen his woman. Yes, Lincoln wouldn't have taken too kindly to that. He was probably the type who viewed women as possessions, their theft being the worst kind of personal insult.

But she wasn't going to concern herself too much with Lincoln. It was Pally she wanted to have it out with, Pally she needed to confront. And she knew where she'd find him. He'd be propping up the bar at the French, trying to think up implausible excuses for his behaviour while he believed she was safely tucked up in her hospital bed. Well, he was going to have to face her sooner than he thought. There was nothing like the element of surprise.

Liv tried to get her emotions under control as she approached the French. Fatigue dogged her steps, but adrenalin spurred her on. She felt angry and betrayed. Pally's deception had cut her to the bone; not only had she been bashed over the head and shot, but stabbed in the back too. Friends weren't supposed to do that kind of thing to you.

She didn't pause when she got to the door, but barged straight in. Pally was standing at the bar and she saw the shock on his face as she approached. 'Surprise,' she said drily.

'Hey, what are you doing here, hon? You should still be in hospital. I was going to come and see you later.'

'So you've talked to Lincoln, then?'

Pally didn't deny it. 'Don't be mad. It's not how you think.'

'You can buy me a drink before you start up with the excuses. I'll have a brandy, thanks. You can bring it over to the table.'

Liv went and sat down, desperate to take the weight off her feet. She felt cold and clammy and had to press her hands together to stop them from shaking. Her gaze fixed on Pally, seeing him as a stranger might – just a tall, blond man with fading bruises on his face – instead of the friend she had come to trust and rely on over the past year. The truth was that she didn't know him, not really, and the realisation caused her pain.

Pally placed two large brandies on the table, took the chair opposite to hers and gave her a rueful smile. 'I know how it must seem but—'

'It seems how it is,' Liv said, before picking up a glass and taking a quick gulp of brandy. The effect was almost instantaneous, like a warm glow spreading through her body. 'You tricked me. You and Lincoln hatched your little plot and kept me in the dark. Bentley told me how the two of you were mates.'

'Mates is stretching it a bit. But, yeah, we knew each other through Rosa. We've known each other for years.'

'So why didn't you tell me, for God's sake? I'd have happily gone along with it if you'd explained. You didn't have to lie to me. You didn't have to do all that George Hallam nonsense, and you didn't have to go through that ridiculous charade of being beaten up.'

Pally's hand rose to his face. 'Not exactly a charade. I don't think Lincoln's pals entirely understood the concept of going easy.'

'Oh, poor you.'

'I didn't mean it like that. Look, it wouldn't have worked if you'd known about Rosa. You'd have behaved differently around Garvie and he would have picked up on it. And you'd have been too keen to find out something about her.'

'So you just decided to send me in clueless? You were sure he was a murderer but that, apparently, didn't matter. Did you think he might kill me too? Is that that what you were hoping for? If you couldn't get him for Rosa's murder then at least you could get him for mine.'

Pally frowned and shook his head. 'Shit, no. How could you ever think ...? No, we weren't even hoping for anything on Rosa, not after all this time. We were just trying to get *something* on him: dodgy dealings, tax evasion, a bit of dirt on his personal life. Anything that might help bring him down. I'd never deliberately put you in danger. You know me better than that.'

'Do I? Only right now I don't feel like I know you at all.'

'Okay, maybe we didn't go about in the right way, but we were always looking out for you.'

'There's no bloody maybe about it.' Liv drank some more brandy and glared at him over the rim of her glass. 'And I don't recall *anyone* looking out for me while Muriel was bashing me over the head or pointing a gun at my brains.'

'No, well, I'm sorry about that. We screwed up. We were so sure it was Garvie—'

'And you were wrong.'

'Yeah.'

'You almost got me killed. If it hadn't been for Bentley, I wouldn't be sitting here right now. I'd be lying in the morgue with a label on my toe.'

'Lincoln was there too.'

'Oh, good old Lincoln,' Liv said. 'And how long would it have taken him to break down the door on his own? Anyway, Muriel only shot herself because she knew the police were there. If it had only been him, she'd have probably put the bullet in *his* head.'

Pally gazed down into his glass before looking up again. 'What did you tell Bentley?'

'I was wondering when you'd get around to asking that.' Liv

gave a hollow laugh. 'I told him everything, all about how you and Lincoln set me up. I'm surprised he hasn't arrested you by now.'

Pally studied her face for a few seconds. 'No, you didn't. You didn't tell him a damn thing.'

Liv hated the way he could read her, how he knew her so well. 'I should have done. The two of you deserve to be locked up.'

'You could have a point.' Then, smiling, he said, 'Geoff's off the hook, too. Have you heard? Cynthia's turned up.'

'I'm glad,' she said.

'Yeah, Geoff's relieved. I reckon he was starting to think that he might have done it after all.'

'That's what happens when people mess with your head.'

Pally reached out and covered her hand with his own. 'Don't hate me, Liv. I should have been straight with you, but I can't do anything to change that now.'

'I don't hate you. I just don't trust you any more.'

'Come on, we're a great team. Once we get back to work, we can—'

'No,' Liv said, sliding her hand out from under his. 'It's over, Pally, you and me. I'm getting out of London. I've had enough of the place.'

'What? No, you're just in shock. Take some time to think about it.'

'I'm not going to change my mind.' Liv thought about her father, who had not been able to walk away from everything that was bad for him. She wasn't going to make the same mistake. 'It's finished.'

'When are you going?'

'Soon. A few days.'

'At least stay and have another drink with me.'

Liv rose to her feet, leaned down and kissed him quickly on the crown of his head. 'Bye, Pally. Take care of yourself.'

75

Ralph McCall was sitting in Joe's, drinking coffee and smoking a cigarette. He had experienced two surprises over the last twenty-four hours, one good and one so bad that he hadn't quite come to terms with it yet. The good one had arrived this morning as he'd been leaving West End Central after attending a press conference on the shootings at Bridle Lane. He'd had a nagging worry that his phone calls to Garvie & Carr, especially the second one, might have been a contributory factor, but Bentley hadn't mentioned it. This had still been on his mind as he'd walked out of the door and noticed a tall, good-looking redhead approaching the police station. It had taken a few seconds for him to put a name to the face, but once he had he'd been quick to intercept her.

Cynthia Crosby had been on her way to explain to the police that she wasn't in fact a missing person, but Ralph – with the incentive of a modest financial reward – had persuaded her to postpone the revelation for half an hour and talk to him first about what had happened to her. The story was hardly novel, but it did contain enough salacious angles for it to demand a prominent position in the next edition of the *West End News*.

Approached by a smooth-talking charlatan, Cynthia had been promised an introduction to a top American film director who would launch her career and make her a star. She had been duped into accompanying him to Manchester but the interview, of course, had never materialised and she had found herself singing instead in a sleazy nightclub with about as much chance of seeing her name in lights as the local road sweeper.

Although Ralph had not been able to squeeze all the sordid details out of her, he had enough for his readers to form their own conclusions. Swept off her feet, dazzled and starstruck, Cynthia had relinquished more than her hopes to the con man. By the time she'd realised it was all smoke and mirrors, it was too late. She had hurried back to London with her dreams in tatters and her tail between her legs. He would present the story as a bleak warning to every other starstruck girl out there – dreams could be dangerous and scoundrels abounded.

All of this was thoroughly satisfying, but Ralph's triumph at securing the exclusive was overshadowed by the horrifying news he'd received last night: Pauline had declared, somewhat gleefully, he thought, that she was pregnant. The announcement had descended on him like a hammer blow. The next step, so far as she was concerned, was a snappy marriage before she began to show. He, alternatively, was working on the feasibility of doing a runner.

Ralph stubbed out his cigarette in the ashtray, cursing softly under his breath. Scarpering wasn't really an option, not if he wanted to continue working as a reporter. Unless he changed his name, moved to the other side of the country and started all over again. But even then, she'd probably track him down eventually. Christ, fate wasn't fair. It gave with one hand and took away with the other. The future stretched ahead of him – a tedious lifetime with Pauline – and he knew he had no choice but to bow down to it.

Bentley sat at the bar of the Black Bull, sipping a Scotch while he thought about recent events. He was aware that he would never know all the details of the Rosa Palliser murder: Muriel had taken those to her grave with her – or, more precisely, to the mortuary. But at least the case had been solved, most of the loose ends tied up and the guilty party finally exposed. Stephen Carr still had some questions to answer over the false alibis, but it was doubtful, after all this time, that any further action would be taken. Carr claimed – probably truthfully – that he'd never suspected Muriel of the killing. Garvie had decided not to pursue Liv Anderson over using a false identity to secure a job, although this was clearly more down to his desire to avoid further embarrassment to the company than any actual generosity on his part.

And what of Liv Anderson? She was a girl who had somehow managed to get herself embroiled in all kinds of trouble. He wasn't fooled by her air of innocence or convinced by her denials of conspiring with Palliser and Lincoln. Hopefully she had learned her lesson, even if it had been the hard way, and would think twice about embarking on any other madcap schemes.

Bentley raised his head and gazed across the pub. Moll Ainsworth had often drunk here, a quick snifter before returning to the streets. Her life had been a tough one. And for what? Who would remember her? A few of the other girls, perhaps, but gradually she would fade from their memories too. He had a vague recollection that she and Slug had once been an item, but it was so long ago – over thirty years – that he couldn't be sure.

As he scanned the customers, he almost expected to see Slug

sitting in the corner with his eyes on a newspaper and his ears pricked for any useful snippets of information. But, of course, his old informer was still in hospital making the most of some free bed and board until his leg healed enough for him to be discharged. The Larry Marks confessions still played on his mind, but he was resigned to the fact that, as with so many other things, the whole truth would probably evade him for ever.

Bentley sighed. Life went on. You did the best you could and hoped it was good enough.

76

Goodbyes were always hard. After severing her ties with Pally, Liv's next farewell, a couple of days later, was with Henry Squires. By then, although her arm still ached and she still had the dressing on her head wound, she was feeling considerably better. Now she'd got over the shock, she felt almost exhilarated at having survived a near-death experience, as though all her senses were heightened and the world was a sharper, brighter place.

There was, however, nothing sharp or bright about the Eagle. It was its usual dingy self, smelling of stale beer and shrouded in fag smoke. Henry was perched on a stool in his familiar position at the bar. He was kind and solicitous, expressing concern over her injuries and how they had happened. She span the same yarn for him as she had for Bentley and anyone else who didn't know the whole truth – a tale of mistaken beliefs and of being in the wrong place at the wrong time. Although he knew a tall story when he heard it, Henry did nothing more than raise a cynical eyebrow.

Liv bought him another pint and ordered an orange juice for herself. Some conversations were best held in a state of sobriety and this, she thought, was one of them. After today it was doubtful that she would ever see Henry again and she wanted to be sure that she learnt everything she could.

'I went to see Irene Forster,' she said, after they'd sat down at a table away from prying ears.

'Now why doesn't that surprise me?'

'I had to. She was the only person left who could help.' Liv threw him a look. 'Well, maybe not the *only* one, but you weren't ever going to go there. She told me everything, in case you're wondering.'

Henry, with all the wariness of an experienced reporter, asked, 'And what exactly does "everything" mean?'

'About who my father was actually in love with.'

'Ah.'

'It's all right. I understand why you didn't tell me. You did know, though, didn't you? All that stuff about Irene was just a smokescreen. It was Nicky he'd really fallen for.'

'I'm sorry. It's not an easy thing to tell a man's daughter.'

'No, I don't suppose it is.'

Henry looked around the bar, although whether he was checking for curious eyes or just playing for time, she wasn't sure. Eventually his gaze settled on her again. 'He tried hard to fight it, but he couldn't. It was like he'd dammed up his true feelings for so long and then the floodgates opened and . . . well, he couldn't return to pretending to be someone he wasn't. He'd crossed the line and there was no going back.'

'Did he talk to you about it?'

Henry nodded. 'I knew something was wrong, that he wasn't his usual self. I had no idea at that point that he was . . . well, he was a married man with a kid; it never occurred to me.'

'You must have been shocked.'

'It takes a lot to shock an old hack like me. I'd say surprised rather than shocked. I told him to be careful, that he could lose everything, but he was in too deep by then. You know what's always bothered me?' Henry sighed into his pint. 'I often wonder if I should have told your mum the truth. Should I? I feel like it was wrong to keep it from her.'

Liv wished she had the answer to that but she didn't. Instead she asked, 'Before or after he shot Nicky Lister?'

'Either. Both. I don't know. After, I suppose. It might have helped her to make some sense of it all.'

'I'm not certain there was much sense to be made.'

'No, maybe not. I thought I was protecting her, but I'm not sure now that was even my place.' Henry scratched his forehead as if he could erase the frown that had settled there. 'I quit reporting for a while after Paul was hanged. The stuff they wrote about him ... it was hard to take. He was one of their own – some of them even used to drink with him – but then he just became a story, another headline in an endless row of headlines.'

'But you went back to it.'

Henry gave a half smile. 'It's in my blood, my dear, for better or for worse. What else would I do?'

Liv wondered what was in her blood, but that was something she still had to discover. She was at least no longer afraid of the madness that could be lurking there. Finally, she had come to understand why her father had done what he'd done. The problem with secrets, she thought, was that they clung to your heels like bitter shadows and, no matter how hard you tried, you could never shake them off.

They talked for a while longer before Liv told Henry that she was leaving London and probably wouldn't see him for a while. What she knew, what they both knew, was that they'd never meet again. As she left the pub, she glanced back over her shoulder. Henry was staring into space, his eyes full of sadness, his thoughts with a man who had once been his friend.

77

Liv's final farewell came on Thursday morning. Goodbyes had already been exchanged with Verity and Aline, who had both left for work. She would miss Verity immensely and, incredibly, would even miss Aline a little too. When you lived with people they became like family and after a while even their gripes and grumblings felt oddly comforting and familiar. Now, standing on the doorstep, she looked at Dora and felt tears pricking her eyes.

'You take good care of yourself, love,' Dora said, dabbing at her own eyes with a handkerchief. 'And make sure you write when you're settled.'

'I will. I promise.'

Not wanting to prolong the parting, or to make it any worse than it already was, Liv gave her a quick hug, grabbed her suitcase and hurried down the street. Dora had been like the grandmother she'd never had – always kind, always looking out for her – and it was hard to walk away. And yes, of course, there had been all that dreadful business with Larry, but she didn't blame her for trying to protect her son.

Even while she was packing Liv had questioned her decision to leave, wondering if she was doing the right thing, but there was no turning back now. It was time to move on, no matter how hard. For the past year Soho had been her playground, the place she could be anyone or anything, but all that had turned sour. If she stayed, she'd be forever running into Pally and it probably wouldn't be long before she fell back into the old ways.

Tube, cab or bus? Her suitcase weighed a ton and she could only use her one good arm to carry it. The Tube was too far to walk to, a cab was too dear – she needed to save what little money she had – and so the bus was the obvious choice. Even at this point she had no idea where she was actually going. She would take pot luck depending on what bus came along and leave it to fate as to which train station she eventually ended up at.

While she stood and waited, Liv's hand rose to the silver cross at her throat. It was the only item she'd redeemed from the pawnbroker and its presence comforted her. Having it back felt like having a part of her mum with her again. Her lower lip trembled as a wave of grief washed over her. She had spent the past year trying to forget, but that was impossible. Somehow, she had to find a way to live with the loss.

A car drew up at the bus stop. Liv was so lost in thought that it took her a moment to realise that the driver of the grey saloon was Lincoln. He leaned across and called her name through the open window.

'Liv!'

She frowned when she saw who it was. 'What are you doing here?'

'I thought you might want a lift.'

'No, thanks.'

'Are you sure? That case looks kind of heavy.'

'What don't you understand by no? Just go away and leave me alone.'

'Aw, come on. I need to talk to you.'

She took a step towards the car and said, 'You've got nothing to say that I want to hear.'

By now all the other people at the bus stop were watching and listening, their morning enlivened by what they probably perceived to be a lovers' tiff. Liv could feel their eager eyes on her, their stares burning into the back of her neck.

'All right,' Lincoln said, raising his voice so everyone could hear clearly. 'Then we'll just have to discuss it here. Where shall we start? How about George Hallam and the day you—'

Liv pulled open the passenger door, leaned down and glared at him. 'What the hell are you doing?'

Lincoln grinned. 'Well, if you won't talk in private . . .'

'Just go away.'

'Just get in. I'm not going until you do. And I'm not going to stop talking, either.'

Liv, left with little choice – she hardly wanted the details of her somewhat dubious past broadcast to all and sundry – got in and hoisted the suitcase on to her knees. 'You're a bastard,' she said.

Lincoln pulled the car out into the traffic, still grinning. 'I've been called worse.'

'How did you know I was leaving today?'

'Verity told Pally.'

Liv rolled her eyes. 'Why is no one round here capable of keeping their big mouths shut?'

'I thought it was keeping our mouths shut that got you so annoyed in the first place.'

'No, that was being lied to, manipulated and presented as bait to a man you believed was a murderer.'

'Fair point,' he said. 'So, where are we going?'

'Any train station. The nearest.'

'Any?'

'Yes.'

'You've not decided where you're going yet?'

'Anywhere but here would be good,' Liv said.

'You must have some idea. North, south? No, I can't see you as a northern girl. If you're going south, you'll need Victoria. Have you thought about Brighton? Lots of fresh sea air, and there's money there too. Yeah, you could do worse than Brighton.'

Liv stared at him. 'What is it you want?'

'Just to explain some things to you. I feel bad about what happened.'

'I don't care how you feel.'

'You might as well listen. It'll pass the time while we're driving to the station.' Lincoln's fingers danced on the steering wheel for a moment. 'I guess you already know that me and Rosa were engaged for a while. It was one of those impulsive wartime things – we'd only been going out for a couple of months – but everything was crazy then. You didn't know how long you'd be alive and so you just made the most of the time you'd got. I bought the flat in Duncan Terrace and she moved in there. I wanted her to have somewhere secure to live while I was away.'

'Why are you telling me all this?'

'Because it matters. I suppose it matters. I don't know. I liked Rosa, she was a great girl, but we'd never have lasted. To be honest, I was relieved when she wrote and said she'd met someone else, a bloke at work. You see, she was decent like that; she wouldn't go behind my back. She even moved out of Duncan Terrace because she felt bad about staying there.' Lincoln paused again for a few seconds. 'Anyway, that's how Garvie became the major suspect after she was murdered, but even though I told the law, they didn't do anything about it. That's when me and Pally took matters into our own hands. Once we were back home, we went to see him, tried to get him to confess but he wasn't having any of it. Called the law on us instead and had us arrested for harassment.'

'Well, you did have the wrong man.'

'Yeah, but he knew who Rosa had been seeing. I'm sure of it. He knew Stephen Carr had been sleeping with her.'

'But Carr didn't kill her, either.'

'No, but if the truth had come out, Bentley might have looked a little more closely at his alibi on the night in question.'

Liv sighed, the sound of her escaping breath making Lincoln turn his face to look at her. 'You and Pally should have told me,' she said. 'You should have told me everything.'

'Yeah, but we didn't. People screw up; they make mistakes.'

There was a short silence before Liv suddenly thought of something. She rummaged in her bag and brought out the tiny box with the heart-shaped locket in it. 'I almost forgot. I've still got this.' She tried to pass it over to him but he flapped it away.

'Keep it. What am I going to do with it? I've never looked good in silver.'

Liv leaned forward and placed it on the dashboard. 'I don't want it.'

'It's only a locket, for God's sake.'

'I don't want it,' she said again.

'Suit yourself.'

Liv, who needed to tie up any loose ends before she and Lincoln parted company, said: 'Did Don Moody know about any of this? I mean, about George Hallam or Lord Carbrooke or anything else you were up to?'

'No, of course not.'

'So you just thought it was fine to put the fear of God in me?'

Lincoln shrugged. 'In my defence, I didn't think you were the kind of girl who was easily scared.'

'Anyone who isn't scared of Moody needs their head examining. He's a vicious sod and everyone knows it.'

'Vicious but stupid.'

'What about Carbrooke? Didn't you tell him his gambling debt would be written off if he played along?'

'It has been written off.'

'And how are you going to explain that to Moody?'

'I won't need to explain it to him. That's what creative bookkeeping is all about. So far as Moody's concerned the debt's been paid in full. No one will ever be the wiser.'

'You hope.'

'Hope has got nothing to do with it.' Lincoln gave her a sideways glance. 'Did you ever get to see Irene?'

The sudden change of subject took Liv by surprise and reminded her of everything that had happened between them last Saturday night. Instinctively she shifted as far away from him as she could within the confines of the car. 'No.'

'You just went to Berkeley Street for the fun of it, then.'

And Liv, a scowl forming on her face, remembered that he'd been following her around. 'If you already knew the answer, why did you bother asking?'

'It was just a conversation opener. I thought you might want to talk about it.'

'I don't.'

'All right.'

Liv stared through the windscreen, wishing the journey was over. For the first time she took notice of where they actually where. 'This isn't the way to Victoria.'

'Victoria?' Lincoln said. 'I thought you'd decided on Brighton.'

'I hadn't decided on anywhere. What are you doing?'

'Driving you there. It's the least I can do after everything I put you through. I mean, do you really want to be lugging that suitcase, standing in queues and waiting around for hours on end on draughty platforms? It's not my idea of a fun morning.'

'I don't need any favours from you.'

'Well, as it happens, it's not that much of a favour. I'm going that way anyway.'

Liv stared at him. 'What?'

'Yeah, I think it's time to get out of London before Moody discovers I've been skimming off his profits for the past five years.'

'Tell me you're kidding.'

'Of course I'm kidding.' Lincoln briefly turned his face to her and laughed. 'He's too damn stupid to ever find out.'

'You're crazy.'

'I prefer to call it entrepreneurial.'

'Call it what you like. He'll still kill you if the truth comes out.'

'Everyone has to die sometime.'

'Stop the car,' she said. 'I don't want to go to Brighton, and I especially don't want to go with you.'

Lincoln kept on driving. 'Come on. It's a lift, not a marriage proposal. Where's your sense of adventure? If you don't like the place you can get on the first train out of there. But you may as well give it a go. What have you got to lose?'

Liv thought about this for a while. None of today was panning out how she'd planned it, but perhaps Brighton was as good a town as any. Summer was ending, a new chapter beginning and if the truth be told she didn't much fancy spending hours on some station platform. 'Just to be clear,' she said. 'Once we get there, you go your way and I'll go mine.'

'Sure. Whatever you want.'

'*That's* what I want.'

Lincoln smiled.

Liv kept her eyes on the road ahead.